My Kingdom is Dying

EVALD FLISAR

MY KINGDOM IS DYING

Storytelling at the end of the world

Translated from the Slovene by David Limon

First published in 2025 by
Istros Books
London, United Kingdom, **www.istrosbooks.com**

Originally published in Slovene as *Moje kraljestvo umira*

© Evald Flisar, 2020

The right of Evald Flisar to be identified as te author of this work has been asserted in accordance with the Copyright, Designs and Patents Act, 1988

Translation © David Limon

Graphic design: Bojana Dimitrovski

ISBN: 978-1-912545-53-7

This publication is made possible with the assistance of ARTS COUNCIL ENGLAND

*Alice laughed. "There's no use trying," she said.
"One can't believe impossible things."*

*"I daresay you haven't had much practice," said the Queen.
"When I was your age, I always did it for half-an-hour a day.
Why, sometimes I believed as many as six impossible things
before breakfast."*

Lewis Carroll: *Alice in Wonderland*

1.

The Carer and me

Often, I admitted to my Carer, I am overcome by a wave of astonishment at the fact that I am not someone else, for there were billions of possibilities that I would perhaps be born as a poor child in sub-Saharan Africa or as the son of a royal family, perhaps even as a girl who as a teenager began to make a living from prostitution, or as a serial killer who killed for fun, or as the dictator of a minor country, whose people rebelled and hung me on a square in the main city, then celebrated, drunk with delight, until I was replaced with another dictator. And why not as a psychopath who did not know he was a psychopath, although he was at least hazily aware that he was different (that he *wanted* to be different) from the majority of "normal" people.

These waves, more common with each passing year, included thousands of possibilities, including astonishment that I hadn't been born as a girl who in her adult years had become my Carer, and who would, by chance or the will of fate, take care of a writer who, through his own stupidity, had suffered a serious accident.

These waves of astonishment which sometimes completely disable me, I told her, also involve questions that do not deny, but rather confirm, that all is not well in my head. Ever more frequently, I am astonished by the fact that nothing in the world fundamentally changes, except the climate, which we are changing ourselves, with all the consequences that we impassively learn about, almost without any sense of disturbance; as if it was a story that we had become accustomed to. It doesn't seem necessary to us, in answer to the question *Granny, why do you have such big eyes?* to reply *Because I'm not granny, but a wolf.* The most necessary shifts in our head do not seem necessary to us. My attacks of astonishment, which from time to time lead to bewilderment, also include the generally accepted belief that the universe is infinite, born out of nothing in the Big Bang; that galaxies are travelling away from each other with ever increasing speed, that the majority of people are convinced that man was created by God and evolution at the same time, while no religion is able to acknowledge that, if God exists, he is only one and that in his name, and in the desire for exclusivity, it is a sin to kill innocent people.

The waves of astonishment also leave me astounded at how frighteningly stupid humankind is not to be aware of this, and this fills me with the greatest fear. Are we here in the endlessness of space to entertain the Creator with the evil that we do, just as we entertain ourselves by watching stupid television programmes before going to bed?

The Carer listened to me patiently, gently smiling as I enumerated the things that astonish me. That became her habit soon after I employed her. I stuck to the agreement that we came to at the very beginning. When in the middle of chatting about something else I, more in jest than seriousness, asked her what would happen if I slowly fell in love with her, she would move away from the stove on which she was making me lunch, lean over me and look me straight in the eye, saying: *would you really fall in love with this?* I would see a slightly wrinkled woman in late middle age, quite tall, already slightly bent at the shoulders, with thick hair, grey in places, the kind of woman I would overlook on the street or in a shop, for there was nothing special about her. But my question – quite a stupid one as I soon realised – was triggered by my awareness of her goodwill towards me, her patience and understanding for the confused individual who had, by a string of coincidences, become her patient. At the same time, looking at her aroused in me the feeling that, in spite of her age and irregular features, she was in fact beautiful, not in the usual, sexual way, but as a human being who understood a thousand times as much as me and who was selflessly trying to keep me outside the circle of madness from which there is no way back. The love that I had felt for her for some time did not involve a desire for brief and forgettable bodily contact; my love was made up of devotion, trust, respect. Most of all, trust. Perhaps all her advice was not the best – after all, she wasn't a psychiatrist – but it helped me, or most of it did, and helped more than I expected or hoped anyone or anything in this world could help me, especially after it became clear that the thoughts in my mind were slithering like worms. First I began to value her, then to respect her, and not long after to admire her, then soon after that to trust her unconditionally and, at the same time believe, completely unreasonably, that she would find solutions to all my problems.

Except to those connected with women. She asked me about them right at the beginning of our conversations, but she soon realised that I was neither prepared nor capable of revealing anything crucial about my experiences with "members of the opposite sex", or at least nothing that would help save me from the fits of depression and hallucinations (as much as she believed that was even possible). My restraint regarding relations with women convinced her that most of the reasons for my problems could be found in precisely this area, perhaps even decisive reasons. There were ideas that had been planted in my life and my head by Scheherazade, whom my Carer saw as an imaginary person resulting from my hallucinations and my inability to make contact with the real world, because I fear it and replace it with stories. These stories are my flight from reality, dreamt up as I go along, knowing that at any moment I can revoke or change their supposed reality, or assign it to imagination, which perhaps really is the basic tool of the writer, but which, if it escapes control, can be fatal.

I had no wish to quarrel, for above all I was afraid of losing her. Without her, without the possibility of being able at any time to ask her about anything at all, I would be compelled to come up with my last, concluding story: withdrawal from awareness of my existence; a story I would not be able to retract. I felt that she did not want that, that she was even afraid, although not because she would lose well-paid employment, but much more because she would be left alone, for at the very beginning she had confided to me that she had no friends, that she was fundamentally lonely. This loneliness she had felt all her life, as her work in various hospitals had not allowed her to establish human relations with her patients. She sought solace in books, in the kinds of novels and stories that I write; she had emphasised during our first conversation that she had read most of my books. She did not do this in order to make an impression or to give her an advantage over the other candidates; she wished to tell me that she knew more about me than I could imagine. That we were bound together by my search for meaning through writing and her search for consolation through becoming close to fictional people.

It's true that because the intimacy of our contact (she had to dress me, undress me one piece of clothing at a time, wash and feed me, help me to the toilet) her curiosity about my experiences with women became ever greater, ever more noticeable, for I felt it even in conversations which were not connected with relationships or marriage or families, and I knew the moment would come when I would have to satisfy her curiosity. On top of this, I had never been willing or able to reply to her oft-repeated question as to why I had never written a love story. Or to the question of whether it seemed to me that novels such as *Madame Bovary, Ana Karenina,* or even *Fifty Shades of Grey* were trivial, less worthy, far from my elevated goals, although we agreed that only two of the mentioned works were worthy of my regard. And how many women there were in my novels, she would ask, why there were so few, why the books were all written through male eyes, that is mine, the author's, and if not through mine then through the eyes of male characters, which were nevertheless, let's be honest, at the end of the day also mine, for although I do not write autobiographies, I make up the characters and what happens to them. Which means that I view women, experience and evaluate them through the eyes of people that don't exist, until I beget them in my imagination, where anything is possible and probable. Including Scheherazade, who I encounter, if I really do, in different parts of the world.

It was in vain that I explained that my male characters were also made up and that not only did they see women through their eyes, but that in the same way they were seen by women who were also the fruit of my imagination. Which in my case, unintentionally, gave precedence to male characters, although that wasn't true for all my novels, for in some of them the story is experienced (and written) from a female point of view, at least as much as I know women and am capable of experiencing the world through their eyes. In the great majority of novels and stories, both sexes are present, each in their own way, and it is always the relation between them that shapes the message of the story, although that is not set in stone, but rather interpreted by each reader in their own way. When we begin to make up the world in which we live and describe it in line with the conundrums that we carry within us, a reality appears that perhaps we are not comfortable with and which we had not been expecting. And this (made-up) reality can prevail over the actual one (if actual reality even exists and does not merely consist of personal interpretations of perceptions and events) to the extent that they swap roles and we find ourselves (perhaps with no way back) in a world that seems real to us, even though it is imaginary. A world of hallucinations?

I persistently and almost stubbornly avoided the Carer's wish that I tell her something specific about my experiences with women. I felt that this was a great disappointment to her, which at first almost indiscernibly and then increasingly obviously, changed into a gradual loss of faith that she could help me also as a psychological carer, which she undoubtedly wanted to become, for in my fear of confessions of an intimate nature she increasingly saw stubbornness and resistance or, equally likely, fear of her as a woman. Can men, when we tell women about other women, be as frank as we would like to be, even when the woman listening to us has no other aim than to direct us on the path that leads away from psychological confusion? We both knew that her job would end sooner or later, that my wounds would sooner or later heal, and that I would be able to take care of myself once again, and what then?

Would we ever see each other again, talk, meet for coffee if nothing else? We both equally feared the separation:

I, because I couldn't deny that soon after her arrival she had also begun to care for my mind (which had been wounded long before my body); she, I believe, because in her conversations with me she was also managing to solve her own problems, perhaps those that she was unaware of, even though she experienced them as a dark and painful shadow in her mind. I often recognised, even felt her pain, which she was unable to hide: the pain of realising that, in spite of our contrasting roles, we were very similar and that she was perhaps in even greater distress than the unfortunate one she was caring for.

She did not want to answer my questions regarding what she did before she ended up caring for me, in the time before I, not through an agency, but following the advice of one of my few friends, employed her; I could only speculate as to why she didn't. Perhaps she wanted to maintain some distance between herself and the patient she was caring for, whose arse she had to wipe because he was not able to do it for himself and whose member she had to extract from his underpants so that he could piss. I didn't want to delude myself: it was no doubt precisely because of these circumstances that she wanted our relationship to remain within the bounds of professional duty, because we were both embarrassed by these intimate interactions, at least at the beginning, until we accepted that such things were an inevitable part of the caring routine.

I respected her taciturnity about the past, for after all, she could have been caring for me in a similar way in a hospital, where it would never even occur to me to ask her about it. But at home, in my house, during the caring that was aimed only at me, my curiosity did not seem intrusive; it was much more a wish that our relationship should change into sincere friendship, into a mutual trust that would not be hindered by the fact that she was wiping my arse and that I was paying her for doing it.

2.

Me and my house

That I encountered her and not some ordinary district nurse who would have been disgusted by my broken body and would have had to bid goodbye after a couple of days, filled me with the same astonishment as most of the events in my life. One day, when she had gone to the shop for food, I called my friend to thank him for bringing her into my life. My gratitude is so great that I wouldn't know how to put it into words, I added. I asked him where he had found her, since such exceptional women are not in the habit of wandering alone along the road. He confided in me, if I swore that it would remain between the two of us, that she was no ordinary carer: she had a degree in psychology, employment medicine and physiotherapy, and she had always been an obsessive reader, and had certainly read more books than the two of us put together. For many years, she had taught at the medical college, then she had lost her son in a traffic accident and for two years was treated for depression. When she pulled out of it and returned to work, she was struck by a new misfortune: her husband, who was the director of a successful bicycle company and, together with her, a marathon cyclist, got Parkinson's disease. It progressed more rapidly than usual: he was soon unable to look after himself and the precious woman gave up her job to care for him. She did this professionally and dedicatedly for three years, and then the husband, who was a few years older than me, died and she was left alone, robbed of everything apart from memories. Since I needed similar care to her husband, it seemed to him that she was most suitable for the role of my carer and that she would also benefit from this kind of work, for since her husband's death she missed caring for someone. As he knew both her and myself well, he was convinced that we would quickly establish good relations and help each other more than we were aware. What I would appreciate and would help me most was that we could talk to each other about books, he added. Moreover, he joked, she was a good cook. But I would have to tell her a bit about myself, he added, about my life and work, about all the unusual things that had happened to me. By doing so, our connection would become stronger.

And all of this really happened. It didn't take long for her to become my most faithful listener, for I succumbed, perhaps because of my immobility, to a loquaciousness the like of which I could not remember. My desire to tell stories would not let me rest; as I was unable to write, I had to narrate and I did so with that much greater enjoyment the more it seemed that my stories were rescuing her from dark thoughts and everything that she would like to forget. In between, we would talk, including about my amazement at the fact that it was precisely her and not someone else who had come to care for me, and that I had been involved in one of the most bizarre accidents that had ever befallen a writer. She asked me what it was that amazed me most and without hesitation I told her it was something that she would perhaps not be able to believe.

I told her that five or maybe six years earlier, I had been taken aback when I realised that the slow disintegration of my house and my body had become synchronised. It hadn't happened overnight, but gradually, barely discernibly, with lengthy periods when I didn't even perceive that time was passing and that both myself and my environment were irreversibly changing, the victims of a process of decay that could not be halted. But then, one night when I couldn't sleep, I was struck by the realisation that my body, my mind and my surroundings were ageing and decomposing at the same speed, as if they had come to an agreement, although that seemed to me neither possible nor logical; at best I saw in this synchronisation the writer's natural inclination to connect separate events into a whole, which would ultimately acquire narrative properties; they would, in short, become a story.

But the moment arrived when I had to admit that it wasn't the basis for the kind of morbid story I liked to write, that everything within me and around me was decaying and dying. I noticed it first in relation to me and within me. Heberden's nodes appeared – the disintegration of the cartilage and the calcification of the lower joints in the fingers of both hands (a consequence of many years of typing?) – and the doctor told me that the severe pain and increased fragility of the fingers might last from ten to fifteen years, and then the process would subside (it's true that for some months I was barely able to turn the key in the lock). I was lucky, God knows why, for the process stopped after a year and although my finger joints were left with swellings on both sides, at least they didn't hurt (except when I ate things from the nightshade family, such as potatoes, tomatoes, paprika, chillies – everything that Columbus brought from the New World).

I told her that during my travels around the world, most often to various symposiums, festivals, readings and presentations of translations of my work, I had fallen ill three times with malaria (on one of these occasions with falciparum, which almost killed me), as well as with typhoid fever, Legionnaire's disease, pneumonia and Dengue fever. But this did not seem to me to be part of the ageing process; these were the consequences of lack of caution or of circumstance; if you stir up a wasp's nest, sooner or later you're going to get stung. But then other things appeared: increased stomach acid (stress, said the doctor), stomach ulcer and duodenal ulcer (stress, said the doctor), acid reflux (the pain was often reminiscent of a heart attack), chronic headaches (stress, said the doctor, or dehydration), problems with my spine and vertebrae, I often had to spend a month immobile in bed (too little movement, weakened muscles and bad posture, said the doctors), pain in the knees, shoulders, ankles, hip joints and pelvis (worn cartilage, said the doctors, a sign of age, although pain in the sacroiliac joints could also mean the start of spondylitis, which with time brings about the seizure of all the joints in the body and to immobility).

And then unexplained pains, sometimes here, sometimes there, in muscles or bones, or projected from one part of the body to another, for one's leg can hurt because of a problem in the neck vertebrae, I was told. In spite of this, amazingly, I had been convinced my whole life that I was generally healthy and that, with occasional exceptions, I felt well and that in the near future I didn't face any major threat to my health, let alone my life. And this was in spite of the fact that the fairly regular blood tests, ultrasound scans, blood pressure checks and checking of my neck arteries revealed an increasing danger that at any moment I might be carried off to another world: high cholesterol, high triglycerides, elevated liver enzymes, high blood pressure, clogged neck arteries, lack of vitamins D and B12, gradually failing memory, and so on.

There were many other signs that my body was disintegrating at roughly the same speed as the house in which I was living.

And which I did not wish to leave. I increasingly saw the house as my refuge from a world which interested me less and less, which seemed increasingly, almost stubbornly, on the road to perdition, which I already knew and which could offer me nothing fresh, just as I could offer it nothing useful, since it would be hard to write a novel that would surpass the quality and significance of my previous ones. The house, my home, presented me with problems reminiscent of problems with novels and stories. The moment came when it needed a new roof (just as my writing needed new thematic and stylistic cover); every summer the garden, small but densely planted, became so overgrown that it needed weekly pruning (climbing a ladder at three or four different places, otherwise it was impossible to reach everything forcing its way over the fences and walls into neighbouring gardens), while the lush greenery at the front made its way towards the road, bothering passers-by (just as it is necessary with novels and stories to keep cutting, chopping, shortening) and it all became increasingly too much for me.

Quite often, I was overcome by the desire to sell the house in Ljubljana and move to an apartment without a single plant, for as soon as you have something growing in an apartment, you can't go anywhere for a longer period without a feeling of guilt that you are neglecting something that Nature put into your care. But I had got used to the house, to the greenery that was impossible to tame without hard and dangerous work (once I even fell off the ladder and injured myself); I had got used to the space, which was actually of no use to me but gave me a feeling of freedom, however false, and to the refreshing coolness which, because of the thick walls and the dense wrapping of greenery, filled the living room even in the midst of the hottest summer. The house was "mine" in a similar way that my body was "mine".

But in the end I had to accept that, in parallel with my health, my house was also losing its peace and its future, and it would have to be treated in the same way as I. At times it seemed to me unusual that, together with my body and mind, everything around me was ageing and getting closer to death: the house, belief in the future, sociability, solidarity, friendship, the desire to visit foreign places, for reputation, for recognition for my work, even to find a friend, if possible of the opposite sex, to whom I could, without shame and hesitation, entrust all my fears and mistakes and sins, without risking that my imperfection would turn them away from me. I increasingly accepted the fact, with ever diminishing anxiety and pain, that such a person did not exist, and that, in spite of my advanced years and plentiful bitter experiences, I was still setting unrealistically high standards, as I did in my writing, where I demanded more of myself than five Nobel Prize winners would have been capable of producing.

The house's ageing told a story of unavoidable decline, of the shadow that increasingly covered not only my efforts, but also the results of those efforts, my literature and everything that I was (or thought I was) during my brief stop on planet Earth. Like the arteries in my body, the house's water pipes were rusting, like the age spots on my face and elsewhere on my body, dirty marks appeared on the white exterior walls; as the plants in the garden and around the house were creeping everywhere and concealing it from the eyes of passers-by, my interior, my mind, my soul, my awareness (possibly even my kidneys and the soles of my feet) were becoming overgrown by the branches of twisted thoughts, fears and doubts, which when I looked at the disintegrating house, wound themselves ever tighter around my neck and sowed in my brain an infection worse than anything I had hitherto experienced: not only the awareness that in the end the house would collapse, but also that my body, too, would soon be reduced to ashes or to bones beneath the earth.

The end. The final act. Nothing.

In senseless fear, I hired a host of craftsmen to return the house to its former glory and youth: they laid fresh floor coverings in every room, renovated the central heating and installed new radiators, replaced metal pipes with plastic ones, painted everything that could be painted, took out the old kitchen and installed a new one, installed a new washing machine and new dishwasher, replaced the old fridge and freezer, put new tiles on the terrace, sealed all the windows that were letting in draughts and causing constant coughing and sneezing, changed the front door lock and the alarm system, put a new mattress on the double bed that at my time of life I had no one to share with, installed a new television with all the available channels, although I don't usually watch, only now and then, most often programmes on ageing and dementia.

In the bathroom, they repaired the bidet, which saved me a lot of toilet paper. I asked the cleaning lady who came to vacuum and iron, for a modest extra payment to get rid of the cobwebs from every corner of the house, even the most hidden corners, and the dust from all the books on the shelves (there were over 4000, most of which I hadn't read, due to lack of time); twice I had all the drains cleaned, including from the bathroom on the first floor, which ran down to the ground floor and on to the sewer (for twice the downstairs drain had got blocked, no doubt because I tipped into the toilet the leftovers of all the greasy food that I didn't manage to eat). Once the water flowed back and flooded the hallway with food remnants and faecal matter that hadn't found its way into the sewer).

I did everything that seemed necessary for me to live in a faultless house, where nothing bad could happen. For if my house was completely healthy, I would also remain healthy. A house and the person living in it are one, I believed.

That this is not the case I had to admit when it became obvious that fixing problems in a house is easier than with a body: physics and biology are far removed from each other. The more my house became suitable for a comfortable and lengthy life, the more obvious it became that my body was falling apart quicker than my house was being renovated. There was no connection between them. Medical examinations became a constant in my life. Luckily, what I earned from my novels and dramas and short story collections was enough for me to be able to afford, in addition to endless house renovations, the most reliable specialists (for among doctors, like writers, some are adequate, some average and some exceptional). I demanded that they examine me from the top of my head to the tips of my toes, and in so doing to make use of all the latest technology. Medicine is a science, they said, so we cannot give you false hope. Above all in your own interest, our professional duty is to tell you the truth.

That's the least I expect, I told them.

They told me the following: at 7.6 my cholesterol was way too high; my triglycerides, at 4.5, likewise; one of the neck arteries that carried blood to my brain was only half its proper width, which meant that in a year or so I would need an operation to fit a stent; due to almost forty years of sitting at a desk and bad posture, the vertebrae in my thoracic spine were so damaged that I would never rid myself of pain between my shoulder blades, except with the most powerful analgesics; my blood pressure was certainly too high, although some say that in later years it is normal for it to increase; my frequent headaches were most probably the result of stress, which I couldn't control, although it perhaps seems to me that I can do so with benzodiazepine, which is part of my daily diet; the intermittent depression from which I could barely dig myself out was probably the result of lack of vitamin D (I should be in the sun more), although it could arise from the feeling that I had not achieved most of my life goals. Or that I had achieved all of them and before me was only emptiness, the wait for death. That was a problem that a psychiatrist might be able to solve.

And so on. And every time the same. The disintegration of my house was visible, tangible and repairable; the disintegration of my body was made manifest through test results and pain, whilst the "repairs" remained within the bounds of probability and the speculations of medical science, which at least at times seemed to me to be striving to fill my decaying body with as many pharmaceutical products as possible.

3.

Death and me

In the end, I realised that the house in which I so much enjoyed living, although it was also a burden to me, would remain standing long after I was in my grave, even if I forgot about it and devoted all my attention and energy (and financial resources) to maintenance and "repair" of my body. From there to the realisation that sooner or later, perhaps sooner rather than later, I would die and avoid further "repairs", was a shorter journey than I had expected. The moment came when I recognised and accepted the fact that death would not avoid me. And that it could come for me at any time. Even the next moment. The numbness that had been growing inside me over the past four or five years meant that this realisation did not throw me, frighten me or make me unhappy; towards the end of our days it seems that even life itself is condemned to diminishment, to expecting the end. More or less patiently, but at the same time with curiosity.

The question began to assert itself as to what form of departure from the world and consciousness of it (and of myself) would I want, if I excluded suicide (for which I wouldn't find the courage, nor the willpower, for birth and death are in the hands of fate). Regardless of the fact that it was a voluntary exit that would make possible what I firmly believe in: that at the end every minute is important, perhaps even every second, for it extends the moments that you can make peace with the fate you have been assigned, with the mistakes you made through awkwardness and which are still within you like implants of anxious guilt, even though you sincerely regret them. In moments of departure you have the last opportunity to make peace with what you have carried within you your whole life and which you referred to as "I", while others called it "you", although this "I" and "you" was a sequence of different people, created by circumstances, experience and everything else that on the journey through life influenced your feelings, worldliness and capacity to look within yourself.

From the age of twenty, I knew that with me would not die the one who was born, or the one I was at the age of fifteen, thirty, or even fifty, but rather a sequence of people, although similar enough in their basic features to be able to call themselves relatives; that together with me, it could be said, would die a family of "I's". Nor would the body be the same, for it changes throughout life – every seven years all the cells of the body are replaced.

What, then, would go to the next world? Certainly the "I" of that moment, with its hazy, incomplete memories, which old age would reduce or even completely erase, a truncated "I" containing only that which at the moment of death was accessible to consciousness, and that may be very, very little. In any case, I would like to be *aware* that life was ending, I told the Carer; I would like to be *present* at my death, at the same time both its victim and its companion.

Whenever an awareness of passing and the inevitability of the end ambushed me like a bandit, I was often overcome with the feeling that I wouldn't experience an ordinary death, but something unique, worth describing in a novel or at least an equally strange end as other world-renowned authors (which, towards the end of my life, I also saw myself as.

The Carer asked me to describe to her some of the weird endings of well-known writers. For a long time (I don't know where I heard this story) I thought that Joyce had died in hospital in Zürich, where, following an operation on his appendix, through negligence a scalpel had been left in his stomach, which caused inflammation, and then sepsis, followed by death. In reality (however much the truth matters at all in such cases), he died due to a perforated ulcer in his duodenum, which led to undigested food entering his stomach cavity, which led to inflammation, leading to death two weeks later, before he reached the age of 59. He died young, although it is questionable whether, after *Finnegan's Wake,* he would have written anything else readable. In every author's life are works that could not be written twice; those who manage to do so risk the second, recognisably different version devaluating the first.

The deaths of other masters of the pen in the history of the kingdom of dying are less banal. When I became familiar with them, it became clear to me that all the unusual deaths of authors and playwrights had already occurred and that I had no chance of an end that would at least be as original as that of some of my works that do not flirt with others and do not belong in the mainstream, but rather are, as the critics observed, "individual" (for the word "original" is avoided by most critics).

One of the most bizarre ends of a master of the written word occurred in Antique Greece, in 400 BC, when a tortoise fell on the head of the barely thirty-year-old Aeschylus (and think of all he managed to write!), killing him instantly. Of course, the tortoise was not thrown by a vengeful Zeus, but dropped by an eagle. Eagles sometimes hunt tortoises for food and in order to get to their flesh easily they drop them from a height onto a rock or rounded stone, so that the tortoise's shell breaks. At the age of thirty, Aeschylus was completely bald. An eagle mistook his head for a stone and dropped a tortoise on it. The creature's shell broke into pieces, as did Aeschylus' skull. It always interested me whether, in addition to the tortoise, the eagle also ate Aeschylus' brain.

A similarly unexpected end was met by the American writers Tennessee Williams and Sherwood Anderson. The first wasn't killed by alcohol, although it came close (which is characteristic of American writers), but at the age of seventy-two either by a sedative or by the eye drops he was using. Or to be more precise, by a plastic cap. For some reason the cap of one of the bottles ended up in his mouth and then in his windpipe, where it got stuck and choked him. If such a thing had happened to one of the characters in his plays, everyone would have said it was not only implausible, but also impossible, and the drama critics would have labelled his play as a construct (as if every play is not a construct, which drama critics, who have never written a play and never will, fail to understand and never will).

The death of Sherwood Anderson at the age of sixty-five was less unlikely. He fell ill when on a cruise with his wife. At the first opportunity they disembarked and hurried to the nearest hospital, where Anderson died of peritonitis. The inflammation was caused by a toothpick, which he had swallowed through clumsiness during a meal on-board and it had become stuck in his colon. I wouldn't like anything like that to happen to me, although a number of times I *have* fallen asleep in front of the television with a toothpick on my mouth while watching the news, which is an endless litany of corruption, scandal, corruption, scandal.

If I had a choice, I'd much rather die like Shakespeare's contemporary, Christopher Marlowe, although he was only twenty-nine years old. After drinking all day with friends, he got into an argument in a tavern, which grew into a physical altercation, during which a friend stabbed Marlowe in the forehead, above his right eye. One version of the story says that Marlowe had attacked his friend first and stabbed him in the stomach, then the friend (Frizer) pulled the dagger from his hand and in self-defence stabbed him in the forehead. Another version states that Marlowe staged his own death because of debts and then fled abroad, where he wrote most of the dramas attributed to Shakespeare.

I wouldn't say no to such a death. It would be painful, it would be violent, but it would go down in history as a great mystery, which would extend the life of my books for several centuries.

To be honest, I'd rather experience a romantic death, like the English poet Shelley, husband to Mary Wollstonecraft, author of *Frankenstein*, who drowned in the Tyrrhenian Sea at the age of twenty-nine. One version is that he drowned while swimming through tall waves, another is that a sudden storm sank the boat on which he was sailing with two friends and the tide washed his body up onto the shore. There, his wife and friends, including Lord Byron, cremated his body using bunches of branches, and in a timely fashion one of his friends pulled out his heart from the flames, handing it to his widow.

"I'd like a roughly similar death or at least one equally tragic," I concluded my narrative.

4.

Scheherazade and me

The Carer wasn't interested in the particulars of my accident. I had broken both wrists and my left ankle, as well losing skin from my forehead, as if someone had scalped me, for it hung down over my eyes to the end of my nose. I needed twenty-six stitches to sew it back. I also experienced a severe concussion, although even with tomography or MRI it wasn't possible to determine how serious the injuries were or how they would affect my life. She didn't want to be intrusive and, from excessive consideration towards her patient, waited for me to choose the appropriate moment to trust her with the details. But I did feel that she was waiting for that moment with ever more impatience.

Then one day I decided it was selfish to leave her in suspense, not only because we were becoming increasingly friendly, but also because of her extreme and admirable selflessness. It seemed to me that my recovery was becoming her life project and so I decided to reveal to her the circumstances that had led to me becoming an invalid, even though they were highly embarrassing. I asked her to open the French windows and to push the wheelchair in which I spent most of the day outside and across the neglected lawn to the other end of the garden. I pointed out to her the rounded, overgrown shelter left over from the time of the Cold War and told her that some steps led to the top of the low rise from the line of garages below it.

One evening, at nine o'clock, with a full moon in the sky, at the top of the slope, I saw Scheherazade, that beautiful woman, who for decades had been following me tirelessly and appearing in the least expected places, now here, now there, as if she was real, and in whose existence I was certain, despite psychotherapists assuring me that she did not exist, that she was a hallucination. Whenever she appeared, I tried to get closer to her, to touch her, to see whether she was alive, with a tangible body, or whether she was just an apparition of a sick mind, something I was unable and unwilling to believe.

When she appeared to me right before my accident, I unlocked the gate that led from the fenced garden and went along the path towards the garages, and then up the steep steps towards the top of the shelter, where she awaited me, hazily lit by the moonlight, sitting on the floor cross-legged. In spite of her bowed head, her pose seemed slightly sinister. It had rained during the day, the steps were covered with wet grass which had grown in the gaps between them and I almost slipped as I was going up. When I got to the top and reached towards my tormentor, she suddenly evaporated. I stretched out my hand and felt emptiness. As so often before.

I turned round to go back down the steps, when I suddenly saw her on a pile of logs that had been stacked in front of the first garage in the row. She wasn't a reflection on the wall, she was sitting on the logs, a real person. For the first time since we met, she looked me full in the face and she even raised her hand and gestured for me to come closer. So that she wouldn't disappear again, I went down the steps faster than I should have; about half-way down I slipped, but I didn't fall backwards – in trying to regain my balance I twisted round, fell down the steps head first and banged my head against the logs in front of the garage.

When I came round in the emergency ward of the hospital, I found that I had been saved from death by a lucky coincidence: I was found by a neighbour who had gone for a walk because he couldn't sleep; he called an ambulance, I was taken away, they awoke me, stitched up the wound on my head, measured everything that could be measured, expressed amazement that I was alive, told me that I had broken both wrists and my left ankle, that for some time I would be like an invalid, with both wrists and my ankle in plaster, with painful stitches on various parts of my head, especially my forehead, and the state of my brain would have to be regularly monitored. Because of the adrenaline built up inside me, none of this seemed particularly strange. It was only later that I gradually became aware of the seriousness of what had happened to me.

"You shall need constant care," I was told. "Would you like to stay in hospital?"

"God forbid," I replied. "Your nurses treat me like an object. I'll hire someone."

The Carer couldn't decide whether or not to believe the details of my accident. Astonishment and scepticism were written all over her face. It all seemed simply too bizarre. In the end, she plucked up the courage to ask me whether it was another of my stories that she had not yet come across, even though she was an avid reader of my short prose, even more so than my novels, although she wasn't implying that my novels weren't equally good. More than once, I had to reassure her that the evidence of the reality of the incident was pretty obvious: why else should she be working in my house as a carer? It turned out that she did not doubt most of the details of my accident, but she couldn't come to terms with Scheherazade. She had read *One Thousand and One Nights,* she knew how Shahryar's wife had prolonged her life, but more than two thousand years later, how could she appear in the visions of a man who told stories himself, and why? When had she first appeared, she wanted to know. How and in what circumstances?

At that point silence would have bordered on cruelty, so I decided to go back to the past and tell her the story of the stories that led to my unusual encounter with Scheherazade. Although certainly not the first, I emphasised.

5.

"The city of dreadful night"

It had started many years before at a literary congress in Kolkata, I began. At that time, I was living in London. In truth, before this, literary gatherings and congresses had not interested me. I was convinced that such events attracted mediocrities who wanted, by taking part, especially if it was an "international symposium", to attain a sense of importance that they could not achieve through their writing. In the normal course of things, I would have turned my nose up at a world congress of short story writers. But there were three reasons why I didn't: first, because I wasn't invited; second, because Peter Evans, who writes prosaic, primitive science fiction stories was invited; and third (and this was the main reason), I saw this congress as the ideal opportunity to resolve the creative crisis that had been destroying me for quite some years and was beginning to eat away at all the layers of my life.

I read in the newspaper that the congress would involve more than a hundred writers from around the world. The theme was *Fiction in today's world: luxury or necessity?* I knew that it wouldn't remain at that. Everyone would ride their hobby horses, the central theme would be spun in every possible direction, the participants would talk about approaches to creativity, structural modes, the metaphysics of short prose; the congress would be a gathering of magicians, and each would show and explain their favourite trick.

I was a magician whose tricks were no longer enough and who wanted to synthesise all the known tricks of all the known magicians, and to perform magic that was more than just a trick, but a miracle. Something that no one could unravel, analyse, invalidate.

After sleepless nights of smoking and knuckle-cracking it became clear to me that I had to attend the congress at any price: through trickery, or through violence, if there was no other way. First of all, I suggested to the writers' association that they send me as an observer. They said they were being represented by Peter Evans, who had been officially invited at the organisers' expense; they didn't see the need to send another author at the association's expense. And even if they did, that individual would have to be democratically chosen by the membership.

I called a friend who was a television producer. I suggested that he should send a small team to film a cheap documentary about the congress. He said that he would need to think about it first and consult his bosses. He called me a half hour later to say it was no go. If it had been a world congress of beekeepers or toppled kings or arms smugglers, maybe. Even a congress of bestselling writers would attract interest. But unfortunately, short story writers were "a minority interest".

I got ready for the journey (visa, jabs against cholera, typhoid, tetanus, anti-malaria tablets, my suitcase, the usual things). The evening before the departure I invited Evans to dinner in the "literary" restaurant, the Gay Hussar, in Soho. I invited him under the pretence that I wanted to discuss with him an adaptation of his stories for a television series. After dinner, during which we discussed all manner of things and eventually got into a spat about my assertion that writers living in countries under authoritarian regimes had a creative advantage that writers in the "free", consumerist West did not have, I invited him to a bar and poured a sleeping draught into his glass of brandy.

He was quite groggy when I stuffed him into the car, drove him home, dragged him inside (he lived alone), turned down the bed, took his shoes off, loosened his tie (there are few science fiction writers who would dare to go to a restaurant without a tie), took his invitation to the congress from his desk and left.

As the plane landed in Kolkata, I thought that only a cynic or a terrible joker would organise a world congress of short story writers in a city that Rudyard Kipling called "the city of dreadful night". (A quarter of a million people live on the streets, while many millions are forced to live in shacks of dried mud).

I recalled Churchill's comment that he was glad he had seen Kolkata so that he didn't need to see it ever again. And Mark Twain's bitter joke that the climate in Kolkata was so hot and humid that even bronze door handles melt into porridge. The name itself, Kalikata in Sanskrit, originates from Kali, the goddess who symbolises fear and evil, and is depicted with snakes around her neck or with a necklace of human skulls and a tongue dripping with blood.

Kolkata is a city of poverty and violence, but at the same time it is one of the biggest and richest cities in India, an industrial and cultural centre, one of the youngest cities in the world in one of the oldest cultures; a wonderful city, according to Bengalis, a city of palaces and temples, museums and luxury hotels, a centre of Indian learning and literature, the city of Rabindranath Tagore. It is said that Kolkata has more poets than Dublin has writers and more publishers than all the other Indian cities together; even the chief of police reviews books in his spare time for one of the many literary journals!

And thus Kolkata (I thought after our landing in the smothering heat) really is the most appropriate city for a world congress of short story writers: a microcosm of everything that is good and bad in the world.

For us, all that is good, since the anonymous sponsors of the congress (the rumours were that it was one of the Birla brothers, the Indian Rockefellers) had enabled one hundred and twenty participants from around the world to stay in the air-conditioned rooms of the luxurious hotel Grand Oberoi, as well as three meals a day, plus afternoon tea for those who fancied that traditional ritual. Also available were unlimited amounts of whisky and other beverages.

I expected problems, but a smiling Mr Banerjee, "the administrator", reassured me that it didn't matter at all if I had come instead of Evans, who had suddenly fallen ill. "The main thing," he explained, "is that I have 120 people on the list and 120 people in the dining room." He gave me a room with a view of the Maidan, the main park, "bigger than Hyde Park," he proudly explained. Finally, he insisted that in an hour I must come to the hotel restaurant, Scheherazade, where the official opening of the congress would take place.

6.

Borges and me

I never dreamed that I would find myself among the *crème de la crème* of the world's short prose writers. The congress was attended by John Updike, Susan Sontag, John O'Hara, Doris Lessing, Nadine Gordimer, Gabriel García Márquez, José J. Veiga, Joyce Carol Oates, Chang Tien, Jaşar Kemal and I could go on. A dwarfish participant whispered to me that, in spite of the general conviction that he would not, even Jorge Luis Borges had turned up. I pushed my way to the front. And it was true, at a table by the wall sat the blind Argentine of whom André Maurois wrote that he "composed only little essays or short narratives, yet they suffice for us to call him great because of their wonderful intelligence, their wealth of invention, and their tight, almost mathematical style."

He was sitting there indifferently listening to Mr Banerjee's bombastic opening speech. As a looked at him, I saw an image that Paul Theroux had described after meeting him: "He was dressed formally, in a dark blue suit and dark tie; his black shoes were loosely tied, and a watch chain descended from his pocket. He was taller than I had expected, and there was an English cast to his face, a pale seriousness in his jaw and forehead. His eyes were swollen, staring and sightless. But for his faltering, and the slightest tremble in his hands, he was in excellent health. He had the fussy precision of a chemist."

When Mr Banerjee finished his marathon speech, grateful applause rang out. Mr Banerjee interrupted it with a gesture of false modesty and said: "Ladies and gentlemen, as it will soon be time for dinner, in the name of the sponsor I invite you to take part in a celebratory banquet, where you will be able to encounter the indubitable excellence of Indian cuisine." These words were followed by even louder applause and it seemed to me that the most enthusiastic were the Indian writers, who represented a majority of those present.

The meal exceeded the expectations of almost all the participants, even the domestic ones, among which the southerners, plump black men with ankle length white robes, ate with their fingers, and their lip-smacking zeal aroused the suspicion that they had been attracted to the congress primarily by the catering and French wine, which the sponsor had supposedly imported specially so that the writers, in the midst of their lively discussions and curry, would not go thirsty. Borges was the only one who didn't touch the food. Nor did he drink the wine, but satisfied himself with a glass of mineral water; he sipped it from time to time, cautiously, as if taking medication.

Beside him sat the Irish-American critic and professor of literature Denis Donoghue, who was asking questions with a full mouth, to which Borges replied more out of politeness than enthusiasm. It seemed to me that he would rather be listening to the whirlwind of sounds around him, the mixtures of languages, accents and cadences, which did not give the impression that they were coming from the world's elite writers.

At a table near the entrance sat Ruth Prawer Jhabvala, a Polish Jew who had married an Indian Parsi and lived in Delhi, writing novels and stories about India, chatting in a dignified way with the bearded Sikh, Khushwant Singh (I had read his collection of novellas *The Mark of Vishnu* and some of them seemed good). To my left, a young writer from Israel was speaking in broken English to a magnificent woman in a sari. They were talking about Indian food. She was warning him to avoid "Bangalore phal" unless he had a fire truck handy. But he was only interested in which of the numerous dishes in silver vessels contained pork. "Ah," said the Hindu woman, "then you eat the beef and I'll eat the pork." "A fine example of cultural-religious cooperation," replied the young author from Israel.

"Do you write stories?" asked a young woman from Hong Kong, who was seated to my right. When I nodded, she asked: "What kinds of problems do you encounter when writing?"

It seemed to me too early to start talking about the essence of my crisis and the environment was too noisy and lively, so I casually replied that when writing I encountered no problems that would not be known to other writers. For me too, I told her, "a short story cannot be finished, but has to be abandoned in despair and published." I, too, had problems achieving a synthesis between my initial vision and the form available for its realisation. And it also often happened to me that I created a sequence of wonderful words, which at the end turned out to be stylistic onanism. I added that she, too, must certainly have encountered and solved such and similar problems.

"Creative problems are universal," she said to me, under the influence of the French wine, "but we all resolve them in our own way and the way that we do so is a measure of the author's originality." I wouldn't have dared repeat this statement anywhere, but at that moment it seemed to me a profound one.

"The theme of my stories is sex," she said. I almost choked on a piece of chicken tikka masala. I looked at her more closely; she was middle aged, skinny, and even in a generous moment you wouldn't describe her face as attractive. I thought that for her writing about sex was a way of exorcising unsatisfied lust, an attempt at self-therapy. But after reconsideration, that thought seemed to me unworthy of the author of *Funeral of Dreams* and *The Night of Deposed Kings*. Where was this sudden shallowness coming from? I was being dulled by the food, dulled by the wine. If things carry on like this, I thought, then the congress will degenerate into a babble of hiccoughing "sages".

"The title of my best story," she said, "is *Woman*. In it I describe how a Chinese girl, first with joy and then with growing horror, awaits the ceremony in which, in the old Chinese way, they will bind and deform her feet." I replied that I had heard of this terrible custom, but I didn't know that it still went on. She timidly admitted that the story was autobiographical.

Then she bleated: "The Chinese deform girls' feet because of their idea of feminine beauty, but in the West you deform the minds of your children to enable them to live in a world of greed and selfishness!" Yes, I nodded, that's true. We are all crippled. And that, more or less, is the theme of my stories.

I wanted to carry on talking but she turned her back on me.

After dinner, discussion groups of various sizes formed. The largest group was crowded around Borges. I wished to join them, but I reconsidered and decided to join a group of Indian delegates, who wanted to go for a walk before bed. "To aid the digestion," one of them hiccoughed, patting his stomach.

On the pavement in front of the hotel the beggars stretched their hands towards us. "Babu, babu," begged the hoarse voices, "paisa, paisa, meharbani se." Some were lying exhausted on the ground and around them squatted ragged, bare-bottomed children. At the edge of the pavement was a boy without arms and legs. He had wooden blocks fastened to his knees and elbows, and on them he rushed towards me, clop, clop, clop. In the metal dish he held in his teeth coins were rattling. He raised the stumps of his arms towards me and moaned; in the light from the streetlights his eyes were glowing imperatively. I reached into my pocket and placed some coins in his dish. This attracted the attention of the others, who leapt on me like wolves, and in a moment I was at the centre of a forest of outstretched arms that refused to withdraw. I was rescued by one of the Indian delegates, who dispersed the mass of beggars with a single hissed word, while he pulled me, slightly pale, along behind him.

"You need to be careful," he warned me. "It's natural that your first response is pity, but there are so many beggars that you can't give to all of them. I pay no attention to them. For you, who come from a different environment, it's more complicated. You are faithful to the tyrant you call conscience. In Kolkata it will give you no peace, it will hound you and whip you like a slave. I advise you to reach an accommodation with it. Tell it that you were not the one who invented poverty. Promise it that here and there you will placate it by tossing the odd coin to a beggar, but only if it stops tormenting you."

Yes, yes, I nodded, disturbed and unable to capture and make sense of my feelings. On the one hand, I felt that Mr Mukherjee was right and that I should digest the moral shock that I was experiencing when confronted with this brutal version of life, and drink it in as potential material for my stories (for my way of dealing with the world is after all literary, aesthetic); but inside me, on the other hand, was swirling a whirlpool of memories of the emaciated bodies of internees that I had seen on footage of Central European concentration camps.

7.

Rescue mission

The next morning only a half of the invitees gathered in the congress hall, the rest were too tired or hungover. A Japanese delegate whispered to me that some East European writers had been drinking and making a racket late into the night, before vomiting on the expensive carpet in the hallways and even on the pictures on the walls, not to mention what their rooms must be like. A disgrace, he said. The people who should be representing the achievements of the October Revolution!

I said that not even revolution can stop a person who, after excessive revelling, needs to throw up. It wasn't every day that comrades from the Eastern Bloc had the chance to guzzle Château du Grand Caumont.

"I drink only tea," he responded sharply. Then he said: "Literature is in crisis, we have come together to look for a way out, not to exchange jokes across the table or spew the contents of our stomachs against the walls of the most illustrious hotel in Kolkata." I advised him to tell this to Mr Banerjee, who might realise that the problems of the world and of literature are not insoluble, and he will fill our glasses with Assam tea, while donating the French wine to the beggars in front of the hotel.

The congress began with the opening papers. I don't know why some thought it interesting to warm up well-known axioms and then explain them as if they were new discoveries. "If the short story is a story that is short," trumpeted some American, "then what are works such as Mann's *Death in Venice* or James's *Turn of the Screw*?" Novellas, shouted some voices in the auditorium. Someone claimed that it didn't matter how long a narrative work was; what separated a story from a novel was not the number of words, but rather that a novel involved a chain of events and the development of characters, whereas a short story was the culmination of what happened before the story began. A novel is a string of pearls on a narrative thread. A story is a single gem in a gold ring.

That's not true, shouted a fat lady from Italy. What about Chekhov, what about Katherine Mansfield and other impressionists, whose stories are often merely extended expositions, emotional locks that are only unlocked in the last sentence? And Moravia, whose stories are notes on the mental state of a handful of characters, often just one? And Borges, whose stories are, at least on the surface, naked formalistic games, mathematical experiments? (We all looked round the auditorium, but Borges was not present.) Wasn't it clear, she continued, that there were as many stories as authors? That some were not better than others because of a different creative approach, but because of a better connection between intention and effect? In short, some stories achieve their goal, while others, exhausted and distorted from excessive effort, fall by the wayside.

And so on.

The level rose when the American, Elizabeth Janeway, provocatively stated that we literati and storytellers had been overtaken by factual literature, which had pushed us from the hands of readers into the hands of academics and literary pathologists, and had seized the privilege of "truth", taking away the value of our writing by criticising it as fabricated. In literature, the truth is only stated between the lines. But modern readers, in their lust for certainty are desperate for "facts", because literature does not mystify, but explains. Modern readers need demonstrable facts that they can cling to and feel safe. And so they prefer to reach for writing that does not demand that they participate in some emotional-conceptual conspiracy, but that "informs" them, giving them "knowledge" about the world. What can the story become (or remain) if we do not wish to get trapped in fruitless, wordy, mind-numbing experimentation on the one hand, or to degenerate into cheap provocation on the other? Should we give up formalism and the idea of the necessity of evolutionary progress and return to our sources? Or should we remain the concubines of psychological, aesthetic, ideological masters?

Pandemonium erupted in the hall. Even the most tired delegates perked up and wanted to express their opinion. I mainly listened. It seemed to me that the question was addressed in a sincere and weighty way only by John Berger and Susan Sontag. John Berger said he saw stories as refuges where the most fragile, but at the same time the most important truths about life were saved from obliteration and oblivion. And through this metaphor he saw the beginnings of narrative art: as a tent or hut or guest house where a group of people gathered to listen to the experiences of a soldier who had survived a dangerous battle, a traveller who had returned from unknown parts, a person who had been affected by unexpected adversity. Story in its original meaning is a vessel in which to store the meaning of life.

Susan Sontag did not agree with this. She said that this was only one among many possible models and that it didn't cover the stories written by Poe, Borges, Calvino and many other writers, including her. Their stories were fantastical, magical, fictitious, they were stories about moral dilemmas, not stories about life, but about fragments of life. Okay, said Berger, but at the end of the day, what do such stories tell us?

We need them, replied Susan Sontag, because we wish to be present when taboos are broken and aesthetic possibilities explored. Why shouldn't experience of life be used also for intellectual speculation, for moral fantasies, for describing probable worlds of past and future? In spite of that, Berger persisted, stories should be read as if we were listening to them, as if they were being told to us by our grandfather by a warm stove, while outside a snowstorm rages. Stories should have a form that is not literary, artificial, but simple and subordinated to content and the message.

Susan Sontag asked him if he was not aware that there had been a radical break between the oral and written traditions. Didn't it seem to him that the eyes perceive differently from the ears? That some things, some shades of life, could be expressed only by words on paper? The eye is quicker than the ear and on the page is a montage of allusions on which the story rests, which is different from what was left unsaid between spoken sentences. John Berger said that that was certainly true, but that he thought of a story even in a written form as a rescue mission, as rescuing the meaning of life from the limitless hollowness of time. A good story enriches the imagination, brings closer to us experiences that we have denied or forgotten about.

Susan Sontag asked whether he thought that life meant something only if it leads to something, but before he was able to reply, a Bengali participant named Dhan Gopal Mukherjee stood up and said that the question facing us as writers of short stories was above all the question of whether the world even needs stories. Are there any experiences in the world that haven't been described? Are some stories worth more than others, and if they are, shouldn't these be the stories we should be writing?

It was as if he had stirred up a hornet's nest, furious comments flew from all sides. There is no future, stubbornly repeated a jaded Scandinavian participant. We had exhausted all our sources – by shifting away from primary sources, we had impoverished all the possible models; the only thing that we could create in the domain of short narrative prose were variations on forgotten themes, illustrations of new literary ideologies, metaphysical intellectual pieces à la Borges and genre stories. That was all, the Scandinavian stopped enumerating. He added that it would be smarter to forget about literature and devote ourselves to planting trees, otherwise we would all too quickly run out of oxygen.

8.

Dancing above the abyss

It seemed appropriate that I should join in the discussion. Of course, every story has already been written a hundred times, I said. Just as it could be said of philosophy that it is merely a series of footnotes to Plato, one could say that all stories are variations (so Gozzi claims) of thirty-six dramatic situations. But in spite of that, we would like to read them again in a new form, in a more immediate, more recognisable shape. The problem I experience as a writer is that I can build a story only on the supposed reactions of readers. That the bricks that I use to build the narrative structure can only be a product of established literary conventions, and that the nature and form of the story are dependent on my selection of building materials. With one selection I get a particular story, with another selection a different one.

It seems to me that the only progress would be a story whose effect, form and meaning would be total and universal, which would have all the available ingredients in the right proportions. A story that would be everything to everybody: a myth, a parable, literary discourse, a fairy tale, a legend, a psychological outline, a commentary on human fate, a philosophical puzzle; equally amenable to all, from a road mender to a mathematician, from a youngster to a literary ideologue. In short, a real shift would be a story that everyone would enjoy, that would charm everyone, strike everyone to the quick, that would reveal something to everyone; a story that no one could reject.

Of course, such a story could embrace only a theme that is present in all of us to the extent that it is almost part of our everyday reality. And what is our everyday reality? It seems to me that it is constructed from wishes and fragments of experience. For between what really exists and what we think exists there yawns such a chasm that we are all, every one of us, trying to balance above it. And it is this hopeless dance above the abyss that I try to capture as a writer. For the only thing that interests us as readers, as observers of the dance: will the person fall or not? Will he plunge into the abyss? For every reader sees himself in the dance of the person that I try to throw light on in that moment of danger, that moment of doubt, that moment of revelation or that moment of enthusiasm. The reader experiences his own dance in the dance of that person. This is what interests me as a writer: how to create a story that captures the essence of the reality of this dance so that it means everything to everyone – not the same to everyone, but in their own way.

When I sat down, there was an unpleasant silence in the auditorium. It seemed to me that my words had fallen on deaf ears. Then they all leapt up at once and in the general scrum it was impossible to catch a single word. Mr Banerjee banged a fat anthology of Indian short stories on the table until the racket died down.

"Ladies and gentlemen, this is not Babylon, this is Kolkata," he rebuked us.

When there was quiet, he gave the floor to a moustached Indonesian. He said that I had succumbed to a lust for perfection, which made sense only as an abstraction, for every effort at embodiment changes it into a construct subordinated to goals that are neither aesthetic nor thematic. Paradoxically, my striving meant that I would be unable to write the kind of story I wanted to. He emphasised that my aspiration was one of the too many literary traps that threaten us and that if none of us was able to write a story that was by definition perfect, as I had expressed it, that was a consequence of the fact that no one can avoid this pitfall. For this reason, most of what we create is maimed.

How many of us are aware of at least the basic pitfalls, such as the tendency to rationalise failure? How often does something seem to write itself and we think that it is the fruit of divine inspiration, because it is unusual? Are we satisfied with what we have written because of laziness and then convince ourselves (which is not difficult) that we 'selected' the words on the basis of aesthetics? How many of us plunge head first into the trap of stylistic innovation? How many of us imagine that we are creating something new and contemporary if we break up sentences or order them in a special way or pad them with parentheses and verbal effects? How many of us choose linguistic skill and showing off as an exit from creative difficulties? And how many of us understand the true meaning of the axiom that literature ought to be challenging? Is there still anyone among us who does not interpret this word in a sensational way? Is there still anyone among us who is aware that the challenge in literature must appeal to the emotions? And so on.

I wanted to wait for a break in his rhetorical flow and to emphasise that it was precisely this that motivated me in my creative efforts: the wish to transcend the intellectualism that stands as the main barrier between the reader and literary art. If I succeeded to raise myself to a level above intellectualism, I would have the kind of story I wished for: a universal 'vessel' in which all readers could pour their own meaning.

I was beaten to it by one of the American delegates, who interrupted the Indonesian. He accused him of distancing himself from the issue that I had raised. Then he turned to me and said that I touched upon the central problem of creativity. He would like to know whether I had already tried to create such a universal vessel. And how. And with what success.

There was a murmur of agreement in the auditorium. All eyes turned to me.

I said that ten years before I had begun to think about the possibility of a story that would occupy everyone's mental space. As the central character I had chosen the person as victim (of society, relationships, his own perception of relationships, perceptions of himself). I described how I had tried to objectivise the image of this character through the eyes of an educated observer, who tries to 'understand' the distress and helplessness of the main figure through the context of his own experience. And how I had added to this main observer two others, who observe not only the main character, but also the main observer and his observing. Both of them also observed each other and the observing of all the others. In this way I wanted to achieve a multi-layered perspective. I wrote the story in such a way that the reader would become the fourth observer and get involved in events, almost like one of the characters in the story. Would help create the story. Would, willingly or not, become my colleague, my ally. It took a long time before I found a suitable form, a suitable style, but eventually I felt that I had everything I needed: simplicity, directness, a narrative thread, tension. All the elements were in harmony and invisibly woven together and set almost like a trap which the reader would be unable to avoid.

But I lacked something. I lacked an ending that came as a revelation, but which at the same time remained open enough to enable the reader's cooperation. I tried pattern after pattern, but rejected all of them. Over ten years, the story acquired a hundred different endings. Thus arose a hundred different stories, but not one of them did I have in mind when I started writing. If it wasn't open enough, if it didn't give the impression that it lacked an ending, then it did have an ending and thus became a story that the reader could not see as part of his experience. In spite of occasional despair, I didn't think that I had reached a dead end, I just needed a flash of inspiration, just a word, and the puzzle would be solved.

There was silence in the auditorium. Then an American delegate stood up and said that I had confirmed everything he had thought when I first mentioned the matter. It was clear that it was not an aesthetic, stylistic, ethical or even a metaphysical problem. It was simply a matter of narrative structure, a trick. He couldn't understand why writers insisted on maintaining their outdated poses, why they delude themselves that writing is the fruit of divine inspiration, when it so clear that we live in a world of a limited number of symbols, from which we can put together only a limited number of conceptual and narrative patterns.

He couldn't understand, he repeated, why we claim to be artists, when we are at best mere craftsmen. Critics had analysed thousands of stories and found in them less than fifty themes. We had to accept the fact that there were no more; that was our building material. Even if we wrote a story that we claimed was completely original, we would find within it traces of many themes and twists that we had subconsciously soaked up and forgotten that they came from outside us. The only possibility we had as writers was to combine the available ingredients in new and appealing ways. But that was never a matter of inspiration, it was a matter of skill, of manipulation.

He opened his briefcase and pulled out something reminiscent of an Indian hundred-year calendar: it was made up of layers of cardboard circles on an axis, which meant that they could revolve and move in different relations to each other, thus creating different combinations of the parts. This mechanical 'plot-finder', said the American, contains two thousand characters, events, circumstances and motives, in short narrative elements from which it is possible to combine the highest number of possible stories following the principles of coincidence, polarity and similarity. He used this creation to synthesise most of his narratives. He was willing to lend it to me so that I could find the most ideal ending for my story.

His offer left me feeling embarrassed. I saw not a few delegates grinning maliciously. I was wondering what to say so as not to offend the bald hack. But Mr Banerjee sprang to my assistance when he clapped and with genuine relief announced that it was time for lunch.

"We have heard," he said, "quite provocative contributions to our basic topic. In the evening, in this hall, there will be a seminar on our beloved Rabindranath Tagore. We shall return to the problems that have been so eloquently outlined tomorrow. Don't forget," he shouted after us as we shuffled towards the exit, "that in the afternoon we have organised a tour of the city!"

9.

Me and Scheherazade

I ate lunch in a hurry. I saw the bald American watching me from the corner of the dining room, waiting for another opportunity to offer his story merry-go-round. I avoided him and rushed from the room. I lay fully dressed on the bed in order to bring some order to my chaotic thoughts and to prepare myself for the monstrous heat hovering outside. Through the double-glazed windows came the muffled sound of traffic, the noise of the masses that poured and splashed around the corner, I heard the grinding of vehicles, horns blasting, the clanging of a tram, I heard the febrile voices of street vendors, shoe shiners, chaiwallahs, and blind beggars rhythmically banging their empty tins on the ground. I even thought I could hear the boy without limbs, clop-clop-clopping along the pavement and blocking people's way.

In the cacophony of noise, my awareness was most deeply pierced by the ringing of the bells from numerous rickshaws. It expressed the whole screeching despair of life on the street. At the same time, I sensed in it something threatening, a warning that I was unable to raise to conscious level; it poured over me like murky water, filling me with a choking tide of exhaustion.

I went over to the window. An ordinary scene was unfolding down below. Guests were entering and exiting, beggars were harassing them, children were getting under their feet, women were nursing babies. Cripples, blind beggars and lepers were banging the pavement with crutches, walking sticks, tins. Every few minutes, one of the two doormen who guarded the door in their fancy uniforms, gestured threateningly towards the mob and shouted something. Usually the doorman's puffed up posture was enough and the wave of beggars flowed back towards the edge of the pavement. But as soon as someone came out of the hotel, the noise rose again and the forest of outstretched arms crept back towards the entrance.

My gaze stopped on a beggar woman who gave the impression that she did not belong among the mob. She was kneeling with a dish in front of her next to the post box. Her knees were on the pavement and her bottom on her heels, she was wearing a dark brown Indian dress that reached to her feet and also covered her head like a scarf. The palms of her hands were turned upwards and resting on her knees. She knelt there, staring into space, placid, resigned, waiting. Sometimes, someone came past and her posture, so different from the trembling agitation of the others, attracted their attention. They would step forward, look into her face, which she never raised, reach into their pocket and toss two or three coins into the dish in front of her. Then they would linger, as if waiting for thanks. But she did not even look up. When the generous one moved on, he often couldn't resist the temptation to turn round: as if hoping that she would move and show that, after all, she was not different from the others.

But she was. When we were boarding the bus in front of the hotel, I deliberately stayed at the back of the line. I approached the immobile kneeling woman and saw that she was roughly my age and attractive in a half-innocent and half-sinful way. She cast her eyes downwards, she had sunken cheeks. She didn't look well. When I placed a twenty rupee note in her dish, it seemed to me that this wasn't alms, but a kind of contribution. I thought she wasn't collecting money for herself, but in order to realise an enlightened idea, to solve the problem that she herself embodied. I felt that such as she was, devotedly innocent, humble, but at the same time proud, she meant something.

That she was telling me something.

"I see that you've discovered Scheherazade," said Dhan Gopal Mukherjee. "She really is something special. Everyone calls her Scheherazade because she never moves from in front of the restaurant of that name. Some romantics claim that is her real name and that the restaurant is named after her. It's interesting that in five years she hasn't aged at all. Nor has she ever looked anyone in the eye. Nor spoken a word. Which is understandable, as she is dumb. Everyone sees her as a kind of saint. Even the hotel doormen, who mercilessly drive away the other beggars, regularly bring her food. No one knows where she came from, but five years ago she turned up in front of the entrance to the most luxurious hotel in Kolkata. And she stayed. As a reminder. Sometimes a trader comes and gives her a hundred thousand rupees. Then he stands in front of her and waits for her to look up at him. They say that in her eyes are hidden the answers to every question."

I said nothing. I had no wish to share my story of Scheherazade with anyone. I didn't want to admit that I had first seen her many years ago, as a schoolboy and many times since, and that over the years she had aged, although no more than I: we had aged in parallel with each other.

The air-conditioning on the bus wasn't working, so the driver opened the door. Through it blasted the hot afternoon humidity, smelling of sweat and cheap petrol, the tarry smell of softening asphalt, thousands of spices and herbs, and of the dung that the sacred cows left in dark cakes on the pavements. Soon, we were all bathed in sweat.

The bus, wildly blasting its horn, inched its way through the crowd of vehicles, bicycles, rickshaws, tricycles, trams, cows and people, people, people, who were hurrying as if fleeing a catastrophe. I saw traffic police dressed in white, guarded by armed police; around us swayed the battered facades of colonial buildings, from which the plaster was crumbling. Everything that we saw and the guide extravagantly praised – the Birla Planetarium, a marble palace, the Dakshineswar Kali Temple, the Ramakrishna Mission, Howrah Bridge, the birth house of Rabindranath Tagore – all of it remained without meaning. While half a million paupers still sleep on the pavements, while some are so poor that they cannot afford to cremate their dead relatives, but throw them in the River Hooghly, where the bleached corpses float back to the shore to be gnawed by dogs...

Only at the botanical gardens in Shibpur did the agitation inside me subside. Perhaps because we got out and walked beneath the trees, or because the thirty thousand varieties of plants for which the gardens are famous created a fresh atmosphere that didn't smother us. The guide took us to the "biggest tree in the world", a banyan tree twenty-eight metres high, which grows in a circle with a diameter of four hundred metres. He explained that forty years previously, the central trunk had been attacked by disease and they had to remove it. Now the 'tree' was made up of six hundred roots, which were also branches of the tree.

We walked beneath the gnarled arches of labyrinthine growth. We enjoyed the freshness of the air. The guide recommended that we should move on immediately, but the murmur of dissent silenced him. Mr Banerjee, who saw that he had no other option, generously announced that we could take it easy for a while.

10.

Criticism of the critics

While strolling in the park, I tried to find Borges, but he was not there; perhaps somewhere behind us. Instead, my attention was attracted by a group of Indian delegates, who gave the impression they were talking about things that others weren't supposed to hear. I strolled towards them. I caught some words about the massacres in Assam, about a plague epidemic that was spreading, and the question as to whether it was even true, since there had been no official reports about it. I went on. Some of them were watching me, giving me suspicious looks and lowering their voices. They quickly agreed that the topic of conversation was not suitable for non-Indian ears, which didn't seem strange to me, for one doesn't discuss family illnesses and tragedies in front of guests.

John Berger approached me. He said that my words had made a great impression on him. Our views were close in many regards, although he thought that the literary 'vessel' that I wished to create did not exist. Of greatest interest to him was the fact that I couldn't find a suitable ending. In his case, his idea for a story usually began with the end and through the story he merely led the reader towards an already prepared effect. It seemed to him that my problem was inherent in my approach, which was more appropriate for a novel than for a short story or at best for a story that was narratively open to emotional impressions. He was also intrigued by my wish to involve the reader in the creative act. What role did I give in that instance to myself, the writer? Would I say that I was an intermediary, that I think up the story or that I merely take part in the creative process, which I triggered as a participant in the event and which I have, if necessary, to subordinate myself to?

I replied that the role I adopt while writing is certainly dependent on what the tone and aesthetic direction of the story will be. So I cannot negate the fact that I am in a certain sense merely a participant in a process that I triggered more or less subconsciously out of a desire to find suitable words for something that was already inside me in the form of an uncertain feeling. At the same time, this of course meant that I had to submit to this primary initiative. But after reconsideration (and because of the events of recent days) these technical problems seemed less important than the question that we should address. The question was a dual one: first, had word inflation devalued our understanding of literature? And second, was the lack of creative courage in contemporary literature a consequence of the success of visual forms, film and television, or a sign of the general paralysis of the human spirit?

John Berger said that he didn't understand what I meant by courage. I replied that we should be writing stories about the most acute problems of existence. Unfortunately, we had in a cowardly and cynical way given up the role of guardians of moral conscience and surrendered to the monsters of literary-aesthetic consumerism, which had turned values upside down and assigned value only to that which, as in fashion, was different from the previous 'new'. We had succumbed to a cult of novelty, so it wasn't strange that literature had become a marginal activity of academics and we searched in it in vain for moral dilemmas, such as the reader confronted in the novels of the nineteenth century. It seems to me, I added, that we have been brought to impotence by our mechanistic conception of reality. We needed to get back to our sources. We must reject the *analysis* of reality and give ourselves up to *experiencing* reality. We needed to take off our intellectual glasses and learn to see without them.

Then we will, perhaps, see what is really happening.

I noticed that Professor Donoghue was listening in with interest. He eventually came up to us. We need a revolution, he said. We must rescue literature from the claws of the tyrant! That tyrant was the reductive nature of science, which had usurped literature as a lawful part of its field. Science (and this applied also to pseudo-sciences such as psychology and sociology) did not recognise mystery. It had swept everything that was mysterious and magical into the lap of religion. And with regard to art, it pretentiously claimed that it was possible to dismantle it into parts, to classify it, periodise it, as if it was something dead, material. The mental arrogance of the discursive approach to literature had created its own fifth column, literature as the result of ideology about literature, so that now waves, which literature ought to cut through, often went before it and directed it. The essence of true literature was something that could not be analysed.

Quite a few writers had gathered around us. Mr Banerjee and the guide stood helplessly to one side. The crowd attracted the others, and among the roots/branches of the biggest tree in the world a discussion developed about critics. When critics are discussed, few writers remain unaffected. The gathering became so clamorous that it could be heard all the way to the road, on which passers-by stopped and collected in curious groups.

The words of some radiated indignation. Why do we even need critics? Isn't it clear that almost every critic is a frustrated writer who, in his inability to be creative himself, takes the work of another and, in the words of Auden, usurps it as a document he has himself discovered? And didn't Tennyson say that critics are the fleas on the coat of literature?

A Danish delegate observed that this was leading nowhere and that we shouldn't be so uncritically sensitive. In his opinion, the real role of critics was defined by Samuel Johnson, who was not only a critic but also a poet, biographer and academic. In Dr Johnson's opinion, a good critic is one who explains how and why he likes a literary work. A good critic doesn't prescribe. At the same time, he does not ascribe his perceptions to some mystical authority and universality. A good critic is intelligent, honest, sensitive, conscientious. He respects the author and does not try to get involved in either a competitive or a conspiratorial relationship.

A delegate from Spain intervened. He said that today not one critic matched Johnson's definition. This was even more true regarding lecturers on literature in universities, who, with the conspiratorial help of students, had changed their subject into an esoteric pseudo-science. And how many living writers become a part of this conspiracy, as if their only ambition is to become the subject of a dissertation? Since today the driving force of intellectual life is trends, critics and literature live in an unhealthy incestuous relationship and give birth to freaks.

A thin, bespectacled delegate from New Zealand then spoke. She said that trends could also play a positive role in art. Of course, shouted some American, but where does their positive role begin and end? Does it end at the point where Harold Rosenberg is compelled to write about the speed with which ever new absurdities appear on the New York artistic scene that "dead art forms are the normal life of art"? Could not these words also be ascribed to critics? Let us acknowledge that criticism of art can succeed only as the opposite of criticism. As long as the critic tackles his work directly, through analysis and classification of form and meaning, he will disable the ongoing understanding of art. In Wonderland, Alice can only meet the Red Queen by distancing herself from her. That should also apply to criticism. Because the method and theory are forged, the only honest and fruitful relationship with a literary work can be achieved by trying to understand what is not told, not by imposing our semantic structures.

"Ladies and gentlemen," said Mr Banerjee. "Please don't be offended, but I have been entrusted with the organisation of this congress and we are currently on a tour of the city. You will have to continue discussions about literature in the conference hall at the right time. I suggest that we visit some other famous sights of Kolkata, which is, to be honest, the most interesting city in the world!"

We drove along the Hooghly River. Sitting next to me was a Japanese writer who in the morning had been boasting that he drank only tea. Although he said nothing for a long time, I could tell from his breathing that he was preparing to say something. I didn't feel like listening, so I closed my eyes and pretended to be dozing. That didn't deter him.

He said that, in comparison with his, my creative problem was a simple one. In his case, the evil fate was at play. Every time he carefully selected a theme and wrote a story, it turned out, usually after publication, that a similar story had already been written by someone else. It might be set in a different time and a different environment, but the narrative was related and he could be accused of plagiarism. For five years now, he had been producing such plagiarisms. He had written stories that had been written before him by Conrad, D. H. Lawrence, Chekhov, Mann, O. Henry, Borges, Saki, Maugham, Bradbury, Maupassant and Moravia.

He went on to explain that two possible explanations came to him. It was possible that he was the victim of an evil deity, who had chosen him as the object of his sadistic games. If he rejected that explanation as irrational and rejected the other possible explanation, coincidence, for coincidence is never reliably consistent, then there was only one possible explanation left: every story has already been written and all writers are now plagiarists, although he, it seems, is the only one who is aware of this. This also meant that he was the only living writer who could write a truly original story: about a writer who discovers, as he goes along, that all the stories he writes have already been written. That was the only story that had not yet been written. That would cross the t and dot the i. It would fill the last creative gap. It would complete the narrative literature of the twentieth century.

"Too late," said Joyce Carol Oates, who was sitting behind us. "I wrote such a story many years ago." The Japanese writer dug his fingers into the leather of the seat in front of him. Then he slowly relaxed and sank into silent reflection.

11.

Bodies in the river

We were driving along the river. The water was yellowish, muddy, with greenish brown patches, full of chemical waste and the overflow from drains. I noticed that there was the bleached body of a child or small woman lying on the riverside mud. Two scrawny dogs were sniffing it. It was the first time I had seen one of the bleached corpses for which Kolkata was famous. It is said that the white coating comes about because of a reaction between the organic acids in the body and the chemicals poured into the river by factories and workshops. A hundred metres further on, I noticed another washed up body: the grossly bloated corpse of a man in a grey robe.

Behind the riverside bushes, a scene was revealed to my eyes that filled me with horror. On the gravel, in many different poses, at different angles, singly or in groups, lay more than twenty bloated corpses. Some were naked, some dressed, some were being rocked and pushed against the bank by the water.

I was overcome by fear that I was hallucinating. Then I noticed that the other writers had spotted the corpses. A wave of agitated whispering rippled through the bus.

Mr Banerjee, trying to retain the appearance of a cool and collected organiser, was consulting with the guide. Then both of them spoke to the driver.

The bus turned off the riverside road. It swayed down pot-holed suburban streets past shabby huts made of mud. In front of them, beside the overflowing drains, swarmed hungry looking children. The poverty was becoming ever more evident and Mr Banerjee realised that he had made a mistake. He leaned closer to the driver. It seemed that he told him to turn right at the first opportunity. The driver complied. Through the low roofs of the slum quarter, we saw that we were approaching through the fog the crooked outline of the Howrah Bridge.

On an open bit of ground by the side of the road was a fire of brushwood and on it a charred, naked bodies were burning. At that moment two men swung another one on, the flames leapt and sparks scattered. In the last flash we saw bent, despondent men bringing the bodies of other men, women and children and laying them in a row not far from the bonfire, where women were stripping them and preparing them to be burnt.

Silence fell on the bus. We felt that something was happening in Kolkata that wasn't usual. Something that wasn't normal even for Kolkata. Our feeling was confirmed by the stubbornly impassive face of Mr Banerjee. But not one of us dared to request an explanation. We were guests in a strange house, we had seen the obscenity of poverty and death, but a guest pretends that he has seen nothing and no one among us wanted to be impolite.

Before the bridge, we were stopped by a military patrol. Mr Banerjee got out and started waving his arms about, explaining something. We saw sweating, dark-eyed soldiers setting up a barricade in front of the bridge. Mr Banerjee was shouting that we must return to the town, we were the delegates at an international congress and that was no small thing. By whining and pleading he finally softened the moustached officer (I saw him press something into his hand) and they allowed us to drive over the bridge. On the other side, Mr Banerjee stood up and, staring into nothing above our heads, said that regrettably we had lingered too long in the gardens, that the city tour would have to end and that we were returning to our hotel.

"Why are they closing the bridge?" asked a brave voice behind me.

"The bridge?" said Mr Banerjee in an agitated way. "No one is closing the bridge, why do you have to be so negative? Surely in other cities the police control the traffic!" He turned his back to us.

Back in my room, I collapsed onto the bed and closed my eyes. In the hollows of my brain bonfires with charred corpses were burning. Splashing water was washing up the bleached bodies of drowned children. I had never before felt more strongly the desire to flee reality, to leave the world of meaning.

From my suitcase I pulled a hundred duplicated copies of an unfinished story entitled *A Lesson in Paralanguage*. I went to look for Mr Banerjee. I found him in the dining room, where he was supervising preparations for dinner. Pulling him into a corner behind the door, I whispered to him that I needed a favour. Would he distribute my story to the delegates and ask them to add to it the ending that seemed best to them or inevitable?

He looked surprised and shook his head. Without embarrassment (as he had done with the moustached officer at the bridge) I pressed a twenty-pound note into his hand.

"Of course," he exclaimed, as his hand disappeared into his pocket, "I am willing to do many things for literature."

He reached for the wad of paper. "I'll distribute them immediately."

I returned to my room and stood at the window, staring at the street. One of the hotel doormen, a powerfully built Sikh with a red turban, was driving away beggars. They poked their tongues out at him. One of the female beggars provocatively rubbed her groin. Children pulled faces. He got fed up and went back beneath the arch of the entrance. After a while, he reappeared. He went over to Scheherazade and placed a dish of rice in front of her, gently bowed and returned to the entrance.

I waited to see what she would do. She did not move. One of the beggar children headed towards the dish, but his mother hurried after him and pulled him back. Scheherazade reached for the dish and placed it into her lap. With the fingers of her right hand, she placed balls of rice in her mouth and chewed them rhythmically. When she had finished, she put the dish down on the ground and remained still in her usual bent posture.

I decided to read once more the story I was unable to finish.

12.

A story without an ending

"It was evening, and in the bay the red lights of fishing boats were twinkling. We were sitting in a taverna in the village of Kotronas in the Peloponnese. *We had met by strange coincidence: Helmut's car had broken down on the road and he'd asked me to drive him to the next settlement.* I had assumed that Paula was his girlfriend, until she explained to me that she was hitchhiking round Greece and that Helmut had picked her up a little before I had picked up him.

At the next table sat three locals, who were watching us with curiosity. It seemed they would like to invite us to join them or that they would join us and engage us in conversation. Unfortunately, none of us understood Greek and there was no sign that they understood German or English. The first one (I found out later) was a young villager called Dinos, who made a living as a lorry driver. The second, older than him, was Filipas, the owner and driver of the village taxi. The third was "Captain" Jovanis, a thin, toothless old man who was all large, timidly curious eyes, with a twinkle of mischief.

Dinos finally plucked up the courage and with a broad gesture invited us to their table. When we joined them, he ordered ouzo for us all. He started to tell us something in Greek, pointed to himself, then his companions, and through gestures indicated that it was necessary to match them glass for glass. We nodded. He shoved back his chair, jumped up, clicked his heels together and shouted: "Atina, Atina!"

When he saw our doubtful expressions, he once more clicked his heels, saluted, removed an invisible rifle from his shoulder, aimed, fired, returned the rifle to his shoulder and saluted again. Now we understood. He was going to Athens to do his military service. We said in German and English, as well as with gestures that were not very eloquent, that he then probably had no option but to get drunk.

There was a short interlude, Dinos was thinking what to say. He raised his glass and toasted us. We all drank. We sat there, looking at each other and our sense of embarrassment deepened. Dinos began to talk to Filipas. We carried on our conversation in English.

Helmut said that it was possible to communicate without words. Gestures, even barely discernible movements, form a 'paralanguage' through which we can express thoughts and feelings as eloquently as through words. Language and paralanguage are of course connected: if we learn a language, then we also pick up the appropriate bodily symbols. We learn that at a funeral we are not supposed to smile. That we cannot communicate as freely with our superiors as with childhood friends. And so on. We always use bodily symbols in accordance with the customs of the social environment. Crying and laughter are the only signs that are widely shared. The meaning of different gestures differs from one nation to another.

So, for instance, a German will ask a question and wait for an answer with a slightly raised head. A Javanese asks a question then lowers his eyes and looks under the table or examines his shoes. If we want to confirm something, we nod. Darwin saw nodding as a reflex resulting from evolution: he ascribed it to the baby's search for the mother's nipple. Now we know that he was wrong, for the members of the ancient Ainu tribe in Japan agree by raising their hand to their chest and waving it; Malayan 'pygmies' throw their head forward like a hen pecking at corn; while Punjabis throw their head back violently. The Afghans, Iranians and even Bolgarians nod for "no" and shake their heads when they mean "yes".

That is why foreign language learning in school is never successful. Language takes on meaning only when it is properly used in communication, when the paralanguage plays an equally important role as the words. It is impossible to speak English and use Italian gestures, while an English man speaking Italian will automatically come to life and will reinforce his words with his hands.

But if we forget about words, said Helmut, and focus all our attention on gestures, language differences are dramatically reduced. At least eighty per cent of the bodily signs used by Germans and English are also used by Greeks. That means that we should be able to communicate in paralanguage without any great difficulties. The deaf can communicate in a similar way.

Paula didn't agree with this. She said that deaf people make use of a series of carefully produced signs, each of which means something specific, agreed. Their way of communicating, although non-verbal, is as precise as spoken language and leaves no room for misunderstanding. The same cannot be said of paralanguage. It's not difficult to assign the wrong meaning to a gesture.

Helmut replied that the precision of the communicative medium did not exclude the possibility of misunderstandings (how else was it possible that even in the most precise languages we cannot communicate about the nature of the reality in which we live?). Thanks to its semantic flexibility, paralanguage facilitates something that spoken languages don't: that we cooperate with the formation of the meaning that the gestures express. Words create boundaries. Gestures bring closer.

Dinos got up, clicked his heels, saluted, took aim with an imaginary rifle and shouted: "Bang, bang!" We raised our glasses and toasted him. Filipas put his right index finger to his temple and turned it slightly: that surely meant that Dinos is crazy. "Captain," Dinos laid his hand on the shoulder of the little old man. We nodded. With gestures that were not difficult to understand, he told us that the Captain was the best dancer in Greece. A few glasses of ouzo and he will begin to dance.

Then the old man looked each of us in the eye. The apologetic glint in his look became a challenging pride. Don't you believe it, said his eyes. Such a bent old man the best dancer? Out of politeness, we nodded in a friendly way. In his younger days, explained Dinos, the Captain was a real hero.

He pushed his glass and cup of coffee into the centre of the table. He settled himself and made room with his elbows. Evidently, he wanted to "tell" us the Captain's story. First he drew a ship with his finger. Then his hand made waves in the air: a boat sailing on the sea. Then he put his left hand on Jovanis's shoulder so suddenly that the old man started. "Captain," emphasised Dino. We understood. The boat is sailing on the sea and Jovanis is the captain.

Then a storm, wind. Dinos blew so violently that the peak of Jovanis's cap stood upright. In the storm the mast broke, the boat turned over and the Captain found himself in the water. Help! Water was running into his throat. Dinos grabbed his throat and gurgled and choked as if he was drowning. Jovanis nodded seriously.

The shipwrecked man got lucky, another vessel came along and pulled him on board. The Captain asked his rescuers to drop him off at the first opportunity, because he wanted to return to Greece, where his love was waiting for him. But the ship, which was five times as big as the Captain's boat, sailed and sailed, hurrying night and day in an unknown direction, and the sailors were very different, for they were dark skinned, almost black, and they all had sharks tattooed on their chests.

The ship finally made port. Jovanis found himself on a tropical island in the South Seas, ruled by a dark princess as fat as a whale. On the island this was a measure of great beauty. The sailors handed the princess numerous presents brought from far away. One of those presents was Captain Jovanis.

Dinos emphasised that this had happened many years before, when Jovanis wasn't an emaciated old crock, but was young and upright, a veritable Apollo. And so it was no surprise that the princess liked her present. Unfortunately, the Captain could summon up no enthusiasm for her. She had too much flesh on her, most of it in the wrong places. When she sat, a wind blew from her arse that pressed the Captain against the wall. And thus, at every encounter with her, his manhood drooped down in a defensive reflex.

When the princess realised that the Captain would be unable to play her favourite game, she ordered him to dance. The poor Captain had to dance from dawn to dusk and from dusk to dawn, day after day, year after year; for five years the Captain danced for the fat princess. He performed all the Greek dances and in the end he made some up. And so it was not at all strange that the Captain was now the best dancer – in such circumstances, even a donkey would learn to dance!

Dinos went over to Jovanis and put his hands beneath his shoulders. Then he changed his mind and grabbed the collar of his jacket. He lifted him and dragged him to the middle of the taverna. Jovanis struggled half-jokingly, his eyes flitting from one person to another, he was afraid we would laugh at him. He was a tiny man, a real clown. The local guests were enjoying themselves. Dinos left the old man in the middle of the taverna and began to clap rhythmically and shout something that sounded like: "Come on old man, dance, dance!"

The Captain stood there as though dumbstruck. He couldn't decide whether to resist or to play his role wordlessly. He once more looked around anxiously. For the first time, I saw suppressed pain in his eyes. Then he began to dance. He clumsily moved his feet and waved his hands. Dinos clapped rhythmically and drove him like the trainer of a dancing bear. And the Captain really was reminiscent of a clumsy, unhappy bear.

After five minutes, Dinos allowed him to sit. The old man slipped back to his seat. Once again, his eyes became eloquent, staring at us both beseechingly and defiantly. It's a devilish life, they said. An old man who has no one, but needs company and a drink, must act the fool.

Soon after that, we went our separate ways. Dinos chugged off in his lorry, Filipas drove off in his taxi. There was silence in the seaside village. Jovanis raised his cap and bid us goodbye. Helmut pressed a banknote into his hand. We watched him go. In the moonlight, we saw that he was going to an old, partially ruined house on the beach. He lay on the ground in front of it and covered himself with a piece of sailcloth.

"Poor old man," I said.

"Why?" said Helmut in surprise. Paula also turned towards me as if I had said something strange. I described how

I had watched the scene and how I interpreted Dinos's dumb show, from the shipwreck to the fat princess to the Captain's clumsy dancing, when it became obvious that it was all a fabrication and that it was all a tasteless joke, unforgivable toying with an old man who could not defend himself.

Interesting, said Helmut. Although we had seen the same gestures, I had placed the Captain in the role of victim. Out of a desire to generalise a one-off event, I had transformed him into a symbol of the neglected, passive half of humanity. And in Dinos I had seen the embodiment of the indifference we feel towards our predecessors, to our past, and our willingness to exploit the past to our own ends.

He had read something else into Dinos's gestures. The Captain had a boat, he made a living from fishing. One day, on the open sea, he had been caught in a storm and the boat had sunk. The Captain swam to dry land. Since had no money to buy a new boat, he got employment as the captain of a fishing boat owned by the company Shark. The Captain had sailed south with a crew of Africans to hunt whales. They returned empty-handed and the Captain lost his job. He became a member of a folklore group that performed traditional Greek dances. They travelled all around Greece and he became a well-known and popular dancer. Five years ago, he fell off his donkey and damaged his back. Now he makes a living by going from place to place and dancing for tourists. At the end, Dinos said he would be happy to dance for us, too. Which he did. He of course expected a tip and he was disappointed because Paula and I had not given him anything.

Paula began to laugh. "That's not right," she said. "Neither one thing nor the other. You two invented those stories."

In reality, he wasn't a captain, she continued. But he dreamed that he would become one and the best in Greece.

But because he was too scared to leave Kotronas, he had to live out his dream in the local bay, where he fished from a small boat. He imagined that the boat was five times bigger than it was, and on the bow he painted a shark. One day, he was caught by a storm in the bay and the boat sank. Jovanis was pulled on shore by a dark-haired villager, whom he married out of gratitude. She didn't have a good opinion about his daydreaming. She was a practical woman who needed a man. Jovanis was on his feet night and day, now he had to go here, now there, he had to work like a pack animal. And since Jovanis was both a coward and a fool, he dared not resist, he was a slave to his wife until she died, five years ago. Jovanis was still the same, he didn't know how to say no, if you tell him to drink, he will drink, if you tell him to get up, he will get up, if you tell him to dance, he will dance. Isn't that right, Jovanis? Dinos had asked him. And Jovanis had nodded. Then he let himself be dragged to the middle of the taverna and he danced.

It seemed to me that Helmut and Paula had confused the order of Dinos's gestures. They said that I had confused them. Paula was of the opinion that Helmut and I were confused. Even when we acknowledged that each of us was slightly wrong, we each felt that our own interpretation seemed the most likely.

And if we were all wrong to some extent, who was closest to the truth?

Whose truth? asked Helmut. The truth of the Captain's story? Or the truth of Dinos's interpretation of the Captain's story? Were we possibly talking about some autonomous truth that exists regardless of the specific semantic framework, within which something becomes perceptible and accessible? There was no doubt that much had happened to the Captain in the past. But the events were not connected by way of natural selection and they certainly hadn't occurred as links in a chain that would conclude in an aesthetic or moral point. The events had had a particular meaning because the Captain had understood them in a particular way. A man's interpretations of the events in his life are subjective. They are understood even less objectively by those who were not present. Even if we neglect the various crossroads through which the Captain's story came to Dinos. Even if we only consider the question as to how precisely we understood what he was trying to tell us through gestures. We have to admit that there, too, reality is only revealed to us through the prism of meanings that we gave things on the basis of the interpretation of our perceptions.

If that's true, I said, everything that comes under the concept of "my life" is fabulated, forced into this or that pattern because in conceptualising our self and our reality, we cannot cope with chaos. And we adapt this story, which we call reality, as we go along, engraving into it new impressions and new explanations of events. Things cannot be like that, I said. At least in one regard we must be fixed, objective and recognisable. Although we had each assigned the Captain a different role – I of the victim, Helmut of the flexible adapter to circumstances, Paula of the dreaming fool – one of our interpretations must be closer to the truth than the other two.

For the simple reason that objective reality of the Captain's life undoubtedly existed.

They both agreed with this. Paula said that there was only one way we could determine which of us had erred the least. We had to find someone who knew the Captain and who could describe his past to us in words.

In the corner of the taverna, three locals were sipping retsina. The owner was leaning against the counter, looking bored. We knew that he knew some German words, but it turned out that he spoke German quite well; he had worked in Ingolstadt for five years and saved enough money to build his taverna. We asked him if he knew Jovanis, the "Captain". Had he seen how Dinos had told us his story using gestures? He nodded. We explained to him that we didn't know whether we were interpreting the gestures correctly. Could he tell us what had actually happened to Jovanis? He nodded."

***

And here my story ended.

The words of the taverna owner would be crucial. They would give the story meaning, a point, a tone. In past decades I had found more than a hundred keys, but not one of them had given a story universality. I knew that the taverna owner's explanation must be as questionable as our three. At the same time, the combination of all four readings should make it easier to get nearer the truth. Not intellectually, like solving a puzzle, but in the form of experience, revelation. In the end, I rejected all the variants. I was too close to the story, I was involved in it, so some of its aspects remained hidden. I needed the help of someone who was not affected.

13.

The plague and me

The next morning, I didn't feel like going into the conference hall. I had a feeling that some writers had already read my unfinished story and would want to discuss it. But it was too early for that. I was also increasingly aware that our discussions were taking place in a luxurious air-conditioned hall, which stood in the stifling heat of Kolkata like a clearing in the jungle and that in this clearing, as self-selected chosen ones, surrounded by intellectual fires protecting us from attacks by the dark animal forces in the bushes, enthusiastic and also indignant, but in reality unaffected, we were discussing the suitability and credibility of a way of living in the jungle, without daring to go to the edge of our operating space. It increasingly felt as if we were having our debates in a luxurious oasis in the midst of misery and death, the symbol of our alienation from that real world which we believed we were writing about. In the circle within which we were functioning, the world of reality was only a semantic-conceptual structure, in which we wandered like half-crazy prisoners of our own inventiveness. I felt that the intellectual fires that had for so long protected us against attack from reality were fading and that the jungle would soon gobble up our clearing. Not victoriously and vengefully, but completely indifferently.

After breakfast, I had the desire to leave the sterile safety of the hotel and to go onto the city streets, not as a tourist with a guide or as a politely interested viewer of architectural features, nor as a writer, a collector of impressions for my treasure store (wasn't I always evaluating experiences and impressions in terms of their literary usefulness?), but as a sentient person, one of the mass. I felt a desire to throw myself into the world of sweat and clamour, into the world of struggle and cruelty, into the inescapable world of the dumb Scheherazade; to cast myself into it like someone who, at first hesitant and following nostalgic impulses, but with an ever greater recognition of affinity, was returning home to the world in which he was born and where he must live with all the responsibility of a local: not only as an observer, but as a participant.

At eleven the main doors of the hotel were still closed. Even bolted. That seemed strange to me. I went into the restaurant, which gave access to the garden and from there to the street. But the door was locked there as well. What was more, someone had placed crates in front of it. I went to the reception desk and asked, slightly impatiently, what on earth was going on. The overweight doorman in white shirt, who could not erase the signs of concern from his face, shrugged helplessly. "A police ordinance, sir. The plague is spreading in the city. The ordinance is temporary, until the situation improves. Experts of the World Health Organisation landed here a few hours ago. You have nothing to fear, you're safe here."

I got the feeling he was trying to reassure himself as much as me.

I returned to my room and looked through the window at the street.

I was stunned by what I saw. There was no longer the bustle of shouting masses and traffic jams. The street, one of the main Kolkata's main thoroughfares, was eerily empty, and above the park on the other side of the road a damp mist hovered. The few groups of people on the street corners and beneath the roadside trees were talking in muffled tones. A lorry drove past, its trailer buckling with the weight of the load of bodies. On the step at the back stood two soldiers wearing gas masks. The driver also wore a mask. Somewhere to the right, towards the city centre, a siren wailed.

I went closer to be able to see the pavement in front of the hotel. Most of the beggars had vanished. Ten or twelve of them were lying on the ground in grotesque poses. Some were clearly dead. Others were dying. The boy without limbs had gone. Overnight, everything had changed. The world had lost its skin, only the skeleton remained.

Only Scheherazade squatted near the post box as if nothing had changed, immobile, with her dish in front of her, her hands on her knees, her head down, staring at the ground.

Why hadn't she left?

I heard knocking. When I opened the door, there stood the Bengali writer Dhan Gopal Mukherjee, with a friendly smile on his face. I invited him in. We went over to the window together and looked at the street.

I didn't feel that he had lost his dignity, his slightly arrogant certainty. Perhaps he perceived the events in the city as temporary nuisance that simply had to be accepted. After all, this wasn't the first outbreak of the plague in Kolkata. The catastrophic extent of the events which I had assumed could be merely a figment of my imagination.

"I read your story," he said. I looked at him in surprise. But my surprise did not arise from the fact that I had expected him to say something about the plague, about our captivity, about the latest news, but at the sudden realisation that my story had sunk into the misty background and had ceased to be, at least for now, the motivating force of my existence. I wanted to ask him whether he thought it was worth adding an ending, but he beat me to it. He began to speak.

But not about the story.

He began to speak about the plague. He spoke in a weary, suppressed and frightened voice. There were rumours that the Americans and Russians had already brought three mobile hospitals into the city. From every corner of the world, more than a hundred epidemiologists were on their way. The civil and military authorities had organised the efficient removal of bodies. They were being burned on bonfires near the airport. In laboratories, three teams of scientists were trying to isolate the virus and find an effective vaccine. Although the authorities were denying it, people were saying that there had also been outbreaks in Delhi, Mumbai, Madras and Hyderabad. Someone had said that on a train journey from Cochin to Benares he had seen no village where they were not burning bodies. There were rumours, although the authorities were denying them, that the plague was spreading towards China, the Soviet Union, Europe. Supposedly, the incubation period of the virus was only four hours. Some were saying that all the roadblocks were a waste of time, this was the end. The rich were blaming the Third World. The rich in the Third World were blaming the poor. The poor were blaming beggars. The virus had appeared among them, due to chronic malnutrition and living in unhygienic conditions.

We stared through the window. A military lorry stopped in front of the hotel. From it jumped two men in gas masks and started collecting the dead. One grabbed the legs, the other the shoulders, they swung each body and threw it on the heap in the trailer. Some were still alive and yelped when they were lifted; they left them and moved on. They collected fifteen corpses. One had light coloured hair and a white shirt with a tie, and I recognised the Danish delegate. Probably he had been out in the town when they locked the doors and he had lain on the pavement, as among equals.

The lorry swayed onwards. It was followed by an ambulance in a great hurry: the sound of its siren drowned in the humidity that was getting ever thicker and wrapping itself around the outlines of the abandoned city. The whole time, Scheherazade remained immobile, indifferent even to the men in the gas masks. In her submission, in the centre of a city sinking in death, there wasn't a trace of resistance.

14.

Borges narrates

I lay on the bed and closed my eyes. Something was resisting my aesthetic sense. Something was wrong in the ingredients of the situation, in the plague that was laying waste to the city and the world so suddenly and so extensively that it was hard to believe; in the fact that a fragment of the world's intellectual elite was locked in a luxury hotel, a victim of its privilege. It was too schematic, there was too much forced symbolism and too many "literary" illusions (Kafka, Camus, Buñuel, Pynchon); almost as if reality wanted to be realised in the narrative text, as plagiarism, as a variant of a story that we had all already written.

Perhaps what was resisting my aesthetic sense was not an image of the state of things, but my inability to understand it any other way than within the conceptual framework of moral symbols. Was the devastation of the world by plague like my "Captain's story": chaos, until it had been given a conceptual dimension based on a personal selection of the narrative possibilities? Is our tragedy (and our fault) here that we know only one language – the language of King Shahryar? That we are all his slaves? That we are also trapped in his concepts, which seem to hold the only reality? Was the plague the end of a story that we did not know how to end successfully, because we had framed it wrongly?

I went into the dining room. They were all there already, even Borges, who was drinking wine. Mukherjee had reserved me a seat at the table where José J. Veiga and Thomas Pynchon were already sitting. The mood of the guests was lighter than I had expected. Mukherjee whispered that most in the hotel felt safe. They were happy that they were here and not somewhere in the city. After the initial doubts, trust in medical science had returned. Trust had hardened into an unlimited conviction that it was only a matter of time before the experts found an effective vaccine and the tide of the plague would recede. But when I looked more closely at the faces around me, I got the feeling that in a number of cases their cheerfulness was fake.

The food was as good as always, nor was there a shortage of French wine. The bottles in front of the delegates from the Socialist bloc were already empty. A Bulgarian writer was trying to convince the waiter to bring another one – the food was too spicy, he needed wine to extinguish the fire in his mouth. All conversations revolved around literary matters. No one mentioned the plague. Just once some smothered words reached my ear that the plague was merely our collective hallucination: a way of assimilating the moral shock we had experienced because of the poverty on the streets.

After lunch, Mr Banerjee got up onto a chair, waved his hands and asked us to listen for a moment. He said that because of the circumstances that prevented us from realising our previously planned afternoon programme, the viewing of the temple of the goddess Kali, some delegates had recommended that we stay in the dining room, drink some more wine ("Bravo! Bravo!" shouted the delegates from the

Socialist bloc, applauding) and pass the time by listening to some stories. It seemed some writers had suggested that it would be entertaining and perhaps enlightening if each of us read the one of our stories out loud. These words were followed by applause and at precisely that moment my eyes stopped on the face of John Berger. I thought how close this was to his definition of the story as refuge; the story that someone tells when people are sheltering from the rain, from a storm. From the plague.

First up, John Barth read a story entitled *Menelaiad*. Menelaus lost the beautiful Helen; her love was not enough for him and he kept pestering her with the question as to why she loved him. The desire for understanding cost him the tangible reality. His search for something that would not evade him became the search for certainty, the fight with Prometheus, whose ability to adopt a hundred different forms personified the fluidity of reality. Menelaus tells a story which includes stories that are told within the framework of the first or second, and so you are never able to say whether he is really hunting Prometheus or struggling against a dream. And when it seems that Helen has returned, he cannot say whether it is really Helen or just a dream cloud. Or perhaps Prometheus, who has adopted her shape. All that is revealed to him as indubitable, measurable fact may be just part of a wider unfathomable fiction. Maybe reality, too, is no more than a form of fiction. In a world where we demand evidence for everything, we are lost forever; in a world where reality, as we get entangled in the strands of analytical fiction, permanently evades us, what certainly remains present is only the endless possibility of love.

We all applauded, some enthusiastically, others out of politeness. The delegates for the Socialist bloc exchanged some sarcastic comments.

Then Jorge Luis Borges stood up. A silence fell over the hall. He said that, as we knew, he was blind. He therefore could not read us a story, but he could tell us one. We all applauded.

Slowly and with carefully chosen emphases, he began to tell us his famous story *Tlön, Uqbar, Orbis Tertius*. Although most of the writers already knew it, out of the author's mouth (and in an environment where we could not forget reality even for a moment) it acquired a mysterious, almost magical power.

It began on the level of accessible reality. The fictitious narrator and his friends discover in an encyclopaedia a reference to a country called Uqbar. The literature of this country was described as a fantastic collection of legends and epics that did not speak of reality but about two fabricated areas: Mlejnas and Tlön. Then by chance the narrator discovers the "First Encyclopaedia of Tlön" with the history of an unknown planet. After careful study it is discovered that this "new world" was created by a secretive society of specialists in every area of human knowledge. What at the beginning gave the impression of chaotic fiction became a coherent cosmic structure based on carefully formulated laws. A particular feature of the Tlön language was that it had no nouns, since for the inhabitants of Tlön "the world is not a concourse of objects in space; it is a heterogeneous series of independent acts". Artists in this world (and in this language) are not seekers of truth but rather "astonishment" and for them metaphysics is a form of fantastic literature. On Tlön, people change the forms of the things around them by moving them and if they forget about them they sink into misty oblivion. In this world, the spirit rules the material and there is no reality that people perceive, but only what they determine with their senses. The mysterious origin of Tlön is clarified only in a postscript in which the narrator mentions a secret benevolent society that met in Lucerne or London in the seventeenth century and decided to make up a country. Two hundred years later, the members of the brotherhood turn up in America, where they are joined by some millionaire who recommends that they make up a whole planet. He also recommended that the truth of the real nature of this planet should remain a secret.

"Proof" of the existence of Tlön enters our world very slowly. First, by coincidence, the "Tlön alphabet" is discovered. Then objects are found which seem to be from Tlön. Then the First Encyclopaedia of Tlön is discovered. All of this is part of the plan of the members of the secret society to project the made-up planet into our world. The planted evidence is received as real. It is received with enthusiasm. Our world longs for order. It is enthusiastic (at least temporarily) about every symmetrical system that gives the impression of order. In different periods people were attracted by different systems, such as theism, dialectical materialism, Nazism, anti-Semitism, Stalinism, positivism. Why not trust clear evidence about a world that is undoubtedly ruled by order? The appeal of Tlön is that it is wholly the product of the human mind and so it understands that mind without difficulty. Because he has created it, man sees meaning in it. At the end, the narrator sees a day when all the world's languages will disappear and all of reality will become Tlön.

Borges sat down. Everyone applauded. For a long time.

I didn't. There was a tempest in my head. What was this story? An illustration of the phenomenal inventiveness of the human mind? Or a warning against the fact that because we feared chaos, we hurried to impose fantastical structures and then begin to perceive them as real? Wasn't the creation of Tlön basically a liberating act? Why, then, did it become a cage? From chaos, the longing for order, we create order. Is it possible that we had accepted one of the constructed systems as the final model of reality? Shahryar's model of reality?

I got up and hurried towards the exit. Everyone was looking at me. Before I got to the door, I noticed that Mr Banerjee had risen from his seat and was waving a sheaf of papers at me. I ran into the corridor and towards the reception desk. Mr Banerjee ran panting behind me, shouting: "Sir, your story, your colleagues have added an ending!"

15.

The end of a world

I shut my ears and ran across the thick carpet towards the exit. The door was open. The stifling heat of Kolkata crashed into me on the pavement. It seemed as if the city was disappearing in a humid haze, concealing itself and retreating into a world of perceivable but unattainable reality. I ran towards the post box.

"Scheherazade," I shouted. "Speak, please! Speak!"

Her copper dish, full of coins and notes, was on the ground. But there was no sign of her.

"Scheherazade!" I shouted and ran along the street, calling her as if that really was her name. From the haze emerged the scarcely visible outlines of houses, streetlights, abandoned cars. I thought I saw her, appearing and again disappearing in the haze, hurrying, impossible to catch.

I ran and ran, determined to find her.

I began to see uncollected bodies on the pavement. They were naked, emaciated, scattered without order, gaping, obscenely uncovered. There were ever more of them, even on the street, I had to step over them. They were gathered in heaps beneath the roadside trees. Out of the mist appeared the outlines of guard towers, from which soldiers with machine guns watched me. They had helmets on their heads. The mist began to thin. I ran past barbed wire towards some low wooden sheds.

Then I saw her. She was standing among the internees in the yard and staring at me. She was wearing the striped pyjamas of a concentration camp prisoner. I ran towards her with a pistol in my hand and a helmet on my head, wearing an SS uniform. I realised at that point that I was SS Sturmbahnnführer Stolz, a character from my collection of stories on World War Two.

How was that possible?

How was it possible that two separate layers of my fictional reality were so incomprehensibly mixing and blocking my exit?

I got up and hurried towards the exit. Everyone was looking at me. Before I got to the door, I noticed that Mr Banerjee had risen from his seat and was waving a sheaf of papers at me. I ran into the corridor and towards the reception desk. Mr Banerjee ran panting behind me, shouting: "Sir, your story, your colleagues have added an ending!"

I shut my ears and ran across the thick carpet towards the exit. For a moment I was blinded by bright sunlight. I felt sand beneath my feet. When my eyes got used to the light, I saw that I was running along the beach in the bay in Kotronas towards the half-ruined house where Captain Jovanis was sitting on a piece of sailcloth. When he saw me, he jumped up and ran towards the small wood on the other side of the bay.

"Captain Jovanis," I shouted, "wait!" In spite of his years, he was as agile as a deer; he tripped a few times but quickly recovered and ran onwards. Eventually, he began to tire. After a long chase, he collapsed onto the sand and lay still. When

I caught up with him, he stared at me timidly, beseechingly.

"Captain," I said and helped him to his feet, "I intend you no harm, I'd just like your story."

He used gestures to explain that he couldn't tell it to me. He was dumb.

I got up and hurried towards the exit. Everyone was looking at me. Before I got to the door, I noticed that Mr Banerjee had risen from his seat and was waving a sheaf of papers at me. I ran into the corridor and towards the reception desk. Mr Banerjee ran panting behind me, shouting: "Sir, your story, your colleagues have added an ending!"

I shut my ears and ran across the thick carpet towards the exit. The door was locked. In despair, I pounded on the door, until I helplessly slumped to the floor. Two receptionists came out from behind the desk and helped me to my feet. Remorseful and slightly ashamed, I returned to the dining room. Mr Banerjee had already returned. Nobody paid me much attention, they were all listening intensely to the story *The End of a World* by the German writer Wolfgang Hildesheimer. I returned to my table. Dhan Gopal Mukherjee flashed me a curious look and then returned to listening.

With elegant and restrained irony, Hildesheimer was describing the end of a world of manners, wealth, style and cultivation. The Marchioness of Montetristo invites Mr Sebald, the narrator of the story, to her artificial island in the Venice lagoon. Mr Sebald got to know the marchioness when he sold her the bathtub in which Marat was murdered; this helped her complete her collection. At a party in her palace, which is tastefully furnished in every possible past style, from Gothic onwards, he meets famous representatives of the cultural elite. Then the famous flautist Beranger begins to play a sonata by the composer Antonio Giambattista Bloch and the Marchioness of Montetristo accompanies him on the lyre. The guests listen intently, with glasses of champagne in their hands. Only the previous owner of the bathtub in which Marat was murdered knows that the sonata is a fake by a nasty musicologist called Weltli. He is also the only one that notices during the performance, in the corner of the chamber, the appearance of two repulsive rats. The other guests are enjoying the music with their eyes closed. More and more rats appear. Distant thunder is heard and the ground begins to shake. When maestro Beranger begins to play *Allegro con brio*, the last movement of the sonata, puddles begin to appear on the lacquered parquet. The waters rise and the artificial island, known as San Amerigo, sinks. But it does not seem appropriate to the guests to forego aesthetic pleasure because of such trivia. Mr Sebald is the only one to hurry into the hallway and wade across the flooded courtyard to the walls.

"It was obvious that all the servants had fled. And why shouldn't they? They had no obligation to real and eternal culture, and the people in the palace no longer needed them." Mr Sebald throws himself into the last gondola and when they row past the windows of the palace, he sees that maestro Beranger and the Marchioness of Montetristo have finished playing and the guests, their hands above the water that is pouring through the windows, are applauding enthusiastically. The water reaches as high as the candles and the interior is shrouded in darkness. The applause stops. "Suddenly, I heard the terrible sound of walls tumbling down. The palazzo collapsed. The gondola changed direction to avoid falling pieces of masonry. After rowing across the lagoon for some minutes towards the island of San Giorgio I looked back. The sea was completely calm, as if the island of the Marchioness of Montetristo had never existed. A shame about the bathtub, I thought, it was irreplaceable. That was perhaps a cruel thought, but experience teaches us that we can judge such events and their significance only from a certain distance."

Hildesheimer sat down. Everyone applauded. For a long time.

All except me. I got up and hurried towards the exit. Everyone was looking at me. Before I got to the door, I noticed that Mr Banerjee had risen from his seat and was waving a sheaf of papers at me. Mr Banerjee ran panting behind me down the corridor, shouting: "Don't leave, maestro Beranger will play a sonata by Antonio Giambattista Bloch and the Marchioness of Montetristo will accompany him on the lyre!" The door was open.

The stifling heat of Kolkata crashed into me on the pavement. It seemed as if the city was disappearing in a humid haze, concealing itself and retreating into a world of perceivable but unattainable reality. I ran towards the post box.

"Scheherazade!" I shouted.

But she was not there. On the pavement was only her copper dish. Empty. Where had the fruits of her begging gone? Had someone stolen them? Other beggars? Had she taken them with her? Had no one, because of the plague, given her even a coin and she had gone to look for a more rewarding location? But then she would have taken the dish with her, for it was all she owned. But something was clear. She had vanished. And I would have to wait for her to reappear once more. I was convinced that she and only she could contribute the right ending to my unfinished story. And I am still convinced of that today, after all the long years, after all that has happened since.

And with that, I ended my narrative about the congress in Kolkata.

16.

Walks up the hill

It did not seem possible to the Carer, who had listened very attentively, that "my" Scheherazade, even if she had been real and not merely an apparition, would know how to contribute the ending that would be the right and only interpretation of the story of Captain Jovanis, for she would not be able to guess how the owner of the taverna would describe to us the truth of the story told through gestures. And why, in any case, did the ending of some unfinished story seem so important that it still refused to grant me peace after three decades? And why after all this time would I suddenly see an Indian beggar woman on the slope of the shelter behind my house? And why because of her in particular would I experience an accident so severe as to put me out of action for six months?

I shouldn't take offence, she said, but she was almost sure that when I fell my brain suffered worse damage than the tomography and MRI had revealed. Didn't I think I should arrange some other tests? And perhaps a session with a psychiatrist? She knew some, she had connections, she could organise something.

I told her I was grateful for her offer, but no, that would merely make the solving of the puzzle that had accompanied me though life more difficult. I had nothing against psychologists, although most of them don't deserve the title, but before they can help anyone, they too must weave a story through which they can clarify to the patient what is wrong with them, and such stories can be self-willed, misguided, "badly written", as one would say in literary jargon, and also without an ending to clarify what is going on in the patient's psyche. It wasn't unheard of for the healers of hallucinations and illusions to cause more harm than good to the patient with their "stories".

To a large extent, human interaction at all levels and in all forms is, more than anything, half-fabrication, arbitrary interpretation in line with particular interests, and so nothing on this earth is a story told to an end that could not be interpreted at least slightly differently. The stories of our lives are also like that, in which we too often see "fate" without being aware what that word means, for fate is also merely a personal interpretation of some general unfinished story or memory formed in our heads over time. The story of "my Scheherazade" was quite different from how it appeared, for I had not only seen her in Kolkata all those years ago and on the slope of the shelter behind my house, but she had followed me through the years and lay in ambush for me on almost every journey that I made. And those journeys were numerous: at least three journalists who had interviewed me for newspapers and magazines after my more visible successes had written that fate had been so generous towards me that I had lived at least three lives.

The Carer, who had read all of my books that had been translated into Slovene and some also in the original English, was of course familiar with the rough outlines of my life story, but not the details. Quite often I felt that she would like to find out more, but in spite of the trust that had grown between us in the first two months of physical proximity, she did not dare to poke around in my past. During the conversations that, with time, began to seem to both of us too personal, there was almost always a moment when one or the other, or both of us simultaneously, was overtaken by embarrassment, which stopped me from revealing less pleasant parts of my past, particularly those that were a secret to me as well. Moreover, I didn't want to praise myself, to present myself as a person incapable of lying, faking ignorance or minor deceptions; I admitted to her quite a number of sins, but none seemed so bad for her that she would doubt in my basic honesty and good intentions towards the people with whom I had forged personal or business connections. The moment came when I got the feeling that her attitude towards me wouldn't change even if I confessed that I had murdered someone. But in spite of this, for a reason that I can't explain, I kept largely quiet not only about my life following the congress in Kolkata and before the accident that led to her nursing me, but also about my life prior to Kolkata, particularly my childhood.

The day came when the condition of my left ankle improved to such an extent that, with the help of crutches, I could walk about the house, a few days later the garden, and a week after that on the road that led to the woods above the house, and onwards along the narrow path that went up among the trees, towards the top of the hill, each day a little further, strictly in line with her instructions that my movements should not bring more harm than benefit. I trusted her completely, for it rapidly became clear that she had mastered a lot more than basic physiotherapy. She was the one who removed the plaster cast from my ankle and exercised it to the extent that I could push it into a special shoe that she brought from a shop selling medical aids; it was she who drummed into me that I had to keep the plaster casts on my wrists for some time yet, before they could be replaced with supports; and she was also the one to arrange appointments for check-ups and x-rays at the hospital.

During our walks, which at the beginning were extremely painful and which I wouldn't have managed if I hadn't been able to lean on her every few steps, I gradually realised that by keeping quiet about the years that formed the greatest and most important part of my biography, I was doing her a disservice. And so during those walks, which each day took us a metre higher towards the top if the hill, my tongue let loose two or three more stories, my sincerity increased from day to day until I felt that nothing more was holding me back, that I could entrust this woman, my saviour, with even the least attractive facets of my character.

Above all, of course, the details of my life, something that most people do only when acquaintances turn into friends, let alone in instances when friendship progresses towards the kind of closeness that we know only in love.

17.

Return to childhood

And so during our walks on the hill, I gradually told her everything about my life. About how I had been born during the final days of World War Two after a short love affair between a village teacher and an English fighter pilot whose plane came down in Slovenia, but who survived, albeit badly injured, after my grandfather, the head teacher of the school where my mother taught, took him in and instructed his daughter to nurse him, which she did with pleasure, for the pilot was young and good looking, as well as being kind and educated, and she could talk English with him, which was the subject she taught. She looked after him until he was well. At the end of the war, like all British military personnel, he had to return to Britain.

For a long time, he didn't know that half a year later his son was born in Slovenia and that barely two years later the boy's mother died from an illness that the doctors were unable to identify, while I was left in the care of my grandfather, who was on the threshold of his eighties. In spite of his age, he was well enough not to hand me over to his other daughter, my aunt, who lived a long distance away but whom he didn't trust, because she had been a Partisan during the war and became a committed communist, while he faithfully attended mass and wanted to protect me from communism. I loved him and so I was happy that I could stay with him in the village, in the big house with its garden, orchard and vineyard, close to the woods, with a wonderful view across the hills to neighbouring Austria.

I was most happy because grandad liked to tell me stories: to begin with, adapted stories from the Bible and then fairy tales, followed by horror and crime stories and, when I started to attend school, it was the turn of the well-known adventure novels. We lived modestly, as grandad's savings didn't stretch far, but a lady neighbour who lived alone cooked for us and helped around the house; she had some land and two pigs and quite a few hens, and in my first ten years I ate more eggs than in the rest of my life. We attended mass together, prayed together and together honoured God, in whom I firmly believed in my childhood years.

Although I found this out only later, my grandfather made great efforts to find the English pilot whom my mother had kept alive though her devoted care and who, my grandfather never stopped repeating, had said goodbye to her with tears in his eyes. "Even though he doesn't know that he has you," my grandfather assured me, "he will be happy to have you live with him in England." I can't imagine how he managed it, but not long after I started the seventh year of primary school, the very school that my grandfather had been the head teacher of before the war and where my mother had taught English, one Sunday after mass, with a mysterious look on his face, he had called me into the garden shed and pulled from his pocket an envelope with four stamps on it, took a letter from it and read it to me.

It was in English. My grandfather had also been a teacher of English before he became head teacher and he knew that he would need to translate the contents, for at the age of thirteen I knew only a few words of "the language of languages", as my grandfather called it. Rather than learning English, I preferred to listen to grandad's stories and much more than in the real world, I lived in my imagination. But grandad folded the letter and pushed it back in the envelope.

"I'll tell you what it says," he said with a bitter voice, such that I had never heard him use before. "Your father says that the story of your birth and your mother's death may be true, but may not be. Although he is eternally grateful to your mother for the care that she offered him after his plane crashed and he is also willing to send us some money, for he knows that we live in poverty here, unfortunately he cannot come for you and take you to England, even if he wanted to. Since his return home, his life has changed dramatically. He is married, he has a child and another on the way. We must understand that, regarding the situation, he cannot satisfy our request."

I shrugged and said that I was satisfied with the reply, for I was very happy where I was; grandad told me stories, I walked to school through the woods, where I often stopped, sat on the moss beneath the trees and made up my own stories, although they weren't yet as good as the ones he told me.

"But who will look after you when I die?" asked grandad, holding back his tears and hugging me so tight that it hurt.

"You'll never die," I tried to console him, "and if you do, then I'll die with you."

"I forbid you to talk such nonsense," he said angrily and pushed me away. "I'll make sure that you don't end up in an orphanage."

Life went on as before. Although I knew, or more felt than knew, that I faced a great deal of uncertainty, I tried to relieve the sense of anxiety with the stories that I made up on the way to school through the woods and wrote down in secret in one of my school exercise books, for I didn't want my grandfather to read them by chance; in comparison with those he told me, they were too simple, too naive. But writing these stories brought me great pleasure, perhaps my only pleasure; I didn't enjoy socialising with schoolmates, I avoided football, handball, volleyball, celebrations, everything where there was no room for imagination. But I did, so as not to disappoint grandad, go to Sunday school, although the Bible seemed increasingly fictional to me, a collection of stories, very interesting and nicely told, but without any guarantee of their truth. From the village library I borrowed increasingly diverse and increasingly demanding stories, including books for adults, although in many cases I had no idea what they were about. Then my grandfather gave me a book for my thirteenth birthday, which he could not know would determine my path through life.

It was *One Thousand and One Nights*. And so I became acquainted with Scheherazade.

I read it three times. Then again. Then twice more. It moved into my head and pushed out almost everything else. It wasn't long before I began to be tormented by the question of why Shahryar had been satisfied with one thousand and one stories, why he hadn't demanded at least one or two more before he gave Scheherazade her life and married her. Had he grown tired of her stories? Had Scheherazade run out of them? Had she told him all the stories there were to tell and she didn't want to repeat them in different versions out of fear that he would recognise one, even though changed, concealed in another or turned on its head?

One way or another, after some time, I began to feel that the stories lacked an ending, a dot on the i, a conclusion that would give them their only real meaning, a message aimed at everyone and which could not be explained by each reader in their own way. At least *One Thousand and One Nights* seemed to lack a satisfactory ending, it seemed too open, insufficiently unique, too beautiful, too romantic. I don't know exactly when I was gripped by the desire to add another story or two, or possibly three, to *One Thousand and One Nights,* but it was at the same time that I was struck by the tormenting question as to whether I could think up a story that Scheherazade had not already told in one form or another. A story not somehow present in any of the millions of books already written.

18.

On the way from school

When I asked grandad why he had chosen to give me *One Thousand and One Nights* for my birthday, he said that the answer was not a simple one and that considering my age and limited experience, I might not understand. It would be better to talk about it some years later, perhaps when I was in secondary school. But even in childhood, patience was not one of my virtues, and so I persisted. He should look for an answer based on his experience, not mine, I said, and then we could talk about what I had understood correctly and what not.

In the end, I convinced him. He told me that the stories in *One Thousand and One Nights* contain all the themes or at least outlines of themes of which it is possible to deal with in novels and stories. The number of these is not unlimited, he emphasised, and many authors had devoted their lives to attempts to create a story that had not been written in one form or another by someone else; some had gone mad out of despair and ended up in an insane asylum, some had killed themselves. Why? Sooner or later, they had realised that even the richest imagination has its boundaries outside which there is nothing that is not already within them, and that there were only six basic themes that can form the basis for a literary work.

The first is the fight between good and evil, between generosity and selfishness, between truth and falsehood, between detective and criminal, between a fighter for social justice and the unjust society, between slave and master, between morality and temptation.

The second literary theme, grandad continued, which for now I would not understand, at least not in all its nuances, was love, probably the most common theme in literature. It can concern forbidden love, as in *Romeo and Juliet,* which ends tragically, or love that ends with "and they lived happily ever after", for fairy tales also belonged under this heading; it could also be family love, where the main role was given to devotion and faithfulness; it could be unrequited love, where someone's feelings are not returned by the object of affection, most often a woman not returning a man's feelings; and it could also be about the highest and purest form of love – friendship. Within this thematic circle there were hundreds of possible variants and sub-variants.

The third theme, explained grandad, that I might understand in five years or so, went under the name of salvation. Stories about salvation usually begin sadly, with failure, error and tragedy, but by the end the heroes recognise the error of their ways, they improve, try to correct their mistakes and often even sacrifice themselves for the happiness of those they have injured, by losing their freedom and not infrequently with their death. Perhaps the best work on this theme is *Les Miserables*, by Victor Hugo; I should read it, they were sure to have it in the library.

Then my grandfather briefly presented three other literary themes: bravery and persistence (the heroes face great dangers and difficulties, which it seems they won't be up to, but in the end they avoid the worst and even win); growing up, the usual expression for a novel on this theme being *Bildungsroman*, in which we follow the development of one or more young people through a series of events, trials, twists and turns to maturity; and then there is revenge, a common and popular theme found in many works from *The Iliad* to *Frankenstein* and *The Count of Monte Cristo*. We shouldn't forget, he added, that the majority of novels and stories kept in libraries and those that will be created by writers until people are tired of reading, are a thematic mixture, a more or less successful weaving together of love, bravery, revenge and all the rest that he had described to me; there were very few thematically uniform books; it could be said that every really good novel is a kind of thematic goulash.

Under the influence of our talk, the stories that I thought up on the way to school and back again, and which I secretly wrote down in the school exercise book, changed, became ever more complex, but also weirder and barely believable; quite a few of them, when I re-read them, I crossed out and wrote alongside them why they seemed wrong. But the whole time I was driven by the failings of *One Thousand and One Nights*, by the "sugary" ending that didn't seem like a real ending, but something deliberately cut off, with no real point, no conclusion that represented an undoubted consequence of the events described in the book. Without telling my grandfather, I decided to try and write a suitable ending, write an extra story or two, to put *One Thousand and One Nights* on firmer narrative foundations. This I did slowly, allowing my imagination to breathe and correct its delusions along the way.

Every day, as long as it was not raining, I stopped on the way home and sat beneath a large chestnut tree, leaned against the trunk and opened my exercise book of stories.

If I managed to write two sentences, I was satisfied, if I wrote three, I was delighted, but if I wrote none I didn't get upset, since I knew that it would be different the next day. Above all, I was in no hurry; at the age of thirteen I didn't have the feeling that time was passing quickly, I felt as if there was eternity before me. I don't remember how many days, weeks, months passed before I felt that the story was finished, concluded, and that any additional sentence could only spoil it.

For some time, I dared not read it to grandad, since the fear that he would misunderstand it was too great. I was even more afraid that he would not like it. However, because he valued my obsession with reading and literature, he would not tell me that, but would merely praise me in a lukewarm way. That would depress me more than anything. I don't remember how long it was before I plucked up the courage (perhaps more despair than courage) and showed him the story. It was not a lengthy piece, so he read it quickly. When he had finished, he was silent for more than a minute, staring into space. Then he read the story again. And again. After the third reading he was once more silent for a while, staring at nothing. I had no idea how to explain this. It seemed to me strange, for the story was not difficult, it was perfectly clear, or so it seemed to me, so clear that nothing would require further clarification.

After the fourth reading, grandad handed me the exercise book and asked me to read the story out loud. Which I did.

19.

One thousand and two stories

"There was a time when I had a kingdom, I lived in Baghdad, I was a shah, a ruler by the name of Shahryar, and the kingdom, which stretched from the Mediterranean across Persia to China, remained enormous even after I gave the eastern part to my younger brother, who had inherited nothing from our father, which seemed to me unfair. People thought highly of my generosity, I enjoyed a respect to be envied by all the world's rulers. I was just and merciful towards my subjects and so I did not offend even those whom I had to punish harshly because of disobedience or laziness or theft. In my kingdom, in my time, the death penalty was a normal thing, and it was carried out in every case by my Grand Vizier, who had to strangle the condemned one himself. If there was any bad feeling among my subjects, it was towards him, for to have a bad opinion of the ruler would be disrespectful. But this was not the only reason why I was exceedingly happy and proud of myself. I had a wife who was a beauty such as could not be found either within or without the kingdom that I ruled. I had a wife who changed my life into a fairy tale. The last thing I expected of her was infidelity.

But it came to my ears that the young, wonderfully beautiful queen was deceiving me with one of the court princes, and not only once, but many times when I was absent. Then it came to my ears that she had deceived me a number of times with an ordinary courtier. This was a sin worse than all other sins together and so the only suitable penalty was death. The Grand Vizier strangled her on the main square, in front of a mass of people, who enjoyed the death of the sinner and immediately afterwards word of the event spread across the whole kingdom, even to its most remote corners.

Since it would not be appropriate for a ruler, especially an all-powerful one, to be without a wife, I commanded the Grand Vizier to bring me a new young beauty in the evening and arrange a wedding ceremony, for the kingdom needed a queen. As my first wife, whom I had loved immensely, had betrayed me in the lowest way I stopped believing in women's faithfulness and so I ordered the Grand Vizier to strangle the young beauty the next morning. And to bring me another one in the evening. And also to strangle that one the next morning. And so on, night after night, day after day. He did not dare disagree, he carried out his duties without objection. But it did not escape my notice that he was increasingly unhappy, even desperate. Rumours began to spread among the people that their formerly beloved ruler was turning into a monster. I lost my friends, I lost the people's favour and I, too, was increasingly unhappy, but the fear of female infidelity did not allow me to cease my cruel behaviour. Fear began to spread among the populace, families were losing daughters; the more beautiful and talented they were, the greater was the likelihood that sooner or later it would be their turn. The future became frightening; in a few years, there would be a shortage of young women, marriages would be called off, fewer and fewer children would be born, the nation would begin to die out, and all because of me. Although when I thought about it, I was still convinced that it was not my fault, but that of my first, unfaithful wife.

And then something happened that I had not expected. One day, the Grand Vizier brought to me for my wife until the next morning one of his own daughters. Scheherazade was her name and she was more beautiful than any of the girls who had found themselves in my bed before, only to be killed the next day. The idea was not his, he had been talked into it by Scheherazade, who gave him no choice, for she was very headstrong. I asked him whether he was aware that the next morning he would have to strangle his own daughter. He said that sadly he had no choice: he had to obey her and he had to obey me. When Scheherazade appeared in my rooms and raised her veil, uncovering the stunning beauty of her face, I saw that she was in tears. When I asked her what was wrong and whether she had perhaps come against her will because her father wished to get rid of her, she said it was nothing like that; she was crying because she had a younger sister, Dunyazad, whom she had been close to since she was little and whom would never see her again. Would I have anything against it if her beloved sister spent her last night close to her, in the same room as us, so that they could spend at least a few hours together?

I did not have the heart to refuse such a sincere request from this beautiful wife for one night, who next morning at sunrise was due to be strangled by her own father. We were joined by Dunyazad and, discreetly distanced from the marriage bed, she spent the night close to her sister. Half an hour before sunrise, Dunyazad turned to Scheherazade and asked her, once more, to tell her one of those wonderful, tense and exciting stories, with which she had delighted her since she was a young girl. Scheherazade asked me if she could grant her sister's request. Since I also loved a good story, I permitted her and without hesitation she began to tell the story of *Ali Baba and the Forty Thieves*. The sun came up before she was able to finish, the story was left at its tensest moment and because I wanted to hear the ending, I gave Scheherazade one more day of life, so that she could finish the story the next morning.

But the next morning, the same thing happened: within the first story, someone began to tell their story, which at dawn was also left at its tensest moment, and although I would have liked to hear the end of this story, I was obliged, just as every other day, to devote myself to my duties as ruler. I gave Scheherazade another day of life so that she could finish the story and satisfy my curiosity the next morning. My desire for stories grew the more of them I heard: my favourites were those about Sinbad, Ali Baba and Aladdin, which Scheherazade had to tell me twice, and before I knew what was happening, a thousand nights had passed and then one more. Then, with sadness in her eyes, Scheherazade told me that she had run out of stories, but she would not like to repeat the ones I had already heard: the end had come, I should send for her father to strangle her, as had been commanded.

Not only did I not do that, but I even married her and publicly, before the masses, who again fell in love with me, for the strangling of young girls was over, the kingdom had a queen with which the king was so in love (with her and her stories) that he did not wish to spend a moment without her. The kingdom flourished once more and the people were once again happy.

The last thing I expected was that something would go wrong. But that is exactly what happened. Two days after the wedding Scheherazade confided in me that her more than three years of storytelling had damaged her vocal cords and she feared that she would lose the power of speech. The kingdom could not have a dumb queen or I a dumb wife; that would be a great dishonour for me. If she did lose her voice, she would have to leave the court and go somewhere where she was not known and where she would live like a beggar. I assured her that this would not happen, that her hoarseness would soon improve and her voice would become as clear and bell-like as it had once been.

She did not believe me. And I, too, had less and less faith in what I said. Two days before she was finally struck dumb, she told me faintly, so that I could barely understand her, that only I could save her. Now it was my turn to tell stories, she said; after a thousand and one nights, and the same number of stories that she told me, her voice would return and her vocal cords would be healed.

But that would not happen if I repeated her stories or if mine, however original and never before heard, remained without an ending that could not be understood in different ways. But I am the king, I objected, I am Shahryar, I am on this earth to rule, not to tell stories. Her last words were that really good rulers retain the good opinion of their people by telling stories that they can take as their own because they speak of them, of their happy and unhappy fates. Rulers who instead of telling stories issue orders and suppress people are not worthy of the respect of those they rule, which sooner or later backfires on them and they are deposed.

Since we had spent more than a thousand happy days and nights together, she added, I would not miss her if she left as soon as she lost her voice and wandered through unknown places, now here, now there, wherever her feet led her. And when I thought up the kind of story she expected, she would return, we would be man and wife again, and we would live happily to the end of our days. But, I asked her, how could I tell her stories if she was not there; did it not seem unfair to her that she was asking for the impossible? She was amazed. Why, I had twenty scribes available, she said, they should write down my stories, copy them and distribute them among the people throughout the kingdom; sooner or later each one would end up in her hands, there was no need for her to hear them, she could read them. And as soon as a story reached her that matched her criteria, she would return. When I awoke the next morning, she had gone. I was alone."

20.

The beginnings of storying

When I finished, my grandfather was silent for some time, staring into space. A good five minutes passed before he spoke. He told me that I had, wittingly or not, mapped out my fate. I had become Shahryar, who by telling stories for many years had searched for his Scheherazade; I would become a writer, whose narratives, short or long, would invite people all over the world into bookshops and libraries, I would be welcome at all the literary symposia, I would make appearances and win awards, beautiful young readers would write to me and want to get to know me, the most eminent people would consider it an honour if they could shake my hand at some event.

I replied that I wanted none of that. Although I really enjoyed making up stories, storying, I would not devote my life to it, for I would rather spend my time on earth in the real world, rather than a made-up one. Maybe I'd become a pilot or a surgeon or a basketball player, certainly something that would involve the use of my hands, as well as my brain. I wanted to touch the world in which I lived. But it was true that from time to time, if I felt like it, I might come up with some story.

"You'll have to," said grandad, "if you want to see Scheherazade again."

"But grandad," I replied, "I'm not Shahryar, I only thought up the story."

"The whole world is made up," he said. "When you reach my age, you'll understand that."

For some time, stories ceased to interest me: the exercise book that before I had carefully hidden among the others in my school bag I left at home, among the books in my room. One day, after coming home from school, I wanted to write a little story in it, but it was not there, at least not where I'd left it. I rummaged through the disorder in my room, then I asked my grandfather if by any chance he had seen it. I had never been angry with him about anything in my life, but his reply put me in such a bad mood that at I wasn't sure what to do. He said that he had taken the exercise book to school and handed it to my Slovene teacher, whom he had thought highly of when he was head teacher. "I wanted to hear her opinion," he said. "I'm sorry, I know I should have asked you."

I was so angry that I wanted to attack him, kick him, but as he had apologised, sincerely and almost remorsefully, I restrained myself, ran into my room, threw myself onto my bed and burst into tears. I was horrified at the thought that my teacher would not like my stories, for they seemed to me, maybe with the exception of *One Thousand and Two Stories,* the work of a novice, superficial, unfinished.

The next day, after classes, my Slovene teacher, with a serious expression on her face, led me to the staff room, sat me at a desk as if she intended to tell me off and said: "Listen." She was silent for a moment and then continued: "I'd like to say something. Write. Write as much as possible. Never give up. Even if it means you get worse marks at other subjects, keep writing. Tell stories. Do you promise me you will?"

I nodded, vaguely, for her words had stunned me. She came to my side of the desk, hugged me and whispered in my ear: "Believe in yourself. Keep writing until you write the story that returns the gift of speech to Scheherazade."

Since I had no choice, I promised that I would.

***

"And so you became a writer," said the Carer, when I had finished my narration and the approaching night forced us to limp back home.

"Not immediately," I told her later, when she had showered me after dinner and helped me to bed, while she slumped in the armchair that she had some time before moved to the foot of the bed. I told her that in a way, the story of Scheherazade had destroyed in me the desire to make up new stories and that already with the next it became clear to me that I would never be able to write a better one, particularly the kind that would bring the speechless Scheherazade back to the court. For from day to day, I increasingly felt that I was Shahryar and that Scheherazade, who had laid on me the burden of telling hundreds of stories in return for hers, must come back to me, otherwise neither of us would ever be happy. I was overcome by fear. I confided in grandad that I had evidently started to go mad, for things I had made up had begun to penetrate reality; I would soon begin to live in two worlds and in the end, I wouldn't know which was real and which I was making up as I went along. I was convinced that grandad would take me to see a doctor, who would send me to a lunatic asylum.

But after brief reflection, grandad gave me a friendly smile, stroked my head and said that this was nothing unusual, and certainly nothing dangerous; most storytellers spend most of their time living in two worlds and for many the made-up world is more real than that in which they are forced to live and survive. I should not avoid the duty laid upon me by the most famous literary heroine. I should devote all my spare time to writing, I should write stories and publish them, and they would certainly be translated into many languages, and wherever Scheherazade was wandering, she would sooner or later read one of them and then another, and when she came across the right one, she would come and take me back to my kingdom.

My grandfather's words confused me even more, I didn't have the slightest idea what he was trying to tell me. But I didn't question him further, I allowed for the possibility that he too had gone a bit crazy, for he was at the age where most people begin to leave their common sense behind and see things that aren't there. After a while, my desire to write returned and I began to weave stories again. Grandad, who wanted to read every one of them, was quite satisfied with them, but he wasn't exactly enthusiastic: he said they were too reminiscent of the stories that Scheherazade told Shahryar, which wasn't good, for he expected something new and different from me, something original, all mine, and not adapted from stories that had already been told. But soon, all too soon, thinking up a story that had never been told before seemed impossible. My courage began to dissipate, there were fewer and fewer stories, and above all, none was good enough for publication. I not only had to show my grandad everything, but also my teacher and she, too, was increasingly disappointed. "Already familiar, already read," was her evaluation of everything that I showed her.

But in spite of that, neither she nor grandad lost their faith in me; they encouraged me, each in their own way, and in the case of my teacher this soon escalated into demands, even orders. One day she said to me: "She's waiting for you. Somewhere she is waiting. She is wandering around the world, lingering here, lingering there, in the hope that she will encounter you or you will encounter her. And you will tell her a story that seems to her original enough for her to return to you. Don't give up. This is your mission. If you give it up, you will suffer your whole life. Even worse, your life will be empty."

I obeyed her. I began to think up stories anew. And write them down. And I wrote. And wrote. And wrote. Until something snapped inside me and I revolted. I can't go on, I said to my teacher and my grandfather. You're demanding the impossible. If you carry on like this, I'll kill myself. This frightened them both. And the pressure relented.

But the consequences of this madness did not disappear. On the contrary, they became ever more serious and soon I began to see things, as well. On the way to and from school I used to pass a gypsy settlement, which was quite a way from the path, a conglomeration of huts on the opposite slope, but beneath them was a wide grassy clearing that reached all the way to the path. And one day while walking past, I saw on this clearing a young girl wearing a brown robe, sitting in the grass cross-legged and with her arms folded in her lap. The robe also covered her head, and on both sides there appeared from beneath it locks of black hair.

I stopped and looked at her. She didn't notice me, as she was staring motionlessly in front of her. Evidently she was from the village, a gypsy, if her appearance was anything to go by. She was very beautiful! This was roughly how I imagined Scheherazade, a bit darker, Arab complexion, large dark eyes and thick black hair. And suddenly I had the feeling that the real Scheherazade was sitting in front of me, not the one from *One Thousand and One Nights*, but the one

I had recreated in the story, where she had left me with the promise that she would return when I wrote a story that no one else had written!

I stopped two metres before her. She didn't look up. I told her that I was trying, as much as time and my capabilities allowed, but perhaps I was too young, too inexperienced, insufficiently imaginative to write the story she expected of me. She should be patient; the moment would come, although not in the near future, but later, when I had more behind me, more experience, when the real story, the first of its kind, a story for her who knew all the stories of the world, would appear of its own accord, and then I would find her, if she did not find me, and we would once again be king and queen, happy in our kingdom, from which we had been driven by a dearth of human imagination, in which there is, so it seems, nothing completely new, no story as yet untold, which could rescue us.

She didn't respond, she didn't look up, she acted as if she was not only dumb, but deaf and dumb. I turned and went home, and started writing stories like one possessed, I read and read, and turned over what I'd read in every possible way, turned them upside down that I might by chance produce something absolutely new, and although it often seemed to grandad and my teacher that I was strumming a tune never before heard, I knew that they were wrong, even though they were much older than me and had read far more stories than I, even though I also read obsessively. Luckily, not only was the library well stocked, I also found a real treasure house at home, for grandad was a passionate book lover; he also sought in stories something that he had not found in life.

21.

The father comes for his son

The next day, the Carer asked me if Scheherazade appeared to me only once in my school years or if I saw her again on the way to or from school. I told her I had seen her at least three times, as far as I remembered, although not always in the clearing near the gypsy settlement, but each time in a different location: once in a field near the school, the second time in some bushes in the middle of the woods, and the third time on the edge of my grandfather's orchard when I was looking out of the window. In a way, I got used to her and I might even have missed her if she hadn't appeared now and again to remind me of my duty: to read stories and to try and write one that no other author in history had managed to write. I included among stories novels, which I saw merely as longer stories.

Some time passed, some attempts to rid myself of the burden, some decisions to leave home and drown myself in the nearest river; but in the end I accepted the idea that my life was something unusual, that something half pleasant and half nightmarish was happening to me. Even if I had become the victim of some psychological disturbance or mental illness, I decided that it was not so bad that I could not live with it.

At that moment, my life was struck by a massive change, which I couldn't have imagined even in one of my stories where I tried to come up with the most amazing details. My father, who some years earlier had said that he could not take me in because he had a family and two children, suddenly appeared. Without telling me, my grandfather had kept in touch with him, writing to him regularly and informing him about the health and school performance of his "Slovene" son, and in each letter expressing the hope that he could finally meet the boy, his own flesh and blood. The replies were polite, but brief and infrequent, my grandfather later admitted to me. So I thought I was dreaming when one day I came home from school and encountered a stranger sitting with grandad at the kitchen table. My first feeling was that, in addition to Scheherazade, another apparition had pushed its way into my life, but when I saw that the unknown man was looking at a heap of photographs of my mother, which grandad evidently wanted him to see, I immediately guessed that it was my father. What was more, because there was a large mirror hanging on the wall, I immediately saw from the reflection that we were unusually alike and that even a casual passer-by would recognise us as father and son. Of course, he also noticed the similarity and we couldn't help smiling at the same time.

***

At this point in my narrative, the Carer pulled a tissue from her pocket and began to wipe away her tears. The story, which wasn't a story but the truth, and difficult for me to have made up, moved her. "And then what?" she said through her tears.

I didn't have enough energy or the will to repeat the story, which she knew from my autobiographical novel, *Flight to the Sky,* one of the ten that had been translated into Slovene. If she had really read all ten, then she must remember the autobiographical one well enough to recall the details that led some reviewers to criticise me for not writing a classical autobiography, but a sentimental novel for women, full of barely believable twists and turns, which could never happen to the same person in two lifetimes, let alone one.

"Have you not read *Flight to the Sky?*" I tried to divert her from further questioning.

"I have," she said, as if defending herself against an accusation, "twice. But I'd still like to know why you didn't mention Scheherazade. Who is, judging from everything you've told me about her, the driving force behind your life and work, responsible even for your accident and, at the end of the day, for my presence here."

I had no reply handy, but it didn't take me long to find one. "Because my life is not the story of Scheherazade," I said. "If I wove her into the narrative, I would be doing something unforgivable: I would be reducing my life to the level of a fairy tale; I would be diverting the reader's attention from what is real and demonstrable and what *is* my life, to a story about an unusual hallucination, and who would then believe that what actually happened really did take place. At the same time, I would also be doing an injustice to my relationship with Scheherazade, who expects from me a story that will compel her to return to me. That is why my autobiographical novel follows the rules of the genre and focuses on provable facts."

I told her that my father, when his wife and two children died in a car accident and because of the shock he spent some time being treated in a psychiatric hospital, was advised by the doctor to find new meaning for his life in the son that he had fathered after his plane crashed at the end of the war. And that he had taken the doctor's advice and, after producing witnesses and endless bureaucratic complications, he managed to prove that he really was my father and took me to London, where he lived alone in a luxurious house in a protected part of Ashchurch Park, not having married again, although he did employ a cook and there was also living with him the lady who had been the nanny to his deceased children.

I told her that I terribly missed my grandfather and often wanted to flee back to Slovenia, even though an exceptionally warm relationship quickly developed between my father and I, for hitherto I had never met anyone so kind and reliable, who acted towards me as if I meant the world to him. With the exception of grandad, of course. That my father hired an exceptional teacher who in one year taught me English so well that I spoke like a native, my accent included. That he then enrolled me at Eton, the exclusive public school, from where I went on to study English language and literature at Oxford; that I made a lot of friends, of both sexes; that a year after arriving in England, I resumed writing stories, this time in English; that my stories began to be read on BBC radio; that prestigious journals began to publish them, even in the States; that soon after graduating I wrote a novel, the subject of a bidding war between two highly regarded publishers; that I soon won the reputation of one of the most important young writers of my generation. That my work began to be translated and to win awards; that I gained quite a few admirers among my women readers, thanks to which my sex life, at the age when such things seem necessary to a man, if not important, certainly wasn't lacking in any way, although I never fell in love with any of them, let alone did I consider marriage and family and offspring.

I told her that from the age of fifteen to forty, life was so generous to me that I couldn't shake off a feeling of guilt that smouldered deep within me, and the fear that for all the blessings, I would sooner or later have to pay a heavy price. These were the things woven together in my autobiographical novel. But not once did it mention Scheherazade.

22.

My father and Scheherazade

That certainly doesn't mean, I continued my narrative, that when I moved to England Scheherazade stopped appearing. On the contrary. I saw her on a London bus, in the next carriage on the Underground, in the library where I used to go to study, in front of the college in Oxford, and a number of times in Foyles bookshop, where, like me, she was looking through the books. On average, she appeared to me twice a month, always far enough away for us not to exchange looks, except once, when she came to a press conference to mark the publication of my short prose collection *Bandits and Rulers,* and sat in the third row, close enough, but with her head down, as if she wanted to avoid eye contact with me; as if she was there by coincidence. But she was always wearing a dark brown, ankle length robe, with a hood over her head; she always looked like a woman from the Middle East; she was always recognisable, slender and tall, almost as tall as me, and always her face was unusual, with her lips lower on the left, and always sad, her eyes staring into an invisible world that I could not imagine. I did notice, though, that she was slowly ageing in parallel with me; just as I was changing from a boy into a youth and then a young man, and then a middle aged man, she was also changing from a girl into woman in her most beautiful years and then a mature woman, and of everything to do with her, I was most amazed that, even scared that, this showed she was not just a hallucination, a delusion, but that she had her own earthly reality, for she was moving through time like a real, living being.

I tried to suppress my thoughts about this, but without success; they kept forcing their way into my consciousness, confusing me, stealing the energy I needed for studying, and so in the end, when I could live from my royalties, I abandoned my studies just before graduating, with the convenient excuse that the most dangerous thing a writer can study is literary theory, for it fills his head with rules and patterns that render originality unattainable. I quite soon came to the realisation that it wasn't even an excuse, but a fact, for my writing suddenly flowed unhindered and my imagination flew to undreamed of heights.

But the originality that I was capable of still didn't help me to find an ending to the story of Captain Jovanis, which it seemed increasingly likely would remain the only unfinished project in my life. Even the friends and literary colleagues that I asked or challenged were unable to contribute the right ending, while those contributed by the participants of the Congress in Kolkata were by and large laughable. I was equally incapable, in spite of repeated attempts, of writing a story that would satisfy Scheherazade's wishes and standards, for if I had succeeded, she would surely have approached me, addressed me, invited me back into her world, into our shared world of imagination, where we could continue our life together. Maybe that was precisely why, in spite of numerous relationships, mostly short-lived, with beautiful, clever women, I never married; there lived within me the conviction that I was already married and that the only woman in my life could be Scheherazade.

Although I knew deep inside that I was connecting worlds that did not belong together, and that this perhaps didn't particularly contribute to my inner peace, let alone my grasp of reality, I tried to suppress my anxiety in connection with this whenever it began to become unbearable. I never spoke to anyone about it, for I knew I would be received by incomprehension and even ridicule, and although in the end everything is forgiven a successful writer, I had no wish to make a fool of myself in front of my readers, for sooner or later everything would come out and, considering my fame, the gutter press would grab the opportunity with more than usual delight, and that was the last thing that I would want to burden my father with.

Actually, I didn't see my father, who brought me to England and Anglicised me, which was still possible because of my age (five years later, at twenty, my "Sloveneness" would be too deeply rooted in me), all that often. In spite of the fact that our relationship remained friendly and that there was a firm bond of trust between us. He was grateful that I had filled the void in his life and given him an heir, while I was grateful to him because he had offered me a path into the world and, as wealthy as he was, ensured me no small advantage both in my private life and in my attempts to establish myself in the literary world. He was upper class, a gentleman, his father (my grandfather!) had for a time been the private doctor to King George VI, the father of Queen Elizabeth, and so my father, when he inherited his father's estate, could afford a lot more than most people I had known in my life, including profitable shares and property. But he didn't seem to be any happier because of this, he was used to it, he had grown up with it, in contrast with me, who in my childhood years had often wanted nothing other than a slice of bread, spread with lard and covered with sliced garlic.

Whenever I looked at my father, he seemed unusually despondent, his smile was almost always forced, his politeness a matter of habit and upbringing, his attitude to me more a matter of duty than love. I kept telling myself that I was mistaken, and maybe I was; maybe my father gave such an impression only when we were together; maybe I reminded him of my mother, who had saved him from certain death. Or of the family he had lost in the accident. Or maybe he was sad that he was unable to spend more time with me, his only surviving son.

For my father, a fighter pilot, after returning home at the end of the war, had decided on a military career; he became a naval officer, the captain of one of the warships which, because of various international complications, spent most of its time in different parts of the world. Whenever he came home for a week or two or, rarely, a month, for him it was leave. For me, it was a true holiday. For to be honest, I had fallen in love with the father I met for the first time at the age of fifteen, not only because he was endlessly kind and generous towards me and did everything he could to understand my wishes and pave the way to my success, but also because of a feeling of pride that I was his son, the son of the captain of a warship, who was (or at least this was my wish) well on the way to becoming an admiral. Because he had joined the navy largely due to family tradition (his grandfather had also been a navy captain), he never felt at home on the deck of the destroyer; he would much rather be, he confided in me during one of his longer visits home, what I am, a writer, an imaginer of worlds in which we do not live, but in which we might perhaps be happier.

It wasn't strange, then, that it was to my father, during one of his visits, that I confided my plight: I told him about the unfinished story of Captain Jovanis, which no one knew how to finish, and the story of Scheherazade, who had moved from literature into my reality, and who was increasingly pulling me away from the self-evident belief that what we live is real. I couldn't help noticing how hard my father tried not to show his concern. It seemed to him normal to try and solve the problem in a military way: simply, according to the rules, efficiently. The story of Jovanis seemed to him the least of my worries. It is a riddle that cannot be solved, he said. Why burden myself with it? Any possible ending to the story would be as valid as any other. Just as all interpretations of the end of the world, when it comes, will be equally valid, none is the only one possible. I could happily forget about that. The last thing I needed in life and the last thing that he would want for me was an obsession with a fixed idea. And that was what worried him, he said, about the story of Scheherazade. If I agreed and it didn't bother me, he would like to introduce me to a friend from university who was a respected psychiatrist and psychoanalyst; perhaps he, if I told him the story of Scheherazade, would be able to help.

23.

The son loses his father

Although reluctantly and with a measure of fear, I accepted my father's proposal and went to see Dr Johnson. We agreed that we would meet once a week at his office. Even at the end of the first session he confidently stated that, although my case was unusual, it certainly wasn't the first and only one of its kind, for the brain is hard to understand, as well as being a flexible organ that follows its own laws and cannot be commanded in the name of common sense or in line with our wishes. Cases such as mine were connected with the visual cortex in the brain, which due to head trauma or even eye injury, can trigger unusual hallucinations and visions, which often look more real than if they really existed.

One of his patients was convinced that he had a chimpanzee sitting in his lap, an older woman saw Disney cartoons unfolding before her eyes, another had seen two miniature police officers pushing a handcuffed miniature thief into a miniature police car, while yet a third had seen an elephant climbing a tree, and quite a number had seen their deceased loved one, husband, wife, brother, sister, standing in front of them or passing by on the other side of the street, but if they wanted to touch them, they always touched themselves, their hand or face or leg, or their hand reached into empty space.

The diversity of hallucinations caused by the visual cortex is endless, said Dr Johnson. It weaves them, completely coincidentally, from fragments of images in the warehouse of memory, from fragments between which there is no meaningful connection, and so with some people the hallucinations are nothing short of bizarre. Had I ever suffered head injury, perhaps from a fall or playing rugby, had I ever been in a traffic accident, had I ever taken part in sports such as boxing or wrestling, had I ever banged my head against the wall or a low ceiling out of clumsiness? I shook my head: nothing like that. Unless I had forgotten.

That's certainly not impossible, replied Dr Johnson. But there was one other possibility, he said. Why had the girl sitting in the clearing near the gypsy settlement reminded me of Scheherazade from my story? Had her figure become so important in my thoughts, my conscious or subconscious mind, that I had to embody it, see it as if it was real? And had I suggested to myself, upon seeing the gypsy girl, that this was Scheherazade from my story, perhaps because that was roughly how I had imagined her? If that was the case, and it was almost impossible it was any other way, then at that moment had occurred a lasting shift in my mind: autosuggestion had become the autohypnosis that had accompanied me ever since. Whenever and wherever I see a woman in a brown robe with a hood, who reminds me of the first girl in whom I saw "Scheherazade", out of reflex I activate this autohypnosis and I see the person that I have unwittingly ordered myself to see. Because of my sense of obligation to her. Because of the desire to once more gain her love.

The brain is a strange thing, concluded Dr Johnson at the end of our last meeting – the last because I decided that I would no longer visit him. Almost nothing of what he had told me seemed possible.

That was also what my father said, when I described to him our "therapeutic" sessions; he said that he had never in his life heard of autohypnosis. Although, he added, he didn't exclude the possibility that such a thig existed, for after all, Dr Johnson was an eminent expert and wouldn't dare to simply make it up. Perhaps the vision of Scheherazade was the manifestation of my lust for writing, for weaving stories, for storying, perhaps without her I would be unable to write anything worthwhile, for after all, she was the one who forced me to give the best of myself, in the hope that in the end I would write something she liked and we would be reunited. Perhaps she was the one steering my life, introducing ideas for novels and stories into my imagination, helping me to persist, to finish writing, and perhaps she was the one who was guaranteeing me the kind of success granted to few authors, even if that success seemed so unimportant to me. Perhaps I should visit the statue of Scheherazade and Shahryar in Baghdad, he said: currently it was relatively peaceful and safe there, and maybe the two stone figures would help me solve the riddle that had accompanied me through the years and prevented me from marrying, settling down, having children. Life without children is like an aircraft carrier without aeroplanes – it serves no purpose. That was why he had come to look for me and to bring me to England, why each success of mine gave him endless delight, why he had named me as his only heir in his will, why he was unhappy whenever I was unhappy.

"Okay," I said, "I'll travel to Baghdad. I'll see that statue. Something is certain to happen when I see it." Actually, until then I didn't even know this statue existed.

He suggested that we fly to Baghdad together; I would stay a few days and see the statue and the ruins of the city left after the war, he would carry on to the destroyer, under the command of his deputy, which was anchored in the Persian Gulf.

Although, half out of curiosity and half because of obligations connected with my work, I had already travelled half the world, I had never thought of visiting Baghdad, not only because of the war and the danger when there was no fighting, but also because the Middle East, for indefinable reasons, had never particularly interested me. Quite a bit of my work had been translated into Arabic, but I had been published primarily in Egypt, Tunisia and Morocco. After landing in Baghdad I was overcome by a strange feeling; something sombre, anxious, something that could be called a presentiment of evil. My father was met by a military vehicle and driven south with an armed guard, while I took a room in a hotel that my father had recommended as one of the safest.

The next day, I went to see the statue. I half expected to encounter an image of Scheherazade such as I had already seen in different parts of the world. But her features were completely different, less attractive, less sad, there was more energy in them, almost drive, as if she was enthusiastic about what she was telling, or as if she was convincing Shahryar, who was listening to her, lying on his side, leaning on his elbow on a stone bench. The statue, created by Mohammed Ghani Hikmat, was a blatant contrast with the well known, oft depicted image of the young woman from the ninth century, who told stories to the bearded ruler sitting at his feet, almost humbly and in fear for her life. But Hikmat was an artist and it is characteristic of artists that they like to break with established concepts, and if they fail to do so are seen as imitators. Although the stone Scheherazade and Shahryar in Abu Nawas Park in the centre of Baghdad was an impressive achievement, it was so different from "my" Scheherazade that it left me cold, without any feeling that lingering in its presence could benefit me. Because of the war and the ongoing clashes, the surroundings of the statue were neglected, with signs of bomb damage nearby, but the worst thing of all was that some vandals, God knows why, had removed Shahryar's left arm. Although later it had been replaced with a copy, the metal joint remained visible.

I took some photos and returned to the hotel with the intention of seeing the monument next morning in the sunlight and perhaps in a different mood. Even in the hope that I would see from close up my Scheherazade. If she had followed me across the world, from Australia to America, from Slovenia to England, why not also to Baghdad where she had (supposedly) lived in the ninth century.

Since it was too dangerous to walk around the city in the evening, for there was still no real peace and I could easily be hit by a bullet intended for someone else, I went to bed early. But a little after ten, I was woken by persistent knocking on my door. When I opened it, there stood the hotel doorman and a sub-lieutenant of a British submarine in full uniform. The expression on his face made it clear he was not the bearer of good news. When he had checked that I was really the person I claimed to be and to whom he had been sent, he told me, in a reserved and slightly embarrassed way, that he brought bad news. My father had had an accident, which he had not survived. The motor boat returning him to his ship had gone over a mine and, blown to pieces, had sunk to the bottom of the sea. The same had happened to the two patrol boats accompanying him. He had been given the sad duty of passing on the news. The funeral ceremony would be held on the ship and if I wanted to attend, I was entitled to and more than welcome; they would take me there by helicopter. But he had to warn me that the flight there would be anything but safe, for skirmishes between different sects had recently flared up again. I had to decide in the next half hour, he said.

Perhaps I should have done. Perhaps I should have taken part in the naval ceremony on the warship, if not out of a sense of duty, then because of a deep sense of affection, gratitude, love towards my father, who I lost only because he wanted to show me the statue of Scheherazade, because in other circumstances he would surely have returned to the ship by another, safer route. Had he been led to his death by Scheherazade, my apparition? Had she realised that my love towards my father was becoming ever more sincere, that we were becoming best friends, while she wanted me exclusively for herself? This and similar stupid thoughts were swarming round my head as I returned to London.

I needed more than two months to recover and, with the help of an unhealthy quantity of tablets, I avoided depression. During this time, Scheherazade did not appear to me. It was thus much easier to decide that I must take life into my own hands, as there was no one left who I could ask for advice. I was alone, for the first time in my life. The woman who had cared for my father's two children, whom he called 'Nanny', was the only person who could offer me any consolation.

The probate process was complicated and long-winded, but it was concluded without any hitches. I became the sole heir to my father's property, which included not only the house in Ashchurch Park, but also five apartments in different parts of London, all let to reliable tenants, shares in three different funds, a summer house in Cornwall, three expensive cars, an immeasurable quantity of books, paintings, statues and other works of art, and I could keep on enumerating. With the property I inherited, I could live comfortably, more than comfortably, until the end of my days.

But I wanted to remain what I was, a writer. I wanted to create stories, long and short, in the hope that one of them at least would satisfy Scheherazade and she would return to my life as a real person. The house in Cornwall, together with the monthly income, I handed over to the kind lady who in the role of cook and cleaner had looked after my father and I since my arrival in London; the house in Ashchurch Park, my home I could say, I left in the care of Nanny and at the same time hired her an assistant, so that she didn't have to do everything herself. And I? I travelled to Slovenia, to the house of my grandfather, who was no longer among the living, but I wanted to get away from everything that reminded me of my father and of my life in London. I was convinced that only in this way would I find a balance again.

Grandad's house was abandoned and needed renovating. But while living in it, alone, cooking for myself, it quickly became apparent that this wasn't what I was looking for, as everything reminded me of my childhood, of school, of my grandfather, who had died right on the day when I was struck down in London by a bad dose of the flu and so was unable to attend the funeral, and of my first meeting with Scheherazade on the way to school, of the gypsy girl, as I called her at the beginning, of the apparition that stalked me as if telling a story about me to King Shahryar. I sold grandad's house and bought an end-of-terrace house in Ljubljana, spacious, with a large courtyard, which I changed into a garden, near to an old, neglected air raid shelter from the time of the Cold War, a convex, tree covered rise that was visible from my living room. And there I lived some of the time, while the rest of the time in my father's house in London, as well as travelling the world to attend literary symposia, presentations of my books, congresses and debates, but never just for fun, since for some time it had not been clear to me what that was.

Fun? My fate was in the hands of Scheherazade. Who, after all the traumas and relocations and uncertainties, ensured that my writerly vein dried up. Not in Slovenia, but in London, but at the moment I signed a contract for a new novel and I was hoping that I would finally write a story that would return Scheherazade to my arms. But maybe I had already written too many that were unsuitable because they were far from her expectations (not that she had told me what her expectations were), maybe she had grown weary of my failures and wanted to save me by preventing further writing.

***

"No!" exclaimed the Carer. "Writer's block?"

I had no choice: I also had to tell her a story about that.

This was easier, because she had in the meantime moved into my house. I had offered her a room on the first floor. That meant she could keep an eye on me and my state of health without coming and going. She could cook for me, bathe me, dress me, undress me, change me without absence in between, and she would no longer have to come to work by bus, which she hated. Her interest in everything I told her about, largely to lessen the growing anxiety inside me, became ever more intense – at moments, it seemed, obsessive.

24.

Nothing new under the sun?

There were no warning signs of my writer's block, but rather it struck overnight. In mid-sentence. As if there had been a catastrophic train crash in my brain, which had stopped traffic in every direction.

When I got up that day, I had felt normal; only when I had eaten a capacious English breakfast and begun to read the morning paper did I have a fleeting feeling that something had happened. Or to be more precise, something had happened to me. Every morning, when I read the news and articles, the "stories" (for in every news report, even on the crime pages, or political analysis, or news about what had happened to this or that famous person, there was concealed the outline of a story or a twist in a novel) sank into my memory as potential material.

But that fateful day, this did not happen. While reading news items and commentary and articles, it seemed to me from the very beginning that I was reading something that really happened, not something that I might, reworked and enriched with sparks of imagination, include in a short story or novel, in something "imagined", in something that is still, at least by some, thought of as literature.

Between the "facts" and opinions that I encountered while reading the newspaper and their story potential there lacked a connection and I felt that my world of imagination had been erased. I won't deny that my first reaction of surprise, even disbelief, rapidly became fear, and then turned into a feeling of anxiety that I wouldn't hesitate to call horror. Never in my life had I been faced with such a monster inside myself. And what was worst (and this was its essence!) I wouldn't have known how to even approximately describe it!

It had never seemed possible that it would be storytelling that would bring me to the edge of a nervous breakdown and change me into the kind of person who I liked to write about. This time it happened, not within the framework of an imagined story, but in the reality where I was forced to live, even if only because of loyalty to the activity that I saw as my "mission", for I knew that withdrawal from the world, when we lack a way forward and begin to psychologically drown, is always possible and, with the abundance of chemical means available, can also be painless, even instant. But each such thought, that I might withdraw from the world before my natural end (thus showing that I was not a victim, but rather the master of my fate), automatically became transformed into a story that I simply had to write and share with others. With that, the wish for a leap into the next life lost its power and validity.

I never imagined that my predicament would get even worse when my fiction began to move into my reality. And that the border separating the two would finally be erased.

But that happened later. At first, I simply got stuck. In the middle of a novel that I was writing for a highly regarded publisher in London, I suddenly found myself faced with an empty screen, or if not empty, then a meaningless confusion of words that I had to delete at the end of the day. I had a contract with a clearly defined deadline for handing over the text, the publisher had already informed the public that I was writing something exceptional (which was of course not true, or at least not verified, for I hadn't finished the book and the editor hadn't read it). I went to see the editor and told him openly that I had become the victim of writer's block, which I had hitherto not believed was possible. Time was mercilessly rushing past, I said, behind me was a week in which I had not managed to move the narrative forward by even a sentence or two. Here and there I manage to write a page which was passable, or so it seemed to me, but then the next day I was blocked again. I didn't know how to connect the individual pages into a meaningful whole and place them in the flow of the narrative. I told him I would have to withdraw from the agreement; my career was over.

He asked me why I had described my writer's block with the words used by Franz Kafka in his diary. Almost word for word. Astonishment was followed by amazement, for I hadn't even read Kafka's diary. Or perhaps I had and had forgotten. I, too, have three or even four copies of the same book at home simply because on an occasional visit to a bookshop I forget that I already have that book on my shelves and even that I have already read it. Besides which, it would not be surprising if I had read Kafka's description of writer's block in some other book, either as a citation or incorporated into the narrative of some other author, for opinions, experiences and visions move from book to book, without the author's awareness. Much of what we read becomes so deeply anchored in our memory that it becomes part of what we think, and then we write it down firmly convinced that it is something original. After all, even the Romans had the saying *nihil novi sub sole*, nothing new under the sun, and if we delve into the history of literature, we quickly realise that the whole rich literary heritage of the West is riddled with themes, characters, motifs and even styles which are present in most literary works, in many almost word for word or skilfully reworked (without the author being aware), which means that the history of Western literature is made up of an endless series of unconscious plagiarisms, although from a legal point of view plagiarism is of course something else, not the transfer of thoughts, forms, twists and ways of realisation from one century to another. I remembered that my grandfather had already told me something similar.

25.

Writer's block and me

Talking to the editor didn't help. On the contrary, it tied my hands even more and additionally paralysed my imagination. I got the feeling that I was *obliged* to finish the novel that I was writing, a novel that was supposed to be different from all the previous ones, and that this duty was a historical one. It's hard to imagine an author for whom such a task would not be a blow that would nullify any possibility of being able to write.

I doubled the dose of sedatives that I had been taking since the start of my difficulty and asked the editor for another meeting. We met over a beer in a sleazy pub in Soho. "I'm afraid that our cooperation is over," I said. I knew he would survive, because his publishing company published books that people liked to read, perhaps because they fall for the tried and tested promotional methods, or more probably because some people get so used to stories that come close to their human essence that they become addicted in a similar way that we become chained to sedatives and opium and heroin. Sadly, I couldn't and didn't know how to write such stories, not only because I had written too many, but mainly because fate had forced me into something that I was just not up to. Perhaps his idea of a novel that would finally uncover the fact that it is impossible to write an original novel and it thus doesn't matter what we read (in every novel and every story there is present at least part of our dreams, wishes and experiences, at least a fragment of the life that we hold to be ours) was nothing other than the selfish desire of an editor who would like to go down in history as someone who redirected the flow of Western literature and even, although it would also harm him, place a question mark over it.

After our second conversation, he was gripped by a deep sadness. I know how to observe people, I know how to discern their feelings, to peep into their interior through their eyes. He wasn't the first person that I had disappointed, but it seemed that he was disappointed less with me than by the fact that he would never see the novel in which he had invested so much of his professional hope, let alone publish it. He was one of those people for whom their career is more important than their health. Like me. For the thought that I had suddenly, and for the first time in my life, become the victim of writer's block, flooded me with a whole assortment of psychosomatic issues, from terrible tiredness and pains in my joints to anxiety, pain between my shoulder blades, upset stomach and a list of maladies that I would need at least an hour to enumerate.

More than anything, I was overcome by the feeling that my life was running out. That I had achieved what I had been destined to achieve and it was arrogant of me, as well as unworthy of an author who had after all achieved more than most of his colleagues, to expect, even demand from life that it should grant him even more. And what would I actually do with this "more"? Would not the world carry on, as it had done for a long time, without my novel about the pointlessness of writing a novel about how pointless it was writing another novel?

Is it not generally known that every author is finally forced to admit (however much he revolts against this) that there is no point in continuing? Some because of their repeated failures, others because of their more than obvious successes, others because their imaginations have run dry, and yet others, like me, who have become afraid of words and can no longer form sentences, which, in the right order, can create or continue a narrative, or because no sentence they write belongs in any of the narratives they wish to share with others. And after all, what would the possible success of this novel, even if it was the best in my body of work, mean after my death? Nothing. And I stand on the threshold of death at every moment. That is also true for those who are half a century younger than me. Death does not evaluate, weigh up, compare, death does not read, death takes us. And then only those who are not dead deal with our work. If at all. And even if they do, we know nothing about it, and sooner or later they will be dead, too. Even a monument on the main square of a city, where they actually prefer to put statues of generals, does not enable us to know anything at all about the traces that we left behind on our way to Nothing.

One way or another, during the second meeting with my editor, who in the years of our cooperation had become a close and trusted friend, after at times heated discussion, I agreed to his request to keep on writing, although with a short pause, for in his opinion, everything that began so originally in my novel should be finished for the sake of posterity, if not for personal satisfaction at one's own achievement. Writer's block, however bad a case it was, could be cured, he assured me. For the problem is not as rare as it might seem. In Switzerland, there was a psychiatric clinic (more a creative sanatorium than a clinic) that specialised in dealing with writer's block; quite a number of famous names had been treated (and cured) there.

Would I at least consider the possibility of spending some time there? My contract could be extended and I shouldn't be afraid that my fee would be reduced because of my sudden creative paralysis. What was more: in order to get my novel, the publisher was willing to pay the costs of treatment in this institution for two months. And if there was no result, not to worry, they were willing to take that risk.

A psychiatric clinic that cured writer's block? It didn't seem possible. Although of course in Switzerland, anything is possible. My editor's proposal was a kind and generous one, but at the same time laughable and humiliating for an author who had never had any problems stringing words together into sentences and sentences into paragraphs and paragraphs into short or long narratives. Perhaps my guardian angel (who was of course nothing other than part of my subconscious) was trying to tell me not to bang my head against a brick wall; the time had come to bid goodbye to writing. I wouldn't be the first and certainly not the only one to withdraw from the literary battlefield; it would be better to do it honourably, on my own initiative, than to be hounded and written off by others.

In spite of that, I eventually accepted my editor's proposal. Most probably out of curiosity than any hope that some psychoanalytic process could free up the brake in my head. I began to be interested in who I might meet in this clinic, perhaps even an acquaintance or two, and how the process of "treatment" would proceed, which I couldn't even begin to imagine. The final decision fell when the editor confided in me something strange. He said that Simon Goldberg, one of the best-known writers of crime fiction, who – and this I didn't doubt – brought the publishers a great deal of money and who thus facilitated, he added, the publication of less widely read but high quality authors of my ilk, had already been under treatment there for two years. Almost overnight, what had befallen me had happened to Goldberg and he, too, had hesitated before he had gone to the Berghof Clinic.

The problem was that since then he had got in touch only twice: once, immediately after his arrival and the other time three weeks later. The first time he reported that he had enrolled on the programme, the second time he offered only the short statement: *Forget about me.* Enquiries with the management of the clinic had brought no suitable clarification; they had replied that the condition of their patients, even the voluntary ones, was a medical secret which they could not reveal to anyone, even close relatives. After two years of silence, my publishers and many others wanted to know what had happened to Goldberg. Had writer's block perhaps become a nervous breakdown and then mental illness? Was he still there, were they treating him, had he died, had an accident, fled? If I went to Berghof as someone suffering from writer's block, I might find an answer. After all, millions of his readers were also asking why Goldberg had stopped writing.

It didn't escape me that the absence of information on Goldberg's fate was something that the "missing" author would know how to incorporate, with enviable effect, into one of his novels. I had never met him, but I had read quite a few of his books and in all of them tension was created by a secret that was not solved until the very end, and then with a surprising twist. This is, of course, a standard formula in all crime stories since Agatha Christie and Inspector Poirot onwards, but Goldberg knew how to add to the formula some original twists, different in almost every book, thanks to which I enjoyed reading his work, and I am not the slightest bit ashamed to admit that as a serious author I read crime novels. Had Simon Goldberg arranged his own disappearance in order to stimulate interest in his next book, in which he would describe the fictional circumstances of his long absence?

It wouldn't surprise me. Whoever knows how to play with the fate of fictional characters in the pages of a novel, would also know how to play with his own life. Even if only with the intention of writing another novel.

One way or another, my editor eventually convinced me that I would find the answer, or at least the path to the answer, only in the Berghof Clinic in the Swiss Alps, where there was a programme for treating writer's block. I left my registration, prepayment and all the other details to him and myself found out only how to get there. I was surprised to find that it was housed in a medieval castle, Schloss Berghof, which stood on an island in the middle of one of the numerous mountain lakes and could only be reached by boat from one of the small settlements on the shore. Whoever found himself in such a building was, technically speaking, a prisoner.

26.

Arrival at Berghof

On the boat that took me from the pier on the lakeshore towards the castle, in the late autumn, just before the onset of winter, I was for the first time overtaken by a feeling reminiscent of fear. What if my editor had set a trap for me? What if he didn't like the beginning of the novel I had sent him before writer's block struck and he wanted to prevent me from completing it before the deadline, which meant that the publishing director could cancel the contract, regardless of the editor's assurance that the deadline could be extended?

All this went through my mind as the slow, dangerously wobbly boat with a coughing motor, which must have been at least fifty years old, drove from Villersdorf on the shore towards the mighty Berghof castle on the island in the middle of the lake. Besides me, there were only five other passengers: three women, who judging by their appearance were nurses or employees of the clinic, perhaps even cooks or cleaners, and two men of unremarkable appearance, one thin, the other fat, who could likewise be clinic employees, although it would be hard to guess in what role. One could be a psychiatrist, the other an accountant; but one could be, like me, a patient suffering from writer's block, coming for treatment, the other, perhaps, an electrician coming to fix a fault in the network, although it might be the other way round.

I don't know why a sense of mistrust arose among us as soon as the boat left the shore, which prevented any of us from speaking, making a comment, engaging in conversation with the others; as if our destination imbued our journey with embarrassment. To some extent, the weather contributed to this, for it was cold, cloudy, windy, almost wintry; the boat rocked on the troubled surface of the lake, and the boatman, with a beret on his head and wrapped in a creased windbreaker, was half concealed behind a heap of bags, which no doubt contained food and other essentials for the clinic.

From close up, the medieval castle that rose above us offered quite a different impression than when seen from the shore; it seemed more frightening than fairy tale, not only because of its cracked walls, but also more specifically, because of the indubitable sense of threat that breathed from its isolation and remoteness from the world that we had left behind. Grey and damp, surrounded by low clouds swirling around its highest towers, it promised anything but health for the mentally ill individuals that it imprisoned, probably in damp cellars, let alone that a writer with creative problems would, upon seeing it, experience a new burst of imaginative energy. But first impressions are usually unreliable, and so I suppressed my anxious thoughts.

We went along the unstable wooden pier, which no one seemed to maintain, for the planks beneath our feet creaked dangerously, to the steep steps that led to the entrance high above us. Carrying two suitcases of clothes and other things I needed for a two-month stay, I soon ran out of breath on the steps; I had to stop and rest, facing up once more to the fact that passing one's half century and lack of exercise lead to many things that are hard to accept, and that perhaps departure from this world, that seemed to me more imaginary than real, was closer than I wished.

They all overtook me, even the fat man, who should have been most out of breath on the steep, winding and at first sight endless steps. I was left alone. That didn't seem a bad thing to me, for it gave me a chance to take in the surroundings in more detail. I saw that the castle stood on the higher of two high points on the island, while on the lower one, which I could see from where I was resting, stood a small, white, freshly painted church with a leaning bell tower, a real foreign body among the late autumn greyness and beside the poorly maintained castle. Evidently it had been painted quite recently, otherwise the wet, windy weather would have left damp stains on it. Did someone go to it to pray, did Sunday services for clinic patients take place there, or even for the staff, although I couldn't imagine psychiatrists who, in carrying out their duties, would not lose their faith? When I looked towards the church, I noticed that on the slope below it, partly concealed by sparse pine and spruce trees, were quite a number of graves with gravestones. There was no doubt that there was a graveyard below the church. But who would have their final resting place there? Patients?

It seemed more likely that the graves were very old and went back to the time before a sanatorium had been established in the castle. The sudden fear that my body might end up among them evaporated. At the same time, I felt an uncertain but recognisable sense of hope that my imagination was perhaps not as blocked as I feared, for my speculations about the church and graveyard beside the castle already contained the seed of a potential story, which might mean that the blockage within me had been freed up and I could head back towards the boat, which was waiting at the pier below me, return to

London and tell my publisher that I was in remission and that they would receive the novel on time.

But the sense of relief that was born inside me did not last long. I realised that I could not betray my publisher, we had known each other too long, they had launched too many of my books. Above all, I could not flee from fate, however unpleasant that might be. In every life there are moments when retreat is the worst option and this, I finally accepted, was one such moment.

Although I expected problems, there were none. The doorman calmly, as if I had just returned from a good lunch, asked me for my name and the reason for my arrival. Without difficulty, he found the data in the heap of papers in front of him, and without any show of surprise or disturbance he asked me to wait for someone to come and take me to the room that I had been assigned.

"Another thing," I said. "I'd like to visit my friend Simon Goldberg, who has been under treatment here for some time."

Perhaps the dim light was at fault, but it seemed to me that the doorman went pale. "Treated here?" he asked in surprise.

"Yes," I said, "treated here. As I myself shall be. Is there anything unusual about that?"

Was it only my impression that the doorman's paleness became panic? He closed the glass window, picked up the phone, typed a number, spun round on the chair with his back towards me, and began to speak to someone. His shoulders were trembling in agitation. Evidently something unexpected had happened.

The conversation lasted a good minute, and then the doorman swung back towards the window and said: "Dr Wagner will receive you." Almost simultaneously, a young man in a white coat and wearing thick glasses approached along the corridor, evidently an orderly, for I could not imagine that a doctor had come for me. He reached for my bags and said in English: "Follow me. I'm Dr Wagner."

It seemed strange that he hadn't sent an orderly or some other member of staff, but no doubt he had his reasons. He was relatively young, perhaps in his late thirties, tall and thin, red-haired and unshaven, which together with his creased white coat gave the impression that he didn't worry too much about his appearance. I followed him until we came, via a labyrinth of narrow corridors and a confusion of staircases, to a large room, almost a small hall, where a fire was burning in the fireplace. Dr Wagner put down my suitcases, asked me sit down in one of the armchairs, and then he left. I remained alone in the room, in which there was nothing but ten armchairs and the fire burning.

For the first time, I thought that in this clinic everything was not as it should be.

Once again, a feeling of loneliness rose up within me, which reminded me of three weeks of solitude in the Sahara Desert, where I had almost died – not because of thirst, but because of the tortuous lack of human proximity. A feeling that had accompanied me ever since in a similar way to my Scheherazade, although not as persistently, for I felt her behind me as a constant presence, whereas the feeling of loneliness appeared only in periods when I was deprived of the possibility of conversation, of communication with my fellow man, with anyone who would understand at least a tenth of what I was trying to say. Usually, the absence of human companionship had to last at least a few days before I was overcome by anxiety. In the large empty room at Berghof castle, I felt pressure in my throat after only a five-minute wait. The feeling quickly became unbearable and I decided to go out into the corridor and onwards, wherever, until I encountered another living being.

I got up, but at precisely that moment Dr Wagner returned. With him was a young orderly of unpleasant appearance, short and stocky, like a wrestler, whose irregular, slightly cruel features were additionally marred by a hare lip. "Take the suitcases to room 13," the doctor ordered him in German. Then he turned to me and in English said: "Simon Goldberg, you said?" I nodded and added: "I'd like to see him, but I really came to have treatment for writer's block. My editor arranged everything. Do you deal with such problems?"

"All in good time," replied Dr Wagner.

"I hear that you are treating quite a number of eminent authors here," I said, in the hope that he would mention some names. But he didn't. In fact, he said nothing, which somewhat concerned me. I expected at least a measure of medical politeness, certainly not a bureaucratic attitude and cold, Germanic dourness. The English, including those who were born elsewhere and been anglicised, know how to at least feign politeness, which had saved me a great deal of unpleasantness in different parts of the world. Dr Wagner had clearly never lived in England. Or he was simply weary of writers with writer's block. "Follow me," he said and headed off down the corridor. "Room 13," he reminded the orderly with the hare lip, when the corridor divided in two. The orderly took my suitcases to the left, while Dr Wagner gestured to me to follow him to the right.

The corridor wasn't straight, it turned left and right, it was without windows and was dimly lit by sparsely distributed wall lights, it had an arched stone ceiling and here and there water dripped down; it smelled of damp and some kind of chemicals, perhaps medical, perhaps for cleaning. We went past three open doors; through them I saw large rooms with daylight in which stood rows of metal beds, on which male patients in striped pyjamas were lying, leaning or sitting in strange postures, most of them staring into space. One old man was sniffing his fingers in amazement and shaking his head in disbelief, a younger one was intently scratching his shaved head, while the others were almost immobile. I thought that these were mental patients; I couldn't imagine that among them might be some internationally known writer being treated for writer's block.

The unusually long corridor then split in two again; the left branch was unlit, the right one widened and on the floor was a dirty, but soft carpet, on which our feet stopped echoing. There was also more light; evidently we had come to the more comfortable part of the castle.

We ended up in front of a thick oak door, where Dr Wagner asked me to wait for a moment. Then he went inside, closing the door behind him; the hinges creaked unpleasantly and the sound echoed within me, until the door opened again five minutes later. Dr Wagner invited me to go in.

I found myself in a room which after the strong light in the last part of the corridor seemed so dark that for some time I could make out nothing more than its hexagonal shape and high ceiling, in which there were small windows. As soon as I grew accustomed to the modest light, I noticed that some daylight was also coming through a narrow window high in the wall, and that in the corner there was an illuminated standard lamp. When my vision sharpened even more, I noticed an oval table, covered with a disorder of papers and books, a brown metal filing cabinet on which stood a vase of plastic orchids, a metal chair that was a distance away from the table, almost in the middle of the room, and on the table also a device that reminded me of an old-fashioned cassette recorder.

The hinges squeaked and the door closed. I looked round and realised with surprise that two men were standing behind me, one on each side of the door. One was Dr Wagner, who was in the process of cleaning his glasses with a cloth, the other was the orderly with the hare lip, who was staring at me rigidly, almost stupidly. How had he managed to get here before us, considering that he had carried my suitcases along the other corridor in the opposite direction? He hadn't overtaken us; had he perhaps entered through another, hidden door? I suddenly felt as if I had been brought here for questioning.

And then I spotted a third man. Like some strange animal, he slowly crawled on all fours from behind the oval table, his eyes on the ground as if he was looking for something.

"Dr Goldberg," Dr Wagner introduced him.

27.

Things become strange

My heart sank. If this is the famous writer of crime novels who came to the Berghof clinic to be treated for writer's block, I thought – and it seemed impossible that he was not, for to have two patients with the same name in the same clinic would be too much of a coincidence – something extremely unpleasant must have happened to him. During his treatment, had the experts at the castle gone so far that he had developed a mental illness? Although we had never met (writers of crime novels attend different symposia and festivals to serious authors), I had read quite a bit about him and knew that he had been, before he took up writing, a locksmith and as such it was unlikely that he had a doctorate.

Was Dr Wagner making a joke, was he using the academic title ironically?

At that moment, the supposed doctor stopped crawling on the floor, he got up quickly and agilely, raised his right hand and exclaimed: "Eureka!" Between his fingers I could see a large brown button, which had obviously dropped off his crumpled jacket, for it was exactly the same as the two which were still sewn on. Simon Goldberg was unusually tall, almost two metres, perhaps he had played basketball in his younger years, I judged him to be over fifty, he had a small, round head, which squatted on the top of an unusually long neck, and beneath his Jewish nose there was a small Hitler moustache; he looked just like he did in the photographs on the back cover of his bestsellers and accompanying interviews that I had come across. There was no doubt that there stood before me the man whose fate was of interest to my (although not his) editor at the publishing house we had in common.

"How is it possible," he suddenly said in English, "that I don't know who invented the button? Considering that I know almost everything, or at least too much for me to sleep peacefully at night. Were buttons used by the Sumerians? The Babylonians? The Egyptians? I'm almost convinced that it was the Chinese who invented them. Like most useful things in the world."

Dr Wagner jerked his head towards me. "You have a visitor."

Simon Goldberg turned his eyes towards me as if he hadn't even noticed me before. It was hard to describe what was in his look. Curiosity? Amazement? Fear? Perhaps even panic? All of those? He began to slowly make his way towards me. He moved with great difficulty, dragging his feet as if he couldn't bend his knees. He stopped right in front of me, so close that I could feel his breath. He looked at my face as if examining a valuable painting, which he suspected was a fake.

"A visitor?" he posed the question to Dr Wagner, without ceasing to avidly study my face.

"A visitor," repeated Dr Wagner.

Simon Goldberg turned and began to shuffle back towards the oval table. "It must be a mistake," he said. "You know that I don't have visitors. Patients have visitors. And other doctors. I am the only doctor in this institution who no one ever visits."

"But that's not possible," I couldn't restrain myself from saying. "How can you be a doctor in an institution to which you came two years ago to be treated for writer's block? After all, you are one of the world's most successful writers of crime novels. I am also a writer, I've read at least three of your books, we have the same publisher." I turned to Dr Wagner, who said nothing, but shrugged almost indiscernibly.

Simon Goldberg turned and rested his bottom against the oval table. "Who are you to say that I don't know what's possible? After all, I am the director of the clinic. Are you saying that I don't know what I'm talking about?"

At this point, I was lost for words. Director of the clinic? Had my editor for some reason spun me a story that had no connection with reality? Why would he do that? It didn't seem plausible. Before me stood, without a shadow of a doubt, Simon Goldberg, the world-renowned author of crime novels. Why was he suddenly claiming to be the director of the clinic? Were they setting a trap for me, was this some kind of "entrance exam" for the programme for treatment of writer's block? I had never read anywhere that Simon Goldberg had a twin, and even if he had, which was not impossible, they wouldn't both be called Simon. Although this wasn't actually impossible; there is no shortage of strange parents in the world.

"Can you answer me at least one question?" I decided to get to the bottom of this mystery.

"I can answer a thousand, many thousand," he said with a wave of the hand.

"Do you have a twin who is a writer and publishes crime novels under your name?"

"Your question is criminal, patient. For you did come to Berghof as a patient, if I'm not mistaken? Certainly, everything is not alright in your head, it is full of illusions and ridiculous suppositions. In your case, the border between imagination and reality has obviously been blurred, if not erased. That kind of flaw is common among writers, but your problem has evidently progressed until it represents a mental disturbance."

"No," I said. "No," I repeated more decisively. "I have another question. Have you, Simon Goldberg, ever written crime novels under your own name? Or even everything that under you name sells more than successfully on every continent?"

"Dr Wagner," said the supposed director of the clinic, turning to his younger colleague, "who have you brought to me? Have you checked his details and those of the people who sent him? You well know that this is an exclusive clinic and that we don't treat just anyone. Have you made notes on his psychological state and placed him in the right group?"

"The gentleman has come for two months' treatment for writer's block," replied Dr Wagner, calmly and politely. "All his expenses have been paid in advance. We accepted him onto the programme, since we had no reason not to. I think that the gentleman has been misinformed about you and your status at Berghof and that we can without difficulty include him in the programme."

Simon Goldberg was silent for some time. Then he moved away from the table and took some shuffling steps towards the metal chair.

"Sit down," he commanded me. "Have you had a long journey? Are you not tired?"

Of course I was, and resting on the chair, although it looked highly uncomfortable, would have more than suited me. I took some steps towards the chair, but as soon as I began to lower myself onto it, I was stopped by Goldberg's imperative voice.

"Not there! I said on the chair!" He looked at me as if I had been about to do something indecent.

I turned to Dr Wagner, but the young doctor remained impassive. As if nothing special was happening. Perhaps there is another chair in the room, I thought. I looked in every direction, checked every corner, also looked behind the table, but there was no other chair, there was only the one.

"I'm sorry, doctor, I misheard, did you tell me to sit?"

"I don't remember saying anything else."

"On the chair?" I asked, to avoid any further misunderstanding.

"Where else?" he replied, slightly taken aback.

Okay, I thought, on the chair – but I had hardly bent my knees when Goldberg's voice rang out in my ears even sharper than before. "On the chair, I said. Are you deaf?"

"Actually," I replied, "I'd rather stand, if you don't mind."

"Why?" Dr Goldberg responded with a note of intolerance. "I asked you to sit on the chair that is right in front of you, what's the problem?"

Okay, I thought. I'll sit. On the metal chair.

And I sat down.

Simon Goldberg tilted his head and for the first time there appeared on his face something reminiscent of a friendly, albeit patronising smile. "So, was that really so difficult?"

Completely confused, I repeated that I was registered for the programme treating writer's block, but that didn't necessarily mean that I wished to take part in the programme, for to be frank, it would make sense to leave the clinic, where I had been told Simon Goldberg was being treated, as soon as possible. Had he perhaps lost his mind during the treatment process and become a patient?

"Of course I'm a patient," replied Simon Goldberg and went on in a tone he might use when lecturing a group of students. "Like Dr Wagner. And all the doctors you will meet. The Berghof Clinic is known for not distinguishing between mental health and, to put it differently, normality and different deviations from the average psychological state. For us, madness and common sense are one and the same thing, we are interested only in deviations from the golden mean. You will surely agree that all of us without exception go through life with some major or lesser disorder in our heads. And that those among us who suffer from the lesser disturbance can help those who do not even know how ill they are."

I got up and, as calmly as my pounding heart would allow me, said: "I am pleased to meet you, Dr Goldberg. No offence, but now I will leave."

I was almost at the door when Goldberg said behind me: "Not today, I'm afraid."

I turned and saw a pistol in his hand. He slowly pointed it at me. "If I remember rightly, you came to be treated for writer's block"

At the same time, Dr Wagner approached from my left with a syringe in his hand.

The confusion that flooded over me was so severe that I didn't even react when he took my hand and pushed the needle into a vein above my wrist.

I was shrouded in darkness.

28.

Prison?

When I regained consciousness and ascertained that they hadn't killed me, which I had feared in that fleeting moment before I blacked out, the first thing that I felt was almost complete numbness. I was lying on a rough reddish-brown mat, beneath a grey blanket, which stank of the absorbed sweat of a number of different people. I was dressed; when I passed out, they had carried me as I was to a cell, laid me on the mat and covered me with the blanket.

I sat up with difficulty, pushed the blanket aside and began with stiff fingers to massage my legs from hip to ankle to get my circulation going. The air was damp and smelled of something rotten, it was smothering me. I was in a cell not much bigger than a bathroom, with slimy stone walls, an irregular floor of brown earth, a black iron door and a small round window with a peephole through which I could see a stone-paved courtyard. Empty, not a soul to be seen.

I sat for quite a few minutes on the mat, massaging my calves and then my thighs, while the morning light entered the cell until the black mass in the corner came to be visible as a filthy bucket and, on the ceiling, a damp stain, from which every few moments a drop of water fell, making a barely discernible plopping sound when it landed on the mat.

With the exception of the dripping and my breathing there were no sounds in the cell for a good five minutes. Then from the underground cells on the other side of the courtyard I heard a muffled cry, which was not the result of joy or pleasure, but definitely rather an expression of fear and suffering. As if someone was being beaten, or threatened with a pistol or a knife to the throat. Similar cries followed and each was noticeably different. With difficulty, I got to my feet and moved to the peephole. I tried to open the tiny window, but the half open shutters were on the outside, as were the smeared samples of fly droppings on the glass. In spite of that, I could still see the spacious inner courtyard and the wall on the other side. The castle was waking up; behind a window on the first floor the shadows of human figures were moving in both directions along the illuminated corridor.

The noise was coming from the cellars. Behind the glass of one of the peepholes, similar to mine, I saw the distorted face of a bald man of about my age, who was staring at the courtyard with a surprised, enraptured expression, as if he was enthused by the gloominess of the dawning winter day. Then the noise ceased and the face withdrew. I thought I could hear doors slamming, the cracking of whips, sharp commands. I pressed my face to the glass and looked upwards to see whether the sky was clearing or whether the first snow was on its way, but I could see only the lower part of the balcony which protruded from the wall above the peephole. I felt dizzy, for a moment it seemed that I would slump to the floor and pass out. I leaned against the wall and waited for the feeling of nausea to pass.

When I again felt some strength in my muscles, I staggered to the door and began to bang on it with my fists. But it was made of iron, so my blows sounded as if I was beating against the sides of a tank. "Let me out, let me out!" I yelled, but my yells sounded equally hollow. As if I had been shut in a tomb. In spite of that, I kept pounding with my fists against the iron and shouting, until I was hoarse: "Let me out, I want to see Dr Goldberg!" The only response was renewed noise from the cellar on the other side of the courtyard.

I suddenly remembered that I had come to the castle with luggage. It was not in the cell. Where had they put it, what were they doing with it? I looked through my jacket pockets. They had even taken my passport and wallet. But not my notebook and pen. As if they wanted me to begin writing about the strange things happening to me. Fuck you, I said in my head, fuck you.

The next moment, I heard the creaking of door hinges on the other side of the courtyard. I looked through the peephole. Someone was opening the door above some steps in the corner that I hadn't noticed before. A chubby man with a fur hat on his head and a bucket in each hand came through it. I thought they probably contained slops from the kitchen. He was holding them slightly away from himself, so as not to dirty his coat, and he waddled across the courtyard towards my door. A good five metres away, he stopped, put down the buckets, bent over, and with both hands lifted with some difficulty a metal hatch in the ground. He poured the contents of the buckets into the drain and with a clang put them on the ground. It seemed then that they contained not kitchen slops but excrement. Of course! A similar bucket stood in the corner of my cell. Then he lowered the hatch and straightened it with a kick from his leather boot.

I began to shout and bang on the glass in the peephole. The man, who had already picked his buckets up, put them down and headed towards me. Evidently, he had heard the rumpus I was kicking up. He looked around discreetly, as if afraid that someone would see where he was going, then he came close to the peephole and pressed his face against the glass. His dark eyes met the ends of the fingers that I was scraping against the glass. "Dr Goldberg!" I shouted. "I want to see him! Now!" The man stretched out his arms, like a bird opening its wings to fly off, and closed the wooden shutters so that they met with a bang in the middle.

I was left in complete darkness.

Next morning, there was a rattling outside the door, someone opened it and a beam of light came from the corridor into the cell. The young orderly had brought me breakfast, which didn't enthuse me too much: a plate of mashed potato and three boiled carrots. Without cutlery. I would have to eat with my hands, which wouldn't be a problem for me, as I had done so many times in southern India. I told him I wouldn't touch the food unless someone, he or someone else, opened the shutters on the cell window; I hadn't the slightest intention of eating in the dark and languishing in a cell without light, without knowing what was going on; he should tell Dr Goldberg that what they were doing with me was a criminal act that someone would have to answer for, and that I would demand such damages that the clinic would be bankrupt. He should remind Dr Goldberg, or whoever was responsible for the business side of the clinic, that there were people outside who knew where I was, and who would sooner or later begin to make enquiries about me. They should be ready, for no excuse would be good enough.

"Ich verstehe nicht," he replied and closed the iron door behind him, so that I was once again in the dark. But soon after, someone opened the window shutters and light from outside poured into the cell. I saw that it was snowing. Large feathery snowflakes were falling from the sky in gentle spirals and melting as soon as they landed on the stone paving.

When I had eaten the potato and carrots, I felt terribly thirsty; the orderly had brought me neither tea nor water, nothing. I began to bang my fists against the iron door, which I did for a good five minutes. No one responded, no one heard me. When I once again looked through the peephole onto the courtyard, I saw that the snow was getting thicker and was quickly building up on the ground. I suddenly felt almost safe in the cell. Especially since the breakfast had shown that they didn't intend to starve me. That they had some purpose for me. Although I couldn't begin to imagine what they could do with me, other than start treating me for writer's block, or drive me mad and include me among the psychopaths. Everything was in conflict not only with my expectations, but also with the remnants of common sense, which still hadn't completely abandoned me. Or at least it seemed that it hadn't. Although at moments I felt as if I was losing it and that everything which was happening to me was one of my hallucinations.

The orderly took away the mat on which I had been forced to spend the night and brought me a relatively comfortable mattress and an extra, somewhat thicker blanket. And he took away the bucket, which I had been compelled to use during the night, as there was no other option. He brought it back washed. It seemed strange to me, in the late twentieth century, to be in a medieval castle, locked in a medieval cell without a toilet or water – and in Switzerland!

Something was wrong, seriously wrong. The orderly wasn't unfriendly, I'd say rather that he was indifferent, behaving like someone going about their routine work. When I asked him to take me to Dr Goldberg, he looked at me as if he had never heard of him.

"I'll take you to Dr Wagner when he tells me to," he said. "Maybe tomorrow, maybe next week, maybe in a month's time." I couldn't say that he saw me as a mental patient, even less that I seemed dangerous to him, for as he came and went the door was not properly closed, and I could have easily slipped into the corridor and gone along it to rooms where I might have found a way out of the castle and down to the pier below.

And then? The distance from the island to the shore was too great for me to swim across and the water, considering the sudden onset of winter, certainly cold enough to kill me.

The next morning, in addition to mashed potato, carrots and a bottle of water, the orderly brought me a bunch of newspaper cuttings. He said that Dr Goldberg had sent them with the instruction that I read them closely, at least twice. The cuttings contained reports in different languages about elm disease and the ecological damage it was causing in extensive parts of Europe, worst of all in England. One of the reports (evidently taken from a British newspaper) informed me that the previous year, in the south of England alone, more than a million elms had died. Why had he sent press cuttings to me, locked in a cell, with no idea when I would get out of it? Was that a puzzle I was supposed to unravel? Did the cuttings contain concealed hints as to how I could escape from the castle? But why should I escape from the clinic when I had come here through normal channels and even paid in advance for treatment?

Had there been a misunderstanding, unintended confusion, had someone in the chain put together two and three and got seven? I read the press cuttings, one after the other, and some again in the hope that it would become clear why Dr Goldberg had sent them to me, and in slight embarrassment that I'd never seen an elm in my life and didn't know what one looked like. The confusion inside me only increased. Because of the sedative that they had injected me with before they dragged me to the cell, and also partly because of the shock of discovering that Simon Goldberg was not only a psychiatrist, but even the director of the clinic, it was increasingly unclear how I should behave towards him. Was he my friend or my enemy? What was he trying to tell me, what was the point of the cuttings?

29.

Elm trees are dying

The next day, two orderlies took me to Dr Goldberg's office. The hexagonal room was as gloomy as when I first arrived at the clinic. Dr Wagner stood near the door, while Dr Goldberg sat on the only chair in the room, with his elbows on his knees and his face buried in his hands. I don't know why, but the last remnants of hope inside me evaporated. There was something too human, too powerless in his posture. He was wearing slippers, through which his uncut toe nails protruded, at least two centimetres long, some of them already broken. Dr Wagner was rubbing his hands together as if he was cold and he no doubt was, since the small electric heater was giving off too little heat for a spacious room with a high ceiling.

I stood and waited. Dr Goldberg finally removed his hands from his face and looked towards me through the frames of his glasses. He placed his hands against his thighs and got to his feet. He shuffled past the table towards the window, scratching his head as he went with the fingers of his right hand. He stopped and stared for some time through the window. It was still snowing.

Then he suddenly said: "Good morning, patient. Satisfied with the breakfast?"

Since he was obviously making fun of me, I decided to keep quiet. He reached into an inside pocket of his dirty doctor's coat and pulled out a creased notebook. He opened it at random, raised it towards the dull light coming through the painted window pane and spent some time carefully, or so it seemed, reading the notes on both pages. Then he closed the notebook, put it back in his inner pocket and turned to me.

"Sit, patient," he said, "on the floor."

This was something new. I could think of no reason not to obey. I thought that sitting on the floor was part of the same puzzle as elm disease, and that sooner or later all the pieces would fit together into a whole I could make sense of. Like some kind of yogi getting ready to meditate, I sat on the floor with my legs crossed and looked at Dr Goldberg.

"I said on the floor, patient!" he almost roared. "Not on the chair. The floor! Must you always do the opposite of what I ask of you?"

Okay, I thought. And was surprised that I hadn't thought of this before. I got up and sat on the chair. Goldberg's eyes shone with approval. "Well, is there anything wrong with sitting on the floor?"

I shook my head and looked at Dr Wagner, who was fiddling with the switches on the recording device; it seemed to me that his lips beneath his moustache were stretched into a barely discernible smile.

"Would you rather sit on a chair?" Dr Goldberg turned to me once again.

"No," I replied, "the floor is fine."

"Quite comfortable, eh?" he responded. "You can always fall off a chair, but from the floor never. The floor is safest for those who are afraid of tipping over. People who think they are clever bombard us with advice about standing on the ground, on firm ground, don't they?"

I nodded.

He looked satisfied. More than that, his smile showed the conviction that he had won an important victory. "Now tell me. What is happening to elm trees in England?"

I had been waiting for this question, which seemed to me a basic part of the puzzle, and I wanted to show him that I had done the assignment he had given me. "Elm trees in England are dying," I said, "but not just there, elsewhere too. The disease began in Netherlands and from there spread right across Europe, without anyone knowing how or why."

His face showed surprise. "Are you joking?"

"No," I replied. "In southern England alone, millions of elm trees died in a few years. Soon, there'll be none left."

"Soon, there'll be none left," he repeated, more to himself than to me. "Is there anything else in the world that will soon be no more?"

Oh, I thought, many things. But it didn't seem wise to engage the doubtful director of the clinic in a debate on ecological problems, on the accelerated disappearance of animal species, on the lack of interest in literature and books, on the growing difference between a handful of rich individuals and the majority of ever poorer people, and on all the other plagues that were spreading and threatening our very survival.

So I said nothing.

"Millions in the last few years?" he repeated. "How do you know? Have you been in England recently, have you counted them?"

The question seemed a stupid one, but I didn't want to argue, and so I shook my head.

"Am I right in assuming that you became familiar with this data that you're citing between the walls of this clinic?" He gave me a smug smile.

"That's right," I admitted, and why not as I was speaking the truth. "I've read quite a few reports about this issue. And analyses. Am I wrong in thinking that it was you who sent me the newspaper and magazine cuttings?"

"I wasn't able to send you anything that hadn't been published," he gave a slight frown. "Which means that the basis for your opinion on this disease is not the fruit of personal experience or research. You have formed an opinion on the basis of printed information, the authors of which and their intentions you do not know, which means that this information does not have its feet on the ground and is sitting on a chair like you."

I couldn't argue with this. I nodded. But he didn't see it because he'd turned back towards the window. "Come here," he invited me with a crooked finger, "come here for a moment."

When I joined him, he tapped with his fingers on the lower, clear part of the window. "Tell me what you see," he said.

It wasn't difficult to oblige. "I see that it's still snowing," I said. "I see the lake, which has evidently frozen, for layers of snow are building up on its surface. I see the pier, also covered in snow, I see the boat, locked in ice. The snow has cut us off from the world and covered us. And hidden us. We've been swallowed by winter, and not only in the literal sense. We've become an island in the middle of the whiteness. Just as I've become an island in the middle of a mystery that I can't get to the bottom of. I also see the church on the neighbouring hillock and some trees."

"Some trees," his response was rapid. "How many?"

"Two by the church and three on the shore of the lake," I said.

"What kind of trees?" he wanted to know. "Apple, pear, pine, spruce, beech, poplars?"

Even if I was able to see the trees clearly through the curtain of snow, I wouldn't be able to identify them, as even in primary school botany was by far my weakest subject; the only thing I was sure of was the difference between evergreen and deciduous trees. And between pines and spruces. Everything else was just greenery on trunks or stalks to me.

"I think they're elms, sir," I said.

I turned to find that I was staring straight into Goldberg's eyes. Grey, half absent, confused. He abruptly turned away, but in spite of that I saw, in the faint light from outside, how pale and tired his face was from close up, and how deep the wrinkles on his forehead. He seemed old, worn out and at the end of his strength.

"Elms?" he said as he shuffled back towards his chair. "Can you tell me which are diseased and which not?"

I replied that that wasn't possible, except from close up, and I evidently couldn't hope for that.

He suddenly replied: "The two near the church are sick. The three on the lake shore are still healthy. Do you know how the disease is transmitted?"

"Of course," I said. "It is transmitted by *Scolytus scolytus*, the larger European elm bark beetle and *Scolytus multistriatus,* the smaller European elm bark beetle."

"Well done!" he said. "At least there's nothing wrong with your memory. And what will happen if we leave the sick trees where they are?" I replied that sooner or later the beetles would carry the disease to the healthy trees on the lake shore. The only solution was to cut down the diseased trees near the church.

"Bravo, patient!" said Dr Goldberg. "Excellent. Would you like to cut them down? As a favour to the clinic where you're being treated?"

Suddenly, all the cells in my body were awake. Yes! Goldberg's idea of how I could flee the clinic was connected with cutting down the two elms beside the church! After all, this was the only way to spring me from the prison of the castle walls – and if I then abandoned the mission and made a dash across the frozen lake towards the shore, nobody would be able to accuse him of anything. Of course, I wouldn't be allowed go to the church alone, but with an axe in my hand who could foresee how things would unfold?

"You'd like me to cut down the elms next to the church?" I asked.

His back was turned towards me. He was facing the door and when he spoke his words were barely audible, as if he didn't wish them to be caught by the recording device.

"If you think that is your duty, I cannot stop you."

30.

An attempt at revolt

Ten minutes later, two orderlies escorted me from the castle and down steep, snow-covered steps to the foot of the hill and along a narrow path to the elms in front of the church. The fresh winter air was so harsh that it pierced my throat and lungs like a knife. I almost lost my balance: the two orderlies grabbed me by my elbows to stop me from falling. The change in the freshness and harshness of the air was too great, too sudden; instinctively, I would have turned round and crawled back up the steps to the castle. I did turn, but one of the orderlies was behind me with an axe in his hand.

"What, sir?" he smirked. "Surely you're not cold? Swinging an axe will warm you up. You'll even sweat a bit!"

They looked at each other and winked. But it turned out to be for nothing, for soon a uniformed guard carrying a rifle came after us and ordered them to return to the castle. They obeyed without a word, one of them shoving the axe into my numb hands. The guard put the barrel of his gun against my back and pushed me forward down the steps. He followed me through the fresh snow, in which there were still no footsteps, towards the elms. For the first time in my life, I held an axe on my hands; for the first time, I would have to swing it and cut into a tree trunk; for the first time, I would have to do it until the tree leaned over and toppled.

Even after two swings, it became clear that I would not be up to the task and that the only option was revolt. I threw the axe into the snow and, without a word, headed back towards the castle, following the trail the guard and I had left.

"Wait!" shouted the guard in German. "Where are you going?"

"Home," I replied, trudging onwards.

"But you are home," I heard behind me. "This castle will be your home until the end of your life."

"I'd rather jump from the castle walls," I replied.

"Come back, or I'll shoot you in the back," he yelled. "Those are my orders."

"Orders need to be obeyed," I shouted back. "Otherwise, you might lose your job. Probably you have children, a wife, who would support them?"

And what do I have, I asked myself as I trudged through the snow and waited to be hit by a bullet. I have no wife (although there has been no shortage of women in my life), I have no children (though I wanted them), most of my friends are writers, who received my international success with envy and one by one fell silent; I have no future, for I am crippled by writer's block, because of which, on the advice of a devious editor, I came for treatment to Berghof and became the victim of an incomprehensible conspiracy, some kind of game that I cannot get to the bottom of; I have neither the ability, nor the desire, to carry on playing the game in the hope of rescue; I have neither the strength nor the willpower to carry on, even just from stubbornness, as one of the characters in a story where it seems someone has mixed up the paragraphs or, even worse, assembled it from individual sentences taken from the stories and novels produced by the imaginations of thousands of "imaginers" over the past three millennia; I no longer have any belief that any story has anything to tell me, let alone that it can say anything redemptive or important to readers who come across it by chance, or in the stubborn belief that they ought to remain faithful to me; I no longer have any hope that my disappointment in literature and my role in it will stabilise at least as satisfaction, even if not in pride due to the admiration for thematically inconsistent stories with which I have charmed a large number of people, who read them in the blind belief that in fictional stories they can find something important for themselves, an answer to a question that the real world cannot offer.

Above all, I no longer have any hope that the desire to write will ever return, and with it belief in the sense of "storying", for in spite of my great optimism even treatment of my writer's block has turned into the most bizarre story that I could imagine.

And so go ahead and shoot, I suddenly thought, send a bullet into my back on the left-hand side, through my heart, so that I am wreathed in darkness as soon as possible, the Great Void, and that I become a collection of molecules of the dark matter that makes up the universe and in which is perhaps concealed the answer to all the mysteries of time and space and of the human mind. If life is too full of questions without answers, or with answers that are undoubtedly just a kind of consolation, it is not all unusual if the mind becomes weary and the desire for an alternative reality comes up against an impenetrable wall.

And so go ahead and shoot me, guard!

But no bullet hit me, the threat was an empty one. Wet through and deadly tired, I once more found myself in my cell with its view of the snowy courtyard, my head feeling so heavy that I could barely raise it from the pillow, with trembling limbs and the feeling that a piece of coal glowing in my chest would any minute burst into flames. At the same time, I felt a terrible chill running from head to toe. Even the feelings within me were out of harmony and unbalanced, a botched story. I opened my mouth to shout for the orderly who brought me my modest meals and took away the toilet bucket; I wanted to ask him to bring me some more blankets, not thin ones such as I already had, but the thickest possible, woollen, warm. But I immediately realised that I would be shouting in vain, even I did it at the very top of my blunted voice, no one would hear me; the heavy iron door would be the only witness to my suffering.

I woke with a start, as usual; from sleep I moved, in fact "jumped", into a state that I recognised as wakefulness. On the chair beside the matress I saw a plate of carrots and mashed potato. My orderly had been and gone. The meal could be breakfast, lunch or dinner. It was cold. I saw through the window that it was half dark in the courtyard, so I assumed this was a late lunch. I ate it almost with gratitude. I had got used to the taste surprisingly quickly. Do we get used to everything in the end? Is existence merely an iterative process of getting used to whatever life brings us? And are the only mentally healthy ones those who get used to change quickly and without resistance? While the others, largely those who resist change, are wretches, mental patients, writers?

Maybe all three at the same time?

When the courtyard in front of the window was shrouded in darkness, the orderly brought my dinner: a plate of carrots and mashed potato. I told him that I felt worse than I'd ever felt in my life and that I would soon die; would he be so kind as to inform Dr Wagner and ask him to hurry to my cell?

Less than five minutes passed before Dr Wagner appeared beside my bed. He put his hand on my forehead and felt my pulse. There's no reason for panic, he said, I had caught a cold. Not surprising, since they had dragged me from the castle into the cold and dressed me insufficiently. "Actions have consequences," he added. I certainly knew that. But he could certainly not take responsibility for the stupid actions of others.

I told him that I would like to see Dr Goldberg. I demanded clarification.

"Dr Goldberg is very busy," came the reply. "Don't worry, your turn will come. But I can't say when."

"Why has he shut me in this uncomfortable cell?" I wanted to know.

He looked at me in surprise. "Didn't you come to be treated for writer's block?"

"I did, but I can't be the only one! Where are the others? I was told that quite a few well-known names were being treated here."

"That's true. But for now, they are all locked in their cells."

"Why?" I raised my voice. "Is that a way of treating writer's block?"

Dr Wagner was silent for some time; I got the impression he was trying to come up with another reply to placate me. "Be patient," he said impatiently. "Everything is under control. We know what we're doing. If you have come for treatment, you can't give orders to the therapist about how he should treat you."

31.

In the snowy courtyard

The weather did not improve. Every day it snowed for two to three hours, often with snowflakes the size of small paper tissues, such as I had never seen the like of. The courtyard in front of the window began to run out of space. Orderlies or hired workers shovelled the snow into four heaps, one in each corner, and another, the biggest, in the centre. But every evening it became necessary to shovel the freshly fallen snow, the heaps kept getting bigger and it was obvious that there would soon not be enough room and that the moment had come for extreme measures, perhaps for melting snow each day with jets of hot water. I had never imagined that winters in the Swiss Alps had such an abundance of snow.

After I'd been in the cell just over a week – or so it seemed, if my sense of time was not deceiving me – something unexpected began to happen in the courtyard. Between eight and nine, soon after breakfast, orderlies with canes in their hands began to herd patients dressed in striped pyjamas and boots into the courtyard for exercise, group after group of them, each made up of ten people, and for ten minutes they ran around the heaps of snow, some of the hesitant encouraged by blows with the canes wielded by the orderlies. When the first group had finished and disappeared back into the bowels of the castle, another one appeared led by a different orderly, which also moved, more or less quickly, around the heaps of snow, and again not without help from strokes of the cane.

Then came a group of ten female patients, also in striped pyjamas and boots. The women ran slower and the orderly accompanying them did not deliver any blows. One even fell down into the snow and lay there; the orderly tried to help her to her feet and spent some time persuading her to run on. She didn't want to, maybe she was unable to, she sat stubbornly in the snow and the orderly allowed her to wait until the end of the exercise; then he helped her to her feet and accompanied her at the back of the line into the castle.

Nice, I thought, that in this institution men are more friendly towards women than to other men. This sign of compassion and understanding in the midst of the general madness gave me hope that I was not going to face violence, at least not excessive or physical, but for the psychological violence that the doctors were practising against me I could find neither reason nor purpose, certainly not as part of the treatment for writer's block because of which I had come to the clinic.

The groups of patients who came to the courtyard for daily exercise kept alternating, men followed by women and they in turn by men. When the last group went back inside, I realised that the number of men and women was roughly the same. But each group behaved slightly differently, perhaps because of the nature of their illness, or, more likely, because of the orderly who led their morning exercise. However, all of them, when they came out into the freezing courtyard, huddled together like frightened sheep. They stayed in groups, as if they felt safer close to each other; some yapped, some stared at the sky from which snowflakes were falling, some indifferently, some with mouths open in amazement, as if they had never seen snow before. Some grumbled, others cursed and threatened, although from opposite ends of the courtyard, and through the closed window I could not hear their words, let alone understand them.

After less than a minute, the orderly who had brought them would hit a random selection, usually the nearest, on the back with a cane, some of them two or three times, thus encouraging them to move and run. Some didn't want to move, they stood there as if frozen to the ground, staring at the sky. Their expressions changed from blind, almost childish trust to fear and the desire to escape. What did they see in the snow that was falling on them? What filled them with hope and joy, and what with horror? If I were to write a story, I would find it difficult to navigate among the complex of endless possibilities: for the first time I felt that my blockage was actually liberating. Would I lose anything important if I never wrote again? Would the world lose anything important?

Most of the orderlies managed to get the patients to run, or at least to stagger around the heaps of snow, but each used a different method. The younger ones were more patient, they didn't use force, even though they also carried a cane; some spoke with the patients, cajoled them, one even began running himself, gesturing for the patients to follow him, to overtake him, and some actually did, which was what he had intended – he wanted to give them a sense of victory.

Among the older ones was one, a shaven headed muscleman with a beard, whose face I would happily slash with a sharp razor if I could get to him. He led into the courtyard a group of ten old men, who smiled the whole time as if afraid something bad was going to happen to them. Their faces reminded me of puppets, their smiles were bitter, desperate and, like a group of living puppets, surprisingly lively for their age, they tottered around the heaps of snow until the orderly got angry with those who couldn't keep up the pace and began to lag behind, and he tried to speed them up with blows to the back. Here and there, some lost their balance and tumbled into the snow. The orderly hit them across the back with his cane until they gathered sufficient strength to get to their knees and eventually their feet. Then they joined the group, which was once more circling the snow heaps and, often with the support of two others, continued their morning exercise.

One of these old men, a little chap with a notably hook nose, liked to make mischief: he would hide behind one of the smaller heaps of snow and throw snowballs at the others as they ran past. Yesterday, one of them hit the orderly full in the face; no doubt by chance, for a fragile old man would not be able to aim so well. The enraged orderly soon found the culprit behind his heap of snow and hit him in the face with his cane, right across the mouth, from which flew not only blood, but also some broken teeth. The old man lay on the ground and I thought he was dead; the fear on the faces of the patients, who gathered round him in a semi-circle, and particularly on the orderly's face, almost convinced me that a crime had taken place in the courtyard.

In a Swiss psychiatric clinic? How was such a thing possible? Was it all happening in my head, considering the terrifying fact that the border between imagination and reality was getting increasingly blurred?

Was I the only patient and what I saw outside merely an apparition?

To my great relief, I soon got evidence that this was not the case; two orderlies came hurrying through the door on the other side of the courtyard, carrying a stretcher; they put it down and rolled the injured old man onto it. He twisted round and tried to tell them something; he wasn't dead. His attacker stood to one side, his head hanging down. Three more orderlies appeared and then two doctors; there followed a series of verbal attacks on the one who had triggered the crisis, who writhed sanctimoniously and tried to pin the blame on the victim – at least, that was what I interpreted from his movements, while the orderlies carried the injured old man inside. Then something unusual happened: one of the doctors approached the attacker and delivered a violent slap with his right hand. His left hand pointed towards the door and commanded the orderly to get out of his sight. Then the two doctors rounded up the patients and led them into the castle.

I was convinced that I would never see the violent orderly again. But the next morning, he appeared with his usual group, including the snowball thrower whom he had almost killed the previous day. The injured man had a swollen and slightly twisted mouth, but apart from that he appeared unharmed; what was more, at the first opportunity, he once again hid behind a heap of snow and began to throw snowballs at those running by.

I decided to stop trying to understand where I had ended up and why and what everything meant; that was the only way I could retain a modicum of sanity.

32.

Let me not be mad, not mad

My stay at the clinic settled into a routine. Every other day, around 7 am, immediately after the carrots and mash for breakfast, my orderly, who had finally confided in me that his name was Lucas, led me along winding, damp, palely lit corridors to a bathroom with rusty showers, probably not the only one in the castle, although it was big enough for fifteen to twenty men to shower at the same time. Some days there were more, others less, but each time we rubbed up against each other while the water sprayed down upon us from large nozzles in the ceiling. Since it was hard in the castle in the middle of winter to dry one's hair, as we entered one of the orderlies would hand us a shower cap with which we could more or less successfully cover our head.

At the beginning, this ritual seemed degrading, especially because my fellow showerers, among which I was the only one who had come here for writer's block (all the others showed symptoms of serious or milder mental illness), kept staring curiously at my above average organ, not with envy, but more with amazement that they were seeing something supernatural; a number of times one of the crowd would sneak up to me and try to grab hold of it and squeeze it, but I quickly developed a way of avoiding this. The temperature of the water spurting down on us was uncontrolled; sometimes it was icy cold and other times so hot that it turned into steam as it fell. Whenever it was extremely hot or icy, everyone tried to avoid the spot where the most powerful jet was falling; none of the patients realised that the nozzles rotated and so it was best to remain in one place.

Then one morning it happened that one of the patients, an emaciated middle-aged man who was constantly blinking, simply could not stand being struck by the boiling water right in his face, and passed out. He slipped onto the dirty, slimy floor, where he remained for some time in a sitting position, supported by the legs of his fellow sufferers, before eventually slumping down to the horizontal. The orderlies present did not want to get wet, so he lay there for a few minutes, the feet of the other patients, who couldn't move far enough away because of the huddle, trampling on him, even on his face. When the orderlies finally intervened and dragged him out, they quite indifferently ascertained that he was dead and it was too late to try and resuscitate him.

Why didn't I revolt, why didn't I yell at the top of my voice and demand that the orderlies pull him out while he was still alive and could be rescued?

Why did I merely observe the terrible events in the shower room as a silent witness, as someone who was completely numb? As someone who had accepted the idea that everything that happened in front of me was in some way unreal, merely a nightmare in which I had no power to intervene? Or was it simply that I didn't want to intervene, to avoid problems?

When the nozzles in the ceiling had stopped spewing out water and we had, one after another, dried ourselves with the damp towels, which had last been washed God knows when, survived a screaming argument about which pyjamas belonged to whom, and finally dressed, Lucas took me by the same route back to my cell, where I spent the next three hours entertaining myself by listening to my stomach rumbling and in driving away the thought that I would at any moment wake up in my bed at home, or that they would finally send for me and let me join the other writers who it had been said were receiving treatment for writer's block. And who were certainly staying in different, more up-to-date, more comfortable, more Swiss, more professional rooms, not in conditions that belonged in the Middle Ages, and which were completely at odds with the regard that this institution supposedly enjoyed.

Around midday, Lucas brought me lunch of mash and carrots, and around five, dinner of mash and carrots. Surprisingly, every three days there was a piece of cauliflower on the plate. And each time he also brought a plastic bottle of stale water. While I ate, he took away (when he felt like it) the toilet bucket; sometimes he brought it back washed, but most often dirty. Quite a few times he only removed my excreta, which did nothing to improve the quality of the air in the cell, when I threatened to complain to Dr Wagner. When I mentioned Dr Goldberg, for reasons I couldn't understand, he remained indifferent.

I imagined that the mental patients were staying in special, group cells and eating together in a dining room. Some of them must have been locked in cells similar to mine, although less stuffy and damp, but there cannot have been many of them. Lucas didn't want to tell me what he did when he wasn't with me, so I had no idea what was happening in this unusual medieval building, so picturesque when viewed from the shore of the lake, and so terrifying when you were inside it. I was so terribly cut off from everything that I didn't even know what the other patients got for breakfast, lunch and dinner. Certainly not only mashed potato and carrots, otherwise they would soon waste away and die, which was surely not permitted in a country such as Switzerland. Although the damp cell had given me a bad cold and I was feeling ever worse, I still remained convinced that I was healthy and psychologically normal.

Why did I have to keep repeating that to myself?

33.

Words are poisonous mushrooms

The assistant doctor, who recorded my next conversation with Dr Goldberg was not Dr Wagner, but a much friendlier man of roughly the same age and build, that is, on the verge of middle age. He had large, friendly, slightly bulging eyes and a nervous habit, if not obsession: he kept scratching various parts of his face with his middle finger. In contrast with Dr Wagner, he was genuinely interested in everything, and he also showed more respect to Dr Goldberg; when I entered the hexagonal room, he helped him to get to his feet and he instructed an orderly to prepare the usual bath for the "director". Dr Goldberg stood in one of the six corners of the room, staring at the floor in front of him.

When the orderly left, the young doctor smiled at me and introduced himself as Dr Fassbinder. He added that I was sure to have heard the surname before, but he was not related to the film director, nor did he like his films. Had I recovered from my cold, he asked me, was I feeling strong enough and willing to talk to Dr Goldberg again? Or would that be too much of an exertion? His politeness so surprised me that for some time I couldn't find the right reply. It would have seemed ungrateful not to reply in similar manner. I told him I'd be delighted, although I was tired, fed up and more confused than I had ever been in my life, I would be grateful for the opportunity to talk to Dr Goldberg again, above all in the hope that I would finally, and please don't be offended by this, I added, like to find out what was happening to me and what intentions Dr Goldberg had regarding me.

"I'll leave that to the two of you," said Dr Fassbinder. He turned on the recorder on the table and went towards the door. I thought he would leave, but he stopped in front of the door and said: "Don't forget that the solution to most puzzles is most often hidden in the puzzles themselves."

Dr Goldberg, who was in an openly good mood, smiled (a miracle!) and said: "Thank God for the young, who see and understand things that we older ones have become unresponsive to, perhaps even blind to."

I didn't know how to reply, so I said nothing, until he asked me: "And where would you rather sit today? On the chair? The floor?"

If the solution to most puzzles is hidden in the puzzles themselves, I remembered Dr Fassbinder's words, it must also be the case when it is more a game than a puzzle; and that could only have three variants. I didn't think for long, but replied almost immediately: "On the floor."

"Then sit down," he nodded in a friendly manner. Pleased with myself, I walked across the room and sat on the chair.

Goldberg's face flushed with impatience. "That's not the floor! You said you wanted to sit on the floor!"

Oh, for heaven's sake, not again. "I know, but I thought..."

"Just thinking isn't enough," he lectured me. "Try again. And this time, think it through thoroughly." He looked at me with a mixture of sadness and hatred; it would be hard to say which predominated.

"Actually, I'd rather sit on a chair," I said.

"A minute ago, you said the floor. Have you changed your mind?"

"No," I slightly raised my voice. "I never wanted to sit on the floor."

"But you said…"

"It doesn't matter what I said. I had a chair in mind. I thought that for you, the floor was a chair and a chair the floor."

Goldberg stared at me as if he'd never heard anything quite so stupid before. "Dr Fassbinder," he turned to his colleague, who was still standing at the door, "did you hear what our patient said? Would you agree with me that a chair cannot be the floor or the other way round, since they are two completely different things, not to say concepts?"

Dr Fassbinder first shrugged and then nodded. Dr Goldberg turned back to me. "Why did you confuse the two?"

"I don't know," I said abruptly, suddenly convinced that Dr Goldberg was trying to break me psychologically.

"From a desire for comfort" he kept enquiring. "So that you don't have to sit on the floor? Because the floor is dirty and the chair clean?"

"No," I said, looking him straight in the eye. "I wanted to accommodate you. I don't understand the game you're playing with me and even less why you're doing it, but I am trying to adapt to you. For your sake, not for mine."

Dr Goldberg put his hands behind his back and took a few painful steps towards the table. Suddenly I felt pity for him, although I wasn't sure why.

"Does that mean you'd do that in every case where the decisive factor is a person who is more important than you because of his position? Would you suppress what you really think and bow to the opinion of someone merely because you wouldn't want to annoy or upset him? Have you been so calculating all your life?"

"Okay," I said, making an effort to suppress the fury building inside me. "I'll no longer make the effort at adapt to you, since it brings me no benefit."

"You've just confirmed that you align your behaviour and statements with what benefits you," he gave a cunning smile. "Why did you want to cut down the trees close to the church?"

"Because you asked me to do it," I responded.

"I?!" he said in amazement. "Never! I asked you if you thought that it was your duty to cut them down. *You* said that it was, not me. I only uttered a question, the answer was yours."

The confusion in my mind was increasing. It didn't seem possible, as it had already been unbearable when I arrived at the clinic, but now it was gradually changing into something hitherto unknown, into something that I wouldn't hesitate to call madness. It seemed to me that the temperature in the room suddenly increased, my whole body was itching. I stared in despair into Dr Goldberg's eyes, looking for the slightest trace of humour or irony – I would much sooner accept that than the suspicion that I was losing my mind. In the hope that I would read something on Dr Fassbinder's face, I turned towards him, but at precisely that moment he was enthusiastically scratching his forehead and his hand was conveniently covering his eyes.

"You know the reason why I wanted to chop them down," I turned back to Dr Goldberg. "I wanted to protect the healthy elms on the lake shore."

"But the trees on the lake shore are not elms," said Dr Goldberg triumphantly. "They are plane trees. And the two below the church that you were unable to cut down are beeches."

"Then why did you say that all the trees on the island are elms?" I demanded angrily.

"I never said that," replied Dr Goldberg calmly. "*You* said it. Would you like to listen to a recording of our conversation?

I was left speechless.

"Allow me to refresh your memory," said Dr Goldberg. "I asked you to look through the window and tell me what kind of trees you saw on the shore of the lake. You said elms. The fact that I didn't correct you seemed a good enough reason for you to rush down to the church in order to cut down two completely healthy beeches. Now you claim that we cannot hold your responsible. That you were the victim of misinformation. Would that be your response if the matter came to court? Didn't you have botany at school? Did you never walk in the woods? Did you never ask yourself what sort of trees you were passing? What, then, interests you? What actually interests you in life, considering you're a writer?"

"I don't understand," I said with an effort. "Please tell me… Clarify…"

He took two steps towards me. "I would like to cure you, Mr Writer," he said. "You're ill. A dying elm. Why else would you come here? From your branches, I call them branches of imagination, no more leaves can grow. You no longer know how to write. You don't know how to construct new stories. And even if you do, you can no longer write them."

He slowly shuffled to the table and picked up from it a fat, leather-bound book. With noticeably nervous, trembling hands, he leafed through it. Then he found what he was looking for. He raised the open book with his finger on the edge to stop it closing and showed me a full-page colour photograph of some trees. "The elm falls ill when a poisonous insect pushes a poisonous fungus beneath its bark. In your case, the role of the poisonous fungus is the printed word.

And straight behind, with its help, is complete or partial misinformation. In which you automatically, without the slightest doubt, see the truth."

"That's not true!" I almost yelled.

"Why, then, do you act in line with what you read? Why, after reading some articles on sick elms, did you believe that elms grow on the shore of the lake, without checking?"

"I made a mistake!" I rose from my chair. "I'm not the only one, we all make them. We are people. I have been too keen to please you, I trusted you, convinced that you sent me the article about sick elms for a reason. I shouldn't have trusted you."

"Me or the printed word?" he asked, his eyes looking straight into mine. "Do you really not know the causes of your problem? The impulses in your life do not come from your heart, from deep within you, as they should. They come from your master, the printed word. You live your life in line with what you read or hear others quote – and most often misquote. It's a kind of addiction. A kind of madness, of psychological perversity. There is only one way we can cure you. By breaking your addiction to the wrong source of truth."

He smiled reassuringly. "But rest assured: you are in the right place."

34.

Rotten in the head

Five days later, they began to prepare hot baths for me. Every morning at nine, I was taken into a chamber full of steam in which there echoed such frightening cries that only a completely deaf person could remain there more than a few minutes. The orderlies on duty protected their ears with earplugs.

Each time, they stripped me naked and laid me in a concrete trough full of water. Then they firmly tied my hands to a steel post at the upper end of the trough and slowly raised the temperature of the water. My cries were soon as loud as those of all the others. I usually passed out after two or three minutes, depending on how quickly the temperature of the water rose. Some patients, especially very young ones, begged and swore a lot longer; the length of the baths was dependent on the mood of the duty orderly.

I also got some injections, after which I was incredibly sleepy. I remember that in this drugged state I was interrogated by Dr Goldberg, but I don't recall the details. Since they began to prepare me baths, I was with him at least once a day. At about half of these sessions, I was in a drugged state. The other half, which I do remember, did not give me enough to evaluate what was going on. Even though Goldberg's theories seemed ever less extreme and I even found myself thinking that I may accept them as a possible solution, in reality we did not come any closer to each other; the hatred between us only got more profound.

Dr Goldberg claimed that there could be no hope of progress or discharge if I kept increasing the distance between us and I refused to accept that I was mentally ill. I felt there was something slightly illogical in his theory. I kept asking him why I had to be subjected every day to the humiliating torture in the chamber with the baths. His reply wasn't always the same. Once, he said that, considering the reason why I was in the castle, I actually had no right to demand free will, which in this case wasn't even my will, but rather one of the symptoms of my illness.

I was unable to avoid frequent outbursts of anger at myself; I should have long ago realised that everything wasn't as it seemed at first sight. I should never have uncritically accepted my publisher's version of the story about the clinic. And I shouldn't have revealed my reasons for coming there when I found out that Simon Goldberg was not a patient, but rather the director of the institution. How could I ever have believed that I was a cautious, circumspect person?

I was increasingly incapable of analysing my own thoughts and feelings. To save myself the pain of self-betrayal, had I perhaps wanted to conceal this superficially genuine change of conviction, with the deception that I wanted to surrender, because Dr Goldberg had opened my eyes? Or had he really opened my eyes?

I could not claim that from many points of view he was wrong; most of my views on life had been formed on the basis of printed data. But the majority of his also! I agreed that half-truths implanted in the mind of the ordinary person would always find fertile ground there. But was there any other possibility?

Once or twice, I tried to express my doubts to Dr Goldberg. I cannot live, I said, without taking certain things to be self-evident and concluding that our means of communication, albeit far from perfect, facilitate the recognition of unclear truths about how the world works. Mistakes, even tragic ones, are of course inevitable. But what if we rejected the unreliable light with which we try to illuminate our way and chose darkness – in that case, would we walk a straighter path?

Dr Goldberg did not take these reservations seriously. He believed that they weren't *my* reservations. Nothing I might say on this theme originated from my direct experience, he claimed. Within me was the flotsam of long years of indoctrination with the printed word, with the words of others. Perhaps somewhere in the depths, my real self was still alive, my unspoilt, primary self that no one had appropriated. In any case, I should know by now that we would never reach it if I did not allow him to remove all the rubbish that concealed it.

Thus he finally made me aware of his goal. When he had negated my will, he wanted to "drill a hole in my head and rinse all that was rotten from it". Then he wanted to "renew my mind with healthy material", as if he were "filling a hole drilled in a tooth". But he didn't even begin to hint what material he wanted to put into me.

I thought at first that my salvation would be passive resistance. When he realised that he could not shape me, he would leave me alone.

Then came the electric shock.

The memory of that moment – of the world that collapsed, the high flames that flared from my core and devoured everything, my past and my future – is still very vivid and will remain inside me until I die. At night, as I shivered in my cell, I would sometimes suddenly curl up and begin to shout from the horror, and a burning pain would twist my spine. Although Dr Goldberg did not repeat the shock, I had no doubt that he would do that in a moment if he suspected that my resistance was increasing.

Or in the moment when Dr Wagner turned his back on me!

For the impression was growing inside me that Dr Goldberg did not have complete freedom to decide which therapy was to be given to which patients, at least not in my case. He never once dealt with me alone. I felt relief when I sensed that his power was not absolute. If his colleagues had not restrained him, I felt that he would have subjected me to every form of torture that psychiatric medicine has so far come up with. Or not. For the relentless doctor, in spite of his crazed commitment, concealed within himself a kind of sober canniness that undoubtedly told him that it would be in contradiction with his goals to break the slate on which he wished to write his message to the world. He just needed to wipe it clean!

I realised that my only hope of being saved was a small deceit: I had to convince Dr Goldberg that his therapies were successfully sapping my will power. If I wanted to rescue my mind, I had to pretend that it was destroyed before that really happened. Dr Goldberg would probably not have me here if he did not intend to send me one fine day back into the world. So why not accept his game and ensure that he released me a week or two earlier?

I decided on an approach of gradual submission. I allowed him to continue the therapy of hot baths and sedatives, while hoping that, if I pretended I had taken a step forward, I could remain a step behind what I had in his opinion achieved. I hoped that in this way I would retain sufficient strength to save my mind, which would supposedly have reached a level of complete emptiness. A dangerous game, for I had no way of knowing to what extent the next level would really influence my behaviour. I could only guess. And hope for the best.

In the following days, our relations really did improve. When Dr Goldberg got the impression that I was being less stubborn, he abandoned his paternalistic approach. Almost overnight, he turned into a good-natured doctor. At times, his kindness was almost embarrassing. He kept asking me how I was. During our sessions, an everyday, almost relaxed atmosphere prevailed. We exchanged opinions in a friendly way, instead of him trying to brainwash me. We continued in the unspoken agreement that I was really ill. One day, he commented that I should see it as a privilege that I was his patient. Just as he was honoured to be able to treat me. My case of printed word plague, he said, was one of the most characteristic he'd seen.

I carried the pretence of tactical submission so far that now and then I allowed myself genuinely warm feelings towards the reshaper of my mind. In any case, I was unsure whether I could control such moments. I was even afraid that the game I was playing to rescue myself was nothing more than a trick by my subconscious to weaken my ego and force its alertness to lapse, for I had already decided that rescue was impossible, but I dared not consciously acknowledge that.

35.

Immunisation

I was moved. Two orderlies that I'd never seen before dragged me out of bed and ordered me to go with them. One of them took the mattress, the other the blanket, while I had to carry the bucket. They took me up two flights of stairs to a new cell. In comparison with the prison from which I had come, it was almost luxurious: there was a bed, a concrete floor, dry walls and a nice view of the lake. There were bars over the window – a waste of iron, since the drop to the lake was too frightening to encourage thoughts of escape. Although it was hard to get used to the sudden glare of daylight, which was even brighter because the sun was reflecting off the snowy ground, I was grateful for the silence. If I hadn't heard the occasional steps hurrying along the corridor and the dull, resounding slamming of doors in a distant part of the castle, I would almost have believed that I was hanging in the centre of a soundproofed cube in the middle of the sky.

No sound reached me from outside. The white landscape stretched out before me like the surface of a planet on which nothing was breathing and nothing moving. The gleam was even more blinding because of the contrast with the dark woods on the other side of the lake. A slight sound reached my ears just once, just before midday: the jingling of bells, a quiet rhythmic ding-a-ling, and when I looked out, I saw something that at first sight looked like a giant cockroach, moving across the whiteness of the lake towards the castle. Then I realised it was a sledge, drawn by a black horse, with shining, sweating flanks; his trot looked oddly uncertain, as if the animal sensed the depth of the water hidden beneath the snow-covered ice. Food was now being brought by sledge.

The next day, just before dawn, two orderlies came to my cell, moving through the hazy light like monstrous shadows. They laid me half asleep on a stretcher and carried me back into the dark, smelly bowels of the castle; their voices, divorced from their actions, echoed down the corridors like thunder. After a quick shower, they carried me one storey higher into some kind of common dining room. There, in the light of a bare lightbulb, sitting at one of the greasy plastic tables, I got my first food since the previous morning: a bowl of hot milk and half a loaf of inedible white bread.

As I ate, the orderlies were talking to the man who was passing food through a hole in the wall. Judging by his outfit, he was a cook. I was too confused to follow their conversation. They weren't discussing me, but something that had no connection with the castle: a football match, the weather forecast. My area of interest had greatly narrowed. Only one spark of curiosity was still alive in my impoverished brain, one question banging against my skull: "What's going to happen to me?"

The orderlies said that I was now strong enough to walk. They leaned the stretcher against the wall in front of the dining room and took me back along the warren of echoing corridors, then pushed me into a hexagonal room. There, I was met by a group of psychiatrists, including Dr Goldberg,

Dr Wagner, Dr Heinrich and two other men that I was seeing for the first time. They sat in a row against the back wall; Dr Wagner was cleaning a microphone, Dr Heinrich was watching him, and the newcomers were looking through a heap of drawings that one of them was holding on his knee.

As soon as I entered, Dr Goldberg got up and shuffled towards me. He shook my hand in a friendly manner and cautiously pushed me towards the armchair in the corner near the door. No doubt the armchair and extra chairs had been brought in especially for this occasion. Although I only remember what followed very hazily, I recall certain moments clearly. I remember that Dr Goldberg bent over and tried to attach some wires to my ankle, but then gave up and left the task to the more dexterous Dr Heinrich. He also fastened me to the back of the chair with a leather strap.

I remember the mysterious light falling through the window, which was not strong enough to illuminate the eyes of the doctors who were observing me, but enough to emphasise the excitement on their faces. I remember Dr Goldberg standing in front of me and talking about my case, praising my visible progress and how wonderfully I had grasped the central point of his theory. All of this was praiseworthy, he said, but the fact remained that I was still far from being cured, for although they had washed the poisonous fungus from my organism, I was still perilously vulnerable to infection.

Frankly, he asked, wasn't I convinced that my return to the world where the printed plague had reached global proportions, without any protection, literally meant suicide? Someone who had progressed as quickly as I had in such a short time certainly could not think of returning without fear to a world dominated by plague. Wasn't that the case?

At first, I was unable to answer. Not only because I hadn't the slightest idea what answer he expected from me, but also because I had allowed them to fundamentally erase my mind. There was little material left with which I could create a suitable picture of my future. I knew that I had one, I knew that they would send me back into the world from which I came, but I concluded that when I was outside, it would all sort itself out.

Before I was able to decide what to say, Dr Goldberg laid his hand on my shoulder in a friendly manner. He carefully explained that above all else I needed immunisation. It was necessary to prevent a return to my previous state. Or even worse, a new infection, which would undoubtedly be fatal. I needed to be made "immune to print". At that moment, one of the new doctors got up and went over to the window. I remember that he bent over and from a folder at his feet took a drawing, which he held so that the light from outside fell on it, and I remember how I asked myself whether they intended to test my sight, for what I could see was not a drawing, but large letters from A to I in alphabetical order.

Dr Goldberg asked me to read them out. I complied. Then he asked me to think up some words beginning with these letters that signified negative human characteristics. I came up with arrogance, barbarianism, conceit. Then they asked me to recite the alphabet. I had barely spoken the letter A, when my body was shaken by a powerful shock. The flames of pain flared from my ankles towards my stomach and onwards towards my eyes. Because they didn't reach my eyes, they stopped in my mouth, which in less than a second became a desiccated, prickling hollow, longing for water. After the first two or three waves, the shock diminished, but the fire remained. I had a feeling in my mouth as if I had swallowed a fistful of chillies, only the taste was drier and nauseatingly painful. I vaguely remember how Dr Goldberg stared at me and asked if I was thirsty. I caught my breath and nodded.

A glass of water miraculously appeared in front of me. I remember trying to reach out for it and to break free of the strap holding me back. Then the glass disappeared and in front of my eyes appeared a large letter A.

"Spit on it, spit on it," a voice said to me, "spit on it and you will get water." And I did, or rather I tried, but I had no saliva. The same voice then said: "The letter A is bad, you must destroy it!" I reached out, grabbed the paper on which the letter was printed and tore it to shreds. I remember the same voice saying: "Good, now you'll get a reward," and suddenly water, cold, gentle, heavenly water poured into my mouth, the fire died down and the pain was extinguished. The sense of relief was so immense that I grabbed the hand holding the glass and gratefully smothered it with kisses.

Then in an instant I sank into sleep. When I awoke I was back in my cell, my face was being bathed in the afternoon sunlight shining through the window. At the foot of the bed, I found a jug of water.

Now the jug is almost empty. I am still recording my delusions in the notebook that they left alongside my bed, along with a pencil. But with each written word containing the letter A, the burning pain in my mouth grows, so that after about twenty A's I am forced to reach for the water. When the water has run out, perhaps I shall have to write down my thoughts by omitting the letter A. But I know that won't save me, for tomorrow it will be the turn of B. And the day after C. And then D...

36.

Revelation

After two weeks, when we reached the letter H, the orderlies Henrik and Peter came to take me for a walk. "Thanks, but I don't feel like it," I said, "I've seen all the corridors a hundred times. And a walk round the wet, shady courtyard didn't particularly appeal to me." What about outside, around the church, they said, to breathe some fresh air and move a little?

They were stunned that I didn't accept the offer. My statement that the air in my cell was fresh enough and that I was too old to want to move too much and far too young to actually need it did not seem to amuse them. I was afraid to leave my cell. I had grown so accustomed to the deceptive sense of security that I saw in the atmosphere, colours and shape of the space that I was like a wild animal, tamed after long years in a cage, thinking with horror of the open. I felt comfortable in the cell. It was warm and dry, I got two meals a day and three cups of linden tea (over the recent weeks, the meals had improved, sometimes they served rice and occasionally a piece of beef, even with salad), and I had a fine view: I could see the frozen lake, the woods on the other side and the shining white of the snowy peaks stretching towards the south. And whenever a sledge was approaching or moving away, I could hear the sad jangling of the sleigh bells.

And I had the sky.

The orderlies said that an order was an order; I could discuss this with the doctors, but not with them. They dragged me from the bed, wrapped me in my clothes and half pushed, half dragged me along the corridors to the courtyard and through one of the doors outside.

Dr Goldberg, who was waiting for me with Dr Wagner and Dr Heinrich, smiled and offered me his hand. But this time his grip was unusually limp. He looked tired. He also had a new facial tic. And he had forgotten to shave. His overcoat, which he had probably borrowed from an orderly, was too wide across the shoulders and the sleeves were too short. He was wearing slippers and pyjamas, as if he also had just been dragged out of bed. Somehow he looked different, unconvincing. His authority, so solid and indisputable inside the castle, had been replaced by a fear that he could not hide even if he tried.

Dr Wagner had a fur cap on his head and was wearing a heavy, ill-fitting coat; he wasn't cold, nor was Dr Heinrich, who was dressed just like Dr Wagner, except that he was also wearing leather gloves. I simply could not understand why they let Dr Goldberg go out in pyjamas and slippers. In spite of the sunshine, it was icy.

"You'll catch your death," I said to him. "You should be properly dressed."

Dr Goldberg smiled, but his eyes remained cloudy. "Cold doesn't bother me. I hope it doesn't bother you, either, for I'm going to take you on a short walk."

He waved towards the church on the slope. "Shall we?"

We set off. The stronger looking of the two orderlies helped Dr Goldberg down the slippery slope, holding him firmly round the waist. Half way down, we came across a dozen female patients, huddled together like a flock of sheep. They were guarded by two ugly orderlies and dressed in greyish brown cotton tunics. They had no coats or gloves. This was the first time I had seen any female patients from close up. Their white faces, almost snow-white, filled me with a sudden longing to see my own face; to see whether it was as absent as theirs. As we passed them, none of the women was speaking. They were sitting on the wall of a well or squatting in the snow around it. Some were shivering, their broken teeth chattering. They were all from the electric shock department. Some were leaning against each other and holding hands.

When we came close to them, a toothless old woman got up and pointed towards a bush higher on the slope. "Goat, goat," she said. A girl of thirteen or fourteen reached for the old woman's tunic and tried to pull her back into the snow. "Goat, goat," the old woman kept saying. The girl half stood, took the woman by the hand and began to moan. Then she slid to the ground, lowered her head towards her lap and burst into desperate tears.

The two orderlies were middle-aged and similar to all the others; they were both wearing leather boots and woollen coats. One of them carried a stick, he reached out with it and rapped the old woman on the hand with it. She sat down in the snow and began to massage the painful spot.

"What's wrong with them?" I asked. "Are they receiving treatment for the same illness as me?"

"No, no," said Dr Goldberg and caught his breath. The effort was almost too much for him, the orderly was practically pushing him up the steps towards the church. "They are being treated by my colleagues, Dr Wagner and Dr Heinrich. You are the only patient interesting enough to be treated by me. Ah-ha, we shall sit here. What do you say, Dr Wagner?"

The young doctor nodded and the four of us sat on a large, smooth log. The orderlies stayed close by. Then Dr Heinrich suddenly got up and headed back towards the castle. He stopped at the well and said something to the orderly with the stick, who listened, his head obediently on one side. When Dr Heinrich went on up the slope, he spat into the snow.

Henrik and Peter went up towards the church. The two doctors and I remained where we were. Our feet sank into the fluffy snow. Dr Goldberg was still catching his breath. There was a glittering layer of sweat on his forehead.

All around us was white, brilliant white: the slope, the castle roof, the frozen lake, the distant fields and meadows, the mountains. There wasn't a cloud in the sky. Everything was still, apart from a gigantic bird, fluttering its wings in a tree by the lake. The sun was pale, distant. I felt the icy cold penetrating the soles of my shoes and nipping at my earlobes. We were silent, watching the women below us and the orderly, who like a bored medieval guard was pacing back and forth along the wall. On the castle walls, there were large wet patches.

After a while, Dr Goldberg said: "I'm very pleased with your progress, patient."

I replied: "Thank you." I felt that I didn't sound sincere.

"Are you glad you came?" he asked.

I said yes and once more felt my voice was insincere. In the open air, all my replies sounded mechanical. Looking at the patients, at their almost dead eyes, and the sound of the girl's desperate crying, all washed over me like waves from a distant earthquake, too weak to break me, but strong enough to paralyse me.

Dr Goldberg went on: "We've got used to each other over recent weeks, haven't we?"

Again I agreed. Why? I wanted to say no, something inside me shouted that I should say no. I wanted to yell: Show me my eyes! I haven't seen my eyes for months. I cannot follow the course of my transformation! I don't even know what my face is like now – maybe I no longer look like me!

"Yes, we have," Dr Goldberg continued, "become much closer. I'm your friend and teacher, I wouldn't say I was your doctor. When you return home, you'll know what to do. You'll burn libraries, printing houses, everything even slightly connected with this repulsive disease. The plague can only be destroyed by fire."

He moved a few centimetres close and gave my hand a gentle squeeze.

And then it happened.

When Goldberg's sweet odour penetrated my nostrils, I was overtaken by an acute feeling, which had never come upon me with such rapidity, even though I knew it. It was as if I had been gripped by sudden nausea. For what I saw in Dr Goldberg's eyes was pride, mixed with patronising benevolence. Seeing him, his Frankenstein-like pride as he smugly examined his finished work, filled my heart with malicious hatred. I felt like taking hold of a knife and thrusting, thrusting, thrusting, and watching how the snow around me became redder and redder. I felt the desire to leap on this mild yet cruel person sitting beside me and with overt brutality, just as his had been covert, to demonstrate that not only had I retained my free will and dignity, but also my ability to resist! My submission, I wanted to scream, was fake!

Dr Goldberg was still looking at me, breathing in my face, while in my thoughts I was shredding his flesh, ripping his heart from his chest, tearing out his intestines, sucking the marrow from his bones. I was taking back everything that I felt he had taken from me.

And then the wind changed direction, and from far beyond the frozen lake, beyond the wooded backdrop, beyond the endless snowy spaces, I heard a train whistle, slow, imploring. The urgency of this call captured me, reminded me of the world outside, the world where I firmly believed there was still a place for me. I felt my pulse slow, the heated violence evaporated though my hands.

But not the hatred in my heart. A wave of that sharp feeling, which I had always tried to avoid in the past, flooded me with a finality which, after all the weeks of emotional chaos, I could not resist. A voice inside me exclaimed with delight: "I hate! I hate! That means I'm alive!" But the wisdom awakened within me by the distant, imploring train whistle compelled me to keep the delightful feeling of hatred inside, to preserve it and keep it burning, for use at a more appropriate moment. First, I had to get out. And recover. Only then would I return and slaughter the lot of them, one after the other. All the doctors. All the orderlies. Everyone on the island. With the exception of the inmates. But perhaps even them.

"What do you wish to tell your patient?" said Dr Wagner, turning to his boss.

"Me?" replied Dr Goldberg, surprised. "Nothing. I have cured him of his addiction to print, which destroys a person's brain, I have cultivated within him a hatred of literature, he'll never again wish to write a short story, let alone a novel. He is liberated, he can now walk freely through life."

"Will he be grateful to you for that?" Dr Wagner wanted to know.

"That's not my problem," shrugged Dr Goldberg. "I've done my job and for me that's enough. I'm cold. I suggest we go back to the castle."

"But *you* wanted to come here," Dr Wagner reminded him. "*You* said that you had to tell your patient something important. *You* said you couldn't do that anywhere other than in the fresh air."

"Sorry," Dr Goldberg looked at him. "Who are you? I don't remember seeing you before."

"Then it really is high time we returned to the castle," said Dr Wagner.

All night I wondered what this exchange between the two doctors might mean. A new puzzle that was still part of the therapy? I had to wait for answer until the next morning, when after breakfast I was once more introduced to the chamber with hot baths. I was so lost in my thoughts that for a few moments I didn't even realise where I was. When the water began to heat up, I roused myself and looked around. I saw two orderlies and Dr Wagner with a portable tape recorder. All three of them were watching me. That was what I thought until I turned my head to the right and saw that their attention was devoted to the patient in the bath on my right. I turned my head a little more.

"Aaah," sighed my neighbour. "There's nothing nicer than a hot bath on a cold day."

The man was breathing quickly and irregularly, but he was not afraid: evidently, he was enjoying the heat. He looked at me with sudden interest. "You face is familiar to me. Have you been here a long time?"

"Yes! Yes!" I yelled. "I'm your patient! Your patient!

I began to sob. Through my tears I saw the offended surprise on Goldberg's face.

"Quite possible," he said. "But you can't expect me to know everyone personally. I've simply got too much work these days." He sighed in delight. "I can't tell you how much I enjoy these baths. How nicely warming the water is! Ooh! I'm going to fall asleep."

Still sobbing, I looked at Dr Wagner.

The young doctor avoided my eyes and for a short while fiddled with the tape recorder. And then, he turned and left; I would swear it was in embarrassment.

The next morning my cell door rattled open and a sleepy voice ordered me to get dressed. Two orderlies waited for me to get ready. Then they gathered up all my things, pushed me out of the cell, and led me through a series of corridors in the part of the castle where there were consulting rooms and offices that I had never seen. In one of them they presented me to Dr Apstein-Müller, head of the clinic.

The doctor's face was almost as pale as the fog outside the double-glazed window. At his elbows lay half a dozen open books, with places marked.

"Sorry that you had to wait," he said in a loud, clear voice, without looking up. He turned the page of the book he was reading.

One of the orderlies left the room. I felt the other breathing down my neck.

"Would you like to sit down?" asked the director.

Now he looked at me and twisted his thin lips into an encouraging smile. But something about me must have bothered him, for in a moment a shadow passed across his face. He pushed aside the papers, tapped on the desk and stood up.

I was surprised: Dr Apstein-Müller's face had prepared me for someone taller and slower, with more considered movements. But he began to jump about the room like a badly coordinated puppet. Eventually, he managed to adopt a relatively static position at the window. He stared out, but couldn't keep completely still and kept rubbing one shoe against the other.

"No doubt you'll be glad to leave here," he said.

He returned to the desk and sat down. He opened a drawer, took from it a sheaf of papers and flicked through them. Behind the desk, he was completely calm.

He leaned back. "You mustn't forget that I am in no way responsible for everything that happened to you. The whole idea was Dr Wagner's, one of my younger colleagues. It probably seems to you like a cruel, pointless joke."

He gave me a sharp look: "Isn't that so?"

I didn't know how to reply. Although I had recovered a little (I could look at the mass of books on the shelves and feel nothing more than a slight prickling in my throat), I couldn't shake off the feeling that I was floating in a transitional world between my old self and a new, as yet unrealised one.

"I don't blame you," said Dr Apstein-Müller, who took my contemplative silence as an affirmative. "Nevertheless, Dr Wagner claims that the experiment gave him a valuable insight into Goldberg's mind. And that is the main reason why we are here. To get an insight into patients' thinking."

Dr Apstein-Müller danced back to the window and stood there staring at the fog.

"I must replay your discussions with Goldberg," he said. "We of course recorded everything. Did you really believe he was a psychiatrist?"

I nodded. As if my nodding had filled some hidden battery in Dr Apstein-Müller's body, he immediately began to jump about again, circling me and then the desk.

"But in reality, Goldberg is exceptionally logical, isn't he? It would be hard to say that he was like an ordinary patient. In his case, we are looking at mental unravelling, a shattered value system or, if you like, a schizophrenic retreat from reality. No, his case is rare and, to be frank, tragic: an example of a brilliant mind, who precisely understands one of the main problems of our time, but offers an imperfect solution to it."

"Is Goldberg the writer of detective stories, who is being treated here for writer's block?" I asked.

"How did you know?" he asked in surprise.

"I'm here for the same reason. And, as far as I know, also some other well-known writers. Have you used Goldberg to turn as all into mental patients? Is there some parallel project which is more important, better paid than treating us for writer's block?"

"All of you who are here for writer's block," he said, "have been through the same or at least similar episode with Goldberg. You came here wanting to be cured. We are treating you. Our method may be unusual, but it works. I recommend that you don't succumb to this current confusion, but stay here and continue your treatment."

37.

Turgenev: "Fuck you!"

The next day, at breakfast, I finally met the other ptients suffering from writer's block. At the beginning, the different descriptions of the same experience we had been through confused us. Most of all, we were thrown off track by the fact that Simon Goldberg had turned from supposed director and then supposed patient into an expert who was supposed to cure us of writer's block. That was purportedly the real and only reason for his presence at the clinic. Everything that had happened to us was meant to be the first phase of treatment and the differences in our descriptions of events were to be a basis for the way forward.

I wasn't the only one who didn't believe the change in Goldberg's role in treatment. Most of my fellow "inmates" thought of the possibility that the second phase of "treatment" might be yet another hoax, just a different story to amuse the psychiatrists, but which would bring us no benefit. All the other patients – Graham Greene, Saul Bellow, David Lodge, Cabrera Infante, Martin Amis, Javier Marías, Javier Cercas and J. M. Coetzee – expressed reservations of some kind. I couldn't have wished for more eminent company; at times, it seemed to me that, regardless of my success on international book markets and among the expert public, I didn't belong among them, although I was aware that I was seeing the others in the light of their achievements, but myself much more in the light of projects that had failed.

But all my fellow sufferers had read at least one of my books, and I had met Coetzee and Marías fleetingly at literary festivals. The others had at least heard of me, if they had not read any of my works; but because even I don't read everybody and everything that deserves to be read, that didn't bother me.

But all were exceedingly happy, with differing degrees of discretion, that our suffering, physical and mental, was at an end, and that we had finally been given comfortable rooms with a cassette player and more than twenty cassettes of good, primarily classical music. And a typewriter, in case we wanted to type up the scribbled description of our "first phase of treatment", broaden it, rework it, perhaps use it as the beginning or end of a novel or short story. And enough paper for five novels. Or for five versions of the same one.

They had also begun to treat us like patients who had, after all, paid for therapy. The rooms had bathrooms; we ate in a special self-service dining room together with the doctors and other medical staff; we had sessions of group and individual therapy, if that's what it was (now one person doubted it, now another, sometimes everyone at the same time); we had a lot of free time for socialising and talks without a therapist, we had the possibility of expressing to each other, openly and without control, our doubts, of which there were quite a few and continually expanding.

We also had entertainment in the form of two fellow patients, one of whom believed he was Shakespeare, the other who introduced himself as Montaigne. Both were part of our therapy groups, which in Simon Goldberg's opinion would help both us and them, for they had transferred their identities into long dead individuals, which was only an extreme phase of what we writers do when we transplant our identity into fictional characters, which in reality are less fictional than we would like to think.

Surprisingly, 'Shakespeare' and 'Montaigne' were facing the same problem: writer's block. But the source of their blockage was the conviction that they had already written everything, and they didn't want to repeat themselves, and certainly didn't want to write something that didn't seem to be a part of literary history and would change it, update it, perhaps divert it, while our problem was that we were unable to write because we simply were unable to. For Shakespeare, and partly for Montaigne, that wasn't even a problem. The world has at least a million times as many books as it needs and as people read, they said; why, then, in addition to the endless virgin forest cut down to make into paper, should we add even more waste, for we must know that it is no longer possible to write anything that is not reminiscent of what they had written and done so a lot better than the best of us might manage. The only solution was for us to stop writing and do something else; if we were unable or unwilling to accept this, we were mentally ill, while they, who would know how to write something that had not been written before, were the only ones who were mentally whole. Which of course we crazy ones, they kept emphasising, were unable to grasp.

On the very first day of our "new" therapy we realised that were going to be involved in a kind of literary symposium, which brought a sense of relief, for we were used to such things, unlike Shakespeare and Montaigne (or even them as well, for all of us in the group were almost convinced that a man does not become Shakespeare or Montaigne just like that; he is first of all a working contemporary writer, when something inside his head shifts, and he begins to believe that he is someone long dead, albeit still present in the European spirit). It seemed to us most unusual that the two patients knew by heart all of "their" works, or at least the majority of them, and kept harassing us by reciting extracts, until Simon Goldberg forbade it. From that point on, they recited the extracts to themselves while pacing around the dining room or therapy room, although in so doing they often raised their voice, so that Goldberg had to threaten to lock them in their rooms.

Montaigne's citations were a lot better than Shakespeare's and at moments were completely in tune with the therapy that had brought this unusual company of people to Berghof. Shakespeare's seemed too familiar, part of the cultural landscape in which we had grown up, and in which our fathers and forefathers had been raised. But Montaigne, surprisingly, was part of the contemporary spirit, so much so that he seemed like a contemporary author.

Simon Goldberg was of the opinion that it would be best to begin as he had done with the group of authors that had preceded us: by defining writer's block and by considering the possibilities of overcoming it. But before he entrusted us with his definition, which we were certain not to agree with completely, he asked us to tell him how familiar we were with statements by well-known authors who had faced writer's block.

I couldn't remember any, as I had never thought about it until it hit me. But my fellow patients had evidently had quite a bit of experience with regard to this and with unusual delight, incomprehensible to me, they rushed to come up with quotations. Saul Bellow quoted his fellow countryman Scott Fitzgerald, author of *The Great Gatsby,* in my mind one of the most over-rated of novels: "For two months I struggled with a short story for a magazine, although I knew in advance that when I finished it, I would throw it in the waste bin. Let this building with all my manuscripts and me burn down as soon as possible!"

No one in the therapeutic group showed in any way that he had never felt like this or worse. J. M. Coetzee, a lover of Russian literature, quoted Turgenev: "In my head I have no text. I began the chapter with the following (how original!) words: 'One fine day...' First I crossed out 'fine', then 'one' and then I wrote in capital letters 'FUCK YOU'. And with that I was finished."

Montaigne intervened, recalling the words of Thomas Mann: "For me, writing is a process where you need to grit your teeth and slowly crawl forward: you wait patiently, roll around half the day, sleep and hope that the next day, when you have a clear head, the work will flow on." He added that this wasn't true, at least in his experience, for when you have a clear head, you have an empty head; you can only write when your mind is crawling with thoughts, ideas, inclinations, memories, hopes, fears; only from disorder can you create order, which in the end, when reducing it is finished, takes on the shape of a story or essay.

His words stunned me: the last thing I expected in life was that my opinion about writing would be most accurately expressed by a mental patient who believes he is a French Renaissance essayist. Others could also have contributed a quotation about writer's block, but Martin Amis insisted that these were stupid games, more a test of chance memory than therapy. He demanded that the therapist tell us how he perceived writer's block, especially since he was not a writer and had never experienced it.

His statement had a more than obvious hint of criticism, even sarcasm, but Amis was known for that; in his reviews and essays he liked to strike to right and left, we all knew that, with the exception of 'Montaigne' and 'Shakespeare', although I didn't exclude even them, for I had a growing suspicion that they were in reality collaborators of Goldberg's who had agreed to play the role of madmen as part of our treatment. After the lies and deceit of the first phase, this was not impossible.

It seemed to me that Goldberg was a cunning old fox, who knew exactly what he was doing and that although his method was unusual, it was ultimately successful. At the same time, I was beginning to suspect that perhaps 'Montaigne' and 'Shakespeare' weren't the only ones pretending to be something they weren't and that some of the patients were lying about their identity, although they all looked like the photographs that I had seen in newspapers and magazines, or on the covers of their books; I had even met Marías and Coetzee at two festivals, so it would be hard for them to trick me.

But the others? Graham Greene seemed genuine enough, if only because of the characteristic lines on his face, but it seemed highly unusual to me that he was still alive; had I not read recently that he had died? I didn't exclude the possibility that I was wrong, especially because in my writer's block I saw – not always, but often enough – the first signs of approaching dementia. For quite some time the fear had smouldered inside me that it was stalking me in the image of the dumb Scheherazade, who had not yet appeared at Berghof, but I constantly had the feeling that I was a man on the run and that I could not escape this fate. No, Graham Greene was certainly genuine.

What about Guillermo Cabrera Infante, Cuban author, former friend of Castro and minister of culture, until they quarrelled and he was sent as a diplomat to Netherlands, from where he moved to London and stayed, although he did not stop writing in Spanish? A big name in the Spanish literary sphere, less well known elsewhere, even in England. Through an unusual coincidence, which in the lives of writers are always miraculous (almost as if thought up by the writers themselves), at my London publishers I got to know the assistant editor Trevor Morris, who was married to Ana Cabrera Infante, the writer's younger daughter. She never introduced me to her father, she said that they didn't get on because in Cuba he had left her mother and gone off with his secretary. In spite of that, she was proud of him, she even gave me some of his books in English translation. His photograph stayed in my memory, but not clearly enough to be able to compare it to the person before me. In spite of that, it seemed to me that in a Swiss clinic it would be hard to play the role of an exiled Cuban writer with such a complicated history, and so I put aside my doubts and decided that this Cabrera Infante was the real Cabrera Infante.

One concern less. But on the list of suspects there were still three names behind which an interloper, or even two, might be hiding: Saul Bellow, David Lodge and Javier Cercas. That one of the doctors or even a professional actor would dare to pretend to be a winner of a Nobel Prize for Literature, seemed impossible; that would seem too risky even to Simon Goldberg, if he had really planted someone in the group. And in general, Mr Bellow gave a very convincing impression of the Canadian-American intellectual, who had married and divorced five times, especially because he was on very good, friendly terms with Martin Amis, who I knew had often visited him, and had written essays and paeans – to my mind over the top, but who can deny the privileges that friendship brings? They showed that they knew each other well at the very first group meeting.

That left two suspects: David Lodge and Javier Cercas. I didn't know enough about either to be for or against; I knew that Lodge had written a quite successful trilogy of novels about academic life, that he was a professor at a university in Birmingham and hadn't written a lot, but that was all I knew, and I had never seen his photograph, so I couldn't swear that the David Lodge who introduced himself as David Lodge really was David Lodge; by name perhaps, but not also an author with writer's block. I knew even less about Javier Cercas, who was the youngest among us; considering his age, he probably hadn't written a great deal. That he was a writer and suffering from writer's block, which was unusual considering his age, I found out only at the first therapeutic session. Since I knew nothing about him and had never seen his photograph, I had no problem doubting that he was the one who had been planted to pretend he was a writer suffering from a blockage.

But in the end, my suspicions seemed like the fruit of the chronic paranoia that has accompanied me though life and whose central character was Scheherazade; whatever Goldberg's therapy was – and it wasn't what we expected – it seemed to me impossible and certainly not useful that he would plant a spy among us, who could, under some pretence or other, be of any decisive help in our treatment.

For this reason, my surprise was all the greater when Goldberg, after Amis's rude comment, said that his therapy wasn't theory, for that usually didn't work, and certainly wasn't a literary symposium at which we should strive to be as original as possible, but was rather a sequence of puzzles, conversations, debates, challenges, detective mysteries and tasks, a kind of writerly-intellectual quiz, during which any one of us might be the first to throw off writer's block, even the one suffering its most acute form (and he looked directly at me).

He emphasised that the reputation of all the participants of the therapy, who had gathered there together by chance, merely on the basis of registrations, and not because they had anything in common (on the contrary, we had very little in common), filled him with what might be called stage fright, for he had never had so many illustrious names gathered together at the same time. Perhaps stage fright wasn't the right expression, perhaps it was an excessive desire to help us to the best of his ability and to succeed, as well as the fear that he might not. During the treatment process, many things would happen that would surprise us and which we would hold against him, and what arose between us would certainly be a kind of love-hate relationship. But he appealed to us to follow his advice and (unfortunately, there wasn't a better word) rules, otherwise we would be the biggest losers. He could always blame us for the lack of success, which he had done a number of times since he came to the clinic to treat victims of creative impotence.

We should on no account think that what we were there for was writer's block; in reality, it was impotence and the sooner we recognised that, the better. "The basis of my therapy is that you cannot and should not trust anyone, and that you must find answers on your own to the questions which at first glance have no answers. If you cannot find them, then simply make them up. When you are able to do so, you are cured."

Then he asked how many of us had guessed that one of us was not a real writer, but had been planted. I hardly dared to raise my hand, I did so only when some of the others did. I was surprised that all of them had thought of this possibility, and judging by the expressions on the faces of my fellow sufferers, most of them had me in mind! "Your first task as part of the therapy," Dr Goldberg said, "is to find the one who does not belong among you, although he is included in the therapy. The only way to solve the puzzle is to talk to each other. Not all together, but one to one, personally, following an agreed order. When you uncover the interloper, when you reach agreement about who is only pretending to be a writer with writer's block, we can continue. This will, I expect, take quite a while. I hope you'll have lots of fun."

With these words, he turned and left, leaving us in an even worse quandary.

38.

Drawing lots

"I," said Cabrera Infante decisively, "am not getting involved in these stupid games. We are not children, to be solving puzzles. How will that help us? They took our money and now they are toying with us as if we were dim-witted."

"And what does that mean?" asked Coetzee. "That you'll drop out of the programme and leave?"

Cabrera Infante hung his head in silence.

"I think that without trust nothing will happen," commented Javier Marías, "even though their methods are highly unorthodox. We are patients, we need to accept that, and patients have no right to advise doctors how to treat them. And for me, it's curative in a way to find myself in the company of authors that I value. We can help ourselves a great deal through talking with each other, as Dr Goldberg advised."

"There's another problem," I observed. "Actually, a puzzle. But a puzzle that may become a problem. Simon Goldberg, as you no doubt know, is a world-famous writer of detective stories that have all been bestsellers. In terms of the number of books sold, he is surpassed only by Georges Simenon and Agatha Christie. My publisher, who sent me here for treatment and is paying for it, told me that Goldberg was here being treated for writer's block. In reality, as we can see, his role is the opposite: he's not a patient, but a doctor. Of course, it's not impossible that there are two Simon Goldbergs, but the likelihood that both should end up here at the same time, one a crime writer and the other a doctor, is so negligible that we can discount it. So, what's going on? Did my publisher have the wrong information, or was he, for unknown reasons, lying to me? Is Goldberg really a psychiatrist who treats writer's block, or a crime writer, whom the clinic has allowed, for a large sum of money – to put it nicely, a donation, which as a best-selling writer he can easily afford – to use and abuse renowned writers of serious literature to try out the plot and possible outcomes of his latest novel, which is set in a Swiss sanatorium for treating writers with writer's block? And it cannot be denied that what is happening to us has all the elements of a detective story. Who's who, who's guilty, what's really happening? It's not impossible, especially considering what has befallen us so far, and which was also only a game, that we are the victims of an unusual conspiracy, which we will understand only when we have read Goldberg's next book."

There followed a silence during which my fellow sufferers exchanged meaningful glances. What is this person on about? I felt even more strongly that they saw me as Goldberg's plant, even those that weren't convinced before. Why otherwise would I be talking about the possibility that Goldberg was toying with us, if I wasn't informed about it? And if Goldberg hadn't put me up to it? On the other hand, the exchange of meaningful looks could be evidence that, each for his own reasons, they liked finding themselves in the middle of a puzzle which was now becoming additionally complex, and saw in this as well, albeit reluctantly, a special feature of the treatment method for which each of them had paid a fair sum of money. And that altogether it was going to be more entertaining than they had expected, primarily because they themselves had become characters in a story that they hadn't written: in a detective story about serious literature, which in itself was something completely contradictory, and perhaps because of that the beginning of a new, original genre, which each would want – as soon as possible and without the others knowing – to launch into the world as something original of their own.

The first to speak was Saul Bellow, who was worth listening to because he was the only Nobel Prize winner among us.

"All of this is alien to me," he said. "I don't read crime novels, although I have heard of Goldberg in passing, but that he would be here, with God knows what intention, pretending to be a doctor, sounds to me like something that is possible only in a bad novel, perhaps one of his. I recommend that we remain serious, that we trust the therapist and his methods, be they highly unusual, as if he really was a psychiatrist, and that we change our opinion of him only when enough evidence for that has accumulated. I suggest, therefore, that we follow his instruction and begin talking with each other about the problem of writer's block until we discover the interloper."

"I agree," said Martina Amis immediately, which was to be expected.

"So, we talk," Cabrera Infante gave in. "The only question is who talks to whom."

"Very simple," said David Lodge, who gave the impression of being the most reasonable among us. "Since we must all talk to each other, we can draw lots for the first round of pairs, and then rotate until we have exhausted all the combinations."

"Excellent," observed Javier Cercas, the youngest one present, taking a coin from his pocket.

"That won't work," commented Graham Greene. "A more reliable method is that we each write our name on a piece of paper and then we fold the papers up and throw them into Mr Bellow's hat, then we draw them out one by one. In that way, everyone will get an interlocutor."

"What if someone pulls out their own name?" asked Cercas, slightly offended because tossing a coin had been rejected. "Will he then talk to himself?"

"You can do that, if you're so inclined," retorted Graham Greene, slightly impatiently. "We shall repeat the procedure. And we shall keep repeating it until everyone has someone to talk to."

It was a good thing that Saul Bellow had a large hat on his head. And that he was willing to remove it.

39.

Graham Greene and me

For my first discussion partner I got Graham Greene, which pleased me greatly, for I had been an admirer of his novels even as a student, especially, I'm sorry to say, his less serious works, which he called "entertainments", because of which, it was said, instead of him the Nobel Prize went to William Golding, for me a much less interesting writer. Saul Bellow got David Lodge, Cabrera Infante the young Spaniard Cercas (no doubt they talked in Spanish), Coetzee was paired with Marías, Amis had to make do with 'Montaigne', while 'Shakespeare' continued to walk around the room, reciting lines from his plays.

And thus, two to a table, we began our discussions.

"What are we supposed to talk about?" asked Graham Greene.

"I think about the potential causes of writer's block," I said, although I was guessing, "and how it can be got rid of."

"Until something happens, everything is possible," he replied, "although I fear that any particular success with this kind of treatment is not to be expected."

"Maybe it's just necessary to awaken the vestigial memory," I said, "only in the memory are the hidden seeds from which something can sprout."

He shook his head. "Every good writer has a bad memory. From what you remember appears at best reportage, but what you forget sinks into the soil of the imagination."

"That's possibly true," I agreed, "but even imagination is limited by memory. It can promote only what we have lived through and experienced, or seen and read."

"You may be right," he nodded. "Everyone, especially writers, experiences a moment in childhood when a door opens and enables the future to enter our life and subordinate it."

Was he talking about my childhood? About Scheherazade?

"I've read almost all your books," I said, "*The Heart of the Matter* particularly closely because it was a set book when I was at college. I still have the copy somewhere from that time, scribbled all over with comments and notes. I cannot deny that it influenced my writing."

"Really?" he said in surprise. "Why?"

"It seems to me, or it seemed to me then, when it was part of my study, that in a special, very subtle way, it revealed the truth about human life."

"Oh," he leaned back and gave a slight frown. "Wouldn't it be easier, for all of us, if we didn't try to understand everything that we came across, but simply accepted the fact that no person ever understands another, no wife her husband, no husband his wife, no parents their children, let alone children their parents? Perhaps that's why we invented God, someone who knows how to understand us."

"In my case it's different," I said. "I try to understand everything I encounter and everything that takes root in my mind. If I fail, a barrier arises within me, which is most reminiscent of a road block. So many of these have arisen over the years that the road is closed and I can't move forward. That's why I'm here. But I'm surprised that you're here, too. Graham Greene and writer's block somehow don't go together."

"I was also surprised," he said. "I strive to be satisfied with what I write. Sadly, that never happens, but I spend a lot of time and effort – perhaps too much – re-reading and revising what I have written so that I am not too unsatisfied with it. And that is possibly why I am here. Because what I am currently writing, or *trying* to write, fills me with dissatisfaction, bordering on perfectionism. Can you imagine a worse malady to afflict a writer? Rather a work that lacks five or six steps to perfection, than endless polishing and prettifying, which almost always results in something average. Rather a bad novel, but original, than a good novel that is nothing special."

I had the impression that I had heard or read all this somewhere before, perhaps in one of his books, and this time, too, I felt that he wasn't just talking about himself, but about me, for whom polishing words so that they shine is the most laborious and almost loathsome thing in the world. There is always a barely audible voice telling me that words need to be left with their natural sound and scope, not to beautify them, as if they were women heading for a party. But often, perhaps too often, I haven't been able to resist. Which no doubt played an important role in finding my imagination blocked.

"It increasingly seems to me that the causes of writer's block are universal," I said. "Impediments that take away our courage or ability to form literary narratives. And create unreal ambitions and over-zealousness, which has buried many potentially great authors."

"I'll say this," commented Graham Greene after a short pause. "Writing is a kind of therapy. I've no doubt you'll agree with that, although I have unfortunately never read one of your books. I often ask myself how people who neither write, nor paint, nor compose, can avoid madness, melancholy, panic and constant suppression of fear in the soul, which are all a constant result of man's situation in the world. None of us who are here, by coincidence or not, for reality is more unusual than we realise, would dare to deny that the most faithful companion in his life is depression. Show me a happy person and I will show you someone who is full of extreme egoism or ignorance."

"It's true," I responded, "all good literature is an expression of the existential anxiety we carry inside us, although almost always we become aware of that too late in life."

"I won't disagree with you," he said. "That's why I've done a lot of things in life unconnected with books. Things I hoped would anchor me in reality, free me from addiction to the imaginary world of literature and enable me to feel the temperature of life, its madness. For life is far too much shaped by books, wouldn't you agree? Much more than by the people with whom we grow up and who raise us. We first find out about love and pain and uncertainty and fear of death from books. Even when we first fall in love, it happens not because our parents have taught us about love, but because books have informed us about its existence and its possible forms. In other words, books are a source of reality, which we think is the source of imagination from which books are born. Simon Goldberg, in his previous role of clinic director, was perhaps right when he said that the main source of delusions and adversity in the world is the printed word. Are you the person he planted, whom I am supposed to unmask? Or is it just coincidence that you are talking to me as if you were?" He looked me straight in the eye.

"I think it's you," I returned his look and added some sharpness. "Everything I've heard from you is in some way familiar, and so it doesn't seem impossible that you're citing ideas from Greene's books which you have read and re-read for your current role, for the real Graham Greene would not know how to repeat statements and thoughts from so long ago with such accuracy. Although I cannot deny that I, too, in at least twenty interviews, have spoken about the same things and expressed the same standpoints, which means that writers repeat themselves, especially when we talk about our work, and why would you be an exception? But I still have my doubts. You really do look like Graham Greene, as I have seen him on photographs, but the exceedingly crafty Dr Goldberg could have chosen you as his agent and prepared you for the role of Graham Greene."

"You are thinking about it logically," he replied, "but you are mistaken. It is more likely that you are the interloper, and thus a psychiatric patient who thinks he is a writer – you primarily because I've never read any of your books and, to be honest, I've never heard of you."

"I see your words as a confession that you don't read very much," I dared to say. "The fact that I know more about Graham Greene than he knows about me is proof that I'm interested in contemporary literature. You are obviously not, for I am, after all, one of the more important contemporary writers. Although not perhaps among the most important. I know that the real Graham Greene was the whole of his life prey to depression and he once wrote to his wife that his character was to *resist* everyday family life and that was also, regrettably, the material from which he drew his ideas. I also know," I added, "that the real Graham Greene, mainly after he had decided, as an Anglican, to adopt the Catholic faith, had cheated on his wife with an enviable number of other women and never regretted doing so, for his Catholic confession washed away his sin and allowed him to continue his behaviour. And that was the main reason he converted from Anglicanism to Catholicism. The only thing that guarantees us a space in heaven is regular confession, he once said."

"You know what," he said, jumping up. "I'm glad our conversation has concluded so successfully. I'm going to the toilet."

40.

Martin Amis and me

My next interlocutor, Martin Amis, also suspected from the start that I was a fake. I knew only three things about him: that his whole life he had striven to become more famous than his father, Kingsley Amis; that he was constantly being nominated for the Booker Prize, which he had so far not won; and that he had limitless admiration for Saul Bellow, whom he never ceased to praise, and that because of him, according to vicious tongues, he had moved to the States, although not to Chicago, like Bellow, but to Brooklyn.

"What instructions did you get?" was his first question. "What do you have to ask me?"

"I'm more interested what you'll ask me," I said. "After all, this is not an interrogation, it's supposed to be a conversation, a dialogue, an exchange of views."

"I've never heard of you," he said. "The reason may be that you write detective novels, a less worthy genre, which I avoid, or that you're not popular enough, for I have very little time for reading."

"I have not read any of your books, either," I replied. "But I have read all your father's books," I said, touching on his sore point.

Although he was trying to, he could not conceal the fact that he liked me even less now than at the start of our conversation and that he would try to get back at me measure for measure. In fact, I hadn't spoken the truth: I had read two of his books – *Time's Arrow* and *Money*, while I had not read any of his father's. In spite of that, I was not offended that he had read none of mine. I had even read interviews with authors (I don't remember which) who said that they avoided reading the work of their contemporaries, so as not to get infected unawares with bad style; they wanted to remain what they were at any price – that is, original and independent.

Amis did not avoid reading his contemporaries; after all, he had written quite a substantial number of reviews, often negative and venomous. He belonged among those writers who try to increase their own worth by "professionally" lowering the value of others; there were more and more such people on the literary scene. It's not hard to find reviewers who began their literary careers with one or two novels that nobody reads and that were received with crushing reviews. The route from incompetent writer to "literary expert" is a surprisingly short one.

Of course, this didn't apply to Amis, who is, not only in my eyes, a very good writer, while his reviews far surpass the average. In spite of that, it always seemed to me inappropriate for authors to write reviews (be they positive or negative) of the works of their contemporaries, who are also, by definition, their competitors (or friends).

"And which of my father's books did you like most?" Amis asked in a conciliatory fashion, evidently not wanting to confirm gossip that he was competing with his father.

"Oh," I replied, "I read them so long ago, as a student, that I don't remember. But that's not important. I'm more interested when and how your writer's block started."

After a short silence, he said: "I see that you're not going to stop and perhaps I should be grateful to you for that. It began when I mislaid or lost the first third of the novel on which I was working, and without it I didn't know how to continue, for I was left without that which needed to be continued. The only solution was to write the missing first part of the novel again and that was where I got stuck. I would have to repeat or create a new version of something I had already written, which would also in the best case be worse than the first text, besides which it would also be different, for memory follows its own laws. Thus everything came to a halt. It was as if a high jumper had run up and lifted off the ground, and during his flight had suddenly frozen and hung in the air. A tortuous feeling. It had never happened to me before. And you?" He gave me a challenging look, as if he had always suspected that I was a fake.

"My case," I said, "is so unusual that I won't be offended if you say that I've made it all up."

"Try me," he replied, "you never know. After all, we make up everything we write. Is Madame Bovary a real person? No. Are Natasha and Vronsky real people? No. Is Hamlet a real person? No. Are we who make up unreal people real? There are moments when I feel that we are not and that someone is making up us, the fabricators of unreal people, and that someone is making that person up, and someone else this third person, and so on, until we come to the greatest and first Fabulist who made up the great and most ambitious novel – known as the world, life, the universe."

"I have similar thoughts," I couldn't help but agree. "But my problem is worse, so I doubt you'd believe me."

"Try me."

"The reason for my writer's block," I said, "is a desire that I have raised to the status of a professional duty. I want to write a novel about a writer who would like to write a novel about a writer who is suffering from writer's block. In other words, about a writer who has become the victim of the novel he wants to write. Who has become the hero of his novel. The problem is so complex, that for me there is probably no solution, but there's no harm in trying, if I can be allowed one of the horde of clichés that we writers use in moments of laziness or inattention. The treatment here will no doubt cure some of us of writer's block, including you, but me certainly not, for I have, as you can see, bitten into an apple made of steel. But even if there is no solution for me, there must be for other members of the crew of Goldberg's rocket, which is, if I may express myself more picturesquely, flying through unknown space to the extreme border of the mental universe."

"Well, at least your problem is original," said Amis.

"Actually, I wouldn't be participating in this therapy, if you can call it that, if I hadn't been forced onto it by my publisher, who also paid for the treatment."

"Neither would I, if I wasn't in such distress. You are older and have probably already written what you wanted to tell us, regardless of the fact that we've probably heard or read it a hundred times, and so we don't read your books. I'm still relatively young and would still like to stomp around the literary landscape. It's important to forget about the past, only then does the present become memorable. Meanwhile, time passes relentlessly and changes us, big and small, clever and stupid, beautiful and ugly, into what is most reminiscent of crap."

"What time changes us into, we do not know," I said.

"That we know nothing," he said, more seriously and more heatedly, "I, at least, find very wearisome. It destroys my nerves. It offers itself as comedy, but I don't understand a single joke. It offers itself as tragedy, but I am increasingly unsure of what is really tragic and what is merely sentimental. Hour by hour, I am losing energy. Not only for the creation of stories, but to understand anything at all in such a way that I really believe at least something that I think I understand. There are moments when I am destroyed just by looking out of the window and wondering why rain is falling."

"I, thank God, have abandoned the desire to understand anything or anyone at all," I said. "Mainly because my understanding is exclusively mine and is never aligned with how others understand themselves or how they are understood by others. We live in a world of speculation and disbelief and uncertainty. I have accepted that this is how it is, for it cannot be different and there's nothing tragic in this."

"If you really believe that, then you'll never write another novel," said Amis. "To delve into other, different people you need a lot of courage and a lot of faith that it is possible. And it *is* possible. We're all convinced that others live in fortresses. But in reality, we all live in tents, which anyone who is humble enough to bow their head can crawl into. In a tent we are one."

"In spite of that," I said, "there are differences among us that we need to take into account if we wish to create in our fiction at least an approximation of reality."

"There's no doubt about that," he agreed. "What did Nabokov and Joyce have in common, other than excellent prose and bad teeth? Exile and decades of poverty. And a sick desire to tip too generously. But above all, they lived in accordance with their goals: they persisted and finished their works. Is there anything more important for a writer?

"Perhaps, at least occasionally if not all the time, enough money to live on?" I dared to suggest.

"Come on," he reacted quickly. "Do you want me to give you some of my income? If you measure the quality of literature by the state of the bank balance, I can transfer all my savings to you, but your work would be no better for that."

I was pleased that he had finally unrestrainedly manifested his ego, which it is said is the driving force of all writers.

"Are you aware of the seven deadly sins?" he went on. "Venality, paranoia, uncertainty, excess, physicality, contempt and boredom."

"And which have I committed?" I asked.

"All of them," he said. "We could continue, the conversation is unfolding in the right direction, but you have unfortunately derailed it. In the West, we say that men go through a middle-age crisis, whereas women experience the biological menopause. Other cultures are unfamiliar with the middle-age crisis. Where I come from, it usually manifests itself like this: riding a Harley Davidson in a suicidal way on the most winding, dangerous roads, teenage lovers, vegetarianism, jogging, buying a sports car, cocaine, a succession of stubborn but unsuccessful diets, a new baby, a new religion, a hair transplant, and other things that do not sit well with the age of the wretched one who is not aware that there is no going back."

"What are you trying to tell me?" I asked, when he was on the point of pushing back his chair and bidding goodbye, satisfied that he had not given me the opportunity to be the one to end the conversation. "That my writer's block is a side effect of middle age crisis?"

"Certainly not," he said, getting up. "You're intelligent enough to understand what I want to say before I speak. I've learned a lot from our talk. I want to remind you of something that you've known a long time, but dared not admit because it would be the final blow, the *coup de grâce*. Does it seem to you that we writers are at war, but on the wrong side? In a war against health, against life, against love? Every day, we increase the dose of suffering, every day we look suffering in the eye and feel that it is right in front of us, although it is distant, ancient, eternal. But still wild. There's probably a simple reason for the tiredness that I feel, for the weariness that permeates me like a cancerous metastasis. Is it any different for you? No. It seems increasingly that it is a kind of moral tiredness. We writers, God knows why, have become tired of being people. If we ever were people. If we didn't stop being people when we wrote our first book. Where does that fear come from, that after all the books we have written, we won't be able to complete another? It's absurd!"

He turned and took three steps away from the table. Then he came back. "Doesn't it seem to you, from your experience, that the life of a writer is made up of encouraging ambitions and destructive anxieties? Fear of impotence? And that we need both to the same extent? It's not good to write a novel where you feel everything is going according to plan, it's even worse to write a novel in an agony of doubt and fear that somewhere, perhaps half way through, we will get stuck. We need both to the same extent. Writer's block occurs when the balance is destroyed. Is it any different for you?"

"Not at all," I admitted. "But all those are general observations that can be of no help to me or to you, or to anyone else. At moments, it seems that we writers are in the education business. It's true we don't teach the usual subjects, like maths, history, chemistry, biology, but we do teach those who read us the capacity for a moral life and for nuanced judgement of events on the way through life. And courage to face up to the fact that most things we shall never understand."

He straightened up and looked at me rather haughtily, I thought. "An excellent citation," he said. "Why did you lie and say that you'd never read any of my books?"

And he marched off, slightly bent over, but with the posture of a victor to whom victory seemed self-evident.

41.

Conversation with a Nobel Prize winner

When the drawing of lots decided that my next interlocutor would be Saul Bellow, I was flooded with a sense of confusion that would be hard to put a name to. I cultivated a very contradictory attitude towards the novels of this gentleman, who I didn't doubt for a moment was the real one. On the one hand, his *Herzog* seemed to me exceptional and the novella *Seize the Day* likewise, but on the other hand, I would say that his *Henderson the Rain King* was one of the worst novels ever written about Africa. Regrettably. Probably the gentleman from Chicago never had the inclination or the courage to visit that continent to familiarise himself with at least some aspects of its reality.

But so what: even Shakespeare himself wrote quite a number of plays that could be accused of sleight of hand. Nobody's perfect. Writers should be judged by their best works. That's where they are at home, that's where you see what they really are, what they are capable of. And because it is characteristic of writers – at least of the good ones and even the best ones – that they never really shake off their doubts about their abilities, my confrontation with Bellow filled me with the fear that we wouldn't be equal partners in our conversation. For I had long before learned that it is not good to hide one's doubts about the quality of one's work, while Mr Bellow was perhaps so convinced of the excellence of his that he would leave the table if the conversation turned to his verbose hack work *Henderson the Rain King*. One way or another, I decided to wait for him to speak first.

He stared at me as if waiting for me to speak. And I, not out of stubbornness, but because I had no idea how to begin, didn't want to ruin everything with my first words, stared back, as if waiting for him to begin.

"Hello," he said after a while. "I'm Saul Bellow. And you are?"

I told him, in the firm conviction that he had never heard of me and that if he had, he had never read any of my books, at least none that would have remained in his memory.

"Ah-ha," he said. "The name is familiar, but in the midst of this terrible over-production of books, even the best works that one reads quickly fade from memory."

"Well, I have read quite a few of yours," I replied quickly. "But I couldn't answer the question as to which I liked more and which less."

"Excellent," he said. "To my mind, readiness to answer every question is an undeniable sign of stupidity."

I agreed and added: "But it's the case that we live in a world that is becoming ever more stupid."

"Stupidity is too mild a word," he grabbed the bone I had tossed him. "We live in a crazy world. The hope that the general stupidity will not touch us is just another form of madness. But it can be equally mad to follow common sense if we overdo it."

Nicely put, I thought, but does that have any connection with the truth? Can it help us in any way? "Doesn't it seem to you, at least partly, if not completely crazy that we are pursuing the possibility that, with a completely weird form of therapy, we can throw off the shackles of our numb, even completely dead imaginations?"

"Wait a minute," he leaned back, "are you misunderstanding the whole thing? There's nothing wrong with our imagination, our problem is that we cannot transform it into the right words. Or into any words at all. Most writers do not find the right words for what they want to say."

"I agree with you. At least, not always and not in every book. Even you are no exception."

"Which of my novels are you thinking of?" he asked, staring at his fingernails as if to check that they were clean enough.

I had no choice but to tell him.

"You're not the first to think that," he admitted. "Perhaps I really did fail with that novel and I sailed into waters that were more or less unknown to me. Perhaps that time, at least that time, I really did rely too much on imagination. But every individual, especially a writer, must know how to listen to and be capable of accepting the negative things said or written about him. Today, even politicians and fools are given freedom of speech, so why not colleagues and critics who see the world differently."

He had not only elegantly beaten off the attack, he had compelled me to take a step back; what was more, he was pushing me to apologise to him. And if I didn't do that, it was because I could find no reason why I should apologise for a negative view of a book, alongside the thousands of others I thought were bad, just because it was written by such an eminent author as Saul Bellow. The only thing I was able to say was the feeble stock phrase: "I didn't mean to offend you."

"You didn't," he almost raised his voice. "You simply do not like one of my novels. So what? Probably I wouldn't like one of yours. You're lucky I've never read any of them. And due to lack of time, I won't. So you have an advantage in this conversation. Or so it seems. Although it is not necessarily the case that you have. Shouldn't we now talk about something else? Really talk?"

He gave me a final blow.

"Suggest a theme," I said.

"Is it in your nature to lay your burden on the shoulders of others?" he responded.

"Okay," I said, suddenly robbed of words and the will to continue the conversation. "What do you think of this therapy? Of this web of deception in which we are cooperating? Doesn't it seem to you that someone is making fools of us? And is using us for God knows what personal goals, maybe for some dissertation or doctorate on the psychological states and characteristics of authors who say they are suffering from writer's block?"

"Oh," he stretched his mouth without actually smiling. "Don't look at things so negatively. This Dr Goldberg is worth at least a novel, if not a series. It *is* a ruse, perhaps a number of parallel or even contradictory ones, but isn't every good novel also a ruse? Goldberg has staged for us a classic detective story – we have to discover who among us is pretending, who is the blackguard, who is not what he says he is. We have to find among us a Sherlock Holmes, or a Poirot, or Sam Spade, or some other famous detective. Doesn't that seem at least original to you? It's true that the early days of treatment in this clinic or madhouse, if I use a more appropriate word, were anguished, at moments tormenting, even frightening, but certainly not without reason. What, after all, do the two of us know about treating writer's block? Which neither of us has succumbed to before; at least I assume that you haven't either. Let alone that we have even the slightest idea about how to cure it. For we hadn't been expecting it. At least, I hadn't. Had you? I can answer for you: no, you hadn't. I must admit that after my initial doubts, I am quite enjoying what is happening."

"I must admit that I find uncertainty deadly," I said. "If I at least knew roughly what was happening and where all this is leading, it would be easier. Unfortunately, I can't find anything that might lead me to greater certainty."

"Don't you read crime novels?" he said with a look.

I dared not admit to him that I did. "Now and then. On a plane, if the flight is more than seven hours."

"Uncertainty is the basis of a crime story," he said. "Without it, you'd put the book down straight away. In fact, you wouldn't even be able to buy it, since no sensible publisher would publish it. Didn't you know that James Joyce loved to read crime and detective stories, and that after his death his wife, Nora, burned all the ones that he had, because she didn't want to mar his reputation? She saw detective stories as less worthy literature."

"And you," I asked, "don't they seem less worthy to you?"

"Oh come on," he said with slight impatience. "Genres are not less worthy – what is badly written is less worthy. At least, that's what I think now; perhaps ten or even five years ago, I would have agreed with you that writers of detective novels were one thing, serious writers something else, although so far, no one has been able to explain to me what is serious literature and what is trivial writing, for the distinction between them is arbitrary, a matter of personal preference and even adaptation to the enthroned rules, which is the worst thing of all. But for heavens' sake, we have found ourselves, and with us a group of serious authors, among the characters in a detective story, which is not made up, but which is really happening. What do you think: who among us is the interloper that Dr Goldberg, astute and self-regarding as he is, infiltrated into the therapy group? Is it you? Is it me? Of course, deep inside I know it isn't me, but why would you and others believe me? After all, they have no evidence. Nor do I. So tell me, are you Goldberg's interloper?"

"As far as I know, I'm one of the patients," I replied. "But I can't prove this in any way. Just as you cannot. Just as none of us can. Except, of course, Montaigne and Shakespeare, who cannot pretend, as they are ill because they believe they are something they are not. Allow me to ask you: from the conversations you've had so far, who among us seems the most suspicious?"

The question caught him unprepared, he probably hadn't even thought about this, whereas I thought about it all the time.

"Can I be frank?" he gave me a look. "The most suspicious one is you."

"Me?" I couldn't hide my amazement. "Why?"

"Perhaps because, although this shouldn't be a good enough reason, quite the opposite, I haven't read any of your books and I cannot imagine how you might be different from what you are now. Which means that as you are, you can easily pretend to be what you say you are. Who in your opinion is the most likely interloper?"

"Everyone," I replied. "Or at least, everyone I've spoken to so far. And that includes you. No offence intended."

"You apologise too much," he said. "You show me too much respect. In a way that a real world-class author would not. That's why you are my main suspect."

"So then, is there any point in continuing our conversation?"

"Precisely for that reason," he said. "If we discover who among us isn't who he says he is, we might be able to work out why it seems necessary to Goldberg to burden all of us, after what he's put us through, with a detective puzzle. And how that will help him free up the blockage inside us. If that really is his intention."

"But you said that I was your prime suspect. Let's say that I really am the interloper we are looking for. How does that help us to understand Goldberg's method, his goals?"

"It doesn't at this moment," he replied. "But when we uncover the interloper and when we reach agreement on who it is, Goldberg will certainly take his next step. And that next step will reveal to us where this stupid, childish game is heading. Which we have all paid for. To be honest, if it wasn't because of the money, I would already have left."

"I, too, have often felt the urge to flee," I admitted. "After all they've done to us, we could easily sue them for torture. The damages would certainly be as high as the cost of treatment, perhaps even higher."

"Let's wait," he said. "Whenever a story gets stuck in a vicious circle, something must happen to release the brake and drive the story forward. Maybe we'll never write again, but the story that we are experiencing here, which is being written by our bizarre therapist, will have an ending, I'm sure of that. It is not necessary to understand everything. Which would you rather do? Sit at a desk and write down some fabrication that your desire for illusion gives birth to, or to experience something real, something unusual, something that no one would believe if it was in a novel? You should be grateful for the opportunity that's being offered us. The opportunity to go mad. And to shrug off the need to spread illusions, for what is literature other than an attack on readers' real experiences, which seem so boring to them that they would rather have made-up ones? The mind, Mr... er, I've forgotten your name, the mind is a space in which the world dwells."

"To some extent I agree," I said, but I was never able to finish the sentence because Saul Bellow pushed back the chair and got up. "I'm sorry. I have prostate problems. I must go to…"

He turned and hurried towards the toilet. A convenient excuse, I thought. I decided that I would use is myself with my next interlocutor.

42.

A visit in my room

I heard a knock on the door, and quickly put my notebook under the mattress. I thought that lunch was over and that one of the orderlies had come to call me to the second part of the therapeutic conversations. But no: when I opened the door, Martin Amis was standing there. "May I come in?" he asked and pushed past me without waiting for a reply. Okay, I thought, he must have a reason for this rude intrusion into my privacy. I closed the door and he sat on the edge of my bed. He looked agitated.

"Can you imagine?" he said. "I went to the boss, that oddball Goldberg, and told him that I was withdrawing from the therapy and leaving. He demanded to know my reasons. I wanted to tell him that his therapy was like something out of a bad novel, a malicious joke, more psychological violence than treatment. But at the last moment I thought better of it. I realised that open conflict with the patient, for Goldberg is sick, there's no doubt about it, would do more harm than good. So I lied. I said that in my case the therapy had been more than successful and that I could, thank God and him, perhaps more him than God, carry on writing. Therefore,

I would like to bid him goodbye and thank him for the successful treatment."

I didn't know how to respond; it seemed to me that he hadn't finished. And his silence didn't last long.

"Guess what he said. That premature departure was not possible. That it would cause irreparable harm to the others. That I must wait, at least until the end of the current phase of treatment. Until the interloper had been unmasked. Only then could I leave, he said."

"But we're not on forced treatment," I said, trying as hard as I could not to show how much his news had shocked me. "Yes, Berghof is a well-known psychiatric institute, but our department is something else, we came here voluntarily and we have paid for treatment. For God's sake, no one can keep us here if we decide to leave. We haven't signed anything."

He bowed his head and said: "I have. I signed a declaration agreeing that I knew how complex it was treating writer's block and for success it is necessary to persist until the experts agree that they can do nothing more."

"I signed nothing like that," I said. "Unless I have forgotten doing so. I forget many things, but something like that I wouldn't."

"Are you sure?" he looked at me. "I've spoken to the others and they all say they've signed a similar declaration."

"I can't believe it," I said. "Except if the declaration was signed by my publisher, who sent me here and covered the cost of therapy. But he shouldn't be able to sign something like that without my knowledge."

"Lucky you," said Amis. "You at least have a theoretical chance of challenging the validity of the signature and winning your freedom. The rest of us are trapped here like prisoners – I can't find a more appropriate word."

"I think you've misunderstood the declaration," I tried to comfort him and even more, myself. "It's probably consent in principle, which can't be legally binding. After all, Switzerland respects the rule of law."

"Come on," he grimaced, "as a writer you know that the law can be abused in a thousand different ways. Unless you really are the interloper we are supposed to recognise, of which I'm increasingly convinced. Italy also accepts the rule of law, so why is it run by the Mafia?"

"I'm not the interloper," I replied, "and your conviction that I am is your affair. The only problem is that if you really think so, then there is no chance of us having a serious conversation."

"But our conversations are not serious," he once again raised his voice slightly. "We already know everything about writing and literature. What's the point of exchanging our views on the problems of writing, if we have nothing new to say to each other? In any case, writing is something different for each of us. Even in a much bigger group, you wouldn't find two individuals who wrote in the same way. If the only purpose of our pointless conversations is to uncover which of us is hiding behind a well-known name and isn't a writer, or at least not the one he claims to be, because we cannot exclude the possibility that he may be a writer, how can that discovery help us rid ourselves of the writer's block which brought us here in the first place?"

"But if you knew that," I objected, "you wouldn't need treatment, then you wouldn't have come here, you wouldn't have signed the declaration, which, it seems, I haven't, the only one who hasn't, for I wouldn't forget something like that, although it's not impossible considering what they've done to us since we arrived."

"They have deliberately pushed us to the edge of sanity," he said in an emphatically accusatory tone. "And where is the assurance that they have not succeeded? Then they changed us into detectives, merely for their own amusement. What if they are all interlopers, except for me and perhaps you and Bellow, who I know personally? And what if there is no interloper and we are all who we say we are? That's not excluded either."

"That's precisely why our conversations can be useful," I suggested, rather than saying with great conviction. "In the end, it may turn out that they are a crucial step in the treatment. For although it seems that we know everything about literature, or considering our fame we should know, it may not be so. It seems to me, at least, that we all know something different, something very personal and special to us, and that through the one-to-one conversations they have prescribed for us, all the individual ideas, experiences and opinions might be condensed into a collective answer to the question as to what the telling of stories actually is and why we need to continue with it. Not for ourselves, for royalties, awards, fame, or for people to admire us, read us, but for the good of mankind, for the good of the world, for the future good."

"You know what," he straightened up and grimaced, "your statements sound increasingly like those of a secondary school teacher addressing his pupils. Such naivety always pains me, but never as much as now. You should be writing fairy stories for children, the kind that teachers like more than children do, with a didactic undertone. Maybe you do write them and I'm not aware of it."

"Thanks for the compliment," I said, which at that moment was the only response I was capable of. I was aware that Martin Amis was cynical, condescending and at moments even malicious, but his disdainful statement exceeded everything that he had ever said or written. That's just the nature of a writer who is striving to match up to and transcend the reputation of his famous father, Kingsley, author of the novel *Lucky Jim,* which after it first appeared in 1954 was to be found in the hands of every literate person in Britain. I decided to respond in equal measure. "Among your father's novels, my favourite was always *Lucky Jim,*" I said. "I doubt you will ever match that. It seems that in almost every case, the sons of successful writers are condemned to limp along behind their fathers. And that at a certain point, they even begin to hate them."

"I don't like to repeat myself," he said, without looking at me, "but what I said before still goes. Fairy tales are your natural domain." He went to the door, opened it, went into the corridor and slammed the door so hard that it almost came off its hinges.

Well, I thought, I've acquired yet another enemy among my colleagues, but so what – considering how many there are, one more won't make a decisive difference.

The door to my room suddenly opened again and who should come in but Martin Amis.

"Look," he said and then paused for a moment. "I didn't come here intending to offend you in any way. The words slipped from my tongue because of my growing anger at everything that has happened to me here. If I decided to write the most unlikely novel, my imagination would come up against a brick wall even before realising that Goldberg isn't the clinic director, but a patient. Is all this just a terrible nightmare? Or does reality have more imagination than we are capable of? Although, hand on heart, what some authors come up with, especially authors of fantasy literature, which is increasingly fashionable because we are increasingly disinclined to understand humankind and its essence, goes far beyond the bounds of common sense. But that's a literary niche that doesn't have to be taken seriously, let the sociologists deal with it. To keep it brief: I came to you to suggest that we escape. Together."

His words were followed by a tense silence.

"Escape?" I finally repeated. "And go where?"

"It's not important where, what's important is that we get away from here. And go home, probably. To where we live and work. It's important that we escape the danger, which is much more real than many of our group take it to be. These so-called therapists scramble our brains and keep us here as objects of their research. They can do that legally. It's not exactly an everyday theme, writer's block. What if someone wants to get a doctorate out of it? To write a book about it? Get a research grant? Can you at least consider that possibility?"

"I can consider it," I replied. "But I also notice that the majority of patients have unusual psychological issues. In fact, I can't claim that for everyone, because psychological instability is characteristic of writers, but I can say so for myself. And for you. In my case, my confusion is growing; in yours, paranoia. How it is with the others I don't know, but I'll try to find out during the following confrontations."

"So, you're going to continue?" he looked at me accusingly.

"I see no other possibility," I replied. "Fleeing from the operating table in the middle of surgery because the anaesthetic is easing off doesn't seem very sensible. Fleeing because, at first sight, I don't like the weird treatment method? I'm interested to see how it will all end."

"And what if it doesn't?" he almost bleated back. "Or if it all ends badly? There's a telephone in the castle, not just one, quite a few. Why won't they let us make phone calls?"

"Probably because," I said, "making connection with our previous world, which is perhaps one of the reasons for our writer's block, would slow down the healing process, if not end it."

"Okay," he said and headed for the door. "I'd hoped you were thinking like me. I'll just have to escape on my own."

43.

Words, just words

I didn't believe that he would. Escaping from a castle in the middle of a lake is not as simple as it might sound in a novel. But when we gathered twenty minutes later in the therapy room for the second round of conversations, Amis was not there. I was already thinking that he had really undertaken the risky venture, perhaps even succeeded, when he came through the door, head bowed. He didn't look towards me, but with a dour look on his face he sat down at the table where his next interlocutor, Javier Marías, was waiting for him.

I stopped being interested in him because opposite me was that outstanding South African writer, J. M. Coetzee, who really deserved a slightly more pronounceable surname. But that offered me an opportunity to begin the conversation, for I wasn't happy that I had almost always waited form the other person to speak first.

"No offence," I said, "but I still don't know how to pronounce your name, and I'm probably not the only one."

"No, you're not the only one," he gave a slight smile. "I have one of those surnames which may be pronounced in a number of ways, in my case seven, and all of them are correct to some extent. Depending on how I'm feeling, even I sometimes pronounce it one way, sometimes another, to amuse myself and embarrass others, or vice versa. It's one of those Afrikaans surnames which show how Dutch settlers in South Africa succumbed to the English, who of course don't know how to pronounce correctly any Afrikaans word, nor quite a number of English words, either, but that's another story. How would you pronounce it?"

"To be honest, I've never spoken it," I admitted, "I always had it in front of my eyes in the visual form that I'm familiar with. If it's possible to pronounce it in seven ways the risk that I get it wrong is that much smaller, so I'd say that one of the possible pronunciations is *Kutsi*, or *Kutsey*, or *Koatsi*. Am I wrong?"

"Not at all," he said, "all three are in use and I don't object to any of them."

"Did you never have the urge to change your name, which is administratively possible, or to use a pseudonym?"

"Never," he shook his head. "Wouldn't it seem disrespectful to you to change the family name just so that people could pronounce it more easily?"

"You're right," I admitted.

"Besides which," he said, "there are quite a few writers who have not changed their name, even though they are harder to pronounce than mine. Or funny, which is worse. Have you heard of Yi-Fen Chou? Petchtai Wongkamlao? Anocha Suwichakornpong? Trinh T. Minh-ha? Nguyễn Nhật Ánh? Loung Ung? Harivansh Rai Bachchan? Krishnaveni Ayyapan Variyath? Alla Al Aswany? Abd al-Wahhab al-Bayati? Pramoedya Ananta Toer?"

"Surely you haven't read all those authors?"

"Difficult, considering that they've hardly been translated into English. I memorised the names to console myself. If hardly anyone can pronounce my name, who can pronounce theirs?"

"But you are famous, they are not," I objected.

"They are also famous," he replied. "In languages spoken by millions. In parts of the world that we Eurocentrics think of as tourist destinations, rather than as places where literature is really alive. Europe and its former colonies are not the world, they are only a part, you could say a small part, of the world. Do you have any idea how many writers there are on the planet? Writers who write excellent books? And have more readers than the patients sitting in this room? Guess."

"I wouldn't dare," I replied.

"No one would. Even just in the USA, almost a million books are published each year. In China, half a million. Even in Indonesia, almost a hundred thousand. As many as in Russia and Germany. Every year, my dear sir, two and a half million books are published worldwide."

"Barely believable," I said.

"Do you ever ask yourself who needs your books?" he looked at me with a friendly smile. "Do I ever ask myself who reads my books? Who needs them? I don't delude myself: almost no one. Yours, neither. So why, then, have we paid strangers an enormous sum to cure us of the block that prevents us from finishing one more book? One of the two and a half million published each year? What damage would the world suffer if a third or half of what we managed to write before we got stuck was thrown into the wastepaper basket. None. We are no longer living in the nineteenth century, when literature still meant something. The world has changed."

"Maybe you're right," I said. "One of us, I won't say who, has already decided to flee: he is convinced that we are caught in a trap which is of use to someone else more than us."

"Martin Amis?" he smiled. "Evidently he's also been to see you. And perhaps someone else. He's too cowardly to make a break for it on his own, he needs a comrade. But he has no need to flee. He is free, he can leave whenever he wants, and I'm surprised he hasn't done so if he has decided that the therapy is a waste of time."

"He says that he signed a declaration that commits him to remain in the group until the end of the programme. Or at least until the moment when we decide which one among us is an interloper pretending to be a famous writer."

"Oh, come on," he leaned back on his chair. "Such a declaration would be illegal. He could sue the clinic and get back all that he paid for treatment. I find it hard to believe he doesn't know that."

"I, too," I admitted, "have an increasing desire to leave. But my fear of returning to a novel that I am unable to finish is still so alive within me that I dare not do so. Besides, I am able to do what I have been unable to do for quite some time: I can write disconnected observations and thoughts in a notebook. I know that those scribblings are not literature, they are not a story, they are not art. They are words, just words, nothing more. Something that perhaps means something to me without meaning anything to anyone else."

"Well," said Coetzee, "you have described very precisely what is happening to me. And perhaps to all the others. I console myself with the hope that this is a necessary step in the healing process. And if it's not, if it's a therapy that someone merely wants to try in the hope that it will prove to be successful, no harm done; I have all too often been cheated in life that I'll survive this, too. It is necessary to believe. Belief is the only source of energy. Belief is the battery that we connect to an idea so that it moves and runs. Especially at a mature age like ours, when we are aware, or at least we ought to be, that the end of longing is also the end of poetry. The end of intensity in the soul."

"We would still have a lot to say," I said, "if we had the time. But unfortunately, the clock on the wall is telling me that this round of conversations ends in one minute."

"Let's leave it," he said. "We've had a nice enough chat, so I suggest that we stop talking and wait for the bell."

And we fell silent. No wiser than at the beginning of our conversation.

44.

A conversation with Montaigne

It seemed strange to me that one of the participants in the conversations was a mental patient who claimed to be Michel de Montaigne, but at the same time I was looking forward to sitting down opposite him. I had seen him talking normally, calmly, confidently with others. He certainly wasn't the interloper that we were supposed to unmask, even though the therapists thought it necessary to impose him on our circle, for we all knew that he couldn't be the real Montaigne (in the whole of history, only Jesus supposedly arose from the dead). And as it turned out, he was my next interlocutor.

When he sat down and gave me a wan smile, I was surprised to discover quite a similarity between him and Montaigne, as portrayed by his contemporaries, with his moustache, triangle of hair and almost bald head. But it seemed unlikely that something so coincidental and approximate had led him to the conviction that he had managed to cheat time and stay alive for centuries, and that he was the real, original and unrepeatable Michel de Montaigne.

He said nothing, but waited for me. There was nothing to indicate that a madman was sitting opposite me.

"No offence," I said, "but it doesn't seem possible that you are the real, only Montaigne from the sixteenth century."

"It's not important how I seem to others, what's important is how I seem to myself," he said calmly, almost as if reading a report that did not concern him personally.

"That sounds learned and wise," I praised him and offered him another opportunity. He wasn't cautious enough, but grabbed it.

"We can become learned by other men's learning," he said, "but a man can never be wise but by his own wisdom."

"You have given me two citations from the real Montaigne's *Essays,* which means that you've read them quite a few times, if you don't have them with you in your room," I pounced.

"Why would I offer citations from my own work," he was almost genuinely surprised. "I hear that you have written quite a number of books, some of them good. I don't doubt that much from those books has remained in your memory. If you quoted some thoughts from one of them, would that mean that they were not yours and that you are only pretending to be the author that you claim to be?"

He had surprised me. And confused me.

"Besides which," he added, "we are not here to decide which of us is mad, for we could all be mad, each in his own way, and I'm increasingly convinced that is actually the case, but to ascertain whether it makes any sense to continue writing at a time when literature is on the threshold of death."

"I don't think so," I said, "I think we are here, except perhaps for you, because we would like to continue, but are unable to do so because of writer's block."

"And what does that mean?" he gave me a sharp look, as if interrogating me. "That you have nothing further to say. Nothing new. Your words have dried up because you have for too long scattered them in every direction, as if they were cheap goods that cannot run out. You cannot continue because you have been gripped by the fear that you will begin to repeat yourself. You are afraid of self-plagiarism and that, only that, is your writer's block."

For a moment, I was overcome by the feeling that his diagnosis was the correct one, and I was surprised that I had never considered that possibility. But no, I said to myself, although I've known from a young age, ever since the unforgotten days I spent with my grandfather, that each story is, in a way, the story of another story, and so on back to Scheherazade; I am convinced that searching for and narrating that handful of stories in which there is no echo of other stories is not only something that we writers are left with, but that it is very necessary for preserving the narrative basis of consciousness, memory and history, through the endless relocation of stories from one time to another, from one environment to another, in accordance with the needs of the spirit, which with changes in the world demands ever new interpretations of everything that we experience and perceive.

I wanted to say all this to the man sitting opposite me, but at the last moment I thought better of it. The last thing I needed was a dispute with a madman. "You," I said, "are obviously not here because of writer's block, but for other reasons. Can you confide in me what they are?"

"No, no," he responded quickly, almost as if he had been waiting for the conversation to veer in that direction, "writer's block is above all my problem, far more than yours. You are sure to find a way back to spinning words about things that have already been written about thousands of times more than they need to be. What about me? How can I make contact with everything, or at least a small part of it, that I wrote about five hundred years ago? How can I add anything, correct anything, complete, delete, when it has already been, a hundred times or more, printed in all the languages that mean something, most often badly translated and very often far from what I was hoping to express? I am cut off from what I created, you are not. For you, writer's block, however unpleasant it is, is something temporary, for me it is final."

"But before you said something else," I objected, "you said that the reason for our problem was fear that we would begin to repeat ourselves, because we had realised that there is nothing new under the sun and even history repeats itself. Now you claim that we shall be cured? And carry on writing?"

My words filled him with amazement. "The reason I speak of myself in a different way should not seem in any way unusual to you, a composer of stories, as you claim to be; you should know that I, too, like all the others, look at myself and my thoughts and convictions differently every day. I am a turbulent river of insights and views, which share only a current, but not content, which is always a thing of the moment, for it can be nothing else. Is it different for you?"

I had to admit that it was not, and the logic of the mental patient seemed increasingly worthy of attention, in contrast to mine, which seemed increasingly inadequate, a mental process that I should not trust.

The patient by the name of Montaigne noticed this. "Regardless of the development of technology, a lot of writers — and when I say a lot, I mean too many — are convinced that since *One Thousand and One Nights* onwards, it is their calling to keep narrating the same stories over and over again. Each time with some changes, which we ourselves are unaware of, but which the readers, who are not stupid, discover immediately, often with the bitter feeling that they have been cheated."

"That may be true," I admitted. "Maybe we have assigned ourselves, or others have assigned us, too much importance and maybe for quite some time our importance was something binding, but now it no longer is, at least not to the extent it was, and maybe because of this we should quit our delusional actions and violating people with our fabrications, in which they then try to find, through various diversions, often arbitrary and very convoluted, a replacement for the life that they cannot live in reality. And fully. But tell me, you who are five hundred years old and can look at your writing objectively from a distance that can cast light on some error you may want to correct, is the era of literary art merely one of the short, perhaps the shortest era in human history? Have we entered a temporary crisis, neither the first nor the last, which we, particularly those of us in whom evil fate has suppressed the ability to spin stories, shall sooner or later overcome? Among the first perhaps those who have taken refuge in this castle for treatment?"

"Dear sir, who believes himself to be a teller of fictional stories," he said, "how many things that yesterday served as the basis for strong belief, today seem like mere stories? The same is true of science, lest you think that literature is the only culprit for the confusion of the human mind, which is sliding irrevocably towards the end of its period in history. There is nothing that we believe as firmly as that of which we know the least."

"Why does it seem to me," I expressed my surprise, "that what we are talking about is more of a problem today than in the Renaissance, when you arrived at your findings and through them earned immortal fame."

"I don't know," he shrugged. "I always strive to tell what I believe to be the truth, but only so far as I dare. But the older I am, the less I dare. Something that those younger than me, particularly the youngest, still full of courage, cannot understand. That with the years, belief in certainty fades and eventually disappears."

"That applies to me, too," I said. "So it is still not clear to me who and what you really are. On the one hand, it seems that you really are the real Montaigne, who by some miracle has stayed alive for five centuries, even though that goes completely against common sense. On the other hand, I am almost convinced that you are bluffing and that the clinic hired you as part of the therapy to play the role of Montaigne. Can you not drop a hint about who you really are?"

"You guessed correctly," he replied. "I'm a professional actor. The clinic hired me to play the role of Montaigne as one of the madmen that they are treating, while at the same time I take part in the treatment of the writer's block, which has brought the clinic quite a bit of money for the treatment of those who really need it. I read Montaigne's essays ten times. But you, if I'm not mistaken, quickly realised that I'm not a madman who thinks he is Montaigne, but that I am the interloper whom all of you are supposed to identify. You succeeded. Congratulations. The others didn't."

"Are they paying you well?" I asked.

"Exceptionally," he gave a broad smile and leaned back, stroking his moustache with both hands as if he wanted to repair the impression he was creating. "I have free accommodation, free food, which is nothing special but at least it involves no effort on my part, I have the opportunity to play secret games with the most respected authors on the planet, who cannot decide what to believe of the lies I spin, I enjoy the thought that I know a lot more than them and that I am perhaps the real Montaigne, who is still alive after five hundred years; what more could a person ask for?"

"You're toying with me," I replied.

"And why not?" he asked in surprise. "You worked out for yourself – as yet, the only one to do so – that I am the interloper who is supposed to be unmasked before the therapists will allow you to proceed to the next phase of treatment."

"Which will be what, in your experience?" I asked.

"I've no idea," he shrugged. "It's the first time I'm playing this role. The last thing I played was Shylock in an amateur performance of *The Merchant of Venice* in southern Germany, just across the border, without payment; then I was offered the chance to earn quite a tidy sum by playing a dead essayist, with the aim of confusing writers suffering from writer's block in order to help them make the quickest possible recovery."

For some time, I said nothing. Nor did he. I got the impression he was enjoying himself.

"Have you told everyone this?" I asked.

"Oh," he gave a bitter smile. "What would I gain from that? In any case, they forbade me from doing so. While in your case, I was told to pretend at the beginning and then admit that I am merely playing Montaigne."

"And why me?" I asked aggressively.

"How would I know?" he replied in surprise. "Maybe because you're the only one who has at least a slight chance of recovery, while the others have no hope. Although I did think of another possibility. You are the only patient and the others, like me, are all actors they hired to play well-known writers as part of your treatment."

"Are your trying to say that from the very beginning, with the exception of me, you are all pretending to be someone that you are not?"

"Maybe you, too," he said, "and you aren't aware of it. What else is literature other than pretending that something fabricated really happened?"

I took a deep breath. "You know what," I said. "You haven't got the slightest idea about literature and its meaning. Whoever prepared you for this role – I assume that trickster Dr Goldberg – didn't do a very good job. Nor have you. Aren't you at all ashamed?"

"Me?" he asked, surprised. "Why? Because in half an hour I'll bank my money and say goodbye to this madhouse, where, it seems to me after all I've experienced, the worst patients are the doctors? Am I not entitled to payment for my work?"

He pushed back the chair and got up. "You were last on my list of conversations. I'm leaving. I apologise profoundly for deceiving you. For an actor, acting is acting, regardless of the location or the public. I bid goodbye with no sense of guilt. I've done what I was hired to do. No offence, but your problem and your literature don't interest me in the slightest."

"Con man!" I shouted after him.

45.

An unexpected visit

In line with the inscrutable laws of fate, we were joined at the castle by Salman Rushdie, who also came as a patient. To me at least, this seemed rather unusual, for the friendly middle-aged man could more easily have found a solution to his creative problem in Buddhism, Hinduism or even Confucianism, or in Tantrism, or Zen, or one of the other branches of Eastern wisdom that in the West, thanks to idiots and self-centred semi-educated individuals, had been degraded, to our immeasurable loss, to "new age".

Mr Rushdie was born to a Muslim family in Kashmir, grew up in Bombay, attended Cambridge University and was infected with the Western way of thinking (at the same time, renouncing the religion of his parents and becoming an atheist). His first novel was a catastrophe, for his second, *Midnight's Children,* he won all the important prizes, and after his *The Satanic Verses* the Ayatollah Khomeini, the Iranian religious leader, issued a fatwa, calling on all the world's Muslims to kill him (the award for his death was at first two million dollars, but was later increased to 3.8 million). He had to go into hiding for years, protected by a special unit of the British police. Thanks to this, more than because of his novels, he achieved world renown, but such is the time in which we live: now it is scandal that determines the extent of one's fame.

Why would an author of his ilk be suffering from writer's block and why would he come to be cured right here in Berghof were questions that would be difficult to answer, even to someone very familiar with both him and his work. That didn't particularly interest me, I was more excited at the possibility of a conversation with him, and as it turned out, Dr Wagner (who would have guessed!) chose me as Rushdie's first interlocutor as soon as he arrived.

Whether Salman Rushdie had also gone through the torments that had been aimed at the rest of us at the beginning, I didn't know. I was interested what he would say when I described to him my problem. He admitted that my name was known to him, but regrettably he had not had the opportunity to read any of my books, mainly because more than literature, he tended towards history, religion, philosophy and similar things. I gave as good as I got, I said that of all his books I had read only *Midnight's Children,* and that fleetingly, for it seemed too extensive. I had deliberately avoided *The Satanic Verses,* I added, perhaps because too much had been spoken and written about it. Of course, I would read them, I concluded, especially now, when fate had planted us at the same table, certainly with the intention of giving us a chance to say something intelligent to each other, or something that might be useful to at least one of us.

"It's very strange that I have encountered you and not, for instance, Bellow," he replied. "Which would, if I'm honest, be preferable. I know his work and we could at least argue honestly, if nothing else. But the Earth creates wonders, it can consume our heart, but the wonders keep coming and our duty is to be attentive, for each one brings new realisations. Let's hope that applies also to our encounter."

"For me, the greatest wonder is that you're sitting opposite me," I said, "for you are the last writer that I would expect to suffer from writer's block."

"I'm not here for writer's block," he gave a cunning smile, "which is perhaps another wonder. I am here to research how writer's block comes about and why even creative writers, like the majority of those being treated here, can be afflicted by it."

I admitted that I had no idea how this would benefit him.

"I'd like to write a novel about a writer who commits suicide because he cannot carry on writing," he said. "Of course, they wouldn't have accepted me here if I didn't pretend that I was also a sufferer, so please don't tell anyone."

"And why confide in me in particular?" I asked.

"Because you are the first I've been asked to talk to," he said. "I'll also tell the others, then I'll wait to see who will be the first to betray me."

"I won't. After all, it's quite possible that I'm also pretending. And all the others. Whatever, one of us is pretending, the interloper, as the therapists call him, and these conversations are supposed to help us uncover which one of us it is."

"And?" he looked at me. "Who do you suspect?"

"If I'm honest, everyone." I decided to keep quiet about Montaigne. "Except myself, of course, for I know who I am. Or at least, I think I do. Of the others, only Graham Greene seems genuine."

"Is he here as well?" he was surprised.

I nodded. "He was my first partner. With all the others I had at least a fleeting feeling that the interloper was sitting opposite me, but in his case I had no doubt whatsoever."

"Strange," he again showed surprise. "Can you tell me what year it is?" The question took me aback. "The year 1993 is drawing to a close," I said, "isn't it for you?"

"Yes," he replied. "Didn't you know that Graham Greene died two years ago, in Switzerland, in Vevey, not far from here?"

It would be hard to say how long I was silent, mulling over his words.

"That's not possible," I said eventually. "Certainly all the newspapers would write about that, it would be on the television news."

"Evidently you overlooked it," he shrugged. "It's not surprising, considering that two people die every second. Since the start of our conversation, more than a thousand have died. Including, I'm sure, some writers."

"It's true that two years ago I was leading a school of creative writing in Papua New Guinea, where the news of Greene's death perhaps didn't reach, but if that's true then the interloper that we are supposed to unmask is the man claiming to be Graham Greene. How is it possible that none of the other patients have heard of his death?"

"How do you know that I'm not also pretending to be Salman Rushdie?" he gave an almost malicious smile. "I do look very like him, but that's no proof. How did I manage to get here, considering that since the fatwa, I've been under the protection of the British police?"

"You know what," I said, "in this clinic, which is basically a lunatic asylum, so many strange things happen that nothing would surprise me anymore. Even one of the patients who is not being treated for writer's block, but who is a mental patient, has been pretending, with the doctors' agreement, as part of our therapy, that he is the director of the clinic. Now, as you probably know, he is leading the therapy for writer's block. In my own case, throughout my life, from when I was a young boy, I have been stalked by a speechless Scheherazade, the image of a woman who appears here and there, in different parts of the world that I travel to, always close by, but without ever looking at me. And if you are thinking that it's a hallucination, the symptom of a deranged mind, I assure you that it is a real, living woman, for I have come close to her and addressed her a number of times, although of course she doesn't hear me, and I could touch her if I dared."

"And why daren't you?"

"I'm afraid I would touch a void," I replied, "which would mean that she really is an apparition, a projection of my mind, and that I am really ill."

"Interesting," he said. "Before we go our separate ways, could you answer one question as if we were both sane and not just me? Why are you convinced that you cannot continue writing? Maybe you're only using writer's block as an excuse to avoid something. Self-knowledge?"

"Self-knowledge?!" I repeated. "Far from it. We writers can only know ourselves through the characters we create and through the stories we tell. It will sound like a cliché, but writing is, more than anything, a search for oneself. Perhaps I can't write anymore because I discovered that I don't actually exist, that I am merely a conglomeration of fabrications, behind which there is nothing tangible, nothing that would have its own autonomy. That what I hold to be reality is actually just the fruit of my imagination. Together with my body and its needs. That there is a network of neurons in my brain that are continually giving birth to my awareness, my thoughts, my feelings, my convictions, which are as firm as nails hammered into wood, until the wood begins to rot and the nails begin to wobble. And to exploit the metaphor to its end: my nails began to wobble, they were left without a firm basis, I ceased to be 'hooked', fixed to the world, I experienced a kind of withdrawal, a turning off. The world and everything that happens in it ceased to interest me to the extent that I no longer wished to think about it, to carry on writing: I got the feeling that I'd said everything I had to say; I don't want to repeat myself. At one moment, I felt myself distant from everything around me; as if I was in a theatre and watching a play that seemed neither particularly good nor interesting. The feeling of distance from the world, from reality, if I call it that for want of a better word, paralysed my fingers, which had for many years enthusiastically, joyfully, even zealously hit the keyboard, and thus every thought that came into my mind sank back into itself and became distant, lost, unnecessary and unimportant. The feeling that I was cut off from the world frightened me, paralysed me. So I came to Berghof. At the wish of my editor, but in the hope that the promised cure would return my drive and élan and the need to keep translating reality into fabrication. Not out of desire for praise and elevation, or to earn a lot of money from it, but because through it I would remain connected with the world, fixed on a hard, solid surface."

And I stopped, almost out of breath.

"You certainly know how to talk, once you get going," said Salman Rushdie.

"I'm sorry. I simply couldn't stop until I'd said what I wanted to say. Although I didn't even know what I wanted to say. But now that I've said what I've said, although I might have preferred to say something else, for as a writer you must surely understand another writer, I feel a sense of relief. Somewhere at the end of the tunnel I've seen a light, to use yet another cliché, but you know yourself how useful they are, and that light is telling me that my writer's block doesn't need treating and that I'm wasting my time here. Perhaps it is time which cut me off from the world, which diminished my interest in it and strengthened my sense of resignation with it and with my fate. Or it was the years, which sooner or later take their toll. The fact is that I don't know what I can still do to reconnect with the world into which I was born. And above all, at this moment I don't even know whether I want to. Wouldn't everything repeat itself? Wouldn't what gets repeated keep repeating? Am I tired of writing or life or both? Would the answer even interest me?"

"I don't know," he shrugged and leaned back. "I'd advise you to become all that you made up in those long years of writing. Realise your imagination, those nails hammered into the ground of reality. Why should not that which grew from the ground of reality return to from where it came? Try. Maybe it won't help you to begin writing again, but you will experience life, from which you have hitherto fled into imagination. Turn around. Each day, each week, each month, become someone else. Not necessarily one of your own characters, it can be a character from world literature."

"Shahryar?" I asked.

"Perhaps him more than anyone. Then your Scheherazade will change from a vision into a real person."

He got up and gave a slight bow. "It's been a pleasure," he said. "I found the conversation useful. I hope you did, too." He turned to leave.

"Just a moment," I stopped him. "There's something else I'd like to ask you."

Without a hint of irritation, he sat back down on the chair and gave me an expectant look.

"Do they let you use the phone?"

His look changed to one of surprise. "Who?"

"The therapists," I strengthened my tone of voice somewhat, perhaps too much. "Do you have access to a phone?"

His surprise also increased. "Don't you?"

"No," I almost bleated back. "None of us who are being treated for writer's block have any contact with the outside world. It is not permitted. They say that it would diminish, perhaps even negate the effect of the treatment."

"I didn't know that," he said. "Maybe they're right, but it seems highly unlikely. Since my arrival here I've called at least ten people. Although, of course, for those of you undergoing treatment it may be different. I'm not here for therapy, but for research."

"But doesn't it seem strange to you," I persisted, "that they allow us no contact with the outside world? That we are in reality prisoners here? Shut away in a psychiatric institution like psychopaths who may not go among people?"

"More than strange," he replied. "So don't be offended if I tell you frankly that I don't believe it. I'll check how it is with the others when their turn comes to talk with me. Do you think it's possible that the prohibition applies only to you?"

"No," I replied. "To everyone, I checked. None of the patients is allowed access to a phone. It seems increasingly to me that everything they do is aimed at turning us into psychopaths and keeping us here until we die, jut to stop us writing again."

"Why are you even undergoing treatment? You've just shown that your imagination is working at full steam. What's to stop you writing all that down? I think that writer's block is a convenient excuse for writers who can't be bothered to write any more. It's already happened to me quite a number of times, but each time I employed the old, unoriginal method that I'm sure you know or at least have heard of. Allow yourself to write badly. Write five to ten pages a day, even if they seem like the work of a novice. Write whatever comes into your head. The next morning you can calmly bin it; no one will read it, no one will know about it. Imagine that you are at work and that you've simply taken a day off. Do that for a few days in a row and you'll soon see that what you've written is no longer suitable for disposal because it reads too well and demands a continuation. It's that simple. Treating writer's block at a clinic in Switzerland? In a medieval castle on a lake? Come on! When I heard about this, I couldn't believe it. That's why I came. I'm really interested to see what the others will tell me. Are all of them so blinded? Or is something else going on here?"

This time, he didn't wait for a reply, he pushed back his chair and left.

46.

Conspiracy?

Rushdie's intention of having thorough conversations with the others was not realised, for the next morning word spread through the castle that my fellow patients had fled. They had done this on the initiative of Martin Amis, who had at first encouraged me to escape, but had evidently then forgotten about me or I had not seemed reliable enough to him. As I waited for the others to join me for breakfast, the only ones to appear were Montaigne, Shakespeare, Graham Greene and Dr Wagner, who silently sat down at my table and for a while said nothing.

Then Dr Wagner told me that during the night a catastrophe had occurred that would seriously damage the reputation of the century-old institution and might even mean its end. Soon after midnight, Martin Amis had led the other patients to the pier in front of the castle, bribing two guards in the process, and because the lake was covered with ice and there was of course no sledge, since the haulier came only at eight in the morning, they had set out on foot across the frozen lake. They did not even think of the possibility that the ice might be of different thickness in different places, but above all, they didn't know that the haulier and his horse-drawn sledge transported people and goods to the castle and back via a well-known zigzag route which stayed firm enough until the start of spring. And so the ice gave way beneath the weight of some of the escapees, the water also sucked in those that selflessly tried to help them, with the result that the only one to get to the other side was Martin Amis, the initiator of the adventure. He was currently in the hands of the Swiss police.

"And why was it necessary to flee the castle?" I asked in agitation. "We came here for voluntary treatment for something that may not even exist, paying a large amount of hard-earned money for the privilege. And you, for God knows what reasons, first tortured us and then turned us into prisoners. Where is Salman Rushdie? I want to see him." When I saw the surprise on Dr Wagner's face, I almost yelled: "I want to see him!"

"That will be difficult," he replied calmly. "Because of the fatwa, he's in hiding and no one knows where he is."

"Do you take me for a fool?" I shouted even louder. "I spoke to him yesterday, we had quite a long conversation, and today he wanted to speak to the other patients."

"I don't know who you spoke to," replied Dr Wagner, "but it certainly wasn't Salman Rushdie."

"How so? The other patients who were having conversations at other tables saw us!"

"Unfortunately, they're not here to confirm that," Dr Wagner gave a sour smile, that even seemed to me slightly malicious.

"And you," I turned on Graham Greene, "you died two years ago, who are you really?"

"Evidently I'm the interloper that you were searching for," he said. "None of you knew that I died two years ago, which means that you well-known authors are not at all interested in other well-known writers. At least one of you should have known that I died."

"I knew," I said. "Not that you had died, but I suspected that you were not Graham Greene. That you were the interloper we were supposed to identify. But God knows how that was supposed to help us. And another thing. Salman Rushdie told me of the date of your death yesterday. How can you claim that he isn't here? Why do you keep lying to me? Why have you lied to everyone from the very beginning?"

"It's not lying," replied Dr Wagner calmly and it surprised me that, in the circumstances, he was ever calmer. "You can learn more about that from Simon Goldberg, the crime writer, who came here for treatment a good year before you. And we convinced him, when he was cured, to stay on and take part in the treatment of others."

"Simon Goldberg?" I almost erupted. "The fake clinic director, the fake psychopath, who is supposedly the famous writer of crime novels, is he really who I think he is?"

"I think he is. But you know: it's hard in an institution like ours to be fully convinced of anything without a shadow of a doubt," replied Dr Wagner. "If you don't want to eat the fried egg, which has now gone cold, I'll call the orderly to take you to Mr Goldberg in his room, where you'll have the chance to talk."

Simon Goldberg, whom I had first met in his role as clinic director and then as a psychopath being treated, had not changed much since I'd last seen him. Fragile and bent over, as if twisted by arthritis, he was sitting on the edge of bed, smiling in a docile, almost apologetic way.

"I was expecting you," he said, when the orderly who had brought me left. He pointed towards the chair by the bed; I moved it away slightly and sat down.

"Did they tell you I was coming?"

"No," he shook his head, "I knew that you'd come sooner or later, since they haven't given either of us much choice."

"What do you mean?"

"They knew that I was the only one who could tell you what was really going on here and they knew that I would want to apologise for everything, as my feeling of guilt gives me no peace."

"Why should you apologise? Evidently, they forced you in one way or another to play a false role. I doubt you enjoyed it."

"You're wrong," he hung his head as if in shame. "I enjoyed it tremendously. Not to my own good, of course, but I wasn't aware of that. The game drew me in and I finally got an opportunity to become an actor, which I always wanted, but no academy would take me. That, and only that, is why I began to write stupid crime novels, about which I still don't have a positive opinion, but people read them and read them, and I earned a lot of money."

"Until writer's block hit you," I said. "And you came here for treatment."

"It would be hard to call it writer's block. I think I just became sick of writing pointless literature, where each successive novel was ever more similar to a previous one. One day, I realised that after thirty years I was once again writing my first novel. Then something shifted inside me and I said: enough. But the publisher didn't want to hear that, I had a contract, I had received a large advance, I was threatened with legal action. He sent me here; he said they'd sort me out."

"And did they?"

"You've been here long enough to know what a charade all this is. Our so-called therapists have no idea what writer's block is. Their intention was never to cure any of us. How could they, considering that I, one of the patients, had to explain basic things to them? Their goal was always different."

"But the best of the best in world literature gathered here," I objected. "On what basis did Saul Bellow, Javier Marías, Martin Amis and J. M. Coetzee come here?"

"On what basis do millions of people buy and read my mediocre crime novels? Marketing, my friend. Marketing is the answer to your question. You know what kind of times we're living in. Someone deliberately sets in motion some gossip, someone else is paid to give some evidence, as we call a certain kind of lie, for the rumour, someone else again is paid to publicly stumble upon this evidence, then the story is grabbed by the media, they inflate it and bang on about it, the so-called evidence is eventually, thanks to suitably awarded journalists, shown to be valid and many of us who make a living by stringing words together, with more or less success, more or less quality, in the fear that our career is at its end, join in, hoping that we can help."

"Did you become a cynic after you came to the castle or were you one before?"

"I speak from the heart and from experience," he replied, "I was never a cynic; if I had been, then perhaps my novels would have been better."

"In short," I said, "your writer's block didn't disappear, you found out that they couldn't cure you here."

"What writer's block?" For the first time since I entered his room, he changed position slightly, leaning forwards, first to the left and then to the right. "Writer's block

is a myth. Sometimes we write and it flows, other times we get stuck and for a while we can't write. It can't be any different for you. Now and then words freeze because it's not the right time for writing; things have to be thought through first. Or we are gripped by the fear – you who are seen as serious authors, probably more often than we poor crime hacks – that what we are currently writing isn't good enough and will disappoint our readers. Perfectionism. No word is good enough, every sentence is lacking something. There are other causes: one of our parents dies, our wife cheats on us, we get flu, we aren't out in the sun often enough and the lack of vitamin D cripples us with tiredness. Some semi-literate narcissist publishes a destructive review and we believe him. But more than that, we are assailed by the fear that others will believe him and our fame will begin to slide down the steep slope to oblivion. We are so good at being stupid. We, who hold ourselves to be intelligent."

Towards the end, he spoke ever faster and almost mechanically, but at the same time more convincingly, of which he was evidently aware, for he suddenly took a breath, paused and relaxed.

"I talk too much," he said. "Maybe because, for the first time in a long time, I do not have to act. After all, you came to me, or were sent to me, so that we could clear things up. Probably you already had enough of me when I was pretending to be the director of the clinic."

"You acted very convincingly," I praised him. "Everything happening here was convincing. Although it was barely believable, I never thought for a moment that I was being conned. As far as your claim that writer's block is a myth is concerned, I cannot agree with you. Many poets and writers have experienced it. Some have killed themselves because of it, some lost their mind and ended up in institutions like this for ever. Even Tolstoy, towards late middle age, fell victim to depression that he couldn't shake off, until he found a solution in religion. Although…"

"Although?" he prompted me. I knew that we had got to the point where I should mention Scheherazade and risk the possibility that he may include me among the mental patients. But no, I didn't want to reveal my secret to Goldberg, who ever since my arrival I believed to be mad and who I still couldn't swear was in his right mind; I was afraid that it would spoil our relationship, which was gradually moving towards reality.

"Although," I led the conversation in another direction, "many successful writers have discovered and published quite a number of ideas about what you need to do to get the writing flowing again. I've tried everything. I've tried, as Maya Angelou advises, simply writing down everything that comes into my head, even if it has no connection with other words, as she wrote every day for two weeks 'the cat sat on the mat, that is that, not a rat' and added similar nonsense until the Muse saw that she was serious and she said: Right, I'm coming back. I've tried that myself, numerous times, but when the words started to flow it was some other, new story, not the one where I had stopped in mid-sentence. Nor was Hemingway's strategy of 'restraining the flow' (of verbal ejaculation) of any help to me; at least, not with the novel which had caused the blockage. Deliberately stopping in mid-sentence or mid-paragraph at a moment when the words are flowing, in the hope that the next day continuing will be that much easier, is certainly good advice (G. B. Shaw used this method), but I have never stopped intentionally, the words stopped on their own. I know that many authors avoid writer's block by following special rituals, such as Toni Morrison, who every morning, before dawn, made herself coffee and then, coffee in hand and with the taste in her mouth, she waited for the first light of day to shine through the window of her workroom; in that way, she felt she was offering a kind of prayer to the Muse, who entered the room together with the daylight. It didn't help me at all."

He was silent for some time, staring into space; it seemed as if the torrent of my words had sent him to sleep.

"You are probably aware," he said eventually, I felt with hint of bitterness, "that we have the same publisher."

"I know," I didn't hesitate, "my editor even told me that you were being treated here. And so I was that much more surprised to come across the clinic director, who was no other than Simon Goldberg."

"Although we publish our books with the same publisher, which is big and reputable, we don't have the same editor. Yours organised payment for your treatment, whereas mine said that I was wealthy enough and that they didn't have enough money for such things. You are, of course, a serious writer who writes serious novels, whereas I am shit."

"Come on," I said. "Why do yourself down? Even James Joyce liked to read detective novels. Sherlock Holmes is the most famous person in the world. Genre writing has its place in the literary pantheon, and I am afraid that, sooner or later, it will be discussed as seriously as other so-called serious novels."

"You may be right," he replied. "But regrettably, I won't live to see that. I've begun to think of committing suicide. Because of all the terrible things I've done to people in this institution."

"You said that you were forced and that you even enjoyed playing your role. Are you finally going to tell me what's behind the events that ended in the drowning of four writers of world renown as they tried to make their escape from a madhouse? For in reality, this is not a clinic for treating writer's block, it is a lunatic asylum; I hope you have realised this yourself and that you won't try to fob me off with yet another fabrication. You are no longer the director of the clinic. The game is over, you're just another victim."

"Do you hate me?" he looked straight into my eyes, almost with fear.

"No," I said. "After everything that's happened here, there's no room for such a sentiment. At the end of every story, all that matters is the truth."

"I agree," he nodded. "But it's not necessarily the case that what appears to be the truth actually is the truth."

"No offence," I said, "but I'm weary of all this beating about the bush. Be glad that your acting career is over – save yourself, it's not too late. What's going on in this castle? Who and what are we, including you, the victims of?"

"Will you believe me," he again looked me straight in the eye, almost pleadingly, "if I tell you what should remain a secret? You won't think I'm still acting and that it is part of the deceit?"

"I can't promise that."

"Okay," he said. "The whole truth, very simply, is that we are here – for some, I should say that they were here – only because the board of the institution signed an agreement with five universities, specifically with five university departments of psychology from five countries – Switzerland, Germany, England, Netherlands and the United States – that the doctors here, headed by Dr Wagner, should carry out research and write an extensive report as to whether there is a connection between creativity and psychopathology. Were the greatest minds in history not only geniuses, but also to some extent mentally ill? The purpose of the research is to find an answer to the question whether every mental patient is really just a patient or should we seek within him the basis of suppressed, inactivated genius? Which would of course change the foundations of psychiatry and bring someone a Nobel Prize."

I was silent for some time. While it seemed possible, I couldn't quite convince myself that medical science could afford something so scandalous. What about Hippocrates?

Primum non nocere; first, do no harm. Of course, many things happen in the world, the worst has already happened and would again, but that kind of conspiracy would involve too many people to remain uncovered.

Had Simon Goldberg been persuaded to reveal the conspiracy to me? To what end? So that they could then say it was just a story from a mentally confused individual, who first pretended to be the director of the clinic and then much else besides?

"And now?" I asked him. "Will they allow you to leave? And me?"

He shook his head. "I'm afraid we'll be here until we breathe our last. If the truth came out, too many important people would end up in jail, or at least in court."

47.

The end of the story?

He was right. The story was just made for a public scandal. The gutter press the world over would write about it. The organs of power would get involved, along with the police, and many people would get what they deserved and more. But the thought of staying in Berghof until the end of days did not enthuse me and so I began to think how to escape without drowning in the lake on the way. I thought that Scheherazade could help me with this. Although she hadn't appeared to me for some time, I knew that she was always close by, visible or not, and that my fate was in her hands, for I had become one of those stories that she was unable to tell to Shahryar because she had become weary and fallen silent.

How could I force her to show herself, to return to the centre of my fate, to carry it forward, to add to it what she had to add, and to conclude it? I had no idea. Because talks with Montaigne and Shakespeare had begun to seriously bore me, I spent most of my time in my room, writing notes so as not to forget anything and every so often I would stare through the window to the church on the hill where, twice a day, two orderlies with sticks would drive groups of patients, men in the morning, women in the afternoon, to get some exercise and breathe the fresh air. They didn't stay long, they circled the church and returned to the castle by the same path. Spring had come very early, the sun was warm and the view of the snow-capped peaks had never been so magnificent.

Several times I told Dr Wagner that I would like to walk to the church, for I hadn't been in the fresh air for a long time, but he didn't allow me; he said that my case still wasn't finished, I wasn't cured yet and that now my writer colleagues had left me alone, that would take a lot longer than it otherwise would have done.

"But I came for treatment voluntarily, my publisher paid for me, you can't turn me into a prisoner, it's against the law."

He shrugged. "Our duty is to cure our patients, and when they are cured they can go where they choose."

Nothing did the trick. I could wander round the castle, but they wouldn't let me out.

And then she finally appeared! One morning, when I was looking through the window, admiring the flamboyance of the sunlit mountains, I saw her. She was leaning against the wall of the church, tiny and barely visible, as if waiting for someone. She kept changing position and then leaning against the wall again. She looked as if she was staring towards the castle walls, towards my window. I opened the shutters, stood on tiptoe, pushed my head outside, and then put my hand out and waved to her. Of course, I didn't believe that she saw me, for apparitions do not see those they appear to, but then something happened that I had not expected.

She waved back. My stalker had come to life and was waving to me! Delusion or reality? Once again I waved to her and once again she waved back. Then she gestured for me to come to her. She pointed to the church three times and then gestured to me decisively. It was more than obvious: she was inviting me to a secret assignation behind the church, God knows for what purpose. It was the first time she had made contact with me, the first time she had shown that she was not an apparition. I was so surprised that I couldn't believe it. However, her invitation looked like both an order and a promise; there was something she wanted to tell me.

But how was I to get to her if I wasn't allowed out of the castle? Even if I managed to slip out of one of the doors, they would see me and catch me before I got to the church. I could climb through a window, but the ground was five metres below and I would be sure to break all my limbs or my skull, and kill myself. I could reach my goal unseen only if I joined the group of men that the two orderlies took to the church and back every morning.

I looked for Montaigne and asked him to lend me for a short while the striped pyjama jacket worn by the patients, which I then put on over a t-shirt. I only hoped that none of the orderlies would notice me, let alone recognise me. Since I knew through which door the patients were led out of the castle and back again, the very next morning I waited for an opportunity, and in the huddle of more or less confused men, made my way to the church without difficulty. Since they always circled it before they went back along the path to the castle, I was gripped with fear that they would spot Scheherazade and so I cautiously dropped back to the rear. The two orderlies were still at the head of the column, where they could talk to each other.

But there was no sign of Scheherazade. When the last of the patients disappeared round the corner, I was left alone behind the church. Once again, the victim of delusion, although this time a different one. Evidently, my self-hypnosis was changing. Had I only imagined that she was inviting me to come to her?

But then I saw something that astonished me, to say the least. Ever since my arrival, I had been convinced, like the other patients, that the castle stood on an island in the middle of the lake. So I expected to see, behind the church, the other part of the lake, which I thought the hill with the church hid when viewed from the castle. But on the other side there was no water! Instead of lake, I saw a narrow, gentle slope overgrown with spruces, which dropped towards a depression with fields and meadows, which soon became an alpine forest that rose into the hills before the mountains in the background. On the left and right of the depression, I could see the rounded edges of the lake, which were not visible from the castle. The castle did not stand on an island, but on a peninsula, which protruded into the lake, along with the hill where the church stood and its graveyard, and with a rocky end on which someone, for some reason, had built a castle.

But why was there no road to the castle, why was the only access by boat from the opposite shore? For I could see a road on the other side of the low area, right beside the forest that rose into the hills; it went to the right, past apparently endless orchards and fields, and on to a small village that was barely visible. Was the area of lowland in front of me owned by someone who had refused to allow access to the castle this way, as it would disturb him or split his farmed land in two?

Finding an answer to this question didn't seem urgent; I rushed down the slope, on the way removing the striped pyjama jacket that I had borrowed from Montaigne, so that no one would see me as an escaped mental patient, and ran on in a long-sleeved t-shirt which I had put on beneath the thin pyjama top so as not to be cold, for in spite of it being spring and sunny, the temperature in the Swiss Alps wasn't at all comfortable; I ran on, stumbled and fell and picked myself up, and tried to find the easiest way through the spruces, to the meadow in the depression, where it became easier; I ran, so out of breath that I was gasping, all the way to the road, where I crept into the trees on the other side and collapsed onto the ground, leaning against the trunk of the nearest tree and rested until I had gathered enough strength to walk along the narrow gravel road, intended more for tractors and small trucks going to the fields than real traffic, and to turn left towards the small village, which I reached after more than two hours walking, including some breaks for a rest. The whole time, in my thoughts and my heart, I was thanking Scheherazade for rescuing me from captivity. And it seemed increasingly unlikely that she was merely an apparition, not also a real person, living in the same world as me.

You can imagine that I had to overcome a number of difficulties after that, but once I could prove my identity with a number of select phone calls, I managed to return to London. Nanny, who the whole time had been looking after the house, almost fainted when she saw me. She hugged me for almost ten minutes, gasping: "Oh my God, oh my God, oh my God! My child has risen from the dead!"

And that was roughly how I felt for some time. I didn't tell her where I'd been or what had happened to me, and she had been trained not to invade the privacy of those she was caring for. I called a number of friends and acquaintances among doctors and specialists, who examined me from head to toe, did all the possible tests and measurements, and in the end told me that everything was okay; to check my mental state, they directed me towards psychologists and psychiatrists, but I didn't believe that they could be of any help. Instead, I began writing: what I had experienced was so unusual that I didn't want to forget it.

My writing flowed, the treatment for writer's block had evidently worked, and the moment came when I plucked up enough courage to visit the editor who had sent me to Switzerland and paid for my treatment. I wanted to thank him and at the same time brutally beat him up.

Sadly, I had no opportunity for either step, for when I arrived at the publisher's I was met by a young man with a short moustache and red hair cut in punk style in the centre of his head; at first I thought he was the doorman. He was polite, but somewhat condescending, as if unaware that he was dealing with an author of world renown, let alone the most illustrious author of the publisher that employed him. He told me that my editor had had a kind of crisis, probably triggered by his wife leaving him, which had grown to the extent that they had to fire him. As far as he know, added the young man, he has set off on a round the world trip, and he has taken his place.

I told him that I had signed a contract with the publisher for a novel and asked him whether, considering the change of editor, it was still valid. "Of course," he replied, "our contracts are legally certified. But I am told that you were being treated for writer's block; did you still manage to finish the novel?"

"Here it is!" I placed on the table five hundred pages of printed text.

"Great. I'll start reading it straight away. I'll call you."

He indicated with a gesture that our meeting was over, and so I got up and left without a word.

He called me two days later. "Unusual," he said. "Barely believable. Did you make all this up or is there anything autobiographical in the novel?"

I told him that I honestly didn't know, probably a bit of both. However, even fabricated things don't fall from the sky, but grow from the soil of reality, where they have their roots, even if their above-ground part is ten times more visible, I explained. I asked him if they would publish the book. There was a short silence.

"In view of the contract, I have no choice."

But ten days later, he got in touch again. "I'd like to inform you that I sent your text to Martin Amis, Saul Bellow, Javier Marías, J. M. Coetzee and Salman Rushdie. All of them, with the exception of the last mentioned, threatened to sue for slander if the book is published. You will understand that because of this we cannot publish your novel."

***

"How could they sue you?" asked the Carer in surprise, when I had finished my narrative about writer's block, "didn't they drown trying to escape from the clinic?"

"I don't know. Perhaps Goldberg was lying, which wouldn't surprise me. Or I experienced the whole thing in my imagination and then wrote the story as dictated to me by Scheherazade, who planted all the details in my head. Often I can almost hear her dictating words to me as I write. I think that most of my works have been written at her dictation."

"You'll find another publisher without any difficulty," said the Carer. "Let them sue you. They would achieve nothing. There'd be a proper scandal and you'd sell thousands of copies!"

"Actually," I said, "that's not a bad idea."

48.

Great changes

Two weeks later, I threw away my crutches, as my ankle had healed to the extent that I could walk without them, although slowly and not too far. And of course, I had a limp. I would have to get used to that, said the Carer, like the pain in my left wrist and the limited movement in my left hand, especially my fingers when I bent them in a particular direction, and I would have to avoid lifting anything heavy. For both my wrists and my ankle I would need physiotherapy for quite some time, she said, at least for three months, and because I'd probably already begun to be bored by her, she would find me a new, equally good carer, for she knew a lot of them.

"What about you?" I asked, aghast, "what will you do?"

"Oh," she shrugged, "I'll find something, at least twenty people a day break a limb."

"I'm sure you won't be left without work," I said, "but there's also me, your patient, to think of. After all we've been through together, you can't just leave me. Have I offended you in some way, have I started to bore you with my stories, don't I pay you enough?"

She was silent, as if looking for the right reply.

"I felt that in the months you've been caring for me, we have become friends," I continued, sounding slightly offended. "After all, we live here like man and wife, if you put aside the fact that we are not sleeping together. Your departure would kill me, I can't imagine the depression I'd sink into."

"You're right," she finally spoke, just when I'd decided she would say nothing. "We do live like man and wife, with the difference that very few husbands and wives get on as well as we do. But we also live like mother and baby. Would you even survive without me? I dressed and undressed you, bathed you, fed you with a spoon while you had both hands in plaster, I combed and shaved you for quite some time, put your shoes on, went to the shop for you, cooked for you, cleaned the house, performed ten different professions for you, including confidant and comforter, which was the least demanding of them all. I enjoyed doing so, it brought me satisfaction and happiness, it gave me the feeling that you saw me as an equal, as someone who understands you."

"That's all true," I said quickly, "but..."

"But," she interrupted me, "if we are already living like man and wife, why aren't we that? Have you never thought of the possibility that we might become so? Officially?"

Her words not only surprised me, but really shocked me.

"Look," I tried to object, "aren't we a little old for that kind of thing?"

"I'm not thinking of sex!" she raised her voice. "I've kneaded and twisted your willy in every possible way while bathing you for long enough that it doesn't give me any particular pleasure. And can't you see that I have drooping breasts and wrinkled skin, and look older than I actually am? I'm talking about feelings, Mr Writer, about closeness, trust, intimacy, about the deep connection that we have felt for some time and which is growing deeper. And which gives me, at least, a feeling of safety that I've never known before."

I saw that she had tears in her eyes. Her words had shaken me. And connected me to the feelings inside that I had been trying to suppress for some time. Although I would dearly like to express them with more or less the same words that she had used. I was flooded with a deep sense of gratitude that she had done so. For if they had emerged from my mouth, they would have sounded sentimental. And the last thing I dared to do was to embarrass myself. Now we were both embarrassed. I knew how I should respond to her words, for our shared embarrassment not to get even worse. For if it did, we would never be able to return to the point around which life could turn in a new direction.

"I didn't dare," I said. "Cripple that I am, I didn't dare ask whether it would be a good idea for us to marry. I mean formally. For in essence, we've been married for quite some time. Allow me to ask you now. Would you take me as your husband?"

The tears that she had kept holding back poured down her cheeks, she covered her eyes with her hands and ran from the room. I sat there like a fool, not knowing what I had triggered, what was happening or to what extent whatever I perceived was real or the fruit of my confused imagination. "Scheherazade," I heard my voice deep inside me, "I implore you, place me for at least some time on solid ground. You are responsible for my unhappiness, I'm broken, please now don't break my heart and soul. Let me not be mad, not mad!" "Okay," responded Scheherazade inside me. "Let's do it. Tomorrow, I'll go to the registrar's office and arrange everything. Where are your documents?"

I opened my eyes and realised that the words had been spoken by the Carer, who had returned and was standing right in front of me.

"Where shall we live? Here or in London?"

"As far as possible from the scene of my accident," I said.

"I knew you'd say that," she replied approvingly, already my wife, already deciding about things that affected not only her but also me.

***

The house in Ljubljana, where we intended to come for short holidays, I left in the care of her cousin, who by coincidence, or so it seemed, had just returned from Austria, where she had lost her job as an accountant. We travelled to London and settled in my house there, where Nanny and her assistant awaited us. They knew that I'd had a serious accident, but they didn't know that I was bringing the Carer, my wife, with me.

I immediately felt that they were not quite alright with this, especially Nanny, who still saw me as her unofficial adopted child, "her boy", who should have asked her whether he could marry, and the assistant probably didn't feel it was alright that now, if she wished to stay, she would have to cook for a stranger, who, I immediately saw, she did not like.

"Facts are facts, Nanny," I said, "so be glad that you will have excellent care available when you need it, for my wife is a professional physiotherapist and carer."

"I'd rather care for her," said Nanny, "the air in London is so bad, she'll immediately fall ill. And in any case, you have become an invalid who can hardly move. And look at the scars on your head. The one on your forehead looks like a devil's sign. Terrible! You almost died before me. Doesn't your Slovakian bride know how to look after you?"

"Slovene, Nanny," I corrected her. "The fact that I am alive is entirely down to her, and her only. She came into my life due to God's will, like a guardian angel."

"Don't talk such nonsense," she rebuked me. "You never did before. Why now? Will you carry on writing?"

"What do you advise, Nanny?"

"You don't know how to do anything else!" she said. "You don't even know how to look after the garden and I won't be able to manage the jungle behind the house for much longer."

"I'll sort it all, Nanny," I said, "I'll hire a gardener, and my wife will care for our physical and mental health. I particularly recommend her massages."

"God massages me," said Nanny, "preparing me for entry to his kingdom. Did you have a lot of guests at the wedding?"

The question was so unexpected that I almost laughed out loud.

"A hundred and fifty," said my wife quickly, evidently unable to accept us talking about her as if she wasn't present. This was of course not nice of us, but I couldn't rebuke Nanny, that would be against all the rules of our relationship. Nor could I correct my wife, for then I would be breaking all the rules of *our* relationship. I couldn't reveal that there hadn't actually been a wedding celebration, it took place in front of the registrar in the presence of two witnesses, homeless guys that we collected on the way, buying them elegant clothes and rewarding them after the ceremony with an additional wad of cash. Nanny would have a stroke if she knew. To us, it seemed something special, something original in a world where things are boringly the same and boringly repeat themselves.

"Is your wife also someone important?" Nanny spoke to me again, instead of her.

"She's important to me, Nanny," I said in a slightly sharper tone, "very important, so please address her when you speak of her in her presence – after all, she's standing right in front of you. And please don't forget that her word will carry the same weight as mine when it comes to life in this house. Please, both of you," I also looked at the cook, "bear this in mind, for she isn't a guest, from today onwards this is her home."

"You've really surprised me," said Nanny petulantly and, bent over as she had become during my absence, she skulked off towards her room.

"I'll go and make something to eat," said the cook. "Anything particular you'd like?"

"Actually," observed my wife, "from now on, I'll cook. My husband has got so used to my food that it will be hard for him to change."

49.

Times of flood, times of drought

So I had to let the cook go. Nanny took this very badly, for while I was away they had grown accustomed to each other. On the other hand, my wife who was also still my carer, was right when she demanded for herself, for both of us, a normal life, a continuation of the relationship we had established in Ljubljana and which continued in London: physiotherapy exercises that became gradually less painful, faster walks in the nearby park, endless conversations about stories and memories and experiences before we slept. We slept in my father's room, in his double bed, which was wide enough for us not to have to touch, although every now and then we could turn to each other and embrace, far from any thoughts of sex (although every day, morning and evening, the Carer massaged my naked body), and remain embraced until we felt that we were safe, that we had each other, that we got on and that was how it would continue.

Nanny spent most of her time in her room and prepared her own food, although she had almost stopped eating, for she didn't want to touch a morsel of what my wife had cooked, regardless of my accusations that she was acting like a child.

I knew that from simple gratitude I had to put up with her, for she had no one else.

My wife advised me to start writing again. After all, I had chosen *storying* as the meaning of life, and sooner or later Scheherazade was bound to appear to me and bring me inspiration that could not be resisted. In the meantime, she became familiar with London, which she had visited only once before, many years earlier, when she was in secondary school; since it offered more than she dared to imagine, I would have enough peace and quiet to write something new. And exceptional.

Regrettably, after my return to London, perhaps because of the stress I was experiencing at my new way of life, one of my dry periods began. Periods of verbal droughts and floods had occurred in my life in their own way, in which I sought in vain an order or pattern that might help me forecast when one would end and another begin. To write persistently, regularly and emphatically, to plan narrative structures and their thematic framework, as if building a rocket for a flight to a planet that I would discover only on the way there – that I couldn't do, it was not me. I really envied "engineers" of novels and stories who knew how to produce and develop a structure in advance, on which they would then merely hang carefully chosen words and sentences. In my case, a flood could be caused by a single chance sentence that I heard at another table in a restaurant or that suddenly arose from the earth of reflection on nothing in particular, and then the next day or even immediately triggered a flow that I was unable to stop; it grabbed me and took me with it like a torrent, washed me into ever deeper and wider waters, even if I resisted and grabbed hold of some branch on the bank, in the fear that I would drown in the stormy flood of words and that water would find its way into my brain.

Most often, the verbal storm would cease as suddenly as it started, and only then, after a short break, could I begin to seek in the flood of words elements of narrative, put them in order, give them meaning and create channels through which the superfluous words could flow away. Quite often it happened that the drainage channels got blocked and too many words remained in the lake for me to be able to order them and form a story that I would dare to offer for reading. Then I had no choice but to get as far away as possible from the misguided mass of words, usually by setting fire to it or setting off on an aimless journey to some unfamiliar part of the world, the novelty of which would ventilate my mind and dry up the remnants of sterile water. If I had merely locked the unmanageable text in a drawer, I wouldn't have been able to resist the temptation to take it out and waste a month or so of my life on trying to salvage the unsalvageable; after two such cases, that was more than clear to me.

Thankfully, the drainage channels didn't get blocked too often; usually, I managed to divert the flood of words into a current that also pulled the reader with it, sometimes into a torrent, sometimes into a slow flowing but powerful river with tributaries that widened it, deepened it and even redirected it, without that being predictable or even indicated at the start of the voyage. In that way, and never differently, did my best works appear, for some of which I had received awards, despite the shabby, personally coloured and clique-based critical attacks. Quite early in my career, if I can call it that, I realised (and changed it into a gospel) that it was not worth writing and publishing books that no one reads. Although experience soon offered me evidence that truly good and important books are read by a lot fewer people than crime novels, sentimental personal confessions and books linked to media scandals.

The verbal floods from which good, successful narratives arose were not always followed by word droughts; often, one flood followed another, and only then, when I was exhausted and "wet through" did a period come when there wasn't a cloud on the horizon and the sun began to scorch, while my brain became increasingly dried out, to the extent that I was gripped by the fear that I would never write again. That wasn't writer's block, it was something else, it was a time when the imagination needed a holiday. But it was precisely in the dry periods when the most interesting things happened in my life; I got the most invitations to international festivals and readings, the most requests to visit this or that university and give a lecture on literature in general, but above all, on my method of writing – the greatest proof that the world valued me.

Of course, many such invitations came during times of flood, but then I threw them in the wastebasket, because I was unable to respond to them; and as soon as I threw them away, I forgot about them. But in times of drought, invitations rescued me from the emptiness that yawned inside me, the emptiness of my imagination, the death- defying wish to create a parallel reality into which others could move through reading. The droughts were the only thing that enabled contact with the world that most people considered real, and so I accepted most invitations and requests, at least with gratitude, if not enthusiasm.

50.

The Booker Prize

I had serious reservations when I was invited to be on the selection committee for the Booker Prize; not only because I had never received that award (just as Martin Amis had not, in spite of numerous nominations, so that he became known as a "perennial nominee"), but primarily because it seems to me that writers should not evaluate the work of our colleagues (each of us has his own style, which may not suit others) for in this case we cannot be completely objective. Of course, there is no objectivity in literature, every book is subject to the subjective judgement of the reader, every reader. It is a question of ethics: writers are people, too, and we quickly succumb, even if we are unaware of this, to low inclinations, such as envy, antipathy, revenge and others that might not even have names.

Convinced that I would know how to avoid all this, I eventually accepted the invitation and confirmed my participation in selecting the prize-winner; this was regardless of the fact that a few days earlier, I had read in the *The Times* that in the last twenty years, on only two occasions had the prize winner acquired popularity among readers. In a way, this fact suggested (to me and the other jurists) that we should choose a text that, without the prize, would be read by very few people. But already after the first meeting, it seemed to us (perhaps especially to me) that the path to our goal would be tortuous and risky. It was clear from the start that each of us would ride his own horse, nor did I delude myself that the choice of winner would be anything other than a compromise between five literary tastes.

I recalled what the editor of a Slovakian literary journal that gave a national prize every year for best short story had confided to me: that they had once secretly nominated three juries and that each had recommended their five nominees, not one of which were among those chosen by the other two. Of course, each jury had also chosen its own prize winner. I hoped, at least in the case of the Booker, that the jury would achieve a high or at least minimal level of consensus, although I didn't delude myself that we would reach this consensus without horse trading or, even worse, mutual insults. Everyone who is nominated as a jury member for such a prestigious prize as the Booker suddenly sees him or herself (even if he did not before) as a "connoisseur of literature", as someone who knows what is good and what is worse, and who, God forbid, in this sudden elevation, from honesty to oneself if not to others, will not doubt in the absolute validity of his or her criteria.

In addition to myself, the jury comprised the novelist Angela Carter, the award- winning literary editor Terence Kilmartin, the Australian poet Peter Porter and the novelist Fay Weldon, who was the jury president. The first meeting was pleasant and sweetened with an abundance of mutual compliments, but this was, we all knew, merely an obligatory but empty formality. The difficulties began when we began to read the recommended books. It turned out that the publishers, a key but most unreliable link in the book production chain, somehow knew which of the books they had published were "Bookerish" and which had no chance of making it among the nominees, and so they sent us primarily works which suited this prejudice. There was nothing for it but to ask them to send us additional works.

When we began reading more than a hundred selected novels, it emerged that the publishers and other recommenders of "Bookerish" works (doubtless on the basis of previous prize winners) saw them as something gloomy and overloaded with words (not to mention "innovative" treatment of words), as well as "literary" and "experimental" (even if the "experiments" were repeating long ago written off experiments), but above all works permeated by feelings of post-colonial or social guilt (and thus politically correct, at least implicitly critical to everything that the United Kingdom had done in the past), plus (even worse) works that painfully anatomised the fragile feelings of members of the upper middle class, very often successful writers who could not stand it that their "realisations" and feelings were not taken seriously.

Among the works I received there was not one that I would read without a feeling of duty, merely because the text drew me in so strongly that I was unable to stop. Not in order to discover who murdered whom, but to see how many of the balls tossed into the air the author finally managed to catch. There are of course a number of different kinds of anticipation when reading, the greatest being curiosity regarding what impression the book will leave at the end. While reading the Booker Prize nominations, among more than a hundred I was "gripped" by a mere seven, and for completely different reasons. At the meeting where the jury was supposed to reach agreement about the list of six finalists, it turned out (as I had expected) that not a single one of my suggestions was approved by anybody else. But as members of the jury (for which we were, who would have thought, paid) we simply had to choose the work to which we would give the award; none of us could see a way out other than quitting the jury (with what arguments?).

We began reading once again, each their own choice of twenty of the more than hundred novels, which at the next meeting we had to narrow down to a shortlist of six – a task which to all of us, especially me, seemed impossible. The administrator of the prize – in spite of numerous attempts I am unable to recall his name – enjoyed our meetings the most; he was able to crack jokes and even make fun of particular works, a luxury that we could not afford. After numerous disagreements, which often grew into loud disputes, we were left only with the novel *Flying to Nowhere* by the poet John Fuller (which none of us was really convinced was a novel), *Shame* by Salman Rushdie, Graham Swift's *Waterland*, a work by Malcolm Bradbury, whose title I've forgotten, and *The Life & Times of Michael K* by J. M. Coetzee, which seemed the least contentious to three out of the five of us, including myself, although we were troubled (how petty jury members can be!) by both the title of the novel and the name of its author.

And even that did not satisfy the three conditions set by Philip Larkin for evaluating the true worth of a novel: "Do I believe all this? Does it even interest me? Will it interest me in a year's time?" Selection of a novel for a prestigious award in the hands of five randomly selected jurists is anything but a hundred metre sprint, where it is completely clear who the winner will be (and this applies to other sports, as well); it is more reminiscent of a hot potato, where any amount of tossing from hand to hand will not remove the danger of the hand getting burnt. Although we agreed that the nominated novels which do not win are often more interesting than the prize winner, not one of us could find the answer to the question as to why that was so.

Must it be so? Often, even novels that publishers, infected with some kind of "award" pattern, do not even send for consideration are better, while some authors, including John Le Carré, do not even allow themselves to be nominated.

Hats off to them. To the devil with awards. The feeling that I experienced as a jury member, an experience for which many people would be willing to strangle their own grandmother, was most similar to the fear that I might find myself among the nominees. What would I do? Would I humbly (I couldn't do it with pride) bow to the conspiracy of the publishing industry, which tries with all its might to sell as many fabricated stories as possible, which people simply cannot stop writing, although there were too many of them long ago, most of them remaining unsold on shelves, and which were increasingly similar to each other, so that it was necessary to read only one to have read at the same time (unless you had a very short memory span) a thousand others?

51.

Cruelty in Mumbai

In the end, I was unable to take part in the final meeting of the jury, at which we were supposed to select the prize winner, for I was attacked in the middle of the night by a severe, unusual headache, which even a double dose of paracetamol did nothing to alleviate. The Carer, visibly concerned, watched over me until morning. When I got up to go to the toilet, I banged into the door frame and felt dizzy, unable to maintain my balance. I made my way back to bed with difficulty. The Carer asked me how much I had drunk the previous day at my meetings. Perhaps too much, I admitted. Perhaps this was just the consequence of overdoing it. Nevertheless, she asked me to pull out of any further involvement in the jury, for my health was more important. I did as she said. And a good thing I did, as headaches, dizziness and problems with my balance stayed with me for more than a week.

"Besides," she said, "your voice is becoming increasingly hoarse. Haven't you noticed?" I had to admit that I hadn't. My whole life I had been slightly hoarse, my whole life I'd had frequent, but fortunately mild, colds. And then, just over a week later, the symptoms disappeared as suddenly as they had appeared. With the exception of the headache, which stayed with me in spite of painkillers.

"It will pass," I reassured the Carer. "I've had headaches my whole life. Like most people."

"But you haven't been hoarse your whole life," she said. "It started in Ljubljana and is getting worse in London. Have you really not noticed?" I told her that she was wrong, I really hadn't noticed any particular hoarseness in my voice.

I passed the next week without any symptoms at all, even without a headache, and a desire to return to literary life reappeared. Fortuituously, an invitation from Mumbai arrived: would I be willing to lead a workshop on creative writing at an important literary festival? As it was a long time since I'd done anything like that and also a long time since I'd seen Mumbai, I accepted the invitation. The Carer was against the idea, she said that I wasn't well, the symptoms could reappear. I could go, but under one condition, she said. That she went with me. Just in case.

"Impossible," I said. "Who'll look after Nanny? You can see she's near the end."

She agreed that Nanny couldn't be left completely alone. But she demanded that before I departed for India I had some medical tests done. After all, when I fell behind my house in Ljubljana I suffered head injuries, and although tomography had showed no signs of serious damage, it was five times less reliable than MRI, which I hadn't had. She asked that I have this test now, before I left for Mumbai. And every possible test for my throat, for my hoarseness was increasingly worrying her.

How could I object? I ordered an MRI and three different tests on my throat and gullet, I had them done, told them to send the results to my home address, said goodbye to Nanny, the Carer took me to the airport and I flew to Mumbai.

At the beginning of my career, I had seen invitations to come and lecture at this or that school of creative writing in this or that part of the world as recognition of the quality of my work and belief in the writing skills that I had acquired, and belief in my ability to teach writing, although on every occasion I remembered the words of George Bernard Shaw: "Those who can't, teach." Whenever my writing flowed and I was fruitfully immersed in a story or a future novel, I would politely reject the invitation (with secret pleasure), often with the excuse that, in my opinion, a writer, like a poet, is born not made, and so beginners may be helped by bad or average writers, most of whom master theory, but not practice.

But in periods of drought, and there were more of those in my life than I would have wished, the invitations became attractive in a way they otherwise would not have been. Of course, I knew that in the general and accelerated commercialisation of literature, "creative writing" was becoming an industry where the most imaginative and industrious individuals could earn considerable sums at the expense of credulous "geniuses", who of course must pay for their lessons, but considering the direction in which mankind was going that didn't seem like the worse thing in the world; if I succeeded in helping someone hold onto their illusions and thus the meaning of their life, or shatter their illusions and free them for an activity where they would have more success, then I could see it as a job well done. Often I accepted some offer out of curiosity: because of a culture that I did not know, because of a desire to find out what they thought of creative writing in, say, Mongolia, Laos or Ecuador, and how the concept of literature in these countries could be compared to that in Germany, Italy or the Anglo-Saxon world. Curiosity was still my prime characteristic and that was an endless comfort to me. While you are still curious, things interest you, and while things interest you, you are alive.

But as soon as an agreement about a lecture or leading a creative writing workshop had been reached and I arrived at the "scene of the crime", as I usually referred to it, I was overtaken by my other characteristic: mischief making. Not mischief in the real meaning of the word, but the desire to completely demotivate as many would-be writers as possible and convince them that there is no sense flogging a dead horse, for everything worthwhile was already written long ago; today, we can create only more or less imaginative summaries or more or less imaginative plagiarisms, and the greatest talent, in reality the only one, in doing this is our ability to conceal it.

I permitted myself the worst attack on young (as well as not so young) potential writers on the creative writing workshop that my acquaintance, the actress Dipika Roy, had organised as part of the Tata Literature Live festival in Mumbai. The fee was pathetic, but the lovely woman had already done me so many favours, besides which she had opened the way to the Indian book market for me, which was rapidly becoming bigger than the American one, that I was not able to reject her request (although she freely admitted that she was inviting me because she could not find any other well-known author who would attract the interest of enough participants; she was paid for organising the festival).

I was not a little offended that she regarded me as some kind of last resort, but because her beautiful face reminded me of Scheherazade, my offendedness soon evaporated, for there was always the possibility that I could direct my anger at the workshop participants. There were more than forty of these gathered in a spacious room, from young girls and boys, evidently students, to older men and women, who were without exception deadly serious, while the youngsters were at least expectantly smiling. I decided that I would cruelly deal with young and old alike; I was curious as to how they would react.

"Why would you like to write novels?" I asked them. Some shrugged, but no one replied (although after all, even I would be unable to answer that question). Are you aware, I went on, that roughly 755,000 books are published worldwide each year, that in the last three years alone two million three hundred thousand have appeared, that since the fall of the Roman Empire 134 million have been published, that most people haven't read them or that most of these books have been read only by a select few, that in the best case only five per cent of people, who are not averse to reading, have read the best and most important books?

Strangely, these statistics did not throw them off track: again, some of them merely shrugged, only this time more than half of them did so. What was even worse, I said, was that every day fewer people read novels, which is no surprise, for they have more sensible things to do, novels are increasingly similar to each other and that when you have read the first one, reading others gives you the impression that you are reading the first again. A nice-looking student raised her hand and when I nodded, she said: "I know you are trying to provoke us and that your provocation has a purpose that will ultimately be revealed, for you certainly wouldn't have accepted the role of teacher if you wanted to take away from us the desire to write. We're all here because we want to hear from you, an experienced and acknowledged author, something useful, for instance, what we should write so that publishers won't keep rejecting us, if they bother to respond at all."

"The fact that publishers reject the work you send them," I said, "has nothing to do with the quality of your novels, although that can be the reason for rejection. Rejections are more often to do with the fact that publishers are not the brightest people on the planet and that in reality they don't know what is good and what is bad, what is new and what has been chewed over a hundred times, what will sell and what will not, what will be read and praised, and what will have to be trashed soon after publication. My first novel was rejected by fifteen publishers, *The Diary of Anne Frank* by sixteen, *Gone with the Wind,* whose author won the Pulitzer Prize in 1937, was rejected thirty-eight times, Samuel Beckett's first novel, *Murphy*, forty times, but when he won the Nobel Prize that original manuscript was sold for one and a half million dollars. Golding's *Lord of the Flies* was rejected twenty times and *Zen and the Art of Motorcycle Maintenance* as many as one hundred and twenty-one times, although when finally published it sold over a million copies.

I could stand here enumerating novels that were rejected more than ten times, but later became best-sellers, for a couple of hours, so please don't tell me about the disappointment you feel when you encounter rejection. Perhaps you really have written a bad novel. Perhaps you've written a good one that is so different that the average weary editor cannot understand it, which also often happens even if the editor is not average and weary. To understand a novel not written in line with the approved format demands more than a degree in literature and a narcissistic faith in one's judgement, and that is true not only for editors, but also for critics, among whom confusion and lack of knowledge – real knowledge, not that acquired through study – is even greater.

I can give you only one piece of advice: write. When one novel is rejected, begin writing another. And then another. And keep offering them. Look for agents, look for publishers.

Keep believing in yourself. Can you imagine how much belief in himself and his work Robert Pirsig must have had to cope with a hundred and twenty-one rejections?"

"Actually," said one of the older participants of the workshop, a grey-haired gentleman with a goatee beard and thick glasses, "we're not here to listen to stories about the rejection of famous works. We're here to learn how to write a good novel instead of a bad one. For you to explain to us what the difference is between one and the other. I imagine that you've already led numerous workshops and that the participants all expected concrete advice from you."

I could feel how a sigh of relief ran through the room; finally, one of them had dared to say out loud why they had paid a not inconsiderable sum for participating in the four-day event.

"I'm not an editor," I said, "I'm just one of you, a writer who strives to write something good, new, different. My only advantage is that I have already had fifteen novels and six collections of short stories published. Which of those are good and which bad, which better and which worse, I cannot tell you because I don't know. To ask a writer to understand and explain what he has written is the worst injustice that can happen to him. In addition to all the others that accompany him through life like shadows that he cannot throw off. As a punishment for the arrogant conviction that he can create the world anew, after even the Creator failed at his first attempt."

"What I want to know," said a young woman with plaits in a rather aggressive voice, which I gave her credit for, "is what is the difference between a good novel and a bad one, and whether a good one has more chance of being published than a bad one."

"That's right," at least five other participants agreed, "we're here to find out how we can improve our writing."

"Okay," I said. "You'll hear many things not to your liking that might plunge some of you into depression, which will eradicate your desire ever to write anything again. But you're right: we're here to establish whether you have talent and whether that talent is sufficient to make it worthwhile developing. So I will not be polite, I will not spare you, I will present to you the problems that I've faced during my long years of writing experience. Beginners too often think that they know how to write better, more originally and more profoundly than their forty-year older colleagues, who they see as redundant and passé, but let's be frank: can someone in their early twenties know the problems of forty-year olds, not to mention sixty-year olds, better than those who have experienced them and felt them first hand? Excessive self-belief is more the rule than the exception at the beginning of a writing career, but that is more a consolation for the ego than a genuine belief in one's capabilities. So do not be offended if I am completely honest, regardless of how many participants I offend."

"From the very beginning," said a young man in the back row, "you have attacked us, accused us of something, although we haven't done anything to deserve it. Why are you doing it? We came here to hear something useful, trusting in your knowledge and your abilities, why are you trying to create the impression that we seem unworthy of your advice?"

The young man was of course right and it pierced me there, where it most hurt. If I'd had no intention of helping potential writers with useful advice, why had I accepted the invitation? My betrayal seemed unworthy of that good that remained inside me, but in spite of that I decided not to console the novice writers with promises which I knew, at the very beginning, were nothing more than the result of false politeness.

"I'm sorry if I've created the wrong impression," I said. "But it is in the nature of a workshop that you will not judge my work, but rather I will judge yours. And so all those who I have already offended, should leave the room; only then shall we continue."

52.

Shaming literature

No one left the room. That gave me enough courage to continue aggressively and, where necessary, insultingly. Even if I insulted someone so much that he would lodge a complaint, I would count as a plus; how could I lead a workshop if I couldn't be honest, would be my defence. "Right," I said. "Can we continue?"

They all nodded.

"The only one among you who has so far contributed to the possible success of the workshop," I went on, "is the gentleman in the back row who said that we are here to learn how to write a good novel, instead of a bad one. Are you still interested in the answer to that question?"

Again, they all nodded.

"About the difference between a good novel and a bad one, a hundred people have a hundred different views. We are not at a workshop for space science, where two different opinions cannot both be right. Literature is a different world, uncertain, fluid, open to a great number of interpretations. We can choose from among those, we can add our own, born of experience or from whatever comes into our mind when we are trying to create the impression that we are clever, but in the end, the decision who to believe more and who less must be ours alone. The critic Toby Litt wrote that bad writing is almost always a hymn of praise directed at the writer and not the reader. That doesn't mean that an author may not write about himself, his feelings, his experiences, his realisations. What is important is *how* he writes about this. Almost all great novels contain at least a fragment of autobiography, some of them a lot and in some the autobiographical is clearly too much. Even in science fiction novels, most of what is supposed to happen in the distant future has already happened in the author's life, although in a different form. Good writing is personal, it springs from life experience, it is familiar to the reader, who can find in what is written at least a small part of himself, and if he finds more, he can identify with at least one character and, while reading, experience the events he is reading about. But there are also novels that we say tell us nothing and that cannot be understood, even if they are, from the literary point of view, faultless, wonderfully written, poetic and a credit to the author, who so brilliantly masters the art of writing. But they do not draw us in and we quickly put them down. On the other hand, there are novels that are abysmally written, repetitious, the sentences are too long, they are padded with descriptions of unimportant details, but they tell a story that grabs us from the very beginning and does not let go of us till the end, even if, while reading, we encounter the odd hurdle. Or two. Or three. A good story is one we want to read to the end, even if it is perhaps stylistically inadequate or demands some persistence and effort. As Arthur Schopenhauer said: to have good style, it's enough that you have something to say.

"At the start of my career," I continued, "one of my editors told me that the value of a book is not in how it is written, but in the effect it has on the reader. And so we read some books multiple times, not just once. And with each reading, who knows why, the story is different. We change from year to year as we go through life and as we read the same book for the second, third, fourth time, someone different is reading it, someone that we no longer are. Thus it is not at all unusual that on our way through a writer's work, our view of what is a good or a bad novel changes. Three or five years ago, let alone ten years ago, I would certainly tell you something different, for I would have a different opinion on what is involved in writing a good novel. To repeat what has, perhaps largely thanks to me, become a cliché: literature is not science. Whoever swears that it is, whoever makes a living by teaching patterns, rules, narrative approaches and stylistic changes, does not have an easy job, and I doubt that he or she enjoys what he does or is proud of it, unless he or she is intellectually undernourished or needs reassurance that his work is important. Of course, this doesn't apply to everyone, and if Harold Bloom heard me now, he would most certainly leave the room in protest, if he didn't whack me over the head with a cudgel. In short, things are and are not, they are anchored in facts and at the same time arbitrary, depending on whether we had a good breakfast or are not in pain."

"Excuse me," one of the younger participants, sitting in the front row, raised his hand. "Everything you are saying is perhaps very interesting in itself, perhaps for the majority or at least half of the people at this workshop, but everything we are hearing is the non-committal speculation of an experienced writer at a certain stage of his life, as you said yourself, and it doesn't give us, at least not me, anything concrete, anything that I could use to advantage in my writing. I came here I the hope that I would get directions that would help me write a good novel. And I'm sure the others agree with me," he looked behind him and was satisfied when he saw that most of the others were nodding. "So I would be pleased, and I see it is not just me, if you could offer us answers to some specific questions. If no one objects, I'll ask them myself." Again, he looked behind him and again most of those present nodded.

"Right," I said. "Let's be specific, if that's what you want. But before you start asking specific questions – and I'd be interested to know what is specific in literature – I would like to tell you why you may remain a bad or average writer. There are more reasons than you can imagine. The first is an insufficiently strong desire to become, or even a fear of becoming, really good. Believe me, a fear of realising what is best in us cripples us more often than we are capable of admitting. Or to ascertan that we don't have it inside us. The second is a kind of contrast with the first: excessive faith in our ability, which leads us to keep repeating the same mistakes. Or trust in the unlimited nature of creative freedom, which all too quickly slips into sloppiness. Or writing without sufficiently researching the theme on which the novel is supposed to be based. Or ignoring, often belittling editorial advice, or even the comments of friends that we have asked to read the unfinished manuscript. Excessive use of adjectives, especially where they are not required. It's good to remember Simenon, who in the last phases of reworking his texts, deleted all the adjectives. Empty words, verbosity, dragging out sentences from a few words that are adequate for a description into long, over-long descriptions that cloud what you want to tell the reader. Underestimating the reader in the belief that you must precisely describe everything, even what they already know, because you have already clearly enough shown it to them. Intelligent readers wish to participate in the story and know how to speculate. In other words: I can tell you what you may not do if you wish to write a publishable novel, but I cannot tell you what you *must* do, because that is not prescribed. That is more a matter of inspiration, rather than rules, although inspiration is not really the right word and it's not good to rely on it. So permit me to lay the responsibility for the success of the workshop on you. You wish to write and be published, whereas I am increasingly unclear why I am here. Please, those who think that they are wasting their time here with me get up this moment and leave, and complain to the workshop organiser. All the rest of you who wish to stay, allow me, and that is my condition, to lead the workshop how I see fit and how I have led at least a hundred similar workshops in different parts of the world."

No one left. It seemed as if they'd all frozen. Even the rebel in the front row. They all waited for me to continue. The pattern of my previous workshops was repeating itself. At the moment when I wanted most of them to leave or for me to pluck up the courage to leave myself, the promising huddle of potential Nobel Prize winners (not in my eyes, but in theirs) stuck to me like a swarm of irremovable insects. I realised that, just as every time before, I would have to see the thing through. And as was my custom at this point in the workshop, I asked those present to spend the next ten minutes writing a short synopsis of a novel which they had planned or were working on, but these should not exceed more than ten to fifteen lines. I said I would go to the nearest bar for a beer, but return in exactly ten minutes, and then each one of them would have to read out what they wished to write, publish and send out among readers. Anyone who thought that this was too much effort would be doing me a big favour by leaving straight away, so that they won't disturb the others.

With a beer in hand in the nearest bar (that turned out to be in the Taj Mahal hotel) I had to admit to myself that I had found myself in one of the worst jams that stubbornly accompany me through life. Once again, I had the feeling that I wasn't where I should be, where I would even want to be, that I was somewhere where my presence would bring me no benefit, except financial, and that very modest. My life seemed to consist of a series of dislocations, for which I was not responsible myself, but which I was directed into telepathically by my Scheherazade, perhaps really present only in moments of hallucination, but evidently the most influential precisely then, and with a purpose that she was concealing from me and which seemed increasingly less benevolent.

I looked around the room to see whether she was sitting at one of the tables, but she was not, although I had the feeling that she was somewhere close by, and that feeling never deceived me. I thought of the possibility that she might even be one of the workshop participants, for there were too many of them to be able to look at each one closely enough; if she had changed her appearance cosmetically, I could easily miss her. And if I did recognise her among the participants, what would I do? Would I there and then, without warning or apology, end the workshop and leave?

Was Scheherazade the one who, telepathically or in some other way, was suggesting that I should not follow the well-trodden path, but should remain "me" even where it was not strictly necessary? Was this happening because, in spite of a number of successful novels, I had no idea how a good novel is written and at such workshops I was both teacher and taught, and was, without being aware of it, teaching myself rather than the others? Did I doubt my own capabilities because Scheherazade doubted them? Was there lurking deep inside me, in some corner of my subconscious, the fear that I was not as good as others said I was and, because of this (although certainly not always), I felt so too? This was almost impossible, considering what great authors had said about the work of other great authors (Tolstoy on Charles Baudelaire's *The Flowers of Evil*: "This collection does not contain one poem which is clear and which could be understood without effort – and that effort is rarely rewarded, for the feelings that the poet is conveying are evil and base"; Vladimir Nabokov on Joseph Conrad: "I cannot abide Conrad's souvenir-shop style, bottled ships and shell necklaces of romanticist clichés." Gore Vidal on Norman Mailer's best novel *The Naked and the Dead*: "A forgery. A skilful, talented, excellently executed forgery.") It has been proved that writers, even the best, do not always understand their colleagues as they are understood by others, even when the others are the majority. Each of us wants to be something special. Alone. The only one. There are exceptions, quite a few of them, but evidently I am not among them.

53.

A sea of synopses

After my fourth beer, I decided that when I returned to the workshop, I would tell them precisely that. And I did. They were surprised, some disappointed, and at least some of them were convinced that I was joking.

"I'll add one more thing," I said. "If you wish to succeed on the battlefield which we call literature, your lust for success must be greater than your fear of defeat. Writing is deadly dangerous. The number of suicides and mental patients among writers is incomparably greater than among other artists. Remember that and be aware of it every time you finish your first sentence. I don't want to scare you, but if all of you sitting in front of me succeed, at least a third will end up with psychological problems or even in a madhouse. Are you willing to take the risk? Don't forget that imagination is more important than knowledge, to quote Albert Einstein. And not to forget Hemingway, who said that writing is nothing special, you simply sit in front of a typewriter, cut your wrists and begin to bleed. I'm sorry that I have to repeat this, but are you prepared for the defeat that awaits most of you? And those few of you who are destined for success, will you know how to live with it in spite of the inevitable doubt as to whether you deserve it?"

My words were followed by silence. Not one of the potential literary geniuses sitting in front of me could find a suitable response. At least, not one that they would dare to express. "Right," I said. "The next and key phase of the workshop. You will read to me one after another the synopses of the novels that you are writing or planning."

The first one to speak up was the annoying young man, who at the beginning of the workshop had complained that I was offering nothing concrete. He read a synopsis of a novel, which he said he had basically already finished, it just needed final editing and, of course, a publisher willing to publish it. So far, he had received only two rejections, although together with the comment that the novel certainly wasn't bad, but regrettably their programme was full for five years ahead. His synopsis greatly surprised me, before it disappointed me, for it was an almost exact summary of a novel that almost everyone who reads has read. His novel was supposed to be an emotional dramatisation of the conflict and lack of understanding between the older and younger generation, with an unpredictable outcome of the conflict between passion and ideology. The main character was meant to be the author's alter ego, a cynical student of medicine, a nihilist, who rejects the feelings of memories of the older generation, defending a pure scientific materialism, but above all rejecting the feeling of love, in which he sees nothing other than sentimentality. The main character is unbearably rude and full of advice and indifferent to the rules of good behaviour and social norms, until he falls in love with the daughter of a rich individual from the highest caste, whereas he himself is from one of the lower castes. In spite of his love for the daughter, he persistently rejects her father's outmoded views of the world and of life, but the novel also talks about being in love against one's own will, about the mutual dependence of old and young, and about parents' love for their children, which remains intact even after they can no longer understand each other.

"Interesting, young man," I said. "Unfortunately, your novel has already been written, and much better than you could write it, by Ivan Turgenev, and the title is *Fathers and Sons*."

I encouraged the others to read me the synopses of their planned works. Over the next half hour, I was forced to listen to summaries of stories which have already been written by Salman Rushdie (*Midnight's Children*), Harper Lee (*To Kill a Mocking Bird*), Ngugi Wa Thiong'o (*Weep Not Child*), Carlos Fuentes (*The Death of Artemio Cruz*), J. D. Salinger (*Catcher in the Rye*), Albert Camus (*The Stranger*), Joseph Conrad (*Nostromo*), Ivan Goncharov (*Oblomov*), F. Scott Fitzgerald (*The Great Gatsby*), John Steinbeck (*The Grapes of Wrath*), and after *The Tin Drum* by Günter Grass I dozed off and quite a bit of originality slipped by me – until I heard a loud, almost shouted question from one of the younger female participants: "Sir, are you listening to us?"

"Of course," I replied, "but not closely, for I have heard all this before, read it too, of course, and perhaps written some of it myself without being aware of it, which sadly means that at this point I must call a halt to the workshop, for rather than that it is a lumber room for redundant models, where neither you nor I have anything to gain. The cruel fact is that in the time that we are living in the hardest and possibly even impossible thing is to be original, unless we are satisfied with being approximately original, which means transferring well known and often told stories to other environments and other cultures, changing the names of the protagonists, their age and education, changing the order of events and risking that our story talks about nothing in particular."

I got up and headed for the exit. At the door, I turned round. "I know that you expected more than you have got, above all encouragement and consolation, some advice and some praise, a lie or two that you are on the right path, but believe it or not today's workshop has taught me more than anyone. We will do the greatest service to the world as it is by ceasing to write and pretending that we are telling people original stories that might amuse them or teach them something useful. They've heard everything before, read everything. Already a thousand years ago."

At the same time, I was struck by the thought that I was doing something I should not. What was happening to me? Why didn't I do what would cost me the least and enumerate the writing tips that too many writers were full of, convinced that it's possible to write well in only one way, their way? Why didn't I quote to them a few useful things from the essay *Philosophy of Composition*, published by Edgar Allan Poe in 1846, at least his basic advice: that you must know how the story will end before you start writing; that neither a novella nor a novel should exceed a length at which the reader would be tempted to put the book down; that you need to decide what effect the book is supposed to have; that you need to determine the tone of the whole work (he recommended it should be melancholy); that you need to determine in advance the theme and characterisation; that you need to select the right point for the climax of the story; that you need to know exactly in which environment the story is taking place; and that the highest literary achievement is in a convincing description of Beauty and Death, or the melancholy of the beauty of death? They would certainly like this more than my vicious attack on their creative hopes. Why did I not know how to, was not capable of, did not want to try to instil at least some hope in them, instead of dispersing their last hope?

Disappointed with myself, I made for the exit. "Be glad," I said, "that you still believe in the salvational power of literature. That it has not driven you crazy yet. I am bidding goodbye. Not only to you, but to myself."

54.

Finally the truth?

I wandered past the Taj Mahal hotel and towards India Gate, without knowing why there in particular and why in general. I had to walk, the only other possibility was to slide down a wall and sit on the pavement. And allow myself to be trampled by passers-by. As if they had not already trampled on me many times in my life in their struggle for their own space, some with the undoubted intention of walking all over me, pushing me out of the queue, excluding me from the competition. I had long ago realised that this would never stop and would even continue after my death.

On the broad space in front of the triumphal arch, which stands in the place where the last British viceroy bid farewell to India, beggars like to gather, primarily because of the masses of foreign tourists who come to view the arch or to have their photograph taken with the Taj Mahal hotel in the background. In the midst of the hordes of pesky traders, I came across a young man without arms and legs, merely a body and head, who lay helplessly on a board with wheels and beseechingly eyed the passers-by. Although I was overcome by a strong feeling that I'd seen him once before, after all I had been at the Gate of India more than once, or that I had described him in one of my stories (it often happened that I would write something that I experienced only later), with a hasty gesture I pulled a banknote for five hundred rupees from my wallet and laid it on the heap of change that covered the bottom of the metal dish beside the unfortunate creature.

When I saw that he was directing his eyes straight at me, and not with gratitude but almost accusingly, I thought that he also was telling us a story, such as every one of us does in our own way in the desire that others respond to it, although I knew that he was not telling his own story, but the story of his owner and master, who early in the morning brought him there and came to collect him in the evening, in order to exhibit him somewhere else again the next day. I had long known that in the Indian countryside, criminal gangs kidnap children, boys and girls, and cripple them, chop their limbs off, break their bones and put out their eyes, so that in locations where crowds gather, they can beg as much money as possible. I also knew that often even parents mutilated their children for this purpose.

For an unknown reason (perhaps I would find it if I tried), tears came to my eyes; I realised that I would never dare write such an exaggerated, unbelievable story, such as is written by life every day in every corner of the world, for exceedingly experienced young men and women would immediately jump on me with the accusation that they were not credible.

I turned to wander into the city.

My footsteps stopped. She was sitting three metres in front of me, among a crowd of other beggars, and for the first time since she first appeared in my life, she was not staring into space, but was looking straight at me. It would be hard to describe what was in her eyes. Not what was in them, but what I *saw* in them. Perhaps I saw something that was more in my eyes than hers, considering that I had never, in spite of endless speculation, unravelled the meaning and the role of her presence in my life, although only in hallucinations that had been, so I was told, part of my life from a young age, and which were increasingly bizarre and frequent, although I had never doubted that her appearances, always where I least expected them, were intended to tell me something, to teach me something, to remind me of something fatefully important, even when she gave the impression that she didn't even see me, let alone that she was there because of me and not merely because of simple coincidence.

But with the years, there had been too many of these coincidences, they had taken on meaning, although one I had assigned myself, and that meaning had to be at least in some way connected with me. When I saw her sitting among the beggars beneath the arch of India Gate and, for the first time, looking straight into my eyes, I was overcome by a desire to check whether she was merely a vision or real. With her face directed towards me and sitting straightened up from her usual hunched posture, it seemed that I was not seeing her face for the first time, but that I had seen it every time she had appeared. Dark brown eyes, slightly irregular features, a self-confident look that did not repel but attracted, as if offering protection. For a moment or two, our eyes remained locked into something that could be described as friendly understanding, into pure empathy, into an agreement, it seemed to me, that we were actually one, locked into one soul, one heart, that we had the same thoughts, the same expectations, the same fears, the same hope that we were not sliding to our doom and that everything that happened in the world was not merely a parting charade.

I went up to her and placed a wad of banknotes for ten thousand rupees in the dish just in front of her knees, which contained only a few coins. When I wanted to look into her eyes from close up, she suddenly bowed her head and bent over again. Had I offended her by giving alms that probably surpassed everything that she had managed to beg in a whole year? Once again, I was gripped by a powerful desire to ascertain whether she was a real person or merely the result of hallucination; I stretched out my hand to stroke her head in a friendly way. That was actually the last thing that a foreigner would do to a beggar at India Gate in Mumbai, but I wasn't an ordinary foreigner. And she wasn't an ordinary beggar.

When my hand touched her head to stroke it, I first felt that I was touching emptiness. But a moment later my hand struck against a temple that was almost burning, heated by the sun, and hair damp with sweat; the contact was reminiscent of an electric shock. I started and withdrew my hand, but I had got evidence: Scheherazade was a real person!

She raised her head and looked into my eyes.

"Why are you pretending that you don't know me?" she asked.

The Carer!

"Why have you followed me here without my knowledge? Dressed as Scheherazade?"

She gave a bitter smile.

"Because I am Scheherazade. And now I shall tell you the story number thousand and two."

55.

Good news and bad

I took a room for two at the hotel where I was staying and we spent the next night there. The whole time she was shuddering and quietly crying. She didn't want to talk, she told me only that in the time of my absence the Nanny had died and that she had organised her funeral. I shouldn't worry about that.

"So what?" I wanted to know. "You could have told me that over the phone."

She promised that she would explain the reason for her arrival when the sun came up, and when she had gathered together enough strength and courage. Before she was overcome by tiredness from the journey and fell asleep, she asked me: "Did you talk a lot when leading the workshop?"

I nodded. "Not only a lot, too much. You know that it's hardest to tell people the simplest things."

"And?" she went on. "Did nobody warn you that your voice is very hoarse? And that you're stumbling over some words?"

"No," I decided to end the conversation about this as soon as she started it. "My voice is not hoarse and I'm not stumbling over any words."

"Haven't you noticed that your voice is a lot hoarser than it was before you left for India?"

"Maybe because of the bad air. It's not as polluted as it is in Delhi, but it's still worse than in most big cities."

She said nothing for some time. I thought she had fallen asleep, but she suddenly moved and said: "Please, hug me. Put your arms around me. I feel so sick at heart that otherwise I won't be able to go to sleep. But I must rest at least a little. I'm deadly tired."

I put my arms around her and held her tight. After some time, she sank into sleep. I tried to sleep, but without success. The puzzle she had brought with her gave me no peace. I sensed that in the time of my absence something bad had happened, perhaps very bad. Was she ill? The next morning, too, she was unwilling to tell me anything; after breakfast, she wanted to go straight to the airport and take the first plane back to London.

"Only at home," she said, "can I tell you everything that I'd rather not."

She had a return ticket with Air India for that same day at two in the afternoon, and because she didn't know when I had a return flight with British Airways, she had also reserved a ticket with Air India for me, for she wanted us to return to London together, sitting side by side. Even on the plane, she wouldn't tell me anything, she said I'd find out everything at home. She ordered three whiskeys one after the other, which wasn't her habit, quite the opposite, and each time one for me as well. Because I hadn't slept all night, I soon dozed off in my window seat; when I woke up, the plane was already descending towards Heathrow.

The house was empty.

"And?" I looked at her as I sank into my usual armchair in the living room, still tired from the flight. "Will I finally find out what's going on?"

"You will," she said and went into the hall. She came back with a handful of documents and letters. She sat on the smaller armchair on the other side of the coffee table in front of the fireplace. "Because I am too upset by everything, I'll go through things one at a time. Which would you like to hear first, the good news or the bad news?"

"The good news," I said.

"First I'll tell you the good news, and then all the bad, and at the end another bit of good news, perhaps the best."

"I don't know why it all has to be so dramatic, after all, you could've told me everything in Mumbai, then we could've enjoyed ten days' holiday in Goa."

"For now, that won't be possible," she said. "What's worse, perhaps it never will be."

"Oh, come on," I shifted restlessly, just about to get up and leave.

She took a deep breath and put a book on the coffee table. "The first news. You novel about the events at the clinic in Switzerland has been published. I, at least, don't like the cover, but I have seen two positive reviews. None of the authors that you mention have sued you. And they won't. What's more, Martin Amis, Saul Bellow, J. M. Coetzee and Javier Marías have all written to you. They all sent their congratulations. They all think that the book is exceptional, and are happy to appear in it. Martin Amis even added that the book reads as if everything you describe actually happened."

"It did," I said. "Surely no one thinks that I made it all up!"

"Let's leave that for now," she said, "and go on to the bad news."

She reached for a large envelope and from it pulled some letters and three x-rays. At least they looked like x-rays. In fact, they were from the MRI that I had before I left for India.

"Test results," she said. "They found something that the tomography in Ljubljana didn't detect. Two haematomas, one large and the other smaller. The larger one is evidently the result of your fall before new year, but the specialist thinks that the smaller one is a consequence of a childhood accident. You never mentioned it to me. Why not?"

"Because I never had an accident as a child in which I injured my head," I said, almost argumentatively. "Why would I keep quiet about something like that?"

"It's quite possible, says Dr Shires, a top specialist for head injuries, that one of the consequences of that early accident was amnesia. So I believe you when you say that you don't remember the event, whatever it was."

"The next thing?" I tried to encourage her to continue.

"The next bit of news," she said, "is considerably worse. The test results for your throat and gullet show that you have cancer of the larynx. You'll have to have an operation, they need to remove your larynx and part of your windpipe, but not so much that you won't be able to breathe. But you will be left without a voice."

"Just like Scheherazade," I said after a long silence. "A dumb Shahryar, who was ordered to tell Scheherazade as many stories as she told to him. Plus one more, a thousand and second. Maybe I went too far and told too many."

"I understand," she said, "that at this news you have nothing more sensible to say. I'd like to know what you'll say at the last piece of news, which in normal circumstances would be the best, but considering all the other, you may think that someone is mocking you."

"The feeling that someone is mocking me, perhaps I mocking myself, has accompanied me my whole life," I said. "After what I've just heard, nothing can surprise me."

She took another letter from a small envelope and unfolded it. "The Swedish Academy informs you that you are this year's recipient of the Nobel Prize for Literature."

These words were followed by silence. Hers and mine.

"Are you making fun of me?" I eventually asked.

She handed me the letter. "They want to know whether you'll accept the award."

"What use will it be to me, with two tumours in my head and no larynx?"

"If you do, and why shouldn't you, I recommend that you begin working on the speech that you must give at the award ceremony."

56.

At the royal court

Just over a week later, a few days before the operation which would leave me without a larynx, a letter came from the Swedish king. Addressed to me and with a signature in his own hand. A personal and at the same time official letter. He congratulated me for the award and expressed his pleasure about the fact that it had been received by one of his favourite authors. He had read more or less all of my work, except my last novel, about which various rumours were circulating and which would definitely be considered to be one of the most controversial of my works. He would be particularly delighted, he added, if I were to spend the two or three days before the award ceremony in his palace as his personal guest. He would also invite some other authors that he valued, Swedish and foreign, so that I would have someone to talk to when I grew tired of him. In the hope that I would not decline the invitation, very best wishes and until we met in Stockholm.

"Never in my wildest dreams did I imagine something like this happening to me," said the Carer.

"Just as I never imagined that in a week's time I would be left without a larynx," I said. "I must write back to him straight away that my visit to his palace sadly won't be possible."

"Why not?" she wanted to know, visibly dissatisfied.

"How can I talk to him without a voice?"

"You won't be without a voice," she said. "I'll be your voice. Whatever you want to say, you'll write in a notebook, tear out the page, give it to me and I will speak your words out loud. Or you'll send me a text message, which will be even more straightforward."

I don't know how she managed to convince me. Although to me she had long been more than just the Carer, and with our marriage had become the Decision-maker, at times, I was still able to go against her will. But this time she won. She convinced me that I *must* accept the award, after all I deserved it, and that I *must* accept the Swedish king's invitation to spend some days in his palace, for this would be an event that I could describe in one of my future novels.

After this, things unfolded with a speed which I'd never known in my life. As if time had begun to hurry. But it's more likely that my perception of time had changed. In the fear that the surgical removal of my larynx wouldn't prevent future metastases, not so much in fear but in certainty that it would not do so and that the end was nearer than I dared to think, into the rest of the time available to me I perhaps subconsciously wished to cram as much experience as life can bring. The operation was a success, the consequences were painful and lasted longer than I would wish, but in reality I recovered quicker than most (so the oncologist assured me). And in a flash, the Carer and I were in Stockholm. On time. With the speech that I wrote when the wounds in my throat were healing.

"Fate is on your side," the Carer consoled me with the biggest lie that I'd even heard from her mouth.

At the palace in Stockholm we were given a comfortable, luxuriously furnished bedroom with bathroom. First we rested, then we were invited to tea with the king and queen Silvia. The king surprised me. I'd never seen such a dignified but stooped person, so kindly and melancholy in his dignity, almost amazed at his destiny that had deprived him of living like a true king with power and authority (on horseback and with a sword on a battlefield, where he could realise at least part of his nature), and at the same time almost humbly and devotedly bearing the burden of a completely unexciting reign. It would be difficult to say how many of these feelings were shared by queen Silvia, but her ever-friendly smile seemed at times so unnatural that it reminded me of the wax figures in Madame Tussaud's. So it did not surprise me when I found out that Carl Gustaf had not smiled for thirty years, let alone laughed.

Of course, this information was not nailed to the palace door; for such confidential information, I had to find a friend among the king's numerous staff. I did not seek one out; after a sequence of embarrassing complications, he offered himself. He was quite a corpulent gentleman in an officer's (or possibly a sub-officer's) uniform of the king's guard, who was usually standing at the entrance where the official car had dropped us off, and where began our daily odyssey through the labyrinth of corridors, staircases, doors, turns, ascents and descents to the room that had been assigned to us, and which even after three days we were unable to find without the friendly assistance of a staff member, who gave many people the impression that he was standing at this key corner only in order to steer confused (or drunk) guests to their rooms.

On the very first day, when we had got out of the Volvo and were standing at the foot of the staircase that led up into the labyrinth, and with a shadow of concern on our faces were thinking of all the possible wrong routes that we would choose before we could get to a five minute rest and freshen up before the next event, the officer of the king's guard in knee high boots and with a ceremonial sword on his belt took a barely noticeable step towards us and in the hope of a friendly response breathed rather than spoke two unusual words: "Dober dan."

Of course, even in my wildest dreams I would never have thought of the possibility that he spoke Slovene! His pleasure at our surprise was unusually genuine. He said that his wife was Croatian and that they spent every summer on the Dalmatian coast, and that he spoke a little Croatian. But how had he found out that I was born in Slovenia? Evidently gossip about the voiceless writer was circulating in the court even among the staff. He knew also that my wife and I were having endless difficulties finding our room, and so he explained exactly where we needed to turn left and right. He asked if we were satisfied with our stay in the palace and the Carer said we were very satisfied, although the king was so serious that she was a little afraid of him. Serious and gloomy.

"Everyone knows that," he replied quickly in Croatian, but to continue he had to take refuge in English. "Every Swede knows that their king has not smiled for thirty years. There are theories as to why not, but the real answer is that no one knows."

"My husband will make him laugh," said the Carer.

"Won't that be difficult, considering that he cannot speak?" the guard asked without hesitation.

"He had his larynx removed," said the Carer, "now I am his voice."

"I know," he said, "the newspapers are competing to tell your story. Tragic. But the gentleman is probably pleased to get the prize."

"I don't think he cares one way or the other," replied my wife and led me inside the castle.

When we got to our room, I scribbled on a piece of paper in the notebook: "You've really embarrassed us."

She disagreed. "Writers are expected not to take normal rules of behaviour too literally. They are expected to behave more freely and take more risks than people in other professions. Writers are allowed to and even obliged to remind those around them that art exists and that it is not subordinate to agreed reality, but rather supplements and enriches it. You are not only shamans, who through prose and poetry treat undefined psycho-mythological conditions, but you are also, in the most noble meaning of the expression, court jesters – that is those who, at least in Shakespeare's plays, the king expects will speak the truth, however unpleasant that is."

Writers, she continued, are expected to transgress occasionally; not, of course, in the moral sense, although readers also forgive them such things, but in the sense of verbal courage, intellectual daring, even social audacity. That does not mean, she added, that they should carouse drunkenly at every opportunity, and vomit on the table or on those they are talking to.

No, what she had in mind was a more noble form of disrespect for protocol finesse: an audacity that shocks because, like a Zen koan, it stuns with its evident truth, with its semantic but not its formal appropriateness. It wasn't enough that, as the guest of honour, I amused and charmed an elderly countess, a vehement feminist, the president of the association of Swedish newspapers and many other fine ladies, to which protocol wisdom, following God knows what rationale, assigned seats on our left or right at the banquet. No, my main duty was to cheer up the king and make him laugh. In that way I would show to the Swedes that their monarch wasn't a mummy, but just a man who is unhappy because the demands of ruling were insufficient to mobilise the best in him and who, in spite of his unhappiness, was capable of genuine human reactions. That he was, in short, if I ambushed him, capable of letting go. This should become my main aim.

I quickly wrote: "But what should I say to him, what should I write that you can say to him? What might stretch his amiably immobile face into a smile against his will? And when? And where?"

At the banquet there was no opportunity to exchange a word with him, as I wasn't sitting close enough; and even if I had been, what could I say with the Carer's help? 'Your Majesty, I'd like to tell you something that will make you laugh.' With any luck, merely a stupid statement like that would make him laugh, but it was much more likely that he would turn aside and pretend that he hadn't heard me.

One way or another, when I was thinking most intensively what I would say to the king during the next formal handshake to make him laugh, my wife and I were just going downstairs, down one of the numerous thickly carpeted staircases, without knowing where we were going, past immobile guards, red-cheeked Viking boys who, in uniforms from the 17th century with rather funny headgear and halberds in their hands, were standing on either side, from top to bottom (which they did twenty-four hours a day, although certainly not always the same ones), and when we went past, they crossed their halberds and shouted out some greeting. They did this for everyone, not just for us, but also, as we realised on roughly the twentieth step, for the king and queen, who were, like ordinary courtiers or members of some delegation, ascending.

The encounter was so unexpected that I didn't even think what an opportunity it offered: for a moment, there were just four of us, the king, the queen, my "queen" and I. I could have carried out one of the manoeuvres that I had been so intensively thinking about, but I hadn't fully thought through any of the possibilities and there was too little time to carry it off. So I greeted the royal couple merely with a movement of my head, as did my wife. The king and queen responded in kind, he seriously, as was his habit, and the queen with her frozen smile.

But it was precisely this encounter that, without me realising it, offered me, at dinner in the Villa Paula the same evening, an opportunity that I was unaware of right up to the moment when the right words simply flew into my head of their own accord. Once again, for the fourth or fifth time, the line of Swedish and foreign invitees at the gala dinner were winding past Carl Gustaf and his queen Silvia (obligatory dinner jacket for the gentlemen, long evening dress for the ladies). Waiting in line, I had just enough time to send my "voice" a text message. When I stepped in front of the king and shook hands with him, I smiled amiably, while he, as I had expected, merely gave a gentle nod. Then my wife shook hands with the king and, without fear or embarrassment, said exactly what I had texted her. "My husband says that your palace is not as big as he had imagined, otherwise we would not keep bumping into each other even on staircases."

A miracle happened: the king, without quite knowing what he was doing, laughed out loud, while his queen also broke into sincere laughter. Evidently, my words had the effect of a good joke: he wasn't expecting them, although in a moment he connected them with numerous other handshakes and with our meeting on the staircase, and in this way had recognised the absurdity of what he had been doing all his life. At the same time, he felt an unconcealed sympathy to the dumb writer, who dared to (freely) communicate with him as an equal. He also felt (I read this in his eyes) that he had to recognise this equality: that he really was the king of his country, but I was the king of my imagination, that he was confined by tradition and in his palace, whereas I was the free conqueror of endless imaginary kingdoms. That his room for manoeuvre was small, mine endless; that his predecessors may have gone back to Napoleon's general Bernadotte, but mine reached back not only to Dostoyevsky and Tolstoy, but to Cervantes, to Homer. That I could set off the next day for India, or Brazil or China and stay there until I ran out of money; but he could not do that, even though he had infinitely more money than I. In that moment, I felt, he recognised that his kingdom was actually smaller than mine and that he would, if the rules permitted it, talk with me about this paradox all night. But the rules demanded that he shake hands with the next in line.

I have been regularly employed only twice in my life, and that only for a short time. Both times I fell ill because I had to sacrifice too much of my freedom. If I had to be king, I would probably want to die.

57.

The Nobel speech

When the Carer and I took our seats of honour in the first row, half an hour before the start of the award ceremony, I was subject to strange feelings. Most people in my place would say that God was very favourably inclined towards them and that this would be a reason for gratitude, rather than gloomy introspection. I felt roughly how someone feels who has been sentenced to life imprisonment and shut between the four walls that are now the only thing (except for the guard who brings him food) that he will ever see again.

I realised that these were the walls of my "self" that I would never cross over. And the food that the guard would bring me until my death was a more or less spiced, more or less edible gruel of my memories with added wishes and goals, made from the same flour. The dream that I could be anyone else or different was just an illusion, a personal, particularly obstinate, really stubborn delusion, which in a universe without hope represented a substitute for hope. Of course, we are all sentenced to our own ego, to a fixed record of our personal history, which is at the same time the melody of our thoughts, actions and decisions. The difference is that many people feel at home inside their ego and find within it enough room for manoeuvre. But some see it as a prison cell. For some of us it is too close for comfort. And so we live (or try to live) a kind of parallel life outside it, strangers to our own self, exiles from the centre of our being, outsiders.

And those that are not, never will be and never have been, because they have a differently formatted egostructure, don't understand us very well. Or (which is worse) they misunderstand us and (which is the worst) they are not even aware that they are misunderstanding us, but are (on the contrary) convinced that there is something wrong with us. That we are narcissistic, burdened with pathological introspection, circling in orbits of our own that in the best case are unusual, but in the worst case problematic. Why would someone study themselves, see in themselves both God and Lucifer, and at the same time the kernel that is common to all people, regardless of how much they are aware of this? Is it not more comfortable to splash around in the shallows, which are not difficult to define, where they remain within generally accepted patterns and are thus within reach of the majority?

That was how I should have lived my life. In the shallows. But now it was too late.

When the ceremony began I was only half present. It felt as if nothing happening in front of me had anything to do with me. A succession of people appeared on the stage, each of which said a number of words, first in Swedish and then in English, but they were pure formality. They couldn't be anything else; a Nobel Prize award ceremony offers no opportunity for originality. I pricked up my ears only when somebody announced that the prize-winner's speech would be read by his wife, since due to illness, his larynx had been removed, which was tragic and unusual not only in its own regard, but also because I was the first winner of the Nobel Prize for literature who was without a voice. I didn't have the time to reflect how many different meaning the expression "without a voice" could have (do we not live in times where every writer is more or less without a voice?) because the Carer stepped up to the microphone and began to read my speech (which I had prepared when I still thought that I had a voice).

"Your Majesty, ladies and gentlemen. In spite of years of writing and a career that many would say had been more than successful (if career is even an appropriate word for the decades of transforming barely understandable events into imagination, and incomprehensible and to a large extent unacceptable realities into stories understandable to all or at least most people, if only because in the transformed stories about me they also see themselves), most writers in their later years (whether they realise it or not) begin to lose faith that what they are doing (and what they've done all their lives) has enough value, has enough meaning, redemptive meaning, to continue doing it until their last breath (risking that they write something that they have already written numerous times and each time worse than at the start of their journey). Although a great deal of literature which is generally agreed to have indisputable quality has been created by authors older than fifty, even sixty, it cannot be denied that most late works, instead of an innovative approach, are distinguished primarily by what some critics call experience, skilfulness. And so it is not unusual that many writers deep within (subconsciously) feel resistance to the idea of adding more kilometres to the marathons already achieved, which are most often part of the same race towards a goal that has perhaps already been achieved, if not surpassed.

Over the last three decades the world as a dish of values and meanings has lost its content, and so in this emptiness all big, important words sound hollow, naïve, out of synch with the spirit of the times. Almost like a parody of their meanings. Over the last thirty years, the world of vertical values has finally tipped over and become horizontal. In such a world, only that which is dangerous can stand out from the crowd and only for as long as it brings someone a profit. In such a world, the hero of the masses can be someone like David Beckham (somewhere I read the shortest summary of the history of mankind: *From Buddha to Beckham!*). But someone who, for instance, invents an effective drug against all forms of cancer (if and when someone invents such a thing) cannot become a hero of the masses. In a horizontal world, quality is increasingly a synonym for media quantity: what is spoken and written about is *ipso facto* good. A world without content. A world in which form and forms prevail.

Why should we delve into the spiritual culture and faith and philosophy of other nations, if the majority of us, including ever more of those who are educated, are happy with common sense? Why should we strive, torture ourselves and others, dig beneath the surface, when (according to Andy Warhol) the surface is all there is? It is more comfortable and elegant to remain on the surface, where the world has changed into a global shopping centre, where everything is marked with a price and laid out on low shelves, easily accessible to everyone, even mental dwarves. Not only material things, but also ideas, philosophy, art, religion. Not to mention the meaning of life. Sale: the meaning of life at half price!

I am convinced that no recent inventions have more fatally deformed the human spirit than the remote control and the supermarket. The remote turns us into neurotics whose concentration fades after even a minute of watching one of the hundred and fifty television channels now available, then we succumb to a tantrum of channel hopping. As if we hoped to find on at least one of these channels something made specially and only for us. It's the same with regard to reading books, which is increasingly becoming page turning. And supermarkets (at a price we are not even aware of) guarantee the illusion of equality, the dignity of the consumer (the customer is king). In front of the shelves, we are all equal, and we must all stand in line at the checkout. The instant accessibility of everything to everyone is (paradoxically) the reason for the devaluation of most of what is accessible to all. Faced with such choice (also of books, ideas, theories, therapies, films, music, television series, the opinions of everyone on everything), we are ever more inclined to turn up our noses at what is on offer. Spoilt and weary, we no longer find anything that completely suits us, in which we would recognise an exceptional, higher value. Something that (if I express myself in a way least suited to the times) we would be prepared to die for.

But the greatest paradox of our time, as we know, is the fact that in the midst of a plethora of everything, where something new appears every day, an increasing number of people cannot afford food for their children. And so we ask: after something goes seriously wrong in the world, can even more go wrong?

I try to find the answer to that question in Jung's favourite story, which speaks of the water of life that sprang up in the middle of the desert and began to water it. People came from all around to drink the pure, invigorating liquid. And life was fresh and rich for all. But not for long. For enterprising individuals fenced off the spring; they passed laws determining who was more entitled and less entitled to the water; then they began to sell it. And eventually, the spring of life passed into ownership of a small handful of individuals. They were so immersed in their ownership game that they didn't even notice how their civilisation was founded on water which was no longer there – for the spring had already dried up, the water of life sprang at a different, distant place.

After some time, it became clear to a few people that the form of life was losing content and so they went looking for the vanished water. They found it. But it wasn't long before the spring of life's meaning in the new location was also fenced off, privatised, patented, reserved for its "owners". And so on, throughout history.

What is that dark force in humankind that makes us feel we have to control, fence off, usurp, "make sense of" everything that is alive and good? The lust to reduce disorder to order (of actual life into abstract meaning) is not only a need in the mind of the individual. It manifests itself in art (aesthetic reductionism becomes cliquish dogmatism), in politics (party utopianism becomes social bureaucratism) and in science (simplification of theoretical complexity becomes conservatism of ideas). Whenever we are struck by a panicked desire to find a fixed place in the chaos, the left hand begins to destroy what was created by the right hand.

But that is not the only thing that has always disturbed me in Jung's allegory. I was equally strongly influenced by the realisation that we can give meaning to our role in nature and our attitude towards it only by linking together experiential fragments into a narrative whole, into a meaningful sequence, a story. Or, to paraphrase E. M. Forster: 'king', 'queen', 'sadness' and 'death' are simply words. 'The queen died and the king died' are words that give facts, nothing more. 'The queen died and then the king died of sadness' is already a story, which gives the events meaning and content. The meaning is in the subtext: the king loved the queen so much that he couldn't live without her. There is no need to spell it out. Actually, the message is stronger if it remains unstated. Stories *must* have a subtext, they must have an allegorical dimension, which (in Jung's terms) connects us with the mythological foundation of the unconscious. Or, as Freud would put it, the subconscious.

Jung claims that the role of mythological and religious metaphors is positive. It is directed towards the maintenance and renewal of life, for stories (be they mythological, religious or literary) connect us with those unconscious forces that we keep losing contact with because of our outwardly directed awareness. Thus by arranging experiences into a narrative whole, we not only create the recognisable and renewable continuity of our presence in time and space, but we keep reconnecting with archetypal forces, which are not only the permanent foundation of the spirit, but in a condensed form represent that fundamental wisdom that has helped the human species survive tens of thousands of years.

By arranging experiences into stories that are meaningful (either at a personal or a communal or a ritual level), we are at the same time striving to integrate the forces of the unconscious into our daily, outwardly directed life, where the attributes of reason and science prevail. Experience shows that the healthiest and most fruitful societies or communities are those that do not renounce either the empirical or the mythological dimension, but rather cultivate a dialogue between the two. It is foolish to think that science and God are mutually exclusive. Such an idea can be held only by someone who conceives of God exactly as he is described in the Bible, and who is unaware that science, regardless of its achievements, is nevertheless just a kind of ideology. At the end of the day, the Bible is more a list of ethical instructions than a criminal code. And science is to a great extent the fruit of unlimited human imagination, no less subjective than is belief in God. A society that values its myths and keeps them alive, says Joseph Campbell, feeds from the healthiest, richest layer of the soul.

What happens when springs of invigorating water are usurped by groups or individuals, who forget about the water and begin to sell or impose the *idea* of water? Or what happens when we are separated from this water source, from our story, due to physiological injury or illness? It is precisely this, it seems to me, which is the source of all misunderstandings, conflicts and wars, all tragedies, disappointments and depressions, all feelings of disunity and exclusion. But at the same time the source of all forms of creativity, the unending human lust to transcend the given, to improve, the desire to help God in the final formation of the world. In the case of some illnesses, creativity is limited to its primary role: renewing identity, the individual story, individual meaning. The Russian neurologist Alexander Luria describes a victim of Korsakoff syndrome who, due to complete memory loss, was forced to make up himself and the world around him from one moment to the next, to search for, to create meaning for himself and his life, so as not to plummet into the abyss of chaos opening up beneath him. Other neurologists, most notably Oliver Sacks, describe similar cases. Not 'I think, therefore I am', but 'I fabulate, therefore I am'.

As tends to happen, in this case, too, the illness is just an enlargement of normal functioning, a strengthened form of aspiration, which is natural and healthy. A teenager who tries to mythologise his life by writing a diary of his romantic peripeteia; a chronicler who records the achievements of his sporting or political organisation; a historian who clarifies the fate of his nation or state by connecting a sequence of supposed causes and results – all submit to the natural tendency to order objective, static events into a subjective dynamic narrative intended to give the events meaning. The lust for meaning and to understand the present and the past is, alongside the instinct for biological survival, the strongest motivational factor of human activity. While it is still possible to satisfy this lust without constraint everything is alright: the person has the feeling that he is appearing in a story that he is realising and confirming – him and his community. At the spring he drinks the clear, invigorating water of life's meaning.

But, as Jung's allegory of water shows us, such moments are anything but the rule. Much more often they are the exception. 'I fabulate, therefore I am' is not enough. The person (as an individual and as a member of the community) is obsessed with the need to say: 'My story is better than the others.' Or: 'My story *has to be* better than the others, otherwise it has no value'. And so stories intended to give life meaning, become means of manipulating others, of outsmarting opponents, of achieving and maintaining power, of validating status and forming different hierarchies. They thus become 'dominant stories' (ideologies) that the masses have to submit to, and 'real stories' (scientific dogma), thanks to which all other stories of a different kind are by definition just stories and nothing more. It's true that the facts try to hold back the march of imagination, but that keeps proving that imagination is in front and that facts are only the traces that it leaves behind it.

When a man and wife, or two friends or colleagues, each make up their own story on the meaning of their relationship, a conflict arises that demands resolution and/or tolerance. It can end with one story prevailing over the other, or with hatred which tries to destroy the 'rebel' story. We begin to pass on grown-ups' stories to children as soon they can talk; when, ten or fifteen years later, they begin to reject these stories and seek out their own source of life's water, we are disappointed, even offended. All of us, from first to last, live from our first to last hour in the fear that our story will not cope with the pressure from other stories that are trying to spread their influence and territory. If necessary, we fight for our stories in court. And if necessary, with weapons. We become cunning and aggressive: we force our story on others, we try to convince them that it is more suitable for them then their own.

And so we sell to others water from the spring that has dried up, for the only genuine source of human meaning is in a man himself, in his own story; everything else is form without content. Or form with content that is impregnated with impure intent. In order to sell non-existent water to others we use language, that 'encyclopaedia of ignorance' as Edward de Bono called it, while those that we are convinced *need* our truth, we see as deprived, misled, sick. We feel called to heal them – with our story, of course, which we would like to believe is a universal cure.

From a very young age we experience the world as a network of various stories, struggling for primacy at the expense of others. Big stories eat little ones. For almost as long as I've been alive, I have had the desire to create a story about a man without a story, about an actor who has forgotten his lines and is left with no other option but to improvise as he goes along or to repeat the words whispered to him by various prompters. There is never a shortage of them. And equally as long, I have been fascinated by the Pygmalion complex, which has been depicted in world literature quite a number of times. Pygmalion, you will remember, is a Cypriot king who carves a beautiful woman out of ivory and falls in love with her. When Aphrodite breathes life into the statue, he marries his creation.

Does not this story contain the answer to the question why it cannot be otherwise than that the source of human creativity is at the same time the source of man's downfall? Dissatisfied with his fragile, fallible nature, man has always longed for perfection, to rise above what comes from the coincidences of nature. He has longed for the ideal person in an ideal world, for the power that would bring him close to God and become his 'creative partner'. The idea of the superman does not arise from racist mythology (which has only usurped it), this idea originates from man's feeling of helplessness, from his fear in the face of his own unimportance. By admiring heroes, geniuses, researchers, sportsmen, man has always valued his own unrealised potential.

At the same time, man was never able to live without self-love. And so he always had the desire to create something that would still be him, but bigger and better than him, so that he could then love himself through his achievements. He created technology, with which he subjugated nature; he created civilisation, that seemed to him so wonderful that (like Pygmalion) he fell in love with his own artefact and married it. What arrogance! Hubris, the ancient Greeks would say. And we all know what follows. Nemesis. When man created the civilisation that allowed him to transcend his own humanity, he also created a killer that threatens to destroy him. Dr Frankenstein did not create a superman, but a monster.

Why has the world gone so far in the wrong direction? When and where did the fateful turning point take place? As always, the devil is in the language, in a single word, the verb 'to have'. A verb that we were unable to understand correctly and so we lost control of it. To have means to be the owner of something. Ownership (of things, money, reputation, power, attractiveness) has become the universal criterion of value.

It doesn't matter how the conversation begins or what it is aimed at, sooner or later it always becomes a comparative evaluation of status. As if without establishing in advance our purchasing and selling skills, we would have no firm basis for an exchange of opinions. As if by way of introduction, it is necessary to determine our relative ownership status, on which the order of value of our words than depends.

Although we have never agreed on this in principle, deep within ourselves we believe that the one who has managed to accumulate more symbols of success, knowledge, experience, awards, property, has a *greater* right to have his opinion respected (or to be seriously listened to). And yet the psychological mechanisms of this game are paradoxical as well as dangerous. For in what we have (be it things, education, reputation, talent or whatever), many see a challenge to their own success, and so their attitude towards us is often based on envy (connected with the desire to reduce our property). But if it is more than obvious that *they* have a lot more, or at least a little more, their attitude towards us is marked by patronising arrogance. In both cases, the possibility of genuine human relations is significantly, if not completely, diminished. Identifying with acquired status symbols is so widespread that the majority of people see it as something natural and ascribe judgement of human value through the prism of ownership even to those among us who have managed to avoid this.

Interpersonal relations are also subordinated to the ownership mentality: people are objects that you appropriate in order to be able to call them yours. *My* friends, *my* acquaintances, *my* connections, *my* idols, *my* allies, *my* admirers. And since they are yours, you can also, without a feeling of guilt, renounce them, reject them, abandon them. Addicted consumers have their habits, ideas and opinions; in conversation, they are often aggressive or dogmatic, as they fear that with the loss of their opinions they will be diminished, impoverished. That's not surprising, considering they believe they are nothing more than what they have. When a person says 'I am what I have', they become an object, for they are also possessed by the objects through which they define their value. They are subordinate to them, a dead thing in a world of dead things. For them, the meaning of life is meaninglessness.

How is it possible that we have so stupidly undermined the ground beneath our feet; we, who were so clever that we landed on the Moon, revealed the secrets of the universe and its origin, invented the Internet and transferred to it most of our knowledge and even an extensive part of our lives? Does life have any meaning at all in a world where nature is no longer our ally, because we have become its enemies through our greed? A world where we are in reality ruled not by politicians, but bankers?

You probably all know the English actor Hugh Grant. When his mother was asked what her sons did, she said: 'Oh, one of them works in a bank and the other is an international film star.' 'Amazing!' they responded. 'Which bank does he work for?'

The same applies to us writers. Who needs made-up stories? Fewer and fewer people. Libraries are closing, reading is on the decline, publishers are collapsing, bookshops are increasingly known for bankruptcies rather than for the books they sell. We are renewing stories that have already been told a thousand times; we are even reviving stories that we wrote ourselves, each time with minimal shifts or with other, slightly different characters. Were not all the possible forms of narrative art exhausted by the stories Scheherazade told to king Shahryar in order to stay alive? Why else would I see her in every corner of the world as a projection from my subconscious, as a vision, an apparition that evaporates when touched? And why would she remain without speech if she still had something to tell? And why was I crippled by writer's block right in the middle of a novel about a writer who is writing his last novel about a writer who has decided to stop writing because he no longer wishes to repeat himself? The apparition of Scheherazade was a warning that I needed to stop because everything belonging to the so/called literary world is just a charade."

58.

Story one thousand and two

The Carer, my "voice", took a bow and the applause that followed lasted longer than I had expected. Politeness was evidently part of protocol. But my wife did not leave the stage, she remained at the microphone. When the applause subsided, she said: "Thank you, Your Majesty and honoured guests, for allowing me to read the speech of this year's winner of the most prestigious literary award. Now please allow me to say a few words as his wife."

She suddenly bent down and from the handbag that had been beside her on the floor the whole time, she pulled a brown robe. She threw it round her shoulders and pulled the upper part over her head like a hood. I felt like rushing forward and dragging her by force from the stage. But it was too late.

"I would like to tell all those who do not know the prize winner too well – and you know even less about me – that there stands before you Scheherazade. Not the one from *One Thousand and One Nights,* but from *Story One Thousand and Two,* which my husband wrote when he was a schoolboy of thirteen. In his story Scheherazade, because of constant storytelling, becomes hoarse and then finally loses her voice. She writes a message to Shahryar that it is now his turn, he must tell her stories, and when he tells her one that is better than hers, different, more original, she will return to him. Until then, she intends to travel the world, for she wants to see whether everywhere is the same as his kingdom, or whether there is perhaps one that she likes more. But he should not worry; even if she finds a more beautiful kingdom, better and less cruel than his, she shall return to him as soon as one of his stories charms her. 'But how am I supposed to tell you stories if you are travelling the world?' said Shahryar in surprise. She told him to tell them to his father, the Grand Vizier, and he should have them written down, copied and sent to every corner of the globe. Sooner or later they would reach her, for wherever she was, she would regularly visit shops with stories. And when one of them surpassed the ones she told over a thousand and one nights, she would return to him. And then they would, as befitted a love story, live happily together till the end of their days. Your Majesty, ladies and gentlemen, the prize winner wrote this at the age of thirteen!

His grandfather, the retired head teacher of the school that he was attending and at which his deceased mother had taught English, was enthusiastic. He showed his grandson's story to his Slovene teacher, who was even more enthusiastic and so all of the pupils had to read the story, including me, who was a year younger and in a lower class. So he did not recognise me when his grandfather asked me to put on the robe that I am wearing now, exactly the kind that Scheherazade was wearing on the cover of *One Thousand and One Nights* which the grandfather had given to his grandson, and every so often to sit in a clearing in the woods that the boy passed on his way to and from school. When he first saw me, because of my slightly darker skin, he thought I was a girl from the nearby gypsy settlement. But the colour of my robe and the way in which I was sitting reminded him of the picture on the cover of the book. He began to believe that Scheherazade, whom he had written a story about, had begun to appear to him. At the same time, he wanted to believe in the veracity of his story, particularly because his grandfather and his teacher kept trying to convince him that he had an exceptional storytelling gift and that he must write, write, write, for this was evidently why he had come into the world. Boys of thirteen quickly believe those who praise them, especially if they love them and are dependent on them, as our prize winner was dependent on his grandfather, who believed in the boy's gift and wanted him to achieve something.

So the boy wrote and wrote. His grandfather asked me to keep appearing to him in different places, dressed in the brown robe, with my head covered. If he ever came close, I was to pretend that I could not see him. He drummed into me that I must not let his grandson touch me and discover that I was a real person; he had to believe that I was a figment of his imagination, Scheherazade from his story, wandering the world and reminding him of his duty. He must believe that he was Shahryar and that he would only lure me back to his kingdom with his best story.

But gradually, I also began to appear to him when I was not really there. He was seeing me because of a psychological disturbance that one of his doctors later referred to as auto-hypnosis. He needed me in order to work, to be able to write at all. But I will admit something else: all the appearances of Scheherazade in his later life were not hallucinations, many of them were me, the real person standing before you. For the fact was that, even at the beginning, as a youngster, proud to be able to participate in such an interesting game, I fell in love with the strange boy that you have today awarded, and

I followed him through life as far as was possible, although that wasn't simple considering that he moved to London, while I went my own way, choosing to study medicine and physiotherapy.

I read everything he published, also in my own way a victim of autohypnosis, in the hope that he would finally write the story that would bring us together. I spent quite some time as a postgraduate student in London, where I appeared to him in different locations. Not once did he think that I was anything other than a vision from his story: Scheherazade, leading him through life, waiting for the story that would change her into a real, living being. And he wrote. He wrote because of me. I became less and less like the girl who appeared to him on the way to and from school; God knows why it seemed normal to him that we were both ageing. When some years later I found out that he had, at least temporarily, moved back to Slovenia, I rented a small apartment not far from his house to be close to him. I was still in love with him, although in the meantime I had experienced the death of both my husband and my child. And there too, close to his house, I began to appear as Scheherazade. To remind him that he still hadn't written the story that would bring me back to his kingdom. For him, this was fateful. Here and now, although not the most appropriate time and place, I feel obliged to admit that I made a terrible mistake. I'd like to unburden myself of the feeling of guilt that has been tormenting me for quite a long time, although not, since my husband fell ill and lost his voice, as the Scheherazade in his story, but as a victim of illness in real life.

One evening, wrapped in a robe, the one that I am now wearing in front of you, I climbed the hummock of the old air-raid shelter behind his house. Of course, he soon saw me through the French windows and rushed out of the garden gate to the row of garages, to the steps that would bring him to me. What happened next is summarised in his official biography, which is known to the majority of you. Although I feel responsible for his accident, it is at the same time a consolation that it was me who ensured that he didn't die, but reached the accident and emergency department in time. And when they sent him home and he published an ad for a carer, I did everything possible and perhaps even more, as a retired doctor and physiotherapist, to get the job for which, it seems to me, I would even have killed if necessary. The accident was the story that brought Schehezarade back to Shahryar. Although illness followed, an intrusion from the real, external world, we achieved the union of which he had dreamed in his imagined, narrative world, I in the role of Scheherazade, as he had described her in the story he wrote when he was thirteen, at the start of the career that brought him, and me with him, to this encounter with the Swedish king and with you all, who perhaps see in this story not the truth but one of his narratives.

Every life, Your Majesty, ladies and gentlemen, has its light and dark sides. Including yours. And so you will understand that what I've just told you is something that is both possible and impossible to believe. Remember the dialogue between Alice and the White Queen, in one of the most beautiful stories, *Alice in Wonderland*. 'There's no use trying,' Alice said. 'One can't believe impossible things.' 'I daresay you haven't had much practice,' said the Queen. 'When I was your age, I always did it for half-an-hour a day. Why, sometimes I've believed as many as six impossible things before breakfast.' The Queen was evidently a great reader. She liked made-up stories that in one way or another expressed what was happening in reality, which it seems, and not only to me, is the hardest to believe in."

Epilogue

After we returned to London, the question arose as to how we would talk to each other, considering that I couldn't speak. It would be too tiring, too awkward to write in a notebook or on a computer everything that I wanted to tell her or to say in response to her words, and sooner or later we would grow weary of this and our "conversations" would be reduced to a minimum. Which would mean that we would stop communicating. It would then be difficult to preserve our marriage, for to the greatest extent family relations are dependent on the words that the spouses exchange; the very tone in which things are said tells a lot, perhaps more than anything. And how could we tell each other stories, which were, after all, the main connection between us?

"What about sign language?" said Scheherazade. "It would take some time to learn, but we'd be able to talk more or less normally."

"We're not deaf!" I scribbled in the notebook. It seemed to me that my anger could be read from the way the letters were written.

to be Scheherazade. I didn't send it to you because it seemed to me that I needed to add certain things. But you found it. And without my permission incorporated it into your new novel. That's okay. At least there'll be something in it that isn't made up."

"Are you going to leave me now?" I scribbled in the notebook.

"On the contrary," she said, leaning towards me and giving me a hug. "I'll stay here and dictate to you the rest of the novel that you are writing. Only in that way will I get the story that you promised me when a long time ago, first hoarse and then dumb, I left your court."

that you describe in the story. Nobody knew anything about Captain Jovanis. Or Dinos. Or of the taverna owner who had lived for some years in Germany and supposedly knew the real story of Jovanis's fate. For thirty years, the owner had been a lady called Dina Sideris. It then became clear to me that you had made the story up. Just like the story about your experiences in the Berghof clinic, where you never even went; you wrote the novel in your house in Slovenia. And your encounters with famous writers that you never even met. It's not surprising that they wanted to sue you when the novel came out. Do you know what led me to the idea that you had never been in the Swiss Alps? The name of the clinic. Berghof. Did you call it that deliberately? Had you never heard that Berghof was Hitler's summer residence in the Bavarian Alps, which was demolished in 1952?"

"I live in the world of imagination," I scrawled in the notebook. "Once a writer, always a writer. You live in the real world. Can we meet half-way?"

"We already have. To me as well it's increasingly unclear what is real and what is imaginary. You've infected me with your stories. After all, Scheherazade infected the cruel Shahryar with her stories. Because of them he granted her life. And that novel that you have begun to write about how you got the Nobel Prize and we were in Stockholm with the Swedish king – haven't you gone a little too far? Aren't you afraid the King of Sweden will sue you? And the speech that I supposedly read out, and the story that I supposedly added about myself. At least that is true. I see you've been going through my files. In reality, that is the letter that I wrote after lengthy prevarication. But I didn't send it to you. I wanted to get rid of the feeling of guilt for having deviously followed you through life – first on your grandfather's instructions and then later because I wanted to – pretending collar of his jacket. He lifted him and dragged him to the middle of the taverna. Jovanis struggled half-jokingly, his eyes flitting from one person to another. He was afraid we would laugh at him. He was a tiny man, a real clown. The local guests were enjoying themselves. Dinos left the old man in the middle of the taverna and began to clap rhythmically and shout something that sounded like: 'Come on old man, dance, dance!'

The Captain stood there as though dumbstruck. He couldn't decide whether to resist or to play his role wordlessly. He once more looked around anxiously. For the first time, I saw suppressed pain in his eyes. Then he began to dance. He clumsily moved his feet and waved his hands. Dinos clapped rhythmically and drove him like the trainer of a dancing bear. And the Captain really was reminiscent of a clumsy, unhappy bear.

After five minutes, Dinos allowed him to sit. The old man slipped back to his seat. Once again, is eyes became eloquent, staring at us both beseechingly and defiantly. It's a devilish life, they said. An old man who has no one, but needs company and a drink, must act the fool."

I raised my hand to stop her. The gesture was paralinguistic, but understandable enough for her to stop.

"Believe it or not," she said, "I've read that story at least ten times. I keep re-reading it. And I try to work out which of the interpretations of your fellow travellers is closer to the truth. Perhaps you won't believe what I am now going to admit. I read the story quite a few years before you told me it as part of your narrative about your symposium in Kolkata. After all, it was published some years before the symposium. One day I couldn't resist a simple desire: I went on holiday to Greece, to the Peloponnese, all the way to the Mani peninsula in the south, to the fishing village of Kotronas, to the taverna

"In reality we are," she said. "I can't hear you and you can't respond to what I say." She turned the monitor towards herself, typed "sign language" into the search engine and clicked on one of the endless results. "Read it," she turned the monitor back towards me.

"Wikipedia." And I read: "Sign language is a means of communication based on gestures, facial expressions and movements. Every verbal, i.e. spoken language, has its sign language counterpart, which is independent from the spoken one and develops within the community of deaf people. The expressive resources used in this language are gestures and signs, not words. Sign language is not only used by deaf people, but also those with hearing impairment, family members and sign language interpreters."

"Gestures and signs," I scribbled in the notebook, which I preferred to the computer. "That's a paralanguage. I wrote a story about it that no one knew how to finish so that the ending would be unambiguous. Neither me nor anyone else."

"I know," she said. "I read it. And then heard it from your mouth. The critics declared it to be one of your most original works." She got up and took a few steps over to the bookshelves. She soon found what she was looking for, coming back with a collection of my short stories. She quickly leafed through it and equally quickly found the story that I had written many years before, based on true events in Kotronas, a small seaside resort at the lower end of the Peloponnese peninsular of Mani. "Can I read it to you?"

"Just a part," I scribbled in the notebook, "I know it almost by heart."

And she began to read:

"Dinos went over to Jovanis and put his hands beneath his shoulders. Then he changed his mind and grabbed the